YOU H

Mhairi McFarlane studied English at the University of
Manchester and went on to work in journalism, a bit. She lives
in Nottingham and this is her first book.

YOU HAD ME AT

Hello

MHAIRI McFARLANE

AVON

AVON

A division of HarperCollins*Publishers*
77–85 Fulham Palace Road, London W6 8JB
www.harpercollins.co.uk

A Paperback Original 2012

First published in Great Britain by HarperCollins*Publishers* 2012
First published in the USA by HarperCollins*Publishers*2014

A catalogue record for this book is available from the British Library

ISBN-13: 978-0-00-755946-6

Printed and bound in the USA by RR Donnelley

Thanks to my brilliant agent Ali Gunn, and the lovely Doug Kean, for making me a proper thing. Huge thanks also to Jo Rees, whose superb critique somehow produced stellar results without destroying my self-esteem, something for which I will always be grateful.

Praise be to my wonderful editor Helen Bolton, who proved her love of the book with her marvellous handling of it, and the whole Avon team at HarperCollins for being so professional and a total pleasure. And so much credit must go to the very talented designer, Emma Rogers, who created such a great cover. It had me at … no, I musn't. But, *thank you*.

My hugest gratitude to my exceptional extended family for all their support and encouragement, I couldn't have done it without you, as you definitely know.

Special mentions to Clive Norman, Chrissy Schwartz and Tom Welch for their early-doors generous help, and my friend Sean Hewitt and my brother Ewan for keeping me going when I had one of my many fits of 'Wail, I can't do this'. The phrase: 'What happens next? Send more' is probably the most helpful feedback you ever get.

Cheers to all the great friends/willing readers/advice givers to a 'I done a book' bore: the lovely de Cozar sisters Tara and Katie, Helster, Tim Lee, Sally, Kristy, Manchester advisor Julia Pride, the frankly inspirational Tree C three, Natalie, Paula, Serry (thanks for the name, Nat!) and my sister Laura.

And many witty people I know – notably Jeremy Lewis, Rob Hyde, David Wood, Stephanie Hale – have had their lines shamelessly lifted: much obliged! I hope there'll be none of that horrid 'legal action'. But be aware, if there is, I am disavowing this paragraph.

Most of all, thank you dearest Alex – like Bon Jovi, you kept the faith.

And thank you if you bought this. I hope you laughed at least once, and at a bit that was intended to be funny.

For Jenny
Who I Found At University

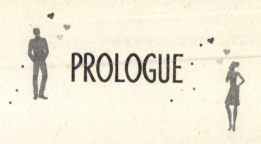

PROLOGUE

'Oh bloody hell, of all the luck…'

'What?' I asked.

I batted a particularly plucky and irrepressible wasp away from my Coke can. Ben was shielding his face with his hand in that way which only renders you more conspicuous.

'Professor McDonald. You know, Egg McMuffin Head. I owed him an essay on Keats a week ago. Has he seen me?'

I looked over. Across the afternoon-sun-dappled lawn, the professor had stopped in his tracks and was doing the full pointing-finger Lord Kitchener impression, even down to mouthing the word 'YOU'.

'Er. Yes.'

Ben peered through a gap in his fingers at me.

'Maybe yes or hell yes?'

'Like a tweedy, portly, bald Scottish Scud missile has your exact coordinates and is ripping across the grass to take you out, yes.'

'Right, OK, think, think…' Ben muttered, looking up into the leaves of the tree we were sitting beneath.

'Are you going to try to climb it? Because Professor McDonald looks the type to wait for the fire crews at dusk.'

1

Ben's eyes cast around at the detritus of lunch, and our bags on the ground, as if they contained an answer. I didn't think an esteemed academic getting a face full of Karrimor rucksack was likely to help. His gaze came to rest on my right hand.

'Can I borrow your ring?'

'Sure. It's not magical though.' I twisted it off and handed it over.

'Stand up?'

'Eh?'

'Stand. *Up.*'

I got to my feet, brushing the grass off my jeans. Ben balanced himself on one knee and held aloft a piece of gothicky silver jewellery I'd got for four quid at the student market. I started laughing.

'Oh … *you idiot* …'

Professor McDonald reached us.

'Ben Morgan …!'

'Sorry, sir, I'm just in the middle of something rather important here.'

He turned back to me.

'I know we're twenty years old and the timing of this proposal might have been forced due to … external pressures. But, irrespective of this, you are amazing. I know I will never meet another woman I care about as much as you. This feeling just builds and builds …'

Professor McDonald folded his arms, but incredibly, he was smiling. Unbelievable. The Ben chutzpah triumphed again.

'Are you sure that feeling isn't the revenge of the sweetcorn and tinned hotdog tortilla you and Kev made last night?' I asked.

'No! My God – you've taken me over. It's my head, my heart, my gut…'

'Careful now, lad, I wouldn't go much further in the inventory,' Professor McDonald said. 'The weight of history is upon you. Think of the legacy. It's got to inspire.'

'Thanks, sir.'

'You don't need a wife, you need Imodium,' I said.

'I need *you*. What do you say? Marry me. A simple ceremony. Then you can move into my room. I've got an inflatable mattress and a stained towel you can fold up and use as a pillow. And Kev's perfecting a patatas bravas recipe where you boil the potatoes in Heinz tomato soup.'

'Lovely offer as it is, Ben. Sorry. No.'

Ben turned towards Professor McDonald.

'I'm going to need some compassionate leave.'

I get home slightly late, blown in the door by that special Manchester rain that manages to be both vertical and horizontal at the same time. I bring so much water into the house it feels as if the tide goes out and leaves me draped across the bottom of the stairs like a piece of seaweed.

It's a friendly, unassuming-looking place, I think. You could peg us as early thirty-something childless 'professionals' in a two-minute tour. Framed prints of Rhys's musical heroes. Shabby chic with a bit more of the former than the latter. And dark blue gloss paint on the skirting boards that makes my mum sniff: 'Looks a bit community centre project.'

The house smells of dinner, spicy and warm, and yet there's a definite chill in the air. I can sense Rhys is in a mood even before I set eyes on him. As I walk into the kitchen, something about the tension in his shoulders as he hovers over the stove makes it a certainty.

'Evening, love,' I say, pulling sodden hair out of my collar and unwinding my scarf. I'm shivering, but I have that weekend spring in my step. Everything's a little easier to bear on a Friday.

He grunts indistinctly, which could be a hello, but I don't query it lest I be blamed for opening hostilities.

'Did you get the tax disc?' he asks.

'Oh shit, I forgot.'

Rhys whips round, knife dangling in his hand. It was a crime of passion, your honour. He hated tardiness when it came to DVLA paperwork.

'I reminded you yesterday! It's a day out now.'

'Sorry, I'll do it tomorrow.'

'You're not the one who has to drive the car illegally.'

I'm also not the one who forgot to go last weekend, according to the reminder in his handwriting on the calendar. I don't mention this. Objection: argumentative.

'They tow them to the scrap yard, you know, even if they're parked on the pavement. Zero tolerance. Don't blame me when they crush it down to Noddy size and you've got to get buses.' I have an image of myself in a blue nightcap with a bell on the end of it.

'Tomorrow morning. Don't worry.'

He turns back and continues hacking at a pepper that may or may not have my face on it. I remember that I have a sweetener and duck out to retrieve the bottle of red from the dripping Threshers bag.

I pour two thumping glasses and say: 'Cheers, Big Ears.'

'Big Ears?'

'Noddy. Never mind. How was your day?'

'Same old.'

Rhys works in graphic design for a marketing company. He hates it. He hates talking about it even more. He quite likes lurid tales from the front line of reporting on Manchester Crown Court trials, however.

'Well today a man responded to the verdict of life sentence without parole with the immortal words: "This wrong-ass shit be whack."'

'Haha. And was it?'

'Wrong-ass? No. He did kill a bunch of people.'

'Can you put "wrong-ass shit" in the *Manchester Evening News*?'

'Only with asterisks. I definitely had to euphemise the things his family were saying as "emotional shouts and cries from the public gallery". The only word about the judge that wasn't swearing was "old".'

Chuckling, Rhys carries his glass to the front room. I follow him.

'I did some reception research about the music today,' I say, sitting down. 'Mum's been on to me fretting that *Margaret Drummond at cake club's nephew had a DJ in a baseball cap who played "lewd and cacophonous things about humps and cracks" before the flower girls' and page boys' bedtimes.*'

'Sounds *great*. Can she get his number? Maybe lose the cap though.'

'I thought we could have a live singer. There's someone at work who hired this Elvis impersonator, Macclesfield Elvis. He sounds brilliant.'

Rhys's face darkens. 'I don't want some cheesy old fat fucker in Brylcreem singing "Love Me Tender". We're getting married at Manchester Town Hall, not the Little McWedding Chapel in Vegas.'

I swallow this, even though it doesn't go down easy. *Forgive me for trying to make it fun.*

'Oh. OK. I thought it might be a laugh, you know, get everyone going. What were you thinking?'

He shrugs.

'Dunno.'

His truculence, and a pointed look, tells me I might be missing something.

'Unless … you want to play?'

He pretends to consider this.

'Yeah, 'spose we could. I'll ask the lads.'

Rhys's band. Call them sub-Oasis and he'll kill you. There are a lot of parkas and squabbles though. The thing we both know and never say is that he hoped his previous group, back in Sheffield, would take off, while this is a thirty-something hobby. I've always accepted sharing Rhys with his music. I just didn't expect to have to on my wedding day.

'You could do the first half an hour, maybe, and then the DJ can start after that.'

Rhys makes a face.

'I'm not getting everyone to rehearse and set up and then play for that long.'

'All right, longer then, but it's our wedding, not a gig.'

I feel the storm clouds brewing and rolling, a thunderclap surely on its way. I know his temper, this type of argument, like the back of my hand.

'I don't want a DJ either,' he adds.

'Why not?'

'They're always naff.'

'You want to do all the music?'

'We'll do iPod compilations, Spotify, whatever. Put them on shuffle.'

'OK.'

I should let this go, try when he's in a better mood, but I don't.

'We'll have The Beatles and Abba and stuff for the older generation on there, though? They're not going to get it if it's all fuck-you-I-won't-do-what-you-tell-me and blaring amps.'

'"Dancing Queen"? No bloody way. Even if your cousin Alan wants to mince around to it.' He purses his lips and makes a 'flapping hands at nipple level' Orville the Duck gesture that could be considered gratuitously provocative.

'Why do you have to behave as if this is such a hassle?'

'I thought you wanted to get married on our terms, in our way. We agreed.'

'Yes, our terms. Not your terms,' I say. 'I want you to have a chance to talk to our friends and family. It's a party, for everyone.'

My eyes drifted to my engagement ring. Why were we getting married, again? A few months ago, we were tipsy on ouzo digestifs in a Greek restaurant, celebrating Rhys getting a decent bonus at work. It came up as one of the big things we could spend it on. We liked the idea of a bash, agreed it was probably 'time'. There was no proposal, just Rhys topping up my glass and saying 'Fuck it, why not, eh?' and winking at me.

It felt so secure, and right, and *obvious* a decision in that steamy, noisy dining room, that night. Watching the belly dancer dragging pensioners up to gyrate alongside her, laughing till our bellies hurt. I loved Rhys, and I suppose in my agreement was an acceptance of: well, who else am I going to marry? Yes, we lived with a grumbling undercurrent of dissatisfaction. But like the toad-speckles of mouldy damp in the far corner of the bathroom, it was going to be a lot of upheaval to fix, and we never quite got round to it.

Though we'd waited long enough, I'd never really doubted we would formalise things. While Rhys still had the untamed hair and wore the eternal student uniform of grubby band t-shirts, distressed denim and All Stars, underneath it all, I knew he wanted the piece of paper before the kids. We called both sets of parents when we got home, ostensibly to share our joy, maybe also so we couldn't go back on it when we'd sobered up. Not moonlight and sonatas but, as Rhys would say, life isn't.

Now I picture this day, supposedly the happiest day of our lives, full of compromises and swallowed irritation and Rhys being clubby and standoffish with his band mates, the way he was when I first met him, when being in his gang had been all my undeveloped heart muscle desired.

'For how long is the band going to be the third person in this relationship? Are you going to be out at rehearsals when I'm home with a screaming baby?'

Rhys pulls the wine glass from his lips.

'Where's that come from? What, I've got to be a different person, give up something I love, to be good enough for you?'

'I didn't say that. I just don't think you playing should be getting in the way of us spending time together on our wedding day.'

'Ha. We'll have *a lifetime together* afterwards.'

He says this as if it's a sentence in Strangeways, with shower bumming, six a.m. exercise drills in the yard and smuggling coded messages to people on the outside. Won't. Let. Me. Come. To. Pub…

I take a deep breath, and feel a hard, heavy weight beneath my ribcage, a pain that I could try to dissolve with wine. It has worked in the past.

'I'm not sure this wedding is a good idea.'

It's out. The nagging thought has bubbled up right through

from subconscious to conscious and has continued onwards, leaving my mouth. I'm surprised I don't want to take it back.

Rhys shrugs.

'I said to do a flit abroad. You wanted to do it here.'

'No, I mean I don't think getting married at the moment is a good idea.'

'Well, it's going to look pretty fucking weird if we call it off.'

'That's not a good enough reason to go through with it.'

Give me a reason. Maybe I'm the one sending desperate messages in code. I realise that I've come to an understanding, woken up, and Rhys isn't hearing the urgency. I've said the sort of thing we don't say. Refusal to listen isn't enough of a response.

He gives an extravagant sigh, one full of unarticulated exhaustion at the terrible trials of living with me.

'Whatever. You've been spoiling for a fight ever since you got home.'

'No I haven't!'

'And now you're going to sulk to try to force me into agreeing to some DJ who'll play rubbish for you and your divvy friends when you're pissed. Fine. Book it, do it all your way, I can't be bothered to argue.'

'*Divvy?*'

Rhys takes a slug of wine, stands up.

'I'm going to get on with dinner, then.'

'Don't you think the fact we can't agree on this might be telling us something?'

He sits again, heavily.

'Oh, Jesus, Rachel, don't try to turn this into a drama, it's been a long week. I haven't got the energy for a tantrum.'

I'm tired, too, but not from five days of work. I'm tired of the effort of pretending. We're about to spend thousands of pounds on the pretence, in front of all of the people who know us best, and the prospect's making me horribly queasy.

The thing is, Rhys's incomprehension is reasonable. His behaviour is business as usual. *This* is business as usual. It's something in me that's snapped. A piece of my machinery has finally worn out, the way a reliable appliance can keep running and running and then, one day, it doesn't.

'It's not a good idea for us to get married, full stop,' I say. 'Because I'm not sure it's even a good idea for us to be together. We're not happy.'

Rhys looks slightly stunned. Then his face closes, a mask of defiance again.

'You're not happy?'

'No, I'm not happy. Are you?'

Rhys squeezes his eyes shut, sighs and pinches the bridge of his nose.

'Not at this exact moment, funnily enough.'

'In general?' I persist.

'What is happy, for the purposes of this argument? Prancing through meadows in a stoned haze and see-through blouse, picking daisies? Then no, I'm not. I love you and I thought you loved me enough to make an effort. But obviously not.'

'There is a middle ground between stoner daisies and constant bickering.'

'Grow up, Rachel.'

Rhys's stock reaction to any of my doubts has always been this: a gruff 'grow up', 'get over it'. Everyone else knows this is simply what relationships are and you have unrealistic expectations. I used to like his certainty. Now I'm not so sure.

'It's not enough,' I say.

'What are you saying? You want to move out?'

'Yes.'

'I don't believe you.'

Neither do I, after all this time. It's been quite an acceleration, from nought to splitting up in a few minutes. I've practically got hamster cheeks from the g-force. This could be why it's taken us so long to get round to tying the knot. We knew it'd bring certain fuzzy things into sharper focus.

'I'll start looking for places to rent tomorrow.'

'Is this all it's worth, after thirteen years?' he asks. 'You won't do what I want for the wedding – see ya, bye?'

'It's not really the wedding.'

'Funny how these problems hit you now, when you're not getting your own way. Don't recall this … *introspection* when I was buying the ring.'

He has a point. Have I manufactured this row to give me a reason? Are my reasons good enough? I weaken. Perhaps I'm going to wake up tomorrow and think this was all a mistake. Perhaps this dark, apocalyptic mood of terrible clarity will clear up like the rain that's still pelting down outside. Maybe we could go out for lunch tomorrow, scribble down the shared song choices on a napkin, start getting enthused again …

'OK … if this is going to work, we have to change things. Stop getting at each other all the time. See a counsellor, or something.'

He can offer me next to nothing here, and I will stay. That's how pathetic my resolve is.

Rhys frowns.

'I'm not sitting there while you tell some speccy wonk at

12

Relate about what a bastard I am to you. I'm not putting the wedding off. Either we do it, or forget it.'

'I'm talking about our future, whether we have one, and all you care about is what people will think if we cancel the wedding?'

'You're not the only one who can give ultimatums.'

'Is this a game?'

'If you're not sure after this long, you never will be. There's nothing to talk about.'

'Your choice,' I say, shakily.

'No, *your choice*,' he spits. 'As always. After all I've sacrificed for you...'

This sends me up into the air, the kind of anger where you levitate two feet off the ground as if you have rocket launchers on your heels.

'You have not given anything up for me! You chose to move to Manchester! You act like I have this debt to you I can never repay and it's bullshit! That band was going to split up anyway! Don't blame me because you DIDN'T MAKE IT.'

'You are such a selfish, spoilt brat,' he bellows back, getting to his feet as well, because shouting from a seated position is never as effective. 'You want what you want, and you never think about what other people have to give up to make it happen. You're doing the same with this wedding. You're the worst kind of selfish because you think you're not. And as for the band, how fucking dare you say you know how things would've turned out. If I could go back and do things differently—'

'Tell me about it!' I scream.

We both stand there, breathing heavily, a two-person Mexican standoff with words as weapons.

'Fine. Right,' Rhys says, eventually. 'I'm going back home for the weekend – I don't want to stay here and take this shit. Start looking for somewhere else to live.'

I drop back down on the sofa and sit with my hands in my lap. I listen to the sounds of him stomping around upstairs, filling an overnight bag. Tears run down my cheeks and into the neckline of my shirt, which had only just started to dry out. I hear Rhys in the kitchen and I realise he's turning the light off underneath the pan of chilli. Somehow, this tiny moment of consideration is worse than anything he could say. I put my face in my hands.

After a few more minutes, I'm startled by his voice, right next to me.

'Is there anyone else?'

I look up, bleary. 'What?'

'You heard. Is there anyone else?'

'Of course not.'

Rhys hesitates, then adds: 'I don't know why you're crying. This is what you want.'

He slams the front door so hard behind him, it sounds like a gunshot.

2

In the shock of my sudden singlehood, my best friend Caroline and our mutual friends Mindy and Ivor rally round and ask the question of the truly sympathetic: 'Do you want us all to go out and get really really drunk?'

Rhys wasn't missing in action as far as they were concerned: he'd always seen my friends as *my* friends. And he used to observe that Mindy and Ivor 'sound like a pair of *Play School* presenters'. Mindy is Indian, it's an abbreviation of Parminder. She calls 'Mindy' her white world alias. 'I can move among you entirely undetected. Apart from the being brown thing.'

As for Ivor, his dad's got a thing about Norse legends. It's been a bit of an albatross, thanks to a certain piece of classic children's animation. Ivor endured the rugby players in our halls of residence at university calling him 'the engine' and claiming he made a *pessshhhty-coom, pessshhhty-coom* noise at intimate moments. Those same rugby players drank each other's urine and phlegm for dares and drove Ivor upstairs to meet the girls' floor, which is how we became a mixed-sex unit of four. Our platonic company, combined with his close-shaved head, black-rimmed glasses and love of trendy Japanese trainers led to a frequent assumption that Ivor was gay. He's since gone into computer game programming and, given there are practically no women in the profession whatsoever, he feels this misconception could see him missing out on valuable opportunities.

'It's counter-intuitive,' he always complains. 'Why should a man surrounded by women be homosexual? Hugh Hefner doesn't get this treatment. Obviously I should wear a dressing gown and slippers all day.'

Anyway, I'm not quite ready to face cocktail bar society, so I opt for a night in drinking the domestic variety, invariably more lethal.

Caroline's house in Chorlton is always the obvious choice to meet, as unlike the rest of us she's married, and has an amazing one. (I mean house, not spouse – no disrespect to Graeme. He's away on one of his frequent boys' golfing weekends.) Caroline is a very well paid accountant for a large chain of supermarkets, and a proper adult: but then, she always was. At university, she wore quilted gilets and was a member of the rowing club. When I used to express my amazement to the others that she could get up early and exercise after a hard night on the sauce, Ivor used to say, groggily: 'It's a posh thing. Norman genes. She has to go off and conquer stuff.'

He could be on to something about her ancestry. She's tall, blonde and has what I believe is called an aquiline profile. She says she looks like an ant eater; if so, it's kind of ant-eater-by-way-of-Grace-Kelly.

I have the job of slicing limes and salting the rims of the glasses on Caroline's spotlessly sleek black Corian worktop while she blasts ice, tequila and Cointreau into a slurry in a candy-apple red KitchenAid. In between these deafening bursts, from her regal perch on the sofa, Mindy is gifting us, as usual, with the Tao of Mindy.

'The difference between thirty and thirty-one is the difference between a funeral and the grieving process.'

Caroline starts spooning out margarita mixture.

'Turning thirty is like a funeral?'

'The funeral for your youth. Lots of drink and sympathy and attention and flowers, and you see everyone you know.'

'And for a moment there we were worried the comparison was going to be tasteless,' Ivor says, pushing his glasses up the bridge of his nose. He's sitting on the floor, legs outstretched, one arm similarly outstretched, pointing a remote at something lozenge-shaped that's apparently a stereo. 'Have you really got The Eagles on here, Caroline, or is it a sick joke?'

'Thirty-one is like grieving,' Mindy continues. 'Because getting on with it is much worse, but no one expects you to complain any more.'

'Oh, we expect you to complain, Mind,' I say, carefully passing her a shallow glass that looks like a saucer on a stem.

'The fashion magazines make me feel so old and irrelevant, it's like the only thing I should bother buying is TENA Lady. Can I eat this?' Mindy removes the lime slice from the side of her glass and examines it.

She is, in general, a baffling mixture of extreme aptitude and total daftness. Mindy did a business degree and insisted throughout she was useless at it and definitely wasn't going to take on the family firm, which sold fabrics in Rusholme. Then she got a first and picked the business up for one summer, created mail order and online sales, quadrupled the turnover and grudgingly accepted she might have a knack, and a career. Yet on holiday in California recently, when a tour guide announced, 'On a clear day, with binoculars, you can see whales from here', Mindy said, 'Oh my God, all the way to Cardigan Bay?'

'Lime? Er … not usually,' I say.

'Oh. I thought you might've infused it with something.'

I collect another glass and deliver it to Ivor, then Caroline and I carry ours to our seats.

'Cheers,' I say. 'To my broken engagement and loveless future.'

'To your future,' Caroline chides.

We raise glasses, slurp, wince a bit – the tequila is quite loud in the mix. It makes my lips numb and stomach warm.

Single. It's been so long since the word applied to me and I don't feel it yet. I'm something else, in limbo: tip-toeing round my own house, sleeping in the spare room, avoiding my ex-fiancé and his furious, seething disappointment. He's right: this is what I want, I have less reason than him to be upset.

'How's it going, you two living together?' Caroline asks, carefully, as if she can hear me think.

'We're not putting piano wire at neck level across doorways yet. We stay out of each other's way. I need to step up the house hunt. I'm finding excuses to be out every evening as it is.'

'How did your mum take it?' Mindy bites her lip.

Mindy understands that, as one of the two slated bridesmaids, she was the only other person as excited as my mum.

'Not well,' I say, with my skill for understatement.

It was awful. The phone call went in phases. The 'stop playing a practical joke' section. The 'you're having cold feet, it's natural' parry. The 'give it a few weeks, see how you feel' suggestion. Anger, denial, bargaining, and then – I hope – some sort of acceptance. Dad came on and asked me if it was because I was worrying about the cost, as they'd cover it all if need be. It was then that I cried.

'I hope you don't mind me asking, it's just, you never said…' Mindy asks. 'What actually caused the row that made you and Rhys finish?'

'Oh…' I say. 'It was Macclesfield Elvis.'

There's a pause. Our default setting is pissing about. As the demise of my epically long relationship only happened a week previous, no one knows quite what's appropriate yet. It's like after any major tragedy: when's it OK to start forwarding the email jokes?

'You shagged Macclesfield Elvis?' Ivor says. 'How did it feel to be nailed by The King?'

'Ivor!' Mindy wails.

I laugh.

'Oooh!' Caroline suddenly exclaims, in a very un-Caroline-like way.

'Have you sat on something?' Mindy says.

'I forgot to say. Guess who I saw this week?'

I'm trying to think which famous person is meant to be my top spot. Unless it's someone I've done a story on, but I spend all day looking at people who are only ever celebrities for the wrong reasons. I doubt a sex attacker on the lam would provoke this delight.

'*Coronation Street* or Man U?' Mindy asks. These are the two main sources of famous people in the city, it's true.

'Neither,' Caroline says. 'And this is a quiz for Rachel.'

I shrug, crunching on some ice with my back teeth.

'Uh…Darren Day?'

'No.'

'Lembit Opik?'

'No.'

'My dad?'

'Why would I see your dad?'

'He could be over from Sheffield, having a clandestine affair behind my mum's back.'

'In which case I'd announce it in the form of a fun quiz?'

'OK, I give up.'

Caroline sits back with a triumphant look on her face.

'English Ben.'

I go hot and cold at the same time, like I've suddenly caught the flu. Slight nausea is right behind the temperature fluctuation. Yep, the analogy holds.

Ivor twists round to look at Caroline.

'English Ben? What kind of nickname is that? As opposed to what?'

'Is he any relation to Big Ben?' Mindy asks.

'English Ben,' Caroline repeats. 'Rachel knows who I mean.'

I feel like Alec Guinness in *Star Wars* when Luke Skywalker turns up at his cave and starts asking for Obi Wan Kenobi. *Now there's a name I've not heard in a long, long time…*

'Where was he?' I say.

'Going into Central Library.'

'How about telling old "Two Legs Ivor" who you're on about?' Ivor asks.

'I could be "Hindi Mindy",' Mindy offers, and Ivor looks like he's going to explain something to her, then changes his mind.

'He was a friend at uni, remember,' I say, covering my mouth with my glass in case my face is betraying more than I want.

'Off my course. Hence, English. Ben.'

'If he was a friend of yours, why is Caroline all ... wriggly?' Mindy asks.

'Caroline always fancied him,' I say, glad this is the truth, if nothing like the whole truth, so help me God.

'Ah.' Mindy gives me an appraising look. 'You can't have fancied him then, because you and Caroline and taste in men – never the twain shall meet.'

I could kiss Mindy for this.

'True,' I agree, emphatically.

'He still looks *fine*,' Caroline says, and my stomach starts flopping around like a live crustacean heading for the pot in the Yang Sing kitchen. 'He was in a gorgeous suit and tie.'

'A *suit*, you say? This man is fascinating,' Ivor says. 'What a character. I'm compelled to know more. Oh. No, hang on – I'm not.'

'Did you and he ever ...?' Mindy asks Caroline. 'I'm trying to place him ...'

'God, no, I wasn't glamorous enough for him, I don't think any of us were, were we, Rach? Bit of a womaniser. But somehow nice with it.'

'Yep,' I squeak.

'Wait! I remember Ben! All like, preppy, smart and confident?' Mindy says. 'We thought he must be rich and then it was like, no, he just ... washes.' She looks at Ivor, who takes the bait.

'Oh, rings a vague bell. Poser who was ...' Ivor flips his collar up '... *Is it handsome in here or is it just me?*'

'He wasn't like that!' I laugh, nervously.

'You lost touch with Ben completely?' Caroline asks. 'Not Facebook friends or anything?'

Severed touch with him. Touch was torn in half, like chesting the ribbon at the end of a race.

'No. I mean, yeah. Not seen Ben since uni.'

And my seven hundred and eighty-one Google searches yielded no results.

'I've seen him at the library a few times, it's only now it's clicked and I realised why I recognised him. He must be staying in Manchester. Do you want me to say hello if I see him again, pass on your mobile number?'

'No!' I say, with a note of panic not entirely absent from my voice. I feel I have to explain this, so I add: 'It could sound as if I'm after him.'

'If you were only friends before, why would he automatically think that?' Caroline asks, not unreasonably.

'I'm single after such a long time. I don't know, it could be misinterpreted. And I'm not looking to … I don't want it to look like, here's my single friend who wants me to auction her phone number to men in the street,' I waffle.

'Well, I wasn't going to put it on a card in a phone box!' Caroline huffs.

'I know, I know, sorry.' I pat her arm. 'I am so, so out of practice at this.'

A pause, with sympathetic smiles from Mindy and Caroline.

'I'll hook you up with some hotness, when you're ready.' Mindy pats my arm.

'Woah,' Ivor says.

'What?'

'Judging from the men you *do* date, I'm trying to imagine the ones you pass over. I'm getting a message from my brain: *the server understood your request but is refusing to fulfil it.*'

22

'Oh, considering your rancid trollops, this is *rich*.'

'No, it was that thundering helmet Bruno who was rich, remember?'

'Aherm, he also had a nice bum.'

'So there you go,' Caroline interrupts. 'Have we cheered you up? Feeling brighter?'

'Yes. A sort of nuclear glow,' I say.

'More serious Slush Puppy?' Caroline asks.

I hold my glass up.

'Shitloads, please.'

3

I met Ben at the end of our first week at Manchester University. I initially thought he was a second or third year, because he was with the older team who'd set up trestle tables in my halls of residence bar to issue our accommodation ID cards. In fact, he'd started off as a customer, same as me. In what I'd later discover was a typically garrulous, generous Ben thing to do, he'd offered to help and hopped over the tables when they'd complained they were short-handed.

I wouldn't have been upright myself, but my hangover had woken me and told me it desperately needed Ribena. The grounds of my halls were as deserted at nine a.m. as if it was dawn. Draining the bottle as I walked back from the shops in the autumn sunshine, I saw a small queue snaking out of the bar's double doors. Being British, and a nervous fresher, I thought I'd better join it.

When I got to the front and a space appeared in front of Ben, I stepped forward.

His mildly startled but not at all displeased expression seemed to read, quite clearly: 'Ooh, and you are?'

This startled me back, not least because it somehow wasn't leery. On a good day (which this wasn't) I thought I scrubbed up reasonably well but I hadn't had many looks like this before. It was as if someone had cued music, fluffed my hair, lit me from above and shouted 'action'.

Ben wasn't at all my type. Bit skinny, bit obvious, with those brown doe-eyes and that squared-off jaw, bit *white bread* as Rhys would say. (He had recently come into my life, along with his definitive worldview that, bit by bit, was becoming mine.) And from what I could see of Ben's upper half, he was clad in sportswear in such a manner that implied he actually played sports. Attractive men, in my eighteen-year-old opinion, played lead guitar, not football. They were scruffy and saturnine, had five o'clock shadows and – recent amendment due to research in the field – chest hair you could lose a gerbil in. Still, I was open-minded enough to allow that Ben would be plenty of other people's type, and that made the attention pretty damn flattering. The low clouds of my hangover started lifting.

Ben said:

'Hello.'

'Hello.'

A beat while we remembered what we were here for. 'Name?' Ben said.

'Rachel Woodford.'

'Woodford…W…' He started riffling through boxes of cards. 'Gotcha.'

He produced a rectangle of cardboard with the name of our halls and a passport photo affixed to it. I'd forgotten I'd sent a handful from a not very flattering session in a shopping centre photo booth. *Really* bad day, Meadowhall, pre-menstrual. Face like I'd woken up at my own autopsy. Might've known they'd come back to haunt me.

'Don't laugh at the picture,' I said, hastily, and potentially counter-productively.

Ben peered at it. 'I've seen worse today.'

He clamped my card in the machine, took the plasticated version out and inspected it again.

'I know it's grim,' I said, holding out my hand. 'I look like I'm trying to pass a dragon fruit.'

'I don't know what a dragon fruit is. I mean, other than a fruit, I'm guessing.'

'It's spiky.'

'Ah OK. Yeah. I 'spose that'd sting a bit.'

Well. That had gone beautifully. Seduction 101: *make the attractive boy imagine you straining on the toilet.*

This was straight from my greatest hits back catalogue, by the way. Quintessential Rachel, The Cream of Rachel, *Simply Rachel.* When put on the spot, the linguistic function of my brain offers the same potluck as a one-armed bandit. Crank the handle and ratchet the tension, it rings up any old combination of words.

Ben gave me a smile that turned into laughter. I grinned back.

He kept the card out of my reach.

'You're on English?'

'Yes.'

'Me too. I haven't got a clue where I'm meant to be for registration tomorrow. Have you?'

We made an arrangement for him to stop by my room the next morning so we could navigate the arts block together. He found a pen. I scribbled my room number down for him on the nearest thing to hand, a spongy beer mat. I wished I hadn't spent last night painting every one of my fingernails a different colour, which looked pretty silly in the light of day. I printed 'Rachel' in un-joined up letters neatly below, as if I was writing out a label for my coat peg at primary school.

'About the picture,' he said, as he took it. 'You look fine, but you might want to jack the seat up next time. It's a bit Ronnie Corbett.'

I slid it out again to check. There was an acre of white space above my dishevelled head.

I blushed, started laughing.

'Spin it,' Ben mouthed, rotating an imaginary photo booth stool.

I went redder, laughed harder.

'I'm Ben. See you tomorrow.'

In the style of a policeman in traffic, Ben waved me away with one hand and the next person forward with his other, mock imperiously.

As I dodged round the rest of the queue, I wondered if the well-spoken girl in the room next door to me was too upper middle class to go for a restorative greasy spoon breakfast. On impulse as I left, I glanced back towards Ben, and he was watching me go.

4

In some workplaces, everyone has clusters of framed family portraits on their desk, a tumbler of those novelty gonk pens with tufts of fluff at the end and a mug with their name on. From time to time they cry in the loos and confide in each other and any personal news is round the office in the morning before the kettle's gone on for a second time. Words like 'fibroids' or 'Tramadol' or 'caught him trying on one of my dresses' are passed about in the spirit of full disclosure.

Mine isn't one of those workplaces. Manchester Crown Court is full of people moving briskly and efficiently about the place, swishing robes and trading critical information in low voices. The mood is decidedly masculine – it doesn't encourage confidences that are nothing to do with the business in hand. Therefore I've masked physical evidence of my emotional turmoil with an extra layer of make-up, and am squaring my shoulders and heading into battle, congratulating myself on my varnish-thin sheen of competent poise.

I'm getting myself one of the Crown Court vending machine's famous dung-flavoured instant coffees, served in a plastic cup so thin the liquid burns your fingertips, when I hear: 'Big weekend was it, Woodford? You look cream crackered!'

Ahhhh, Gretton. Might've known he'd burst my bubble.

Pete Gretton is a freelancer, a 'stringer' for the agencies as they're known, with no loyalties. He scours the lists looking for the most unpleasant or ridiculous cases and sells the lowest common denominator to the highest bidder, often following me around and ruining any hope of an exclusive. Misdeed and misery are his bread and butter. To be fair, that's true of every salaried person in the building, but most of us have the decency not to revel in it. Gretton, however, has never met a grisly multiple homicide he didn't like.

I turn and give him an appropriately weary look.

'Good morning to you too, Pete,' I say, tersely.

He's very blinky, as if daylight is a shock to him, somehow always reminding me of a ghostly, pink-gilled fish my dad once found lurking in the black sludge at the bottom of the garden pond. Gretton's evolved to fit the environment of court buildings, subsisting purely on coffee, fags and cellophane-wrapped pasties, with no need for sunshine's Vitamin D.

'Only joking, sweetheart. You're still the most beautiful woman in the building.'

After a conversation with Gretton you invariably want to scrub yourself with a stiff bristled brush under scalding water.

'What was it?' he continues. 'Too much of the old vino collapso? That fella of yours tiring you out?' He adds a stomach-turning wink.

I take a gulp of coffee with the fresh roasted aroma of farming and agriculture.

'I split up with my fiancé last month.'

His beady, rheumy little eyes lock on mine, waiting for a punchline. When none is forthcoming, he offers:

'Oh dear … sorry to hear it.'

'Thanks.'

I don't know if Gretton has a private life in any conventional sense, or if he sprouts a tail and corkscrews into an open manhole in a cloud of bright green special effects at five thirty p.m. This topic of conversation is certainly uncharted territory between us. The extent of our personal knowledge about each other is a) I have a fiancé, now past tense, and b) he's originally from Carlisle. And that's the way we both like it.

He shuffles his feet.

'Heard anything about the airport heroin smuggling in 9 that kicks off today? Word is they hid it in colostomy bags.'

I shake my head.

'For once they really could claim it was the good shit!'

He honks at this, broken engagement already forgotten.

'I was going to stick with the honour killing in 1,' I say, unsmiling. 'Tell you what, you do the drugs, I'll do the murder and we'll compare notes at half time.'

Pete eyes me suspiciously, wondering what devious tactic this 'mutually beneficial diplomacy' might be.

'Yeah, alright.'

Although I can get ground down by the bleak subject matter, I enjoy my job. I like being somewhere with clearly defined rules and roles. Whatever the grey areas in the evidence, the process is black and white. I've learned to read the language of the courtroom, predict the lulls and the flurries of action, interpret the Masonic whispers between counsel. I've built up a rapport with certain barristers, got expert at reading the faces of juries and quick at slipping out before any angry members of the public gallery can follow me and tell me they don't want a story putting in the bloody paper.

As I swill the remains of the foul coffee, bin the cup and head towards Court 1, I hear a timid female voice behind me.

'Excuse me? Are you Rachel Woodford?'

I turn to see a small girl with a halo of straw-coloured, frizzy hair, a slightly beaky nose and an anxious expression. In school uniform she could pass for twelve.

'I'm the new reporter who's shadowing you today,' she says.

'Ah, right.' I rack my brains for her name, recall a conversation about her with news desk which now seems a geological era ago.

'Zoe Clarke,' she supplies.

'Zoe, of course, sorry, I'm a bit brain-fugged this morning. I'm doing the murder trial today, want to join?'

'Yes, thanks!' She smiles as sunnily as if I had offered her a walking weekend in the Lakes.

'Let's go and watch people in wigs argue with each other then,' I say. I point at the retreating Gretton. 'And beware the sweaty man who comes in friendship and leaves with your story.'

Zoe laughs. She'll learn.

At lunchtime, I open my laptop in the press room – a fancy title for a nicotine-stained windowless cell in the bowels of Crown Court, decorated with a wood veneer desk, a few chairs and a dented filing cabinet – and check my email. A message arrives from Mindy.

'*Can you talk?*'

I type '*Yes*' and hit send.

Mindy doesn't like to email when she can talk, because she loves to talk, and she's a phonetic speller. She used to put 'Vwalah!' in messages to myself and Caroline, which we assumed was a Hindu word, until under questioning it became clear she meant 'Voilà'.

My phone starts buzzing.

'Hi, Mind,' I say, getting up and walking outside the press room door.

'Do you have a flat yet?'

'No,' I sigh. 'Keep looking on Rightmove and hoping the prices will magically plummet in a sudden property crash.'

'You want city centre, right? Don't mind renting?'

Rhys is buying me out of the house. I decided to use the money for a flat. Originally a city centre flat from which to enjoy single-woman cosmopolitan living, but the prices were a wake-up call. Mindy thinks I should rent for six months, get my bearings. Caroline thinks renting is dead money. Ivor says I can have his spare room and then he has a reason to finally kick out his flaky, noisy lodger Katya. As Mindy says, he could do that anyway if he 'found his cojones'.

'Yeees...?' I say, warily. Mindy has a way of taking a sensible premise and expanding it into something entirely mental.

'Call off the search. A buyer I work with is stinking rich and she's off to Bombay for six months. She's got a place in the Northern Quarter. I think it's a converted cotton mill or something, and apparently it's uh-may-zing. She wants a reliable flat-sitter and I said you were the most reliable person in the world and she said in that case she'll do you a deal.'

'Erm...'

Mindy quotes a monthly figure which is a fair amount of money. It's not an unfeasible amount, and certainly not a lot for the kind of place I think she's talking about. But: Mindy's encroaching madness. It'll probably come with an incontinent Maltipoo called Colonel Gad-Faffy who will only eat sushi-grade bluefin and has to be walked four times a day.

'Do you want to come and see it with me, after work?' Mindy continues. 'She flies on Friday and a cousin of hers is interested. She says he's a bit of a chang monster and she doesn't trust him. So you're front runner but you're going to have to be quick.'

'Chang monster?'

'You know. Coke. Dickhead's dust.'

'Right.'

I think it through. I was really looking for something longer term than a fixed six months. Six months with option of renewal, I'd thought. But this might be a way to live the dream while I look for something more realistic.

'Yeah, sure.'

'Great! Meet you by Afflecks at half five?'

'See you there.'

As I walk back into the press room, I realise why I've dragged my feet in moving out of the house, however uncomfortable it is. My decision to leave Rhys is about to turn from words into action, become real. Splitting equity, dividing up our worldly goods, coming-home-at-night-to-empty-rooms-and-a-big-yawning-maw-of-an-empty-future real. Part of me, a shrill, cowardly part, wants to scream: 'Wait! Stop! I didn't mean it! I want to get off!' Motion sickness kicking in.

Yet I remember the text I got from Rhys a few days ago, saying, in what sounded as much like sorrow as anger: 'I hope you're looking for places because the end of living together like this can't come fast enough for me.'

I flip my notebook open and wonder if I want another cow-shit coffee.

Zoe enters and hovers, giving off a static buzz of nerves.

'Feel free to go and get something to eat. You can leave your things here if you like,' I say.

'Thanks.' She puts her coat and bag down, and places her notebook on the table carefully.

'Unless you fancy going to the pub for lunch?' I continue, not sure where this magnanimity is coming from. Trying to atone for what I've done to Rhys, possibly. There will never be enough entries in the good deeds column of the Great Ledger of Life to offset that one.

'That would be great!'

'Give me five minutes and I'll show you why The Castle has earned the accolade of "pub nearest court".'

Zoe nods and sits down to transcribe her copy, longhand. I glance over while I'm typing. I knew it – her shorthand's so perfectly formed you could photocopy it for textbook examples.

Gretton saunters in, squinting from me to Zoe and back again.

'What's this, Bring Your Daughter To Work Day?'

Zoe looks up, startled.

'Welcome to the family,' I say to Zoe. 'Think of Gretton as the uncle who'd make you play horsey.'

I apologise to Zoe for not drinking alcohol when we get to the pub. I feel like I'm letting the profession down in moments like these. At every paper you always hear tales of great mythical beasts of olden times who could drink enough to sink battleships and still hit deadline, get up at first light the next day and do it all again. They're legend, usually because they died in their fifties.

'It's soporific in court at the best of times, what with the heating and the droning on. If I hit the bottle I'd probably end up snoring,' I say.

'Oh, it's OK, I'm a lightweight anyway,' Zoe says. 'I'll have a Diet Coke as well.'

We scan the laminated menus on the bar, hearts sinking. The Castle's menus have clearly been written by marketing managers who think they are conversant in the foreign language of 'funny'. We try merely pointing at our selected lunch items to save our dignity. No dice with the morose barman.

'I've got astigmatism,' he says, as if I should know this.

'Oh,' I reply, flustered, trying for the last route out. 'Then we'll both have the Ploughman's.'

'Naked, Piggy or Extra Pickly?'

Dammit. 'Piggy,' I mumble, defeated. 'Naked for her.'

'You want that as a melt?' he sighs, in a way that suggests most of the world's problems are down to people like us wanting melts. We decide we do, but both pass on a squirt of the chef's special sauce, given we're not on nodding terms with him.

We make small talk, battling the octave range of Mariah Carey and multiple televisions, while two microwave-warm plates are banged down under our noses. As soon as Zoe finishes her meal, she says 'Here's what I wrote', brushing crumbs off her hands and producing a spiral-bound notepad from her bag, flipping to the right page. 'I wrote it out longhand.'

I feel a twinge of irritation at being expected to mentor while I'm still eating, but swallow it, along with a mouthful of rubbery cheese. I scan her story, braced for, if not car crash copy, a fender bender at the very least. But it's good. In fact, it's very fluid and confident for a first time.

'This is good,' I nod, and Zoe beams. 'You've got the right angle, that the father and the uncle don't deny that they went to see the boyfriend.'

'What if something better comes up this afternoon? Do you stick with your first instinct?'

'Possible but unlikely. The wheels turn pretty slowly. We probably won't get on to the boyfriend's evidence this afternoon.'

I hand Zoe's notepad back to her.

'So how long have you been here?' she asks.

'Too long. I went to uni here and did my training in Sheffield, then came to the *Evening News* as a trainee.'

'Do you like court?'

'I do, actually, yeah. I was always better at writing the stories than finding them, so this suits me. And the cases are usually interesting.' I pause, worried I sound like the kind of ghoul who goes to inspect the notes on roadside flowers. 'Obviously it's nasty sometimes.'

'What's it like here?' Zoe asks. 'The news editor seems a bit scary.'

'Oh yeah.' With the flat of my knife, I push away a heap of gluey coleslaw that must've been on the plate when they heated it. 'Managing Ken is like wrestling a crocodile. We all have the bite marks to show for it. Has he asked you the octuplets question yet?'

Zoe shakes her head.

'A woman's had octuplets, ninetuplets, whatever. You get the first hospital bedside interview, while she's still whacked up on drugs. What's the one question you don't leave without asking?'

'Er ... did it hurt?'

'Are you going to have any more? She'll probably try to throw the bowl of grapes at you but that's his point. You're a journalist, always think like one. Look for the line.'

'Right,' Zoe's brow furrows, 'I'll remember that.'

I feel that hopeless twinge of wanting to save someone the million cock-ups you made when you were new, and knowing they will make their own originals, and trying to save them anyway.

'Be confident, don't bullshit and if you do mess up and it's going to come out, own up. Ken might still bawl at you but he'll trust you next time when you say it's not your fault. Lying's his *bête noire*.'

'Right.'

'Don't worry,' I assure her. 'It can be a bit overwhelming at first, then sooner or later, you start to recognise all human experience boils down to half a dozen various types of story, and you know exactly how desk will want them written. Which of course is when you've achieved the necessary cynicism, and should move on.'

'Why did you want to be a journalist?' Zoe asks.

'Hah! Lois Lane.'

'Seriously?'

'Oh yes. The brunette's brunette. Ballsy, stood up to her boss, had her own rooftop apartment and that floaty blue negligee. And she went out with Superman. My mum used to put the Christopher Reeve films on if I was off sick from school and I'd watch them on a loop. "You've got me, who's got you?" Brilliant.'

'Isn't it weird how we make big decisions in life based on the strangest, most random things?' Zoe says, sucking the straw in her Coke until it gurgles. 'Like, maybe if your mum had put *Batman* on we wouldn't be sat here right now.'

'Hmm,' I murmur indistinctly, and change the subject.

7

I see Mindy a mile off in her purple coat and red shoes. She looks like a burst of Bollywood sunshine compared to my kitchen-sink-drama drab black and white.

She calls it her Indian magpie tendencies – she can't resist jewel colours and shiny things. The shiniest thing about her is always her hair. For as long as I've known Mindy, she's used this 99p coconut shampoo that leaves her with a corona of light around her liquorice-black bob. I used it once and ended up with an NHS acrylic weave, made of hay.

She spots me and swings a key on a ribbon, like a hypnotist with a fob watch. 'At last!'

Mindy isn't kidding about it being central. Five minutes later we're there, stood in front of a red-brick Victorian building which has changed from a temple of hard toil to a place of elegant lounging for the moneyed.

'Fourth floor,' Mindy says, gazing up. 'Hopefully there's a lift.'

There is, but it's out of order, so we huff up several flights of stairs, heels pounding in time.

'No parking,' Mindy reminds me. 'Is Rhys keeping the car?'

'Oh yes. Given the way negotiations have gone so far, I'm glad we don't have any pets or children.'

My mind flashes back to hours of my life I'd pay good money to have erased. We sat and worked out how to pick apart two totally meshed lives, me effectively saying 'Have it, have it all!' and Rhys snapping 'Does it mean so little to you?'

Mindy slots the key in the lock of the anonymous looking Flat 21 and pushes the door open.

'*Shit the sheets,*' she breathes, reverentially. 'She said it was nice but I didn't know she meant *this* nice.'

We walk into the middle of a cavernous room with exposed brickwork walls. A desert of blonde wood flooring stretches out before us. Pools of honeyed light are cast here and there from some vertical paper lamps that look like alien pupae, or as if a member of Spinal Tap might tear their way out of them. The L-shaped sofa in the sitting area is an acre of snowy tundra, scattered with cushions in shades of ivory and beigey-bone. I mentally put a line through any meals involving soy sauce, red wine or flaky chocolate. That's most Friday nights as I know them buggered.

Mindy and I wander around, going 'woooh' and pointing like zombies when we discover the wet room with glass sink, or the queen-sized bed with silvery silk coverlet, or the ice-cream-pink Smeg fridge. It's like a home that a character in a post-watershed drama might inhabit. The sort of series where everyone is improbably good-looking and has insubstantial-sounding and yet lucrative jobs that leave plenty of time for leisurely brunching and furious rumping.

'Not sure about that,' I say, indicating the rug in front of the couch. It appears to be the skin of something that should be looking majestic in the Serengeti, not lying prone under a Heal's coffee table. The coarse, hairy liver-coloured patches actually make me feel unwell. 'It's got a tail and everything. Brrrr.'

'I'll see if you can put that away,' Mindy nods.

'Tell her I'm allergic to . . . bison?' It's fake, I tell myself. Surely.

Standing in the middle of the living room, we do a few more open-mouthed 360-degree revolutions and I know Mindy's planning a party already. In case we were in any doubt about the flat's primary purpose, the word 'PARTY' has been spelt out in big burnished gold letters fixed to the wall. There's also a Warholian Pop Art style print – an Indian girl with fearsome facial geometry gazes down imperiously in four colourways.

'Is that her?'

Mindy joins me. 'Oh yeah. Rupa does have an ego the size of the Arndale. See that nose?'

'The one in the middle of her face?'

'Uh-huh. Sweet sixteen present. Before . . .'

Mindy puts a finger on the bridge of her nose and makes a loop in the air, coming back to rest on her top lip.

'Really?' I feel a little guilty, discussing a woman's augmentations in her own flat.

'Yeah. Her dad's, like, one of the top plastic surgeons in the country so she got a discount. So, what do you think to the flat, then?' she says, somewhat redundantly.

'I think it's like that advert where they passed the vodka bottle across ordinary life and everything was more exciting looking through it.'

'I remember that ad,' Mindy says. 'It made you think about people you'd slept with when you had beer goggles on though. Shall I tell her you'll take it? Move in Saturday?'

'What am I going to do with my things?' I chew my lip, looking around. I was going to spoil the view by sitting down as it was.

'Do you have a lot?' Mindy asks.

'Clothes and books. And … kitchen stuff.'

'And furniture?'

'Yes. A three-bed houseful.'

'Do you really love it?'

I think about this. I quite like some of it. I have chosen it, after all. But in the event of a house fire, I couldn't imagine protectively flinging myself on the occasional table nest or the tatty red Ikea couch as the flames licked higher.

'Why I ask is, you could make a deal with Rhys to leave it. You said he's keeping the house on? It's going to be expensive for him to go and re-buy some of the bigger items, and a hassle. You could get money for them and then get things that suit wherever you end up buying. Or you could sell everything you own and buy one amazing piece, like an Eames lounger or a Conran egg chair!'

The Mindy paradox: sense and nonsense sharing a twin room – or even a bed, like Morecambe and not-so-Wise.

'I suppose I could. It all depends how badly Rhys wants me out, versus how badly he wants to make life difficult for me. Too close to call.'

'I can talk to him if you want.'

'Thanks, but … I'll give it a go first.'

We walk over to the window and the city rooftop panorama spreads out before us, lights winking on as dusk falls.

'It's so glamorous,' Mindy sighs.

'Too glamorous for me, maybe.'

'Don't do that Rachel thing of talking yourself out of something that could be good.'

'Do I do that?'

'A bit.' Mindy puts an arm around me. 'You need a change of scene.'

I put a reciprocal arm around her. 'Thank you. What a scene.' We study it in silence for a moment.

I point.

'Hang on, is that…?'

'What?' Mindy squints.

'…Swansea?'

'Piss off.'

8

Mindy has to go home to work on reports for a meeting the next day so we say our goodbyes outside the flat. I'm walking to the bus home when I find my feet taking me towards the library. A few days earlier, loitering in Waterstones, it had occurred to me that if I decided to start learning Italian, I could revise at the library. Revise for the night classes I am definitely going to sign up for, soon. And then, if I ran into Ben, it'd be chance. Just fate, giving a tiny helpful shove.

As I approach, my posture gets better and my height increases by inches. I try to look neither left nor right at anyone as I walk in but can't resist, my line of sight darting about like a petty con on a comedown. Central Library has the reverential atmosphere of a cathedral – it's a place so serene and cerebral your IQ goes up by a few points simply by entering the building.

Inside, I unpack the *Buongiorno Italia!* books I happen to have on me, feeling intensely ridiculous. OK, so ... wow, for a romantic language, this is harder work than I imagined. After ten minutes of intransitive verbs I'm feeling pretty intransitive myself. Let's try social Italian: *Booking a room ... Making introductions ...* and my mind's already wandering ...

♥ ♥ ♥

Ben knocked on my door bright and early on the first day of lectures, though not bright and early enough to pre-empt Caroline, who's the one to call the lark a feathered layabout. I was anxiously turning my face a Scottish heather/English sunburn hue with a huge blusher brush, pouting into the tiny mirror nailed over my sink. Caroline stretched her flamingo legs out on my bed, cradling a vast quantity of tea in a Cup-a-Soup mug. It was a relief to discover that the girls in my halls of residence weren't the demented, experienced, highly sexed party animals of my nightmares, but other nervous, homesick, excited teenagers, all dropped off with aid parcels of home comforts.

'Who's calling for you again?' Caroline asked.

'Someone on my course. He gave me my ID card.'

'He? Is he nice?'

'He seems very nice,' I said, without thinking.

'*Nice* nice?'

I debated whether to oblige her. We'd only been friends for a week and although she seemed sound, I didn't want to abruptly discover otherwise when she started yodelling '*My friend fancies yooooooo!*' across the union.

'He's quite nice, yeah,' I said, with more take-it-or-leave-it insouciance.

'How nice?'

'Acceptable.'

'I suppose I can't expect you to do thorough reconnaissance,' Caroline says, looking at the photo of me with Rhys on my desk.

46

It was taken in the pub, both squeezed into the frame while I held the camera above us. Our heads were leant against each other – his tangly black hair merging with my straight brown hair so it was hard to tell where he ended and I began. *Rhys and Rachel. Rachel and Rhys.* We alliterated, it was obviously meant to be. I'd daydreamed the two intertwined 'Rs' we'd have on our trendy wedding stationery invites, and would've put a firearm to my temple if he found out.

I glanced over at it too and felt a small tremor. Things were new and passionate, and unstable, like new and passionate things usually are, and we were forty miles apart. I'd been so elated when he'd said he wanted us to keep seeing each other.

We'd met a few months previously at my local. I used to go with my friends from sixth-form and we'd all sit with pints of snakebite and black and make moony eyes at the cool lads in a local band. They even had cars and jobs, their few extra years in age representing a chasm of worldly experience and maturity. This hero worship had gone on from afar for a long time. They were never short of female company and clearly content to keep a gaggle of schoolgirl groupies at arm's length. Then one night I inadvertently found myself in a two-player game of call-and-reply on the jukebox. Every time I put a song on, Rhys's selection straight after would pick up on the title. If I chose 'Blue Monday' he'd get up and play 'True Blue' and so on. (Rhys was in his ironic cheese phase. Shame it was long over by the time we really were planning our wedding.)

Eventually, after a lot of giggling, whispering and twenty-pence pieces, Rhys strode casually over to my table.

'A woman of your taste deserves to be bought a drink.'

In a moment of sangfroid I've never since equalled, I found the words: 'A man of your taste deserves to pay.'

My friends gasped, Rhys laughed, I had a Malibu and lemonade and a welcome for me and mine to join the corner of the pub they'd colonised. I couldn't believe it, but Rhys seemed genuinely interested in me. The dynamic from then on was very much his man of the world to my wide-eyed ingénue. Later I'd ask him why he'd pursued me that night.

'You were the prettiest girl in the place,' he said. 'And I had a lot of pocket shrapnel.'

There was a knock at my bedroom door and Caroline was up and over to answer it in a flash.

'Sorry. Wrong room,' I heard a male voice say.

'No, right room,' Caroline trilled, throwing the door open wider so Ben could see me, and vice versa.

'Ah,' Ben said, smiling. 'I know there were a lot of freshers and cards yesterday but I was sure you weren't blonde.'

Caroline simpered at him, trying to work out if this meant he preferred blondes or not. He looked at me, obviously wondering why I was the colour of a prawn and whether I was going to do introductions.

'Caroline, Ben, Ben, Caroline,' I said. 'Shall we get going?'

Ben said 'Hi' and Caroline twittered 'Hello!' and I wondered if I wanted The First Person I'd Met In Halls to get it on with The First Person I'd Met On My Course. I had a suspicion I didn't, on the basis it'd be tricky for me if it went badly and lonely for me if it went well.

'Enjoy your day,' Caroline said, with a hint of sexy languor that seemed at odds with it being breakfast time, trailing out of my door and back to her room.

I grabbed my bag and locked my door. We'd almost cleared the corridor without incident when Caroline called after me.

'Oh, and Rachel, that thing we were discussing before? Acceptable wasn't the right adjective. If you're studying English, you should know that!'

'Bye Caroline!' I bellowed, feeling my stomach shoot down to my shoes.

'What's that about?' Ben asked.

'Nothing,' I muttered, thinking I didn't need the bloody blusher.

Surveying the Live-Aid-sized crowds milling around for the buses, Ben suggested we walk the mile to the university buildings. We kicked through yellow-brown leaf mulch as traffic rumbled past on Oxford Road, filling in the biographical gaps – where we were from, what A-levels we did, family, hobbies, miscellaneous.

Ben, a south Londoner, grew up with his mum and younger sister, his dad having done a bunk when he was ten years old. By the time we'd passed the building that looks like a giant concrete toast rack, I knew that he broke his leg falling off a wall, aged twelve. He spent so long laid up he'd had enough of daytime telly and read everything in the house, all the Folio Society classics and even his mum's Catherine Cooksons, in desperation, before bribing his sister to go to the library for him. A splintered fibia became the bedrock of his enthusiasm for literature. I didn't tell him that mine came from not being invited out to horse around on walls all that much.

'You don't sound very northern,' he said, after I'd briefly described my roots.

'This is a Sheffield accent, what do you expect? I bet you think the north starts at Leicester.'

He laughed. A pause.

'My boyfriend says I better not come home with a Manc accent,' I added.

'He's from Sheffield?'

'Yes.' I couldn't help myself: 'He's in a band.'

'Nice one.'

I noticed Ben's respectful sincerity and that he didn't make any cracks about relationships from home lasting as long as fresher flu, and I appreciated it.

'You're doing the long-distance thing?'

'Yeah.'

'Good luck to you. No way could I do that at our age.'

'No?' I asked.

'This is the time to play the field and mess about. Don't get me wrong, once I settle down I will be totally settled. But until then ...'

'You'll collect lots of beer mats,' I finished for him, and we grinned.

When we neared the university buildings, Ben got a folded piece of paper with a room plan out of his pocket. I noticed the creases were still sharp, whereas my equivalent was disintegrating like ancient parchment after too many nervous, sweaty-handed unfolding and re-foldings.

'So, where is registration?' he asked.

We bent our heads over it together, squinting at the fluorescent orange highlighted oblong, trying to orientate ourselves.

Ben rotated it, squinted some more. 'Any ideas, Ronnie?'

My cheerfulness evaporated and I felt embarrassed. How many women did he meet yesterday?

'It's Rachel,' I said, stiffly.

'Always Ronnie to me.'

Our conversation about the stumpy passport photo came back to me and in relief and self-consciousness, I laughed too loudly. He must've seen my moment of uncertainty because there was a touch of relief in his laughter, too.

The best friendships usually steal up on you, you don't remember their start point. But there was a definitive click at that moment that told me we weren't going to politely peel apart as soon as we'd signed in and copied down our timetables.

I referred to the map again and as I leaned in I could smell the citrusy tang of whatever he'd washed with. I pointed confidently at a window.

'There. Room C 11.'

Needless to say, I was wrong, and we were late.

9

Hope has leaked out of me, collected in a puddle at my feet and evaporated into the roof of Central Library, joining the collective human misery cloud in the earth's atmosphere. No Ben, only the unavoidable evidence of how much I wanted to see him. On reflection, I'm not even sure Caroline wasn't mistaken. She wears contacts and has started doing that middle-aged thing of not being able to tell the girls from the boys if they're goths.

If Ben *was* here, it was only a flying visit for some obscure research purposes, and now he's back in his well-appointed home, far, far away. Putting his Paul Smith doctor's bag down in a black-and-white tiled hallway, leafing through his mail, calling out a hello to the equally high-powered honey he's come home to. Blissfully unaware that a woman he used to know is such a pathetic mess she's sitting a hundred and eighty miles away constantly re-reading the line: '*Excuse me, which way to the Spanish Steps?*' in a bid to appear complicated and alluring.

I get out of my seat for a wander around the room, trying to look deeply cerebrally preoccupied and steeped in learning. The toffee-brown parquet floor is so highly polished it shimmers like a mirage. As I trail my fingers along the spines of books, I start as I see a brown-haired, possibly thirty-something man with his back to me. He's sitting at a table tucked between the bookcases that line the edge of the room, so if you had an aerial view, they would look like the spokes inside a wheel.

It's him. It's him. Oh my God, *it's him*.

My heart's pulsing so hard it's as if someone medically quali-fied has reached through my sawn ribs to squeeze it in a resus-citation attempt. I wander down past his seat and pretend to find a book of special interest as I draw level with his table. I pull it out and study it. In an unconvincing way, I pivot round absent-mindedly while I'm reading, so I'm facing him. It's so unsubtle I might as well have shot a paper plane over to him and ducked. I risk a glance. The man looks up at me, adjusts rimless glasses.

It's not him. A rucksack with neon flashes is propped near his feet, his trouser hems are circled with bicycle clips. I sag at the realisation that this must be who Caroline's seen, too, and decide to gather my things. I pack up in seconds, no longer bothering to look appealing, on the final gamble that the law of sod will therefore produce him.

I shouldn't have come here. I'm acting out of character and hyper-irrational in the post-traumatic stress of splitting up with Rhys. I don't know what I'd say to Ben or why I'd want to see him. Actually, that's not true. I know why I want to see him but the reasons don't bear examination.

A clutch of people in fleeces and hats, who appear to be being given a guided tour, block my exit from the library. Like an impatient local, I retreat and double back round them. Deep in thought, I smack straight into someone coming the other direction.

'Sorry,' I say.

'Sorry,' he mutters back, in that reflexive British way where you're apologetic that someone else has had to make an apology.

In order to perform the little tango of manoeuvring past each other, we exchange a distracted glance. There's absolutely no way this man can be Ben. I'd know, I'd sense it if he was this close. I glance at his face anyway. It registers as 'stranger' then reforms into something familiar, with that oddly dull thud of revelation.

Oh Judas Priest! *There he is.* THERE HE IS! Plucked from my memory and here in the real world, in full colour HD. His hair's slightly longer than the university years' crop but still short enough to be work-smart, and they're unmistakeably his features, the sight of them transporting me back a decade in an instant. And, despite the world's longest ever build-up to a reappearance since Lord Lucan, Caroline's right – he still takes air out of lungs.

He's lost the slightly unformed, baby-fat look we all had back then, sharpening into something even more characterfully handsome. There's a fan of light lines at the corner of each eye, the set of his mouth a little harder. His frame has filled out a little from the youthful lankiness of before.

It's the strangest sensation, looking at someone who I know well and don't know at all, at the same time. He's staring too, although it's the staring Catch-22: he could be staring because I'm staring. For an awful instant, I think either Ben's not going to recognise me or – worse – pretend not to recognise me. But he doesn't take flight. He opens his lips and there's a pause, as if he has to remember how to engage his voice box and soft and hard palates to produce sounds.

'…Rachel?'

'Ben?' (Like I haven't given myself an unfair head start in this quiz.)

His brow stays furrowed in disbelief but he smiles, and a wave of relief and joy crashes over me.

'Oh my God, I don't believe it. How are you?' he says, at a subdued volume, as if our voices are going to carry into the library upstairs.

'I'm fine,' I squeak. 'How are you?'

'I'm fine too. Mildly stunned right now, but otherwise fine.'

We laugh, eyes still wide: *this is crazy*. More than he knows.

'Surreal,' I agree, feeling my way tentatively back into a familiarity, like stumbling around your bedroom in the pitch dark, trying to remember where everything is. 'You live in Manchester?' he asks.

'Yes. Sale. About to move into the centre. You?'

'Yeah, Didsbury. Moved up from London last month.'

He brandishes a briefcase, like the Chancellor with the Budget.

'I'm a boring arse lawyer now, would you believe.'

'Really? You did one of those conversion courses?'

'No. I blag it. Thought there was a saturation point when I'd seen enough TV dramas, I could go from there. Like *Catch Me If You Can*.'

He's straight faced and I'm so shell-shocked that it takes me a second to process that this is humour.

'Ah right,' I nod. Then hurriedly: 'I'm a journalist. Of sorts. Court reporter for the local paper.'

'I knew you'd be the one to actually use that English degree.'

'I wouldn't say that. Not much call for opinions on Thomas Hardy when I'm covering the millionth car jacking.'

'Why are you here?'

I'm startled by this, classic guilty conscience.

'The library, I mean?' Ben adds.

'Oh, er, revision for my night class. Learning Italian,' I say, liking how it sounds self-improving even as I cringe at the lie. 'You?'

'Exams. Bastard things never end. At least these mean I get paid more.'

The fleecy crowd are pouring round us and I know there's only so long we can conduct this conversation, stood here.

'Uh. Got time for a coffee?' I blurt, as if it's a mad notion that's popped unbidden into my mind, tense with the fear of seeing him grasp for an excuse.

'If we've got a decade to cover, we might even need two,' Ben replies, without missing a beat.

I *glow*. Rough-sleepers outside could huddle round me and warm their hands.

10

We make jittery small talk about revision, both real and ficti-tious, until we reach the half-empty basement café. He goes to get the coffees, cappuccino for me, filter for him. I sit down at a table, rub my sweaty palms on my dress and watch Ben in the queue.

He digs in his suit trouser pocket for change, under an expensive-looking military-style grey coat. I see he continues to dress as if he's starring in a film about himself. It's completely unnecessary to look like that if you're a solicitor. He should be lounging about in an aftershave advert on a yacht, not navigating ordinary life with the rest of us, showing us all up.

It wasn't so much his looks that always had females falling all over Ben, I realise, though they hardly hindered. He had what I suppose actors call 'presence'. What Rhys calls *tossing about as if you own the place*. He moves as if the hinges on his joints are looser than everyone else's. Then there's his dry humour: light, quick remarks that are somehow rather unexpected coming from someone so handsome. You're conditioned to expect the beautiful to have less intellect to balance things out.

Yet while I'm gazing at him and feeling my insides liquefy, he's chatting to the middle-aged lady serving the coffees, totally normally and unperturbed. To me, this is a monumental event. To him, I am a historical footnote. This huge disparity spells huge trouble. If this was a fairytale, I'd be staring with unquenchable thirst at a bottle labelled POISON. For now, it's going to taste like milky coffee.

As Ben returns and sets my cup down, he says: 'No sugar, right?'

I nod, delighted he retains such trivia. Then I spot a new and non-trivial detail about him – a simple silver band on the third finger of his left hand. It was absolutely bound to be the case, I told myself that many times, and yet I still feel as if I've been slapped.

'You know, Italians only have cappuccinos in the morning. It's a breakfast drink,' I blurt, for absolutely no reason whatsoever.

'Something you learned on your course?' Ben asks, pleasantly.

'Er. Yes.' Here's the point where fortune farts in my face and Ben's wife turns out to be half-Italian. He rattles out some lyrical phrases, and I have to pretend I'm only on my first few lessons. Ben's *wife*.

'Have you been in a cryogenic chamber since uni?' Ben continues. 'You look exactly the bloody same. It's a little freaky.'

I'm relieved I don't look raddled, and try not to blush disproportionately at an implied compliment. 'No ageing sunlight penetrates courtrooms.'

'Same apart from your hair, of course,' he adds, gesturing the shorter length with a chopping motion of his hand at his neck. It was longer, at university, then I got a more businesslike on-shoulders 'do after a few occasions in court when I was mistaken for the girlfriend of a defendant.

I tuck a strand behind my ear, self-consciously: 'Oh, yeah.'

'Suits you,' he says, lightly.

'Thank you. You look well, too.' I take a sharp breath. 'So, tell me all about your life. Married, two point four kids, belter of a pension plan?'

'Married, yes,' Ben says.

'Fantastic!' I make sure every last syllable sounds robustly delighted. 'Congratulations.'

'Thank you. Olivia and I celebrated our two-year anniversary last month.'

The name gives me a twinge. All the Sloaney-I've-got-a-pony girls on our course were called things like Olivia and Tabitha and Veronica and we used to take arms against them in our non-posh gang of two. And he traitorously married one of them. I momentarily wish I had a Toby to wield in retaliation.

'Well done,' I waffle on. 'Did you have the big white production?'

'Urgh, no,' Ben shudders. 'Registry office at Marylebone. We hired an old Routemaster and had posh shepherd's pie wedding breakfast in a room above a pub. A nice one, I mean, Liv chose it. All idyllic with kids running round in the garden afterwards, we had great weather.'

I nod and he suddenly looks self-conscious.

'Bit cliché, trendified Chas'n'Dave, Beefeater London, I guess, but we liked it.'

'Sounds great.' It does sound great. And cool, and romantic. I don't care what the bride wore or want to see the album though. All right, I do.

'Yeah, it was. No faceless hotel, DJ with a fake American accent, three million relatives glumly picking at a duff carvery that cost three million quid, none of that rubbish.'

'That's only a quid per head budget. Quite tight really.'

Ben smiles, distractedly, and I see the wheels turning, him remembering things that have nothing to do with this weak joke, things he's not going to mention.

For a split second, sensing his discomfort, I marvel at my own masochism. Did I really want to sit here listening to how he promised all his remaining days to someone else? Couldn't I have taken that as a given? Did I want to discover a broken man? No. I wanted him to be happy and it was also going to be the thing that hurt the most. That's the reason this was such a bad idea. *One* of the reasons.

We sip our coffees. I discreetly wipe my mouth in case of chocolate powder moustache.

He continues: 'Kids, not yet. Pension, yes, really cuts into my having-fun fund.'

'Still able to spend harder than Valley girls?'

I remember days trailing round clothes shops with Ben, waiting outside changing rooms, enjoying the gender reversal. He even took my advice on what to buy – it was like having my old Ken doll become self-aware. ('Not that self-aware if he's behaving like a southern poof,' Rhys said.)

'Oh yes,' Ben says. 'I have to hide the bags from Liv as principal earner. It's emasculating. What about you? Married?' He picks up his spoon and stirs his coffee, although he didn't add any sugar, and drops his gaze momentarily. 'To Rhys?'

If we were hooked up to polygraphs, the line would've got squigglier.

'Engaged for a while. We've just split up actually.'

Ben looks genuinely appalled. Great, we skipped schaden-freude and went straight to abject pity. 'God, sorry.'

'Thanks. It's OK.'

'You should've stopped me going on about weddings.'

'I asked. It's fine.'

'Is that why you're moving?'

'Yeah,' I nod.

'No kids?'

'No.'

'That's funny, I was sure you would have, for some reason,' Ben says, unguardedly. 'A little girl with her mother's attitude problems, and the same stupid mittens.'

He gives me a small smile and looks into his cup again. The warmth of this – the reference to something obscure that only we'd understand, the fact it reveals he's thought about me – prompts me to emit a small, strangled noise that approximates a giggle. Then, in a moment, it drenches me with sadness. Like my chest cavity is full of rainwater.

We avoid each other's eyes and move on. Ben tells me about the law firm he's joined, how his wife's also a solicitor. She got transferred from her London practice to their Manchester office so she could be up here with him. They met at a Law Society dinner. The crowded room, black tie. The scene plays in my head like a trailer for a Richard Curtis film I most definitely don't want to see.

He concludes, jokily: 'If I'm a solicitor and you're a court reporter, perhaps we shouldn't be speaking?'

'Depends. What department are you in?'

'Family.'

'Divorce settlements, that kind of thing?'

'Yeah, access arrangements. Sometimes grim. Other times, if you can get the right outcome, grim satisfaction.'

I understand why he'd want to work in that area, and he knows I know, so I nod. 'I think there'd be more of a conflict in talking to a reporter if you were in criminal.'

'Couldn't take the hours. The friend who got me the job up here is in criminal. He's on call all the time, it's punishing. Actually, he was saying he wants to talk to the press about a case. Shall I give him your name?'

'Of course,' I say, eager to please and forge a connection.

We get to the end of one coffee and, despite my offer to buy the second, Ben checks his watch and says he'd love to but he probably ought to be going.

'Yeah, me too, now you mention it,' I lie, twisting my watch round and glancing at it without looking at the time.

Ben waits solicitously as I pull my coat on. I hope he's not noticing the stone I've gained since university. ('Stone,' Rhys used to snort. 'A stone weighing thirty pounds? Did I miss the latest barmy Brussels directive?')

We walk outside together.

'It's great to see you, Rachel. I can't believe it's been ten years, it's incredible.'

'Yeah, unbelievable,' I agree.

'We should keep in touch. Me and Liv don't know many people up here. You can tell us where's good to go out in Manchester these days.'

'I'd love to!' Like I know. 'I'll get Caroline, Mindy and Ivor out, too.'

'Wow, you still see them?'

'Yeah. I see them all the time.'

'That's really nice,' Ben nods, yet I feel it's another example of my decade-long stasis, as if I sit around in a moth-eaten Miss Havisham graduation ballgown, listening to a crackly recording of Pulp's "Disco 2000". 'I'll let you know about that story, too. What's your number?'

Ben keys it in while I try to remember the numbers in the right sequence, awash with adrenaline.

He checks his watch again: 'Crap, I'm late. What about you? Need walking to your stop?'

'It's only round the corner, I'll be fine, go.'

'Sure?'

'Yes, thanks.'

'See you soon, Rachel. I'll call you.'

He ducks down and pecks me on the cheek. I hold my breath in the shock of the contact and the brush and warmth of his skin against mine. Then there's a horrifically awkward moment when he unexpectedly goes for the other cheek too in that media London/sophisticated European way. I don't expect it and we nearly bump faces, so I have to put my hand on his shoulder to steady myself and then panic it looks too forward, over-correcting by leaping backwards.

'See you!' I say, though what I really want to do is re-run the action without me being such a gauche fool, in the manner of a bossy child directing a play in their front room. 'Right, you stand there, I am here again … Go!'

I walk to my stop in a semi-trance-like state, cartoon stars circling round my head, the two recently kissed places on my face burning. There's the illicit rush at seeing him – and he asked to see me again! – combined with the spirit-flattening confirmation that his life's shiny and joyful and functional and mine isn't.

An hour after I get home, when the fixed grin has faded and I'm watching the old telly in the spare room, I let tears fall. Once the dam has cracked, there's a deluge. Married. Happily. Olivia. *What's even in a posh shepherd's pie?*

I feel as if I've woken up after a coma, been jolted back to life by a favourite song. I'm not sure I like the view from my bed. The experience of meeting Ben again is the very definition of the word bittersweet.

Then two very clear questions form in the tears, snot and inner maelstrom: how am I going to feel if he doesn't call? And what good's going to come of it if he does?

11

I don't ask Rhys to borrow the car so I can move my things because I know he'll want to use the car to be nowhere near the house on the day I leave.

The evening before last, I was coming out of the shower with a towel wrapped around my body and another around my head. I was moving quickly because any extra amount of skin on show feels inappropriate, post-separation. Rhys charged up the stairs. I thought he was going to dodge past, or argue about the cavalier use of the hot water, but he stopped in front of me, looked me in the eye. His eyes were unexpectedly moist.

'Stay,' he said, thickly.

I thought I'd misheard. It sunk in.

'I can't,' I blurt.

He nodded, not even angry, or resentful. He galloped back down the stairs and left me standing on the landing, shivering. Turns out the consequences of a huge decision don't all tumble down at once like opening an over-full cupboard; they keep hitting you in waves.

When I tell Caroline I'm going to hire a removal van, she asks what I'm taking with me and decides it can be done in a few runs in her car. She turns up early on a Saturday to find me, lightly sweaty, standing in a hallway crammed with everything I own that's portable. It feels strangely like leaving for university, only with bleak despair where all the bright hope used to be.

Rhys went for Mindy's plan about the furniture. I saw the thought scroll across his face – 'Screw making life easier for her' – then imagining those flat-bed-truck-style trolleys in IKEA, and he grunted his agreement. So it's clothes, books, DVDs, a surprisingly huge haul of bathroom toiletries, and then 'odds and sods', a category which sounds like it should be the smallest but turns out to be the largest. Photo albums, plants, accessories, pictures… I've been scrupulously fair whenever encountering something the house only has one of – hot water bottle, mop bucket, cafetiere, engagement ring – and left it for Rhys.

Caroline casts an appraising eye over the junk and decides it's two journeys, three at a pinch. We start heaping it into the back of her Audi saloon and, with the back seats folded down and some determined pushing, we make decent in-roads.

'Definitely two journeys,' Caroline concludes, as I lock the front door, saying what I'm thinking, minus the part about how much I'm dreading coming back for the next and last time.

We set off, me blithely chattering about the flat to distract from the inner turmoil, Caroline casting worried glances at me whenever she can take her line of sight off the road.

'We don't have to go, you know. If you've changed your mind…' she starts, and I bite my lip hard and furiously shake my head to indicate *please, not now.*

Caroline pats my knee and asks about the route. When we arrive at the flat, I'm grateful for all the tasks – paying the car-parking meter, unlocking the flat, running relays with armfuls of clutter – to occupy me. Eventually it's all piled up and time to collect the rest. I deep breathe and blow the air out as if I'm an athlete limbering up for a feat of exertion.

Back at my house, or what used to be my house, the rest of the packing is completed in minutes.

I can't go yet. I can't. I sit down on the front door step and try to gather myself, instead I feel myself unravelling. A bit of a sniffle turns into whole-body sobbing and I feel Caroline's hand on my shaking shoulder.

When I pull my messy face back up from my knees I say, through all the liquid that's leaving my body via my eyes, mouth and nose, 'I don't have anything to sleep in.'

'What do you mean?' Caroline asks, crouching down in front of me. 'Rupa's got a bed, hasn't she?'

'No,' I gesture downwards. 'To sleep in. I always wore one of Rhys's t-shirts. A Velvet Underground one. I've left it behind.' I wipe my eyes. 'Is it mine? Or is it his? I don't even know.'

I recommence sobbing while Caroline rubs my back.

'You've been together such a long time and this has all happened so quickly. You've got to expect it to hurt, Rach.'

There's something about Caroline's kindly no-nonsense that really sorts you out when you're in a spiral. She's sympathetic without being indulgent. The difference between seeing the school nurse instead of your mum when you've grazed your knee.

'I'm going to miss him,' I say.

'I know you are.' She rubs harder, as if I might be able to cough the hurt up and get it out that way.

'I can't tell him that.'

'Why not?'

'Because I'm leaving him!' I bawl, and break down again.

She moves in beside me on the step, I shift across, both of us ignoring the kids kicking a ball across the street who are looking at us curiously.

'Look,' she lowers her voice slightly, 'I don't want to sound too much like a therapist but I think you're bound to feel guilty, and you're going to feel sad. You have to simply feel it. Don't hate yourself. It is what it is. God, that sounds so trite …'

'No it doesn't. It actually makes sense.'

'Really? Well, good.'

We sit in silence for half a minute.

'We don't have to do all this now if you want to stay another night,' she adds.

This surprises me. Caroline is usually of the 'have at it' school. I have a feeling she'd like to see a rethink, and a reunion.

'No, no, I'm OK,' I insist. 'I want to get it done now.'

Or maybe it's some damn smart reverse psychology.

Caroline stands up, brushes her knees off and holds out her hand to help me up.

'I'll get Mindy to choose some pyjamas for you. You know how she loves a shopping project.'

I smile, weakly, take her hand and haul myself to my feet.

'Sure you want to leave so much behind?' Caroline says, as she checks she's squeezed the boot shut fully. 'I know Mindy thinks it's a good idea, but Mindy thought her last three boyfriends were good ideas.'

'Yeah. I'll have the money to buy it all again. I'm not leaving that much.'

I look up at the house and it stares down at me blankly, in agreement. I think about the envelope I left next to the telephone, containing the ring I'm no longer wearing.

Caroline says nothing more, pats me on the shoulder and gets into the driver's seat. I take a deep rattling breath and walk round to the passenger side.

This is it. I'm leaving. And there was nothing to mark it. Not so much as a significant look passed between Rhys and I. Maybe this is how it always is. It feels like something more formal should be required: an official handshake, a splitting up ceremony, a certificate. As Rhys said, is this all it's worth, after thirteen years?

12

Caroline eventually breaks the waterlogged silence in the front of the Audi.

'I was wrong about buying straight away. Maybe Mindy is right and this... interlude is exactly what you need.'

'Thanks. I thought you were saying Mindy's judgement is dubious?'

'Not always.'

I know they'll have discussed me, worried about me, and there's a question that I can't put off asking any longer.

'Do you all think I'm making a massive mistake?'

There's a tense pause.

'There isn't an "all"...'

'Oh, God.' I put a hand over my face. 'Three different types of disapproval.'

'It's not disapproval, you're thirty-one. It's not for us or anyone else to say what's right for you. I suppose I was surprised you didn't mention any problems before, that's all.'

'I didn't want to talk behind Rhys's back. I wasn't sure how I felt, truth be told. I was being carried along by the wedding planning and then he was being a shit about it and it came tumbling out and there it was.'

'It wasn't worth giving him a shape-up-or-ship-out? You never put your foot down enough, in my opinion, and it might've led to ... laziness.'

'I did try suggesting a counsellor or whatever. He wasn't interested.'

'I doubt he wanted to lose you. He's stubborn ...'

'You can't ask someone not to be who they are. That's where we were.'

'Couldn't you ... if you'd ...'

'Caro, please. I can't do this now. I will do soon, over wine, for hours. We can thrash the whole thing out until you're sick of hearing about it. But not now.'

'Sorry.'

'It's fine. Let's talk about something else.'

Hmm. Not sure when this 'soon' will arrive. I possibly want to wait until 2064 when she can put a data stick in her ear and download the information straight into her frontal cortex.

Then on reckless impulse I add: 'Oh, I saw Ben.'

'Ben? Ben from uni? Where? I thought you weren't going to look him up? How was he?'

I'm grateful that Caroline can only fix her eyes on me momentarily before she has to return them to the road.

'Uh, the library. I decided I wanted to learn Italian as part of the New Me, and there he was. We had a coffee. Seems well. Married.'

Caroline snorts. 'Hah! Well he was *bound* to be. Anyone as attractive and house-trainable as that gets snapped up mid-twenties, latest.'

71

'Anyone decent's married by now?'

Caroline realises what she's said and grimaces. 'No! I mean, men like him are. There are more good women than men, so supply and demand dictates his sort are long gone off the market.'

'Doesn't bode well for my prospects in finding someone then.'

Caroline is crunching the gears, and looks like an Egyptian terracotta head I once saw in the British Museum. 'I didn't mean … oh, you know …'

'Don't worry,' I say, 'I agree with you. Ben was always going to be married, and maybe choices post-thirty aren't great. The divorces are going to start soon, I'll pick someone up on their second lap.'

Caroline gives me a laugh that's more grateful than amused. 'You'll be fine.'

'Mindy and Ivor are still single, and they're normal and nice. Well, fairly normal.'

'Exactly!'

I'm not feeling half as casual as I'm trying to sound, for both our sakes. Starting again. From the beginning. With someone who doesn't know the million important and incidental things about me, who isn't fluent in the long-term couple language that I've taken for granted for so long with Rhys. How will anyone ever know as much about me again, and vice versa? Will I find anyone who wants to learn it? I imagine a York Notes revision style aid on Rachel Woodford. Or a Wikipedia page, lots of claims from Rhys followed by [citation needed].

And is this a brutal truth, everyone good has gone? As if soul mates are one big early-bird-gets-the-worm January sale. Buy the wrong thing, have to return it, and you're left with the stuff no one else wanted. This is the kind of thinking I'd scoff at from my mum, yet I was always scoffing from the security of a relationship. I feel a lot less sure of my 'Don't be so Stepford' stance now I've got to test the truth of the hypothesis.

A few circuits of the apartment building to find a parking space demonstrates why it's as well Rhys has kept our car.

'I'll stay here so I don't get a clamping,' Caroline says. 'If I see a warden I'll go round the block, so don't panic I've legged it with your towels.'

I discover how unfit I am as I run from car to flat door, and Caroline manages not to get ticketed the whole time.

When I take the last of it, she says: 'So I'd stay but I'd have thought you want to show your mum round, now she's here?'

'Uh? My mum's not here.'

'She's there.'

Caroline gestures over my shoulder. My mum is counting out coins from her big snap-clasp purse into the upturned hat of a man with a dog on a string, her black Windsmoor shawl coat billowing like Professor Snape's cape. She's always immaculately turned out and a ringer for Anne Bancroft, circa *The Graduate*. I think she wonders how she gave birth to someone inches shorter, and many degrees swearier and scabbier in her habits, though she might want to look to my dad for at least part of the answer.

'Oh, bloody hell…'

Caroline smiles and climbs back into the car, waving farewell to my mum.

'Hello darling! Was that Caroline? Delightful girl. Still has the metabolism of a greyhound, I see. Some have all the luck, eh?'

'Hi Mum. Uhm. What are you doing here?'

'I'm off to Samantha's make-up rehearsal thingy at John Lewis, with Barbara. You can come if you like?'

'Come to the wedding make-over of a family friend I haven't seen for fifteen years, while thinking about how I'm not getting married and making it completely awkward for them?'

'Oh, nonsense. They'd love to see you.'

'I'd have been useless enough company when I *was* getting married. And I seem to remember Sam's a "squee!" type girl.'

'"Squee" girl?'

'Squee wee! Fun-a-roonie dot com! Let's go get scrummy cupcakes and have proper giggles.'

My mum leans in to give me a kiss on the cheek. 'Come on, no one likes a bitter lemon. Show me your new digs.'

We take the stairs instead of the lift, me walking with the heavy tread of someone on their way to the electric chair, not the kind of lifestyle flat that has a pink fridge. I pull the key out of my pocket and let us in. It smells strange in here, as in, not like home. I stare balefully at the mini-mountain of my crap that's blotting the manicured landscape.

'Goodness me, very gaudy, isn't it. Like the 1960s have been sick.'

'Thanks Mum! I like it actually.'

'Hmm, well as long as you do, that's the main thing. I can see that it's different.'

Different is usually an innocuous word, but it's one of my mum's most damning verdicts.

She unhooks her handbag from her shoulder and sits down next to me. I know exactly what's coming. She clears her throat. Here it comes …

'Now. You and Rhys. I understand you're going through a crisis—'

'Mum! I'm not going through it, like a squall of bad weather on the road to still getting married. We've broken up.'

'If you'd allow me to speak, as someone who's been married forty years...'

I pick sullenly at a seam on the sofa.

'...Marriage is difficult. You do get on each other's nerves. It's relentless. It's very, very tough and quite honestly, even in the good times, you do wish they'd go boil their head, most days.'

'I'm not too bothered about missing out on it then!'

'What I'm saying is, what you're feeling – it's perfectly normal.'

'If relationships are only ever what we had, I'd rather be on my own.'

Pause.

'You could be throwing away your only chance to have children, have you thought of that?'

My mum: not a loss to the world of motivational speaking.

'Amazingly enough I had factored it in, but, thanks...'

'I simply want you to be very sure you're making the right decision, that's all. You and Rhys have been together an awfully long time.'

'That's why I'm sure.' Pause. 'It'd mean a lot to me if you took me seriously and accepted I know my own mind about who I do and don't want to marry, Mum. This is hard enough as it is.'

'Well. If you're *absolutely sure*.'

'I am.' And of course as I say it, I realise I'm not absolutely sure. I'm as sure as I assume you need to be, given I've never broken off an engagement before and have nothing to compare this to.

My mum stands up.

'Your dad and I will be round soon. Let us know if we need to bring any odds and sods you're short of.'

'OK, thanks.' Suddenly my throat has furred up and I give her a tight squeeze, inhaling her familiar scent of YSL Rive Gauche in place of Rupa's flat's olfactory newness.

With my mum's departure, relief though it is, I feel almost as bereft as I did when waving my parents off from the halls of residence car park. I need a massive cup of tea, one that requires two handles on the mug in order to lift it. With a tot of Maker's Mark in it.

I stare out of the huge window and suddenly the vastness doesn't seem glamorous, but precarious. I imagine how tiny I'd look from the other side of the glass. A little scared sad insignificant figure peering down over the Manchester rooftops.

For a lurching moment, I'm so homesick I almost shout out loud: *I want to go home.* But home and Rhys are indivisible.

13

In late afternoon, when I've filled dead air with impersonal radio, a weird additional sound echoes round the room and I realise it's the doorbell. I unlatch the chain and swing the door open to see an explosion of pink and white flowers and a pair of legging-clad legs beneath them.

'Happy Moving-In Day!' Mindy shouts.

'Hello, wow, lilies. That talk. That's lovely of you.'

Mindy pushes her way through the door, Ivor trailing behind, hands in pockets. He leans in and gives me a peck on the cheek. I can tell from his reluctant demeanour that Mindy's given him a 'Congratulate Her On Making A Good Choice' lecture on the way here. He holds out a Marks & Spencer bag.

'From me, but not chosen by me, I hasten to add,' Ivor says. 'I did not touch cloth, as they say.'

I peer inside. Pyjamas. Really nice ones, in cream silk.

'You're not going to cry are you?' Ivor says. 'The receipt's in there.'

'I'm not going to cry,' I say, tearing up a bit. 'Thank you.'

As Mindy turns this way and that, looking for the right

surface to put the flowers, she leaves a massive sweep of ochre pollen on the pristine, wedding cake wall.

'They're from Ivor too,' she adds, finding her pitch and marching over to the coffee table, more pollen from the trembling flowers shaking a fine, fire-coloured powder in her wake.

I discreetly put a hand over my mouth, surveying the mess.

'You're welcome!' Mindy sing-songs, turning round and seeing me, taking it as being agog at the gift.

Ivor has followed my line of sight. He adds under his breath: 'Let's say they're from you. I'll clean up, shall I?'

'What do you think, Ivor?' Mindy calls, doing a gameshow-girl twirl to indicate she means the flat.

'I think it looks like a female American Psycho's lair. Patrick Batewoman.' He rinses a chamois under the tap, which is on one of those bendy arms you usually see in industrial kitchens. 'In a good way.'

As Mindy potters around in vermilion ankle boots, taking it all in for a second time, Ivor gingerly dabs at the damage. He turns to me and nods, to say *it's coming off*, and gestures for me to join Mindy.

'Drink?' I ask, wondering as I say it where my kettle is and what I'm going to do for milk.

'I can't stay actually, I've got a date,' Mindy says.

'Bo... Robert?' I ask.

'Bobby Trendy's been given his cards,' Ivor interjects, breaking off from his cleaning up.

Robert was always head-to-toe in All Saints with bicycle chains hanging out of his back pocket and got the nickname 'Bobby Trendy' from Ivor. Unfortunately, once uttered, it was hard to un-stick it from your mind.

'Yeah, he sacked my family dinner off for a paintballing thing with his brother-in-law.' Mindy waves her hand. 'Enough was enough. There should be a TripAdvisor on dates, so you can give feedback. Nice view. Bad service. Book waaaay in advance.'

'Small portions,' Ivor coughs into his fist.

'Who's this one from, Guardian Soulmates?' I say.

'My Single Friend.'

'Is that the one where a friend recommends you?'

'Yeah. I posed as a man and sold myself as a low-maintenance mamacita who "works as hard as she plays".'

I make an 'oh dear' face.

'It only means solvent, not a clinger, potential for sex,' Mindy adds. Ivor grimaces.

'Yes, I know,' I say. 'Isn't someone else supposed to do it?'

'How could anyone else describe me better than I can describe myself?'

'Why join a site where that's the point then?'

Mindy shrugs. 'Men trust tips from other men. Recommendations from other women are like, "bubbly, great social life" and they think, ho hum, hooched-up woofer.'

'Narcissism and deception, the classic inceptors of healthy relationships,' Ivor says, dropping down on the sofa next to us.

'Anyway. I've kind of over-fished on Guardian Soul Destroyers. Waiting for stocks to replenish. This one's twenty-three.' Mindy chews her lip. 'And he likes grime. The music, you know, not dirt. God knows what we're going to talk about.'

'Well, *him*, if your previous experiences are anything to go by,' I say, and Ivor laughs.

'But his profile picture – young John Cusack,' Mindy sighs. Ivor gives me a look. I return it. Neither of us say anything.

Mindy has a theory of compatibility and none of us have ever been able to persuade her out of it. She says instant physical attraction is a pre-requisite for any successful relationship – it's either identifiably there, or not, from the start. Thus she's only ever bothered with boys who she thinks are good-looking, reasoning she needs to find a handsome man with whom she has other things in common. No amount of contradictory examples or criticism about being shallow has ever moved Mindy an inch on this. Of course, it means she's dated a procession of vain Prince Charmings with the souls of frogs.

I check my watch.

'When is this date? Are you going for high tea?'

'It's not until eight but I've got to get ready. I'm going to get some pure oxygen and have my eyebrows threaded.'

'You know how it works. Mindy goes into pre-production, like an over-budget Hollywood blockbuster. Development hell,' Ivor says.

'Obviously, I should just change my t-shirt and pour a bottle of Lynx Caveman all over myself,' Mindy snaps back, standing up.

'I wouldn't do that,' Ivor says, mildly, 'Lynx is for men.'

Mindy shakes her head at Ivor and gives me a hug. 'Start planning the party. Who knows, if this goes well, I might bring Jake.'

'Jake,' Ivor scoffs. 'He's even got a name that dates him as post-1985.'

'Says *Ivor*.'

'My name's never been in fashion so it can't go out. It only dates me as post ninth century, dear.'

'Whevs! Bye, Rach.'

'Good luck with the Relic Hunter!' Ivor shouts, as I show her out.

Mindy turns in the doorway and gives him two fingers.

'Do you think,' I drop down on the sofa and squeeze an oyster coloured cushion to my body, then feel the shop-fresh plump starchy newness of it and realise these cushions aren't for squeezing and put it back, 'Mindy will ever revise this ruthless policy of looks first, personality a distant second, compatibility irrelevant?'

'Probably not.'

We shake our heads.

'What're your plans? Want me to stay?' Ivor asks, and I wonder why today feels like a series of polite rejections. 'Or go?'

'Erm,' I say, trying to work out what he wants me to say. I feel as if a strange stigma is clinging to me. I have some insight into how the newly bereaved crave people who don't walk on eggshells around them.

'I was going to make use of Katya being away for the weekend and have a *Grand Theft Auto* marathon and eat vacuum-packed pork products,' he continues. 'You're welcome to join me.'

'Hah, no, thanks, I'm fine. Enjoy killing all those hookers.'

I see Ivor out and tell myself sternly that I'm very lucky to have supportive friends, and being single means getting used to your own company and not inventing excuses to keep people around you. None of which makes me feel any less bereft. The latest revelation: you have to relearn being on your own again. Rhys and I had separate interests. We didn't live in each other's pockets. Yet the empty quiet of the flat stretches like an island around me, and the city an ocean beyond that.

I do some more unpacking until the discovery of the old framed photo from university starts me crying, and the intensity of the urge to call Rhys and say I've changed my mind is like

Class A withdrawal. I sit scrolling up and down to his name in my mobile phone address book. I wouldn't have to say anything desperate: all I'd be doing is checking in on him. I stop. However he's getting through today, I need to let him get on with it. I've put myself beyond being able to help him, on this. I imagine him alone in that bed tonight and think: I'm lucky. I get a fresh start in new surroundings. He has the site of our old life, minus me.

Unbidden, my mind starts playing me a montage of our edited highlights. The first night we spent together at his old flat and me falling out of bed and onto his effects pedal, which was a baptism of fire for new love – I screamed the place down and had a bruise the size of a handprint on my back. The run to the shops to get painkillers and the breakfast he made me the next day, involving seven pans and three types of eggs. The day I met his family, when I was virtually levitating with nerves, and Rhys saying on the doorstep: 'They'll love you. Not because I do. Because everyone with eyes and ears does.' The weekend in Brighton with the world's worst car journey down, the dubious Nazi-run B&B that was nowhere near the seafront and the bistro with the horrible waiters. It could've been awful but instead I remember laughing like a pair of school kids for two days solid. The day we moved into our house and drank champagne out of mugs, sitting on the stairs, in a furniture-free desert of sandy carpet, arguing about whether his frightening Iggy Pop photo had too many pubes on show to be fit for the 'reception rooms'. The scores of in-jokes and shared history and special knowledge I couldn't imagine having with anyone ever again, not without a Tardis to whisk me back to being twenty.

What was I doing, throwing all this away? Did it all add up to say I should stay with Rhys? Was I making the biggest mistake of my life? Probably not, purely on the basis that award has already been handed out.

I tell myself, this day is as bad as it's going to be. This is a day you have to get through. It occurs to me that it'd be easier to get through unconscious. I crawl to the huge bed, cover my face with my arms and weep myself to sleep.

As I drift off, I imagine the supermodelly Indian girl animating in her portrait, looking down, saying: 'Well, *that's* not what this flat is for.'

14

I awake to an odd noise, like a bee trapped in a tin can and something scuttling over a hard surface. I sit bolt upright in the twilight and think, Mindy better not have neglected to mention some kind of vermin infestation of B-movie proportions. As I shake off the sleep I see that the noise is coming from my vibrating mobile as it pushes itself around the nightstand. I pick it up as it's about to clatter to the floorboards and see it's Caroline.

'Did you nick my towels after all?' I mumble, sleepily.

'Are you drunk?'

'No! Been asleep.' I rub an eye with the heel of my hand. 'Although that sounds an interesting idea.'

'I wanted to see how my policy of leaving you in splendid isolation was going. I've started to feel guilty, which is downright inconvenient.'

'What do you mean?'

'I laid down the law that we should give you tonight on your own.'

'Cheers!' I splutter, incandescently annoyed for a quarter of a second.

'If we came round tonight and got drunk, you'd have hungover Sunday night blues on your first night alone in the flat. This way, it gets it out of the way.'

'Or it'd bundle all the bad things together,' I grumble.

'Is that how you feel? I can come round now if so.'

I look around at the strange and new surroundings. Rupa's got some sort of fairylight addiction: strings of red roses, the stamens replaced by pinprick bulbs, those snakes of clear tubing with a disco pulse throbbing along them. Even through the grey filter of my misery, I concede it looks rather beautiful. And, as ever, Caroline's tough love is a good thing.

'Ah, I'll cope.'

'Go and get yourself a bottle of wine, order a takeaway, and I'll come round tomorrow.'

After I hang up, I discover I'm not hungry, but I do recall spying a bottle of Bombay Sapphire on Rupa's shelf. I swipe it and tell myself I'll replace it twice over before I leave. I don't have any tonic so it has to make a rapper's delight of gin and juice with a carton of Tropicana. As I switch the television on and let a medical drama wash over me, another worry surfaces. One I hadn't wanted to admit to having. It's just, Ben hasn't called. And I've started to think he's not going to.

I shouldn't be thinking about it. It's positively distasteful, he's a married man, not a potential date. Only: if he never calls, it's going to say such an awful lot. It would be an extremely eloquent silence.

Half an hour of you was enough. In fact, it was too much, but I grinned and bore it. The past is the past and you're the only one living in it. See you again, on the tenth anniversary of never. And by the way, that haircut makes you look like Tom Hanks in The Da Vinci Code.

In my heart of hearts, I know that's my guilty paranoia talking, not Ben. Ben is the person who irrationally apologised for so much as mentioning his wedding when I told him about my ex-engaged status. So why is it, when I examine every exchange between us so many times, perspective collapses? I can't help but think about the killer detail – he took my number, but he never volunteered his, did he?

He was the one saying it'd be great to go out, reassures the angel on my shoulder.

That's the kind of thing you say to be nice during the social disentanglement process and don't necessarily make good on, counters the devil.

Oh God, he's never going to call and I'm going to see Ben and his Olivia of Troy examining high thread count linen in John Lewis and fall backwards over someone in a wheelchair in my haste to escape.

As the patient on TV goes into something called 'VF' and the crash team swing into action, I settle on a theory that suits both my fatalism and my knowledge of Ben's character. He did mean everything he said about it being nice to get together. He asked for my number in good faith, he probably believed he'd use it. Then he thought it through, debated how to describe me to his wife. That consideration alone could make him reassess whether it was a good idea. I can imagine a few memories that might've helped him come to a conclusion. And at that moment, he scrolled down to my name in his phone, felt a pang of regret. Then found his resolve, hit delete, and continued with his charmed, Rachel-less life.

Half an hour later, my phone starts flashing with a call. Mum, I think. I prepare myself to be falsely positive for five minutes. I check the caller display: unrecognised number.

'Hi, Rachel?'

I recognise the warm male voice instantly. I go from someone half asleep at six in the evening to the most awake person in the whole of Manchester. *He called! He doesn't hate me! He didn't lie!* Adrenaline shot with endorphin chaser.

'Hi!'

'Are you OK?'

'I'm fine!'

'It's Ben.'

'Hello, Ben!' I say this in a voice that people usually reserve for 'Hello, Cleveland!'

'Are you sure you're OK? You sound a bit odd.'

'I am, I was – I was …' Christ, I don't want to admit I've been asleep this afternoon, like an eighty-two year old '… having a lie down.'

'Ah. Right. I see.' Ben sounds embarrassed and I sense he thinks I mean some sort of afternoon singleton lie down, with company. 'I'll call back.'

'No!' I virtually shout. 'Honestly. I'm fine. How are you? It's weird you called now, I was just thinking about you.'

Mouth, open. Foot: placed inside.

'All good things I hope,' Ben says, awkwardly.

'Of course!' I squeal, with the ongoing note of hysteria.

'Uhm, I wanted to see if you wanted to meet my colleague after work one night next week to discuss this story?'

'Yes, that'd be great.'

'Thursday? I'll come along, if that's OK?'

'Totally fine.' Totally, amazingly, wonderfully fine.

'He's all right, Simon, but he's a bit full of himself. Don't let him take any liberties if he starts up about the evils of the press.'

'I'm sure I can give as good as I get.'

'So am I,' Ben laughs. 'Right, I'll email a time and a place at the start of the week.'

'Great.'

'Have a nice weekend. I'll let you get back to your lie down.'

'I'm standing up now, think I'll stay that way.'

'Whatever works best.'

We say a stilted goodbye and ring off, with me on a strange, pain-free, woozy high. Onscreen, the patient's heartbeat has returned.

15

I should be listening to the details of when, on or about the 26th of August last year, Michael Tallack of Verne Drive, Levenshulme, obtained monies by deception by strapping on his brother's leg iron and claiming spurious disability benefits.

Instead, mentally, I'm far, far away and long, long ago: part of a group watching a fireworks display at Platt Fields Park in the autumn of my first year of university. I 'oohed' and 'aahed' as each explosion bloomed and faded into spiders of glittering dust. I turned to Ben to say something and saw he was watching me instead of the night sky. It was an intent look and gave me a sensation similar to when you think a fairground ride has come to a stop and it hasn't, quite.

'Uh…' I stumbled over the words that were previously on the tip of my tongue, 'I'm cold.'

'In those?' Ben asked, sceptically, pointing at my gloves. They were Fair Isle, multi-coloured. Admittedly, the size of hot water bottle covers.

'They're nice!'

'If you're seven.'

'Aren't you cold?' I asked him.

'Not really,' Ben said. 'Hadn't noticed.'

His eyes sparkled. In the freezing atmosphere, I felt heat rise to the surface of my skin. I breathed deeply and clapped my mittens together.

A girl joined us, winding her arm through Ben's in familiarity. I angled my body away from them and when I turned back to say something, they'd slipped away. I found myself craning my neck to try to spot them in the crowd. I felt ever so slightly abandoned. Which was ridiculous, and clearly a sign of how much I was missing Rhys.

'All rise,' barks the court clerk, snapping me back to the here and now.

I wait politely for everyone to file out ahead of me, instead of overtaking to slice the fastest path to the door, in my usual tetchy work mode. My mind's very much on my after-work appointment with Ben. Equal parts terror, anticipation, excitement, guilt, confusion ...

I get a cow-shit coffee and go to the press room to drink it in peace. I see Zoe has got there before me. Despite her doubts, she's taken to court reporting brilliantly. The ability to spot a story is one you can't really teach, and she clearly has it. She's also had the confidence to leave a courtroom where nothing much is happening and seek something better. It took me ages to find the guts to do that. I'd be pinioned to the bench listening to a ten-a-penny aggravated twokking, doing side-to-side slotting eye movements, like a portrait in a haunted house when backs turn.

'Sodding Gretton,' she says, by way of greeting, over her takeaway spud, spearing discs of cucumber with a white plastic fork and placing them in the opened lid.

I sip my coffee. 'Is he stalking you now? I thought I'd seen less of him.'

'Yeah. I got this nice story about a have-a-go hero pensioner chasing toerags off his allotments, think I've got it all to myself, and then I turn round and he's breathing down my neck.'

'Uh oh, there wasn't a joke about hoes, was there?'

'The deadly or dangerous weapon was a rake, thankfully.'

'Take it as a compliment. He wouldn't bother if he didn't think you knew what you were doing.'

'I suppose.'

I reflect that this is truer than I'd like. It's an uncomfortable discovery that Gretton's instantly switched to targeting Zoe. Am I that dispensable? I haven't had anything great lately. This must be how fading movie stars feel when they lose a stalker to a younger rival. Even rodents like him are fleeing sinking HMS *Woodford*. Admittedly, Zoe looks like she's going to go far. I think people once said that about me. This bothers me more than it would have done, now that I've broken off my engagement. Funny how, when one part of your life falls away, the other bits that are left start looking rather feeble. I've always thought I had a good job. Now I'm thinking I've never exactly chased promotion, and here's Zoe, probably going to overtake me in a few weeks flat and then be on to the next thing.

'I'm getting off on time today. If news desk ask, I was here until the bitter end,' I say. 'I don't need to file anything until tomorrow and the progress in Court 2 is on the stately side.'

Zoe makes a salute. 'Understood. Anything fun?'

'What, in Court 2?'

'What you're off to.'

That's a good question. 'A drink with an old friend.'

'Ooh. A *friend* friend or a friend?'

For some reason the question irritates me. 'Friend, female,' I snap, then realise my guilty conscience is making me antsy.

Zoe nods, spearing a slice of woolly tomato and then plunging through potato flesh the way gardeners work over soil.

16

The Tallack trial continues, and my afternoon passes in a similar reverie. This time I'm back in my study period before first year exams. Ben left me a cryptic note in my pigeonhole in the university's arts block with the venue, time and 'come alone', as if we were secret agents.

I'd never been up to Central Library in St Peter's Square, content to make do with the university library, John Rylands. In acknowledgement of this, and to take the mickey, Ben drew me a map with the whole route described, eventually arriving at what resembled a blue-biro-inked cake, the Tuscan colonnade standing in for candles. He drew a goonish face, captioned 'Ben', and an arrow to indicate he was inside.

On arrival, as I admired the architecture, I saw Ben waving at me from a desk.

'Hi. Why are we here?' I hissed, sliding into a chair next to him.

'I didn't want anyone overhearing us in the uni library,' Ben whispered. 'And it's an outing. Look at these.'

He pushed a stack of exam papers towards me.

'Past papers?' I asked.

'Yep. Going through them, there's a totally obvious pattern. There's only a question about *Beowulf* every *other* year.'

'Riiight…' I said. 'So…?'

'It was on last year's paper and there's no way it's going to come up this year. We don't have to revise it.'

'A risky strategy.'

'I'm one hundred per cent sure it'll work.'

'Really?' I said, sarcastically. 'One hundred per cent? As sure of the laws of gravity, or the laws of… of…'

'You don't know any other laws, do you?'

'Sod?'

'OK, I'm ninety per cent sure then.'

'There's an equally failsafe fallback.'

'Yeah?'

'Without tutors suspecting a *thing* is happening, we covertly put information into our brains. Then we smuggle it into the exam room behind these faces. No one would ever guess our secret.'

Ben stifles a laugh. 'Smart arse. I knew you wouldn't appreciate my efforts.'

I pointed up at the inscription on the ceiling.

'Wisdom is the principal thing, therefore get wisdom.'

Ben shook his head. 'Get degree is principal thing, not sermon off Ronnie.'

'Look. It might work, but you're clever, you don't need to play games.'

'Ack, I hate Old English.'

'Would your mum want you to do this?'

Ben wrinkled his nose. 'Don't drag my mum into this.'

I'd met Ben's mum by chance, the previous week. I called

in on his shared flat to drop a textbook off and a slim young woman with short hair and Ben's same neat features was stood chatting in the doorway, jangling car keys.

'Hello, I'm Ben's mum,' she'd said, as I approached, in that *yes I will speak to your friends if I want to* teasing way.

'Hello, I'm Rachel. Ben's friend off his course,' I added, in case she thought it was a booty call.

'Oooh Rachel!' she said. 'You're the lovely, clever girl with the musician boyfriend.'

'Er, yes,' I said, flattered I'd been described at all, let alone in such a nice way.

'Now your boyfriend lives – wait, wait – I know it ...' Ben's mum held her hand up to indicate she was thinking.

'*Mum*,' Ben said, in a low growl, face reddening.

'Sunderland!' she announced.

'Sheffield,' I said. 'You got the "S", though. And the north. Very near, really.'

'Honestly, you don't know how healthy it is for my son to have a young woman around who's immune to his charms, so good for you and your Sheffield-or-Sunderland boyfriend.'

'MUM!' Ben shouted, in a rictus of agony, as I'd giggled.

In the library, I said: 'I liked your mum.'

'Yeah, don't remind me. She liked you too.'

'Plus if you fail the first year, who am I going to sit with in lectures?' I asked Ben.

Someone nearby coughed, pointedly. We opened our books. After ten minutes I looked up and saw Ben deep in concentration. He had this habit of clutching his shoulder with the hand on the opposite side of his body, chin on his chest, as he squinted at the text. I had an unexpected urge to reach across and brush the marble-smoothness of his cheekbone with the back of my hand.

He glanced up. I quickly reassembled my features into exaggerated boredom, faked a yawn.

'Drink?' he whispered.

'Triple shot espresso with ProPlus ground up in the coffee beans,' I said, closing my reference book with a thud, half-expecting it to throw up a cloud of talcum-like dust.

Settled in the cafeteria, Ben said: 'I can't fail the first year, I have to get this degree and earn some money because my waster of a dad isn't going to help my mum or sister any time soon.'

'Do you see him?'

He shook his head. 'Not if I can help it, and the feeling's mutual.'

Chin propped on palm, I listened to his account of his dad's abrupt departure from their lives, his mum working two jobs, and felt guilty I'd ever complained about the boring dependability of my home life. I also thought how, with some people, you feel like you'll never ever run out of things to talk about.

When Ben got to the part where he tracked his dad down and his dad told him he didn't want to be found, he was suddenly, to both our surprise, on the verge of tears.

'I couldn't believe it, you know, I thought all I had to do was tell him we needed him around and he'd be on the next train, or send my mum something.' Ben's eyes had gone shiny, his voice thick. 'I felt such a dick.'

I sensed he needed a way out of the moment. I wanted to make the grade as a confidante. And I wanted – given at least one important person had fallen short on this score with Ben – to be caring.

I said, with feeling: 'I know he's your dad and I hope it won't offend you if I say he sounds like an utter bastard. You did absolutely the right thing trying to get him to face up to his responsibilities. If you hadn't tried, you'd always wonder about him and regret it. This way, at least you know it's a hundred per cent on him. You think it was nothing but pain, but it removed all doubt. Consider it what you had to do for peace of mind.'

Ben nodded, grateful, having had the time to get his emotions back under control.

'Cheers, Ron.'

I realised then that, underneath the clean-cut clothes and breezy air, Ben was as much of a work in progress as the rest of us. He simply wore it better.

17

'All rise!' barks the court clerk, for the last time today.

As I scrabble to put away my notebook and float out the door, this semi-dream state is tested to its limits by the appearance of a fulminating Gretton.

'You can tell that bird-faced bitch that I'm after her, right? Press on press is *not on*,' he splutters.

I wasn't aware Gretton operated by any code of honour. This is a retroactive one because he's lost out on a story, no doubt.

'Who …?'

'Your little sidekick!'

'You mean Zoe? What's the matter?'

I try to get him to lower his voice by speaking more quietly and hoping he'll match my volume. A few people are glancing over at us.

'She DELIBERATELY…'

Tactic failing, I clutch his elbow and steer him alongside me as I walk away. 'Shhh, not here. Follow me.'

Being taken seriously seems to calm Gretton slightly, and he just about keeps a lid on his simmering rage until we're in the street.

'She tampered with my court list.'

'How do you mean?'

'I was missing pages on 2 and 3, and when I go and get a replacement, I find those pages have today's best stories on them.'

'How do you know it was Zoe? Couldn't the pages have slipped out? Loose staple?'

Loose screw, possibly. We're each given our computer print-outs with lists of the daily hearings in sealed envelopes every morning by the front desk staff, so I don't see how this trick is meant to have been played.

'That happen to have her cases listed on them? I'm not fucking stupid.'

At this moment, Zoe sails past. 'Alright, Pete?' she asks, cool as the cucumber she doesn't eat.

'I'm on to you, you conniving little cow,' Gretton barks.

'Stop talking to her like that,' I say.

'What's the problem?' Zoe asks, girlish eyes wide.

'Ripping pages out of my lists. If you want to play dirty, we'll play dirty. You've been warned. And you —' he wheels round to jab a finger at me '— better watch out too.'

'Why? What have I done?'

He stalks off, smoothing his rusty flyaway hair with one hand, the other jammed in his pocket, seeking out his fags.

Zoe adjusts her bag on her shoulder. I hadn't noticed how appealingly shabby and insufficiently smart it is — a student-market-looking thing in sludgy colours, covered in little mirrors and tassels. It reminds me how new she is to all of this. She'll probably get her first briefcase from her parents this Christmas. She's smiling, a little too contentedly.

'How'd you do it?'

'I pulled the pages out of mine and swapped our lists over when he was busy looking at that leggy barrister who got her robe caught on a door handle.'

We look at each other and start laughing.

'The fight back starts here,' Zoe says.

I've always put up with Gretton as an unfortunate fact of life, but Zoe's showing significantly more resourcefulness. Perhaps if I'd had this kind of energy ten years ago, I'd be in a very different place right now.

I put my hand out and she shakes it. 'You should be very proud of your first week.'

'Drink?' Zoe asks.

'Ah, no. Next time. I've got this meet-up with my friends.'

'The female friend,' she nods.

For a moment, I struggle to remember my untruth, and stare blankly.

'Have a nice time,' Zoe says, though I have a feeling her smirk says she's rumbled me.

I walk away silently saying to myself: *and you are learning Italian, and you are learning Italian.*

'You look nice,' Caroline says as I pick my way to our meeting point by Piccadilly Gardens, taking in my shirtdress and my higher-than-usual heels. 'All for my benefit, is it?'

'You look nice too,' I say, defensively.

'I always look this nice for work.'

'Show off.'

I hoped to convey 'professional and together.' And, OK, maybe a little bit hot. So far it's earned: 'Ahoy hoy, soliciting under the Street Offences Act, 1959? Court 7!' from Gretton.

I asked Caroline to come in a fit of pre-match nerves when I realised I wanted support in facing Ben and this scary bloke. And maybe, possibly, it occurred to me that four was a better number for one-on-one conversations. I knew Caroline would relish the opportunity to do some hands-off, safe-distance admiring of Ben.

'Graeme didn't mind you coming, did he?' I ask, as we set off, me trying to keep lock step with Caroline's long stride. 'Sorry you had to rearrange your evening.'

'Yep, you've ruined our annual trip to the cinema. I rule out anything with submarines and he rules out anything with Meryl Streep and we stand in the foyer arguing until Gray buys me off with Revels.'

'Sorry…'

'Joking. It was cancelled anyway. He fobbed me off with some bullshit about spreadsheets so he can sit in picking his feet. Who are we meeting again? Apart from Ben?'

'His friend, Simon.'

She raises an eyebrow.

'What is this, matchmaking?'

'Don't be stupid. That's not Ben's kind of thing.'

'Errr…'

'What?' I ask, nervily.

'You haven't seen Ben for ten years, his *thing* could've changed completely.'

18

Ben nominated a fashionable bar in the city centre that I haven't got round to visiting yet, rather giving lie to the idea that I can show him where to go out. It's all poured, polished concrete surfaces, with dramatic under-lighting, tropical flower displays and chairs that are so low-slung you end up talking to a collection of windpipes and kneecaps.

As we enter I see Ben at a table in the far corner, chatting to a tall, blond-haired, mid-thirties man whose expansive body language implies that all the world's a chat show and he's the host. The would-be Michael Parkinson gives us both a languid up-and-down full airport body scan as we reach their table.

'Hi … Ben, you remember Caroline?' I say.

'Of course,' Ben smiles. 'How are you? Simon, this is Rachel, who works for the paper.'

Ben stands up, still in his work clothes, an artfully rumpled (as opposed to the crushed it'd be on a lesser mortal) cornflower blue shirt and dark navy suit trousers, jacket with bright lining slung over seat next to him. Part of me, the part of me that Caroline rightly points out has failed to notice a decade has elapsed, wants to whoop with excitement and throw my arms around him. *It's you! It's me!* I know I have to stop. This is nothing. This is a drink with an old face from university days. He leans in to peck Caroline on the cheek and naturally she goes gooey. Ben and I nod in acknowledgement towards each other, communicating that we did the kissing thing the other day and neither of us fancy a repeat.

Simon unpacks his collection of rangy limbs and rises to his feet also.

'Delighted. What're you having, ladies?'

'Uh, no, it's OK, I'll go, what are you drinking?' I say, realising as I do that resistance is futile: alpha male Simon's never going to allow it. I am far more used to beery betas.

'No. What are you having?' he repeats, firmly.

'Vodka tonic,' Caroline says to Simon, sweetly undermining me.

He turns expectantly.

'G&T? Thanks.'

'How are you, Ben? Rachel says you're married, and a solicitor?' Caroline asks.

'Yeah, family. My wife's in litigation.'

'You studied English at uni, didn't you?' Caroline asks.

'Yep. I did the wrong degree,' Ben says, bluntly. 'Good for almost nothing.'

This hurts. Not because I have huge pride about my qualifications. More that we wouldn't have spent three years in each other's company if he hadn't done that degree.

'Good for nothing if learning has to be vocational,' I say, prissily.

'Yeah, sorry, I didn't mean good for *nothing*, obviously – you've done really well,' Ben says, remembering himself, and I can see he's surprised at his own lapse in tact. 'I was skint after graduating that's all, and I was only qualified to study more. Can't even teach English abroad without a TEFL. And I'm not cut out for journalism like Rachel. I could never buckle down and hit deadlines the way she could.'

I know he's trying to repair the 'good for nothing' damage and, while I appreciate it, I still feel a little wounded. I feel his eyes on me and pretend to be fussing with putting my coat on my chair to avoid his gaze.

Simon returns with two chunky lowball glasses full of ice. 'Lemon in the vodka ... lime in the G&T.'

'Thanks,' we twitter in unison.

He gets a round in without getting another for himself? I'll have to tell Rhys these men do exist. He'd probably recommend Simon donate his brain to medical science. Immediately.

We do the obligatory amount of 'getting to know you' chat, and after establishing Caroline's an accountant, Simon goes off on a tangent with her.

'How's Abigail?' I ask Ben.

Abigail, Ben's bug-eyed, skinny little sister, was around thirteen or fourteen when we were students. Ben doted on her in the way much older brothers usually do. Ben warned me before I met her that she had Asperger Syndrome, which meant she said whatever was in her head, with no checks, balances or social graces. *Sounds no different to most of my family and my boyfriend*, I joked, though privately I was apprehensive. What if she asked why I had sideburns? When I met her, I found she was one of those rare people who have few unkind impulses or nasty thoughts so it didn't matter as much as it might have. She admired a knitted hat I had bought at the student market, with: 'Can I have it, please?' Ben was appalled.

Afterwards, I sent her one similar. Ben said she was so pleased she was 'practically in tears, the gimp', even though it was so large for her it made her 'look like one of the aliens from *Mars Attacks*'. He reported this in a letter, having taken the unusual step of writing to me during the holiday break.

'Abi is,' Ben smiles, '*really* well, actually. She has a part-time job in a travel agent's. My aunt works there so she looks out for her. And she still lives with my mum, so it's good knowing neither of them are on their own.'

I remember how much he used to worry. 'That's great.'

I recall the way Abigail once attached herself to me, and say: 'I bet she loves having a sister-in-law.'

Ben grimaces. 'Hmm, she did at first.'

I make a questioning face.

'Abi assumed she was going to be a bridesmaid at our wedding. Liv had already asked her two friends. She said she wasn't going to sack one of them because Abi jumped the gun. And Liv said if she had Abi, she'd have to have her demonic nieces and she wanted to avoid that at all costs. I tried to explain Abi's not manipulative, she doesn't understand. Well, you know how she is.'

I find it touching he presumes I understand Abi, despite all these years.

'You couldn't have intervened, somehow?' I ask. 'I know how tricky these things get.' Do I ever.

'I wanted to. I tried. Ultimately I couldn't tell Liv who to have as bridesmaid.'

'Ah. Sure.'

'Abi dug her heels in, got into a "bridesmaid or nothing" mindset. It was so political between my mum, Abi and Liv. I stayed out of it. Anyway, upshot is that things have been a bit strained between all of them since. Or they are between my mum and Liv. Abi's forgotten about it. I'm sure they'll sort it out eventually.'

I think of Ben's mum's easy laughter when she met me, and for a split second imagine a parallel universe where I'm her daughter-in-law and Abi was my bridesmaid, and how well we'd all get on. More of my fantasy fiction: I should throw in a few elves as ring-bearers.

'Will you give Abi my regards, if you speak to her?'

'Course,' Ben says. 'She used to ask after you a lot.'

We both pause, at the 'used'. How did he explain our terminated friendship, I wonder? How did he think of me? If he thought of me at all…

This is the first conversational pothole of many on the road that lies before us, if we're going to be friends. It's possible Ben doesn't see the start of anything here, only a favour to another friend. A trip down memory lane, a swift three-point turn and back out again, foot firmly on accelerator.

Ben's obviously thinking this way too, because he says: 'This is mad, isn't it?' gesturing at me, him, our being together. 'Where does the time go?'

I'm sure it went faster for you, I think, nodding. Caroline and Simon's tandem conversation about high finance shows no signs of stopping. Ben therefore obviously deems it safe to ask: 'What happened with you and Rhys? If you want to talk about it? Totally fine if you don't…'

'It was everything and nothing in particular. We reached the end of the line. Cockfosters.'

'Sorry?'

'The end of the line. The Underground? Never mind.'

'Ah.' Ben smiles politely, bemused.

At university, I'm sure that would've made him laugh. *I don't know him any more. He's changed.* Or maybe I should try again with a better joke.

Half of me wants to throw myself on Ben and tell him every last thing, gesturing to the barman to bring us the rest of the bottle and telling Caroline and Simon they're good to leave us. The other half of me knows not only is this the wrong person to seek sympathy from, I can't bear to see a grain – the smallest speck – of relief in his eyes. Relief that he got away from me.

'Anyway. What made you want to move back up here?' I continue, slightly desperately.

'Apart from the fact that Simon said his firm had a job going? Dunno, really – I was fed up with London, couldn't face the commuter belt, I couldn't live somewhere too small, and this is the other big city I know and like.'

'Was your wife keen to move too?'

'Not exactly. We reached the decision through a process of mature debate. And, er, compromise and … concession.'

Simon overhears this and interrupts: 'What he means is, they're here, but Olivia gets her way now until either of them dies.'

He adds: 'And while we're on the subject of pushy women, Caroline thinks Ben should get some more drinks.'

'I didn't say that!' Caroline protests, enjoying Simon's teasing. She's always liked cocky blokes.

Ben shakes his head in mock disapproval. 'Come on, Caroline. We're not doing slammers in the union bar any more. She was monstrous at university …'

'Really?' Simon says, contemplating Caroline, obviously hoping 'monstrous' is code for 'open to suggestion'.

'What was Rachel like?' Simon asks Ben.

Ben mutters 'Worse' and gets up swiftly.

19

'Are you going to tell Rachel about this story, then?' Ben asks Simon, on his return. I'd have liked to sustain the illusion that this isn't about business for a little longer.

Yet I add: 'Yeah, what is it? I'm curious.'

'Can I trust you? Is this off the record?' Simon says, warily, pushing forward on his seat, eyes darting round the bar as if my plainclothes associate might be loitering by the fag machine.

'I don't come to wine bars wired for sound.'

Simon glowers at me.

I make a cross on my chest with a fingertip. 'Promise this goes no further. On my life. You are safe to speak.'

Simon leans further forward. 'I've got an important client who's ready for an interview. With the right paper.'

'We can't pay big money,' I say.

'I said the right paper, not the one that can pay the most.'

'Who is he?'

Simon leans back again, scrutinises my face as if it's a map that contains the key to my trustworthiness. 'She. Natalie Shale. So wife-of-client, strictly speaking.'

My pulse quickens, before natural pessimism returns it to normal.

'She doesn't do interviews.'

'She didn't, I'm advising her differently.'

'To who?'

'Her husband's last solicitor,' Simon says, mouth twitching slightly, possibly in irritation at being doubted. 'I've taken over from a colleague who's snowed under.'

'You must be doing well to get given it…?'

'Simon's in line to be made a partner,' Ben supplies.

'So, you up for it or what?' Simon asks me.

'Natalie would do a face-to-face piece, photos, everything? An exclusive?'

It's been a while since I got truly excited by a story, but I can feel the proper journalist in me stirring after a long, deep, Rip Van Winkle length sleep. My news editor will do somersaults.

'Yes. But no spoilers on the fresh evidence for the appeal, and I'd want your assurance that it wouldn't be a dredge of hubby's murky past. She's very sensitive about it, as you can imagine. She doesn't want to do anything that's going to dim the glory when he's freed.'

'What if he isn't?' asks Caroline.

'He will be,' Ben says.

I make a noise of agreement.

'Why?' she persists.

'Because he's innocent… and because he's got a great legal team,' Ben says, tipping his bottle to clink it against Simon's. Ever the optimist.

Caroline glances at me and I know she's thinking, since when was that a guarantee? Ever the pragmatist.

'He needs great barristers,' Simon says, evenly. 'And as a miscarriage of justice he needs attention, so Johnny Judge accepts you don't get that many people holding placards outside the Court of Appeal and tooting vuvuzelas unless there's a bloody good reason. We need to keep it in the public eye. Natalie's interview could help with that.'

Simon pronounces bloody as 'bladdy' and I wonder if he went somewhere properly flashy like Eton or Harrow.

'And Natalie's very media friendly,' he concludes. 'If you get this right, it's *made of win*.'

'I thought you said she doesn't do interviews?' Caroline asks.

'He means she's attractive,' I say.

'Correct,' Simon says. He reclines, so laidback he's practically horizontal, figuratively as well as literally.

20

Having university friends studying accountancy, business management and cognitive science meant one thing, for sure (apart from them all ending up considerably better paid than me in later life): I had many, many more hours wafting around on 'free study periods'.

Naturally, Ben and I finished our end of first year exams about a week before everyone else. For reasons lost to history, we did our celebrating in a hideous Scottish-themed pub called MacDougal's in Fallowfield. If it honoured the ancient MacDougal clan, I never much wanted to meet them. It had tartan curtains, upholstery the colour of a livid wound and smelt of carpet cleaning agent and Silk Cut. Ben summed it up: 'Och Aye The *No.*'

Despite Ben and I spending almost every day together, and finding each other so effortlessly entertaining that we would've been able to wring laughs out of a night in the cells, I was perfectly clear in my mind there was no risk of me falling for him. Not only was he not my type, it was so easy. Attraction, I'd decided, required friction. It was based on conflict, mystery and distance. Rhys could be decidedly remote at times, in more than one way. He'd even asked me to stop coming to his gigs as it 'put him off'. I was treated mean and, never one to defy a cliché, I was keen.

'I am really really good at drinking shots,' I announced to Ben, two vodka and Cokes down.

'Really?' he asked, dubiously.

'Oh yeah. I can drink vodka to a band playing,' I said.

'You've only had two.'

'I'll drink you under the table!' I cried, with the gung-ho spirit of someone who'd had a couple of large measures on an empty stomach and was talking total shit.

Ben sniggered into his glass.

'You choose,' I added, slapping the table for emphasis. 'You choose the drink and I'll match you, then carry you home.'

Ben cocked his head to one side. 'Ever done flaming Drambuies?'

'Nooooo. Bring it on.'

He darted off to the bar and returned with a cheap match-book and glasses holding an inch of copper liquid. Under Ben's creative direction, we lit them and made tiny lakes of fire, then clapped our palms over the rims to form the seal. We tried to whirl them over our heads before drinking, with predictably messy results.

'You're not like other girls I've met,' Ben said, lightly, wiping his mouth, after round two was aflame in stomachs instead.

'More sweary?' I asked.

'No, I mean … you're, you know. Like my best friends back home. Not a girly girl. You're *sharp*.'

He mumbled the last word so I had to strain to hear it, while he busied himself with the cocktail list.

'What, you've never met an intelligent female before?'

'I didn't mean that. I've never had a laugh with a female friend like you.'

I could imagine Ben hadn't had many platonic friendships with women, and I wasn't about to inflate his ego by speculating on why this might be.

'You're not like other boys I've met,' I said, with the loose lips of someone half-cut, without considering it wasn't a train of thought I especially wanted to pursue to its destination either.

'How?' Ben said.

'You look like you could be in a boy band,' I offered, with a drunken giggle.

Ben's face twisted into something that looked like genuine offence. 'Oh, wow, ta.'

'What? That's nice!'

'No it isn't.'

I continued to insist it was praise and Ben muttered something about needing to have had his sense of shame taken out along with his appendix to have gone that route. I regretted I was so bad at being sincere.

As time started to expand and contract in the warm boozy haze, Ben's mates from his flats joined us, and I found myself the only female in a whooping gang of seven lads. Not only that, they greeted us with 'Oi oi!' and a 'Here with the wife again, eh?'

This didn't bother me, especially in my relaxed state, but when I glanced at Ben he was glowering.

Amazingly enough, I was soon surpassed in the shot-downing stakes: one of them returned to the table with a full bottle of tequila, complete with plastic sombrero lid, a jumbo chip-shop-sized tub of Saxa and a pile of rather withered looking lemon wedges.

'Truth or dare!' the ring-leader, Andy, announced. 'You game?' He was addressing me directly.

'She's not playing,' Ben said, abruptly.

I turned to him. 'Excuse me?'

'Ron, you're the only female here. All the dares will involve flashing them.'

I opened my mouth to object.

'Trust me, they have bigger tolerances than you and much lower standards,' he added.

'Why do you call her Ron?' one of the boys, Patrick, asked.

'Long story,' Ben said.

'They have a secret society of two,' Andy told him.

'Any interesting rituals for membership?' Patrick asked, pulling a leer.

'Why do you have to be so infantile?' Ben said.

'Being oversensitive where this lady is concerned is certainly one of them,' Andy said to Patrick.

I felt Ben's pain increasing by degrees and didn't know how to help. I didn't want to be the meek little woman in a slew of nudge-nudge-wink-wink but I sensed anything I said would be used against us, so I stayed silent for Ben's sake.

'You in, then, or is your keeper calling the shots?' Patrick said to me, in his Captain of the Debating Society voice. I realised I disliked Patrick quite a lot.

Andy shouted: 'Yeah. Let her play! It's feminism, innit!'

'I'm not being a knuckle-dragger, I'm looking out for you. What would Rhys want you to do, faced with this shower?' Ben said to me, quietly.

Invoking my boyfriend had the intended effect. Rhys would be cracking his knuckles and offering them outside.

'I've had a head start on you, I'm going to sit this one out,' I smiled, and they all booed.

The game rolled round the group, with confessions of kinky fantasies about double-teaming crusty tutors, downing pints in one, and Andy rushing over to a window and mooning passers-by. The barmaid merely grimaced and kept flicking through the magazine she was reading at the bar, content that, despite the arses, we were more than doubling MacDougal's take on a slow weekday evening.

'Ben Ben BEN BENNY!' Andy howled. 'Your turn. Truth or dare?'

Andy's eyes flickered maliciously in my direction. I had an irrational fear the 'truth' might involve me somehow. But what truth was there to fear, exactly?

'Uh. Dare,' Ben said.

Andy leaned over to Patrick and they conferred in whispers, punctuated by evil snickering. I gripped the sides of my chair.

'Ben's dare is decided! Kiss her,' Andy said, gesturing towards me.

'No way, she's not playing,' Ben said, with a dismissive laugh.

'So? Were the people on the street outside who were treated to my sweet cheeks playing?'

Ben took on a very steely look. 'No. Bloody. Way. Truth, or – I'm out.'

'You don't get to choose,' Andy shook his head. 'Get busy.' He waggled his tongue at me.

'Urgh. I'm not going to say no again,' Ben said

It was irrational and ridiculous but with the emphatic *urgh* noise I felt wounded. Ben's determination was understandable and respectful and yet so vehement I couldn't help but wonder if the idea genuinely repulsed him. OK, he thought I was 'sharp'… that didn't equate to not thinking I was a hag, did it? We all admired the work of Charles Dickens in tutorials but it didn't mean we wanted a ride on his moustache.

'OK. Ben's a wuss. Truth! Truth.' Andy waved his hands around in a solemn bar-room call for quiet please and attention. 'Right.'

Andy and Patrick went into their snickering huddle again, soon emerging.

'Given you seem something of a swordsman, your truth is – who have you had since you got here? Names. Details.'

'Ahhh, yeah, well, a gentleman doesn't tell,' Ben said, but the table banging had already begun.

'No way. Truth, or dare!' Andy shouted. 'Truth-truth-truth-truth…'

Ben chewed his lip. I was seized by a powerful desire to not hear his score sheet. I wasn't bothered, as such, but his lady killing was something very separate from our friendship. I suspected he'd politely failed to notice Caroline's crush because she was too close to me for comfort. If they were all itemised, these encounters, with a bunch of names, I'd be strangely compelled to go round putting faces and sketchy biographical detail to them, like a repentant hit man revisiting the stories of his victims.

'This isn't fair…' Ben was struggling to be heard among the jeers and the catcalls '…on the people I'd be talking about, is it?'

People. There it was, the plural that signified a vast hinterland of conquests. The Drambuie sat uneasy in my gut.

'Fuck's sake. We're not asking for a blow-by-blow – haha,' Patrick said. 'No need to be coy. If you're a good hunter, you hang a stag's head on your wall.'

'I'll start you off, there was Noisy Louise in the first week…' Andy said, with a cackle. I gripped my chair harder, knuckles whitening.

Ben flicked a beer mat across the table. 'No. I'm not doing any of this bullshit.'

'Oh, don't make us punish you,' Andy said. 'You don't want to discover the punishment but it does involve being upside down in that bin without your clothes.'

There were a lot of them, and Ben's fight club numbered only me. I started to feel genuinely worried for him. I didn't want the extent of my protectiveness to be revealed. I was bothered enough that it had been revealed to me. As an only child, I'd never had a sibling to look after in the playground, but I guessed this was how it might feel if someone threatened them. Quite primal.

'Do the dare,' I nudged Ben in the ribs, acting casual, 'I don't care.'

'Don't you?' he said, looking vaguely horrified. OK, my feelings were definitely hurt. I was offering him a spade and he was reacting it as if it was digging his grave, rather than an escape tunnel?

'Ahahhha!' Andy whooped and the table-banging recommenced.

'Ben, who gives a shit, really?' I hissed. 'It's only a kiss, we know it doesn't matter. If you can face it…'

I nodded in encouragement as he stared at me, weighed things up.

118

He leant down, swiftly, and gave me a closed-mouth, firm kiss on the lips that lasted only seconds. Despite its brevity, I responded, kissing him back with a bit more passion, lips slightly apart. (After all that, didn't want him to think I was a rubbish kisser.)

He pulled back a small distance, as if he was going to stop. Then he unexpectedly moved forward and kissed me again, something more like a proper kiss, open mouths, tips of the tongues touching. I felt his hand on the side of my midriff as he steadied himself.

He tasted of alcohol with the tang of salt, and oh God, completely unexpectedly, I dissolved like a teaspoon of sugar in a mug of hot tea. While my brain stayed fairly on-message, my body rebelled. It was as if it registered superior genetic material and issued immediate instructions to my nerve endings to have thirteen of this person's babies and sod whether I liked his CD collection. In seconds, I crossed the line where I didn't know if my willingness to collaborate to a respectable standard was authentic passion. Ah. Life lesson. *This is why you don't kiss friends for dares.*

Ben broke away again abruptly, making no eye contact at all. We quickly started assembling tequila slammers to stay busy and take the taste of each other away, while everyone clapped. *So*, I thought, regrouping: the problem wasn't a bad kiss, it was a good kiss. Perhaps even a spectacular one. I couldn't deny there was some kind of technical physical chemistry thing there, even if I didn't fancy Ben. I felt like I needed to go sit in an ice bath.

I also knew I'd committed my first crime against Rhys, the sort he'd sternly warned me about when I left Sheffield. Is a kiss still a kiss when it's a functional, enforced kiss, to save someone from a naked violent prank? Surely I was only as guilty as women who get captured by the villain and forced to wear a bikini/evening gown until the hero arrives to save the day...? I mean, Han Solo never gave Leia any crap – it was gratitude for being defrosted and no blame attached. Leaving aside the point about who exactly was Mr Solo in my scenario.

'Good effort,' Andy said, determined to keep stirring. 'You two ever thought about it?'

'I know you find this hard to comprehend, but we're *friends*,' Ben said, scathingly. 'Like kissing a sister. Dare done.'

'Ooh, ouch,' Andy said, glancing to me for a reaction. Yep, it had hit its mark. Hard. I hid the twinge with a cowboy swig from my shot glass.

Under the table, to my surprise, I felt Ben grasp for my free hand and squeeze it, supportively. I tried to calculate precisely what had passed between us, in my impaired state. I knew I was vibrating like a tuning fork.

As the evening came to a messy close, Ben walked me the few yards to my block of halls. We were both finding an awful lot of neutral conversation topics quite fascinating, speech over-lapping, with no silences allowed to develop.

'Hey, I'm so sorry about what happened with that bunch of idiots,' he said, in parting. 'I should've bailed as soon as the game started. Blame the booze. And sorry, for, you know. What I said.'

'No problem!' I said, desperate for him not to repeat or expand on it, adding a hearty: 'Night!'

Apparently Ben had suffered that experience, but I only knew that for the period our mouths were connected, I hadn't. The long summer break had arrived just in time.

21

'I didn't want to admit to the extent of my ignorance in company,' Caroline says, in the taxi home, while I try to quell car sickness by concentrating on the troll figure in Man City strip dangling from the rear view mirror. The seats are covered in de-stress wooden massage beads, presumably to compensate for the effect of the driving. 'But I'm guessing the Natalie Shale interview is a big deal then?'

'It'd be great to get it. You remember the case?'

'Only that it wasn't very nice, really.'

'An armed robbery at a security depot, the guard got thumped with the butt of a gun and lost an eye. The case against Lucas Shale was mostly circumstantial. No one on the press benches thought he'd done it, anyway. He'd been straight for twenty years, gorgeous wife, cute little twin daughters, and everyone thought her evidence that they were at home that night would get him off. The feeling at the time was that the police were under pressure to find someone fast because it was so violent.'

'Why didn't she talk before?'

'I suppose she's had no reason to, till the appeal. Other than money, and it doesn't look like she's bothered. That's the thing,

I see a lot of people in court and both of them came across really well.'

'Well, I'm pleased for you. Nice to have something to take your mind off…everything else.'

'Yes,' I say, thinking it won't be the case on my mind as I go to sleep tonight.

'And Simon's single? Good job, good-looking, smart…' Caroline ticks them off on her fingers.

A pause.

'You're not serious?'

'Why not?'

'Because,' I splutter, as if she's announced the world's run by a coalition of lizards in a bunker, 'for one thing, he's not my type.'

'Talk of "types" should probably end around the same time you stop having pin-ups on your wall. I like to think I have a happy marriage, and I never watched Take That thinking "I wish there was a prematurely grey one who wears loafers".'

'I know, but I mean, come on. Simon's a million miles from Rhys.'

'Do I have to point out that a plan to find someone like your ex contains a fatal flaw?'

'You're wasting your time. I don't fancy him and men like him don't fancy women like me, they fancy women like you. Or they marry women like you and fancy slim-hipped Cuban boys.'

'This is typical.'

'What?'

'You spend one evening with a perfectly charming man and because his background's different to yours you don't just rule him out, you accuse him of being a closet case or a paedophile. You're a raging inverted snob.'

'I didn't literally mean he's a paedophile! And "different background" hardly covers it. He says "hello" as if it's got all five vowels in it. He's got one of those drawls where it sounds like his batteries are running out.'

'It's harder to meet people at our age. I mean, is there anyone with potential at work?'

'Huh. Not without leaping the species barrier.'

'Ben, though. Wooooh,' Caroline makes a low whistle. 'Forgive me for using Mindy lexicon, but, please serve me a slice of *that*.'

I grind my teeth.

'Were you never tempted?' she adds.

'By Ben?' I snort, over-acting a little.

'Yes. I mean, I know he doesn't look like he needs a good wash, as per your usual type, as we were just saying.'

'Oh, no. More like the brother I never had.' The brother I never had if we were raised in a cult in the Fens, under surveillance by the vice squad.

'You were the perfect friend for him, then. Shame you didn't stay in touch. Why didn't you?'

'Is it that strange?'

'I suppose not. You're normally good at that sort of thing, that's all, and he seems fond of you.'

I say nothing, replying both too risky and too painful.

'So if we can establish Simon's at least AC/DC, there's still no potential?' Caroline asks.

'Don't let me be single for more than five minutes before you try to pair me off, will you. *Jeez-us*.'

'Kidding,' Caroline says. She's trying to lean over to nudge me playfully when the car takes a corner and she gets thrown back against the door.

22

My anticipation of announcing the Natalie Shale exclusive to my news editor, Ken, is put on hold when Vicky spies me as soon as I put foot on carpet inside the hum of the newsroom. Vicky is a news desk deputy, and a kind of half-maiden, half-serpent creature, like something out of Greek mythology.

'Rachel!' she barks.

Duly summoned, I pick my way through the desks to her side.

'Your story about the cripple fraud trial that finally ended,' she asks, tapping the screen with her pen, employing her usual charming turn of phrase, voice all honey laced with arsenic, 'limped to the finish line, I should say. Why does Michael Tallack turn into Christopher, five paras down?'

I feel my face grow hot.

'Does he?' I say, a light sweat breaking out on my top lip. I've recently emerged from a sentencing for manslaughter, this story already a distant memory. 'Sorry.'

'Yes. Hopalong Cassidy's brother was cleared of any involvement, wasn't he?'

'Yes, sorry…' *Shit, shit.*

'Try to not to put actionable defamations in your copy, if it's not too much trouble.'

'Really sorry, Vicky, I don't know what I was thinking.'

'It's lucky I spotted it,' Vicky concludes.

'Yes, thanks.' I bet she didn't, and a sub-editor brought it to her. Certain members of news desk are known for dishing out bollockings, not their ferocious work rate. 'A riding crop in one hand and an éclair in the other' is how my friend Dougie once put it. He eventually tired of grumping and went off to Scotland to be a successful crime correspondent. Not for the first time, I have the feeling of being a barnacle-clad rock that time has flowed around like water.

Journalism, probably like most jobs, comes with the paradox that the more successful you get, the less you do the stuff that initially appealed: namely, finding stories and writing them. I could apply for news desk positions but I'd answer phones and argue with people all day. And have to sit next to people like Vicky.

'Is Ken about?'

'Yeah, somewhere.' Vicky loses interest in me and picks up on a flashing phone line.

'What up, Woodford? To what do we owe the honour?'

I turn to see Ken, the news editor, fishing in a bag of Wotsits, a copy of the paper tucked under one arm. He has a thatch of wiry grey hair that looks as if it's clipped into a cube shape with shears. I'm sure it gets squarer every time I see him. He could wear a box as a hat.

'I popped by to tell you some good news.'

'Christ. You're not pregnant, are you?'

'No…' *Possibly the least pregnant I've ever been, cheers, Ken.*

125

'Thank God for that.'

Ken Baggaley is known for being 'firm but fair', even though he's more than firm and not particularly fair. In newspaper-speak, it's because his rages are reactions to actual events, rather than tremors in a psychological fault line.

'I've got an interview with Natalie Shale,' I conclude.

He looks unmoved. 'She's doing a press conference?'

'No, just us. An exclusive. Her solicitor's a contact.'

Ken lifts eyebrows, grunts, and I sense I am briefly Number 1 in interest stakes over cheese-flavoured puffed corn.

'Good stuff. When?'

'Date's being finalised but it'll be in the bag soon, before Lucas Shale's appeal is heard.'

'Let me know how it goes. Well done, Woodford.'

Ken drops into a chair and continues his assault on the Wotsits. I walk out of the office with a spring in my step: now *that* was Ken gushing. Ben's a lucky charm.

On the way back to court, I decide to make a detour via Marks & Spencer. It was impressed upon me when I unpacked my rancid collection of underwear (from the 'L'Amour Longtemps' extra complacency range) that an upgrade is required. At first I thought 'But who's gonna see it anytime soon anyway?', then I mentioned it to Mindy. She explained the feng shui of lingerie: that if I'm in old cotton faded saggy things, a size too small, good things will not come to me, even if I'm not looking. I'm not sure I accept her reasoning.

I don't feel any degrees more sexually energised once I'm

gingerly fiddling with turquoise lace balcony cups. I'm wondering if anyone will ever want to see me naked again, or more to the point, see me naked the first time and then want to see me naked regularly, on a rolling basis, going forward, as Ken would say.

Part of the pact of long-term relationships is that they're sometimes as much about the things they take out of your life as put in. If it's no longer a rollercoaster, more of a monorail, that means you avoid the lows as well as the highs. If your loved one barges into the bathroom and catches you bending over with a gut like an apron made of Babybel cheese, they don't go off you, or expect you to slink about in deep plunge this and Tanga that, waxed into the middle of next Wednesday. They've taken you on, bought the product. Singledom, a new relationship: you have to repackage your contents and sell them all over again, body and soul.

These not very inspiring thoughts are rolling round my mind as I twang a violet triangle of something that appears to be made out of fishing net and an elastic band. My phone goes. *Ben*. Now his number has his name. There's that shiver.

'Hi, Rachel! How are you? I wanted to say thanks for helping Simon out with that story.'

I'm blushing. I'm actually standing here, looking at tiny pants, with a burning face because they're juxtaposed with Ben's voice. *Sex and the City* this ain't.

'Good thanks. And no, thank you for introducing us. That's a great story and it's not done me any harm at work. I owe you.'

'No worries, it solved a problem for Simon. He didn't know how to go about contacting your paper. He thinks journalists are feral creatures. He was scared stiff.'

Crazily confident Simon?

'I'm struggling to imagine Simon being scared stiff.'

'Imagine him being scared flaccid then.'

'Nooo, my eyes are bleeding!' I giggle, aware of the firework of happiness that starts fizzing in my chest at the slightest return of our old rapport.

Ben laughs. 'He was quite complimentary about you. He said you had "sass".'

'He means I was rude.'

'I told you, he needs a bit of fight. He likes it. Anyway, I have something else to ask of you.'

'You do?'

'Yeah, I was wondering if you were free to come to ours on Saturday night. Liv wants to do a "meeting people in Manchester" dinner party. We're bourgeois bastards nowadays, y'know. Liv particularly wants to meet you.'

'Right,' I say, feeling the fear. Why would Olivia particularly want to meet me, unless it was to do a risk assessment? He could tell her she absolutely doesn't need to worry. MI5 Threat Level: Brew Up, Kick Back. Oh God, oh God – what does she know? Reason tells me she has the official history, and this invite is proof of that. Emotions are telling me to use this thong as a slingshot to fire my mobile into the bargain briefs bin and run for the Peaks.

'You will come?' Ben says, into my silence.

'Sure.'

'I don't want to kill your cool single Saturday night stone dead. I know we're old boring marrieds.'

'Are you kidding? I'd love to come.'

'Honestly? That's great.'

Although I meant *love* with a substantial dollop of *bloody shitting self*, Ben sounds so pleased that it almost becomes true.

'I'm a fan of eating. And I'm in awe of anyone who's prepared to make food for visitors,' I say.

'You're a good cook, aren't you?'

'Nah. I gave up when I moved in with Rhys. He was the cook.'

'Ah.' Awkward pause. 'And Liv asked, do you want to bring anyone? A date?'

This is the moment where I'm supposed to have a wacky idea about hiring an escort for appearances' sake. I consider it for the maddest of moments, then firmly dismiss it. One of Mindy's chiselled internet Romeos, it transpired, used to work as an escort. Worse, he wore the 'Canadian tuxedo/Texas two-piece' of double denim. With cowboy boots. And awful shirts. Ivor nickname: Bri–Nylon Adams.

'Er. No.'

After I ring off, I guesstimate my sizes and buy a handful of stuff in safe black. It's a beginning.

23

I returned for the second year with a light tan that I was trying to prolong with Nivea tinted body lotion. It was from a fortnight in Paxos, a gift from Rhys.

While my friends from home had boyfriends the same age who were pot-washing and berry-picking, I had a grown-up one with an actual real proper full-time income who whisked me away for impromptu package holidays. My parents were less delighted: Rhys turned up at our local with a bag packed for me, losing me a week's pay in hand and a job for walking out mid-shift. He'd forgotten I needed my passport though, so we still had to run the gauntlet of my mum and dad's disapproval at the devil-may-care attitude to temporary employment and foreign travel.

I excitedly outlined the whole drama to Ben at the launderette's, as I loaded the drum with my clothes. Normally, the start of the second year and 'living out' would herald having a washing machine. Ours was broken, and the lack of turnaround time between holiday and back-to-uni had left me with a dirty laundry backlog. Ben had volunteered to sit with me during the spin cycle and then go get a coffee. He was house sharing with the lads from the flats, and although he'd filtered out the worst of them, the best of them still wasn't exactly panning for gold. (For example, even he'd admitted it wasn't advisable for me to use their Zanussi unless I wanted to return from the coffee to find them all wearing my smalls on their heads.)

'How did he have a bag packed for you without telling your folks?' Ben asked, as I boasted about sapphire seas and cultural sightseeing.

'Oh, it wasn't my stuff. He went to Boots and bought me a toothbrush and got me a bikini. And some other things.'

Actually, it was a comically stripped down, in more than one sense, male fantasy idea of what a woman might need on a surprise sunshine getaway. The detour to my family home had the benefit I could get the things I needed without hurting his feelings.

'Right.' Ben glanced down at what was in my hand and with some horror I realised it was a school-girlish broderie anglaise bra that was a good few shades away from Daz bright. I hastily bundled it into the machine, slammed the door and fed it with coins.

We sat down together on the slatted wooden bench.

'The look on the warlock of a landlord's face when I left,' I crowed. 'It was great.'

'Sounds it. Greece with Rhys,' Ben said.

'It was amazing!'

'Sure. Lots of sun and … swimming and stuff?' Ben rubbed his chin.

'Yeah.' I sighed. I knew I was being insufferable. I was in that vile realm of 'all broadcast, no reception' smug coupledom where I couldn't stop.

The bell on the launderette door jingled and a girl entered. A girl in the same way an Aston Martin Vanquish is a car: it was Georgina Race. This was a name that any male of the under-graduate population was incapable of uttering without the accompanying exhalation. She was instantly identifiable by her sheet of incredible shiny copper hair, a colour so intense it was as if she walked the planet with a Royal Albert Hall follow-spot on her. It was impossible for your eyes to slide past her – and once they were on her, there wasn't much to quibble with, as my dad would've said. She had a porcelain, doll-like face that looked as if it had been sketched for the cover of a Mills & Boon paperback. You could absolutely imagine her in a ragged blouse, wilting in the bulky arms of the arrogant Prince Xaviero.

Georgina was on my course. She had perfected the art of the lecture hall entrance, standing at the front of the room and scanning the half-empty rows for a spare seat, knowing every male in the place was trying to will her near. Ben would usually nudge me, clasping his hands in a 'prayer' gesture under the desk, to which I'd make a hand-shaking 'wanker' gesture in return. They were all shit out of luck, though: rumour had it she was dating some soap actor in London.

This crisp September morning, Georgina was looking equally crisp: she had an apple-green scarf knotted at her white swan throat and a short swingy patterned dress that served to highlight her long long legs that didn't appear to get any wider as they went up. Over the top she was wearing a navy frock coat that clung to her waist and flared out in folds around her violin-shaped hips. All in all, she looked like she should be striding down Carnaby Street a few decades ago with men who looked like a young Michael Caine lowering their spectacles and wolf-whistling.

She was clearly a bitch. I just had to find hard evidence.

'Hey Ben!' she trilled, spotting him and breezing over. 'What're you doing here?'

She knows Ben? And what the hell do you think he's doing here, I thought. Ordering a frittata, getting a slippy gearbox checked out, waiting for the results of a splenic biopsy?

'Waiting with Ron here. Her washing machine's knackered.'

Georgina's eyes moved reluctantly to me, only for a moment. 'Ahhh. Nightmare, right?'

I nodded. Annoyingly, I felt a little of that beautiful person dazzle, as if a celebrity had acknowledged me, and couldn't speak.

'What're you doing here?' he asked. 'Getting clothes washed, I guess?'

'Dropping some stuff for the dry-cleaning service,' she said, unlatching some probably-incredibly-expensive slinky things in monogrammed garment bags from her shoulder, by way of demonstration. 'Cashmere, etcetera.'

I couldn't help but notice she had slender arms like carved willow and tiny, fluttery-butterfly, delicate hands, screws of translucent tissue paper. In the genetic lottery, she'd won a triple rollover.

'Listen, we should totally do that thing we talked about? The dinner?' she said.

'Sure. Let me know when?'

'Certainly will,' she said, with a little feline moue, and a flirtily-eyelinered wink. 'See you around, yeah?'

She left her dry cleaning, breezed out and did a tips-of-the-fingers coy wave to Ben as she went. I said, trying very hard not to sound like a bitter nosy nag and failing: 'Uhm. What thing you talked about?'

I fully expected Ben to dissemble about some vague plan to hit up the Pizza Hut all-you-can-eat buffet for a gorge-til-you-gag.

'A date.'

'*A date?*' I repeated, as if he'd said 'bumming otters, hanging on to their whiskers like they're handlebars'.

'Yeah. Is it that amazing?'

'I didn't think she went out with students, that's all. Thought it was strictly cool successful older guys in other cities.'

'Like you, you mean?' Ben smirked. *Touché.* And before I could retort, Ben continued: 'Everyone was second guessing so I thought I'd ask her. He who dares wins.'

This got worse. He'd asked her? I couldn't deny that in some ways, it was a match ordained by heaven: the prom king and queen of English Literature & Language.

'*Cashmere, etcetera,*' I mimicked.

Ben didn't rise to it. I had a sense that karmically, I'd pushed hard on a swing door.

24

Pete Gretton and I share the press bench in the later half of the week for the opening of a medical negligence trial. It concerns the very untimely death of a twenty-nine-year-old woman in a liposuction procedure, and two NHS doctors and a nurse at a private practice being prosecuted for negligence and manslaughter. There are several stringers from the agencies – a more geographically mobile, less seedy strain of freelancer than Gretton. He's here because we've heard there'll be some fairly gory details of operative complications and dislodged fat particles. Gretton is a rogue collection of cells himself, travelling around the arteries of the building and causing dangerously high blood pressure whenever he comes to a halt.

'They can't all be to blame,' he mutters, before the court's in session. 'How many people does it take to stick a drip in an arm? CPS are simply chucking a handful of mud and hoping something sticks. Chewit?'

I shake my head at the proffered packet. 'No thanks.'

'On a diet?'

'Get lost.'

Gretton bares yellow incisors. 'Not to worry, most men like some meat on the bones. Hey, mind you, sounds like this 'un was taking it too far. Pushing twenty stone, I heard. Spherical.'

He chews noisily, giving me a view of his half-masticated sweet.

'Shut up,' I hiss, glancing at the heavy-set family in the public gallery, and twist my body as far away from him as possible. I need an *I'm Not With Stupid* t-shirt.

Solicitors are in hushed conference with barristers, papers are shuffled, people in the public gallery cough and shift in their seats.

A couple of the wigged-and-gowned fraternity are having a quiet chuckle about something that's probably hilarious if you're familiar with the intricacies of malpractice, and I see the family peering at them in irritated disbelief. I sympathise. It's hard to believe that your earth-shattering calamity is merely another day at the office for people who do this kind of thing for a living.

Most of the time, journalists are rubber-necking tourists who can grasp the basic concepts involved. Dog bites man, man bites dog, man bites man because his dog looked at him funny, and so on. With a case like this, you have to become a short-term expert in a specific area of a highly skilled profession. Whenever a judge tetchily instructs a barrister or witness to simplify the terminology for the sake of the jury, the press bench heaves a near-audible sigh of relief.

As I leave the courtroom at lunchtime, I see Zoe in conversation with a woman I recognise from the public gallery.

Gretton's seconds behind me, as ever.

'What the fuck is she up to?'

'Talking,' I say.

Zoe and the woman look over at us; Zoe bends her head conspiratorially.

'You want to grow some fuzz on your balls,' Gretton says. 'She's talking to someone involved in this case. Don't you care?'

'Not really. She might be asking the time, for all we know.'

'You're bloody naïve, you are.'

'It's called trust.'

'Trust? That girl doesn't lie straight in bed.'

'You didn't like Zoe from the start, did you?'

'I've got her number.'

I smile. 'Takes one to know one, perhaps.'

Gretton trousers his Chewits and marches off, nostrils flaring.

Zoe walks up to me. 'Pub o'clock?'

I nod. Since I took Zoe to The Castle, she's assumed it as a weekly routine, and I surprised myself by not only acquiescing but actually enjoying it. Normally my lunchtimes are spent in jealously guarded semi-seclusion in the press room. I didn't expect to make a friend.

Outside, I say: 'Gretton got all unwound about you speaking to that woman. Who was she?'

'Guess!'

'Sister of my lipo victim?'

'Mum. I saw them milling around earlier and I could tell she was going to appoint herself the gobby spokesperson so I got in early. I told her what Gretton said about how her daughter would be still be alive if she'd had her spoon surgically removed from the Häagen-Dazs.'

I stop in my tracks. 'You didn't?'

'I did, and I said if she wants to talk afterwards, she should talk to you.'

'But ... Gretton said that in the press room.'

'So?'

'I know that was Gretton at his worst but we all say off-colour things about the cases in there from time to time. You shouldn't share them round.'

'Why not?'

'It's just not done.'

Zoe bites her lip. 'I went too far, didn't I?'

We start walking again, I shift the weight of my bag to the other shoulder. 'It's definitely playing dirty. If Gretton finds out, he'll go ape.'

'Sorry. He was so nasty about her I thought it served him right.'

'I know. Bear in mind you could've messed it up for all of us. The public don't tend to make much distinction between good journalists and Grettons. A lot of them don't even under-stand about open court. They're amazed they can't have us thrown out.'

'I'm really sorry.'

'Ah well … sensitive "our pain" interviews aren't his forte, I can't see him cosying up to the mum, so it probably won't become an issue anyway. And he'll hack them off by doing lots of gratuitous exploding arse stories during the trial.'

Conversation's interrupted while we negotiate road crossing. When we resume progress, Zoe says: 'My mum's large.'

'Really?' I glance doubtfully at her sapling limbs.

'I got my dad's metabolism,' she says. 'Yeah, she looked into gastric banding at one point. But she was too big.'

'Why would they …' I start again. 'Isn't that the point?'

Zoe mutters something about surgery and anaesthesia risk.

'Then she finally lost the weight and got the band, and started drinking those chocolate-flavoured protein shakes for body builders.'

'Right. Liquids are probably best, at first. What with the smaller space.'

'Not if you chug them all day and end up the size you were when you were turned down for surgery.'

'Ah,' I say. Poor Zoe – her jet-propelled ambition is probably a result of wanting to get a long way from problems at home.

'Gretton hit a nerve,' she concludes.

I feel bad for telling her off. I squeeze her arm.

'Gretton hits all our nerves. Don't dwell on it.'

'Should I take back what I said? Tell the mum I misheard or something?'

'I doubt she'd forget the ice-cream gag. Nah, leave it. Thanks for pointing her my way, too,' I add, not wanting to sound ungrateful.

'Any time,' Zoe says. 'We're a team. Lunch is on me today. I'm going to try a Piscine Ploughman.'

'A pissing ploughman?'

'Smoked salmon sandwich.'

'Oh.'

'I made that up.'

'Thank goodness.'

'They call it Fishy on a Dishy.'

'You're ordering,' I say, opening the pub door and ushering Zoe through. 'I suffer enough humiliation without going looking for more.'

25

'Oi!' Caroline shouted, over the aircraft-like noise of my travel hairdryer. I clicked it off. 'Ben for you!'

I galloped down the stairs of our student house to the hallway. We rarely made outgoing calls – our landlord had installed a payphone at his own rate that gobbled up coins like a sweating diabetic with Giant Smarties.

'Ron! Culinary SOS!' Ben said. 'I'm making dinner for Georgina and it has TURNED TO SHIT.'

'You're cooking?' I said, laughing and simultaneously envying Georgina for being the kind of woman men sweat over a flambée to impress. 'Why not go out?'

'She got the wrong end of the stick and I didn't know how to set her straight. She was all …' Ben affected the breathy, 1950s starlet voice she used with men rather well '… I can't wait to try your cooking, Ben.'

'Haha, this is going to be great! You best call on the little hombre from Homepride.'

'She's not the kind of girl who's going to find it funny to be served a Findus Crispy Pancake sandwich, is she?'

Ben lived with boys who re-used dirty plates by putting clingfilm over them instead of washing up. Georgina was going to need a *robust* constitution and all her vaccinations, I thought.

'I can't vouch for her sense of humour but I've never seen her crack a smile. Even in those laugh-a-minute linguistics lectures.'

'Help! What do I do?'

I gave an exaggerated sigh.

'How long have you got until she comes round?'

'Three hours … no, wait, two hours forty-five minutes!'

'And what's my budget if I go to the supermarket on the way to yours?'

'Whatever it takes! You're my angel.'

'Yeah yeah.'

I turned up at Ben's house in my knitted woolly hat carrying misshapen supermarket bags with steadily lengthening handles in each hand.

'Lemme in, these are going to break,' I said, barging through the porch and plopping them unceremoniously on the hallway floor.

'Ah Ron, bless you.' Ben rescued a tub of crème fraîche as it rolled towards the coat-stand.

'I've bought you flowers too,' I said, producing a cellophane cornet of white hothouse roses from one of the bags. 'I feel as if I'm seducing someone by proxy, like Cyrano de Bergerac.'

'Superb!'

I knew I must've been fond of Ben, 'cos I sure as hell didn't want to be seducing Georgina Race with anything more than a bouquet of stinging nettles, severed rat tails and tampon strings. And yet, apparently, I was.

With the help of supermarket recipe idea cards, we assembled something fairly respectable: asparagus starters, stuffed chicken breasts, potato gratin, white chocolate mousse with raspberries. I delegated tasks to Ben and he put music on while we worked. He actually proved quite an able deputy. The fridge gradually filled up with foil-wrapped dishes.

'I didn't know you could cook,' he said.

'I can't, really. I'm making it up as I go along.'

'Now she tells me.'

'Here are the timings.' I jotted down oven temperatures on a scrap of paper and tucked them behind the kettle. 'Follow them in that order and give her the bubbly as soon as she arrives. You can get away with much imperfection when people are pissed. What are you wearing?'

'A shirt?' said Ben, uncertain. He was in a red '66 World Cup top. It directly contravened Article 7.1 of Rhys's Wanker Law that stated you didn't advertise any event you hadn't attended, any place you'd never been, or any band you didn't really listen to.

'Think smart. No sports-related casual wear.'

'Got it.'

'I'll leave you to get ready.'

I pulled my coat on, picked my hat up. 'Good luck,' I said.

'You are my angel and your reward is in heaven,' Ben said.

'It's certainly not on earth,' I grumbled.

As I walked back to my house, something niggled, and it wasn't the fact I'd cooked a meal I wasn't going to eat.

Knocking round with Ben platonically – catching the odd envious look from girls who misconstrued the situation – obscured something that could be decreed by any efficient eugenics programme: boys like him dated and procreated with girls like Georgina Race. I didn't want to date, much less procreate with, either of them, but there was something diminishing in having it confirmed.

I was back at those fireworks, remembering that there were females for fun sexy secret times, and then there was good old doughty Ronnie. A minx for spotting a discount deal on Sainsbury's *pain de campagne*.

The next day, we met up at our ten o'clock lecture, Ben sliding into the seat beside me, wearing a sly grin.

'Soooo … how did it go?' I said, grinning back, chewing on my pen lid.

'Good,' Ben said. 'She loved dinner. Absolutely loved it. Thanks.'

'You're seeing each other?' I asked.

'Doubt it.' Ben shook his head.

'Oh.' I didn't know if I should ask any more questions, or if Ben wanted me to. I thought he was turning away from me to bring an end to the topic, then realised he was making sure we weren't being overheard.

'She was boring! Christ, she was boring. At first I thought it was nerves, but she's *so* dull. And self-absorbed. The weird thing is, I don't even think she's that fit any more. The shine's rubbed off. Nice girl and all that. But … not for me.'

I ignored the lightning-flash of joy that zapped across my insides.

'Never mind. At least I shopped for dinner. You only wasted a trip to Lloyd's Pharmacy...'

'Oh, we still did it,' Ben replied. 'Not going to all that effort for a conversation about Hertfordshire prep schools and collecting Tiffany bracelet charms.'

I looked at him. His expression was impassive. I remembered the conversation in MacDougal's about swordsmanship. There was a strange churning where the lightning had been.

'What? That's grim!'

'Eh?'

'You don't like her as a person, but you still had sex? That's shallow and appalling. Poor Georgina, you're calling her boring after she's become a notch on your bedpost? Talk about disrespectful.' Rachel Woodford, defender of Georgina Race's maidenhood. This was a new one.

'Alright, settle down.'

'I thought more of you than that,' I said.

'People do have casual sex out here in the real and imperfect world, you know, it doesn't have to be seen as an aggressive act,' Ben hissed.

'What's that supposed to mean?'

'I mean, we're not all lucky enough to be with our soul mates, but we're not going to be celibate while we wait for them to turn up.'

I could've said something here about not harbouring any delusions that he was living like an ascetic monk, but Ben had matched me in righteous anger. I'd never felt so grateful for a lecture starting.

Soul mate. Had I said that? In the Greek holiday blather? Oh God. Maybe I had. I realised now I'd laid it on thick in case Ben had sussed the fact I'd swooned during last year's kiss. In actual fact, Rhys and I had definitively exited the honeymoon period. Being treated as an equal by peers at university had made me less willing to tolerate the slightly domineering, aloof manner that had felt so Mr Darcy in our early days. In turn, he accused me of 'getting up myself'. If I was truly honest, I knew Rhys's surprise holiday stunt was as much about him re-establishing who had the whip hand as it was about summer lovin' and dolmades.

After a while, Ben pushed his notes towards me so I could see he'd written in the margin: '*Joking.*'

I scowled in incomprehension, drew a question mark underneath it, pushed it back.

'*We didn't,*' he wrote, underscoring the second word several times to make his meaning plain. '*What's the matter?*'

Good question. I read it, shrugged, passed it back. Was I really so uptight I expected my single friends to live by my rules?

Lecture over, we had tutorials in different parts of the building. I was out of my seat, down the steps and by the door in seconds. Ben caught up with me, grabbing my arm before I could stalk off.

'Look, I was being laddish, you usually find it funny,' he said, under his breath.

I rudely shook my arm free, even though his hold had been gentle.

'For the record, we didn't do anything and I didn't want to,' he added. 'I still can't see why it would've been some moral failure.'

'None of my business,' I said, haughtily, heart suddenly

banging against my ribs as if it wanted to make a break for it and scuttle off to the Victorian Essayists ahead of me. My behaviour suggested I'd be a good fit for the era.

'I'd have had a better time if you'd stayed,' Ben said, nailing the source of my anxiety more accurately than I wanted.

'Why do you say it like that? Like it's the lowest standard – "I'd have had a better time *even* if Ron had stayed."'

'That wasn't what I said.'

No, and that wasn't what I meant. *I don't want you to want to do that, with her. When she's nothing like me.* What was I on?

Ben looked out of the window, back at me, opened his mouth to say something, hesitated.

'I can cook,' he said, flatly.

'What? You conned me so I'd do your shopping?'

He glared at me. I glared back.

'Pleased to see you two were paying such rapt attention and that the academic debate now rages,' our tutor cut between us. 'And I'm certain those notes you were passing were on the rise of the middle classes in the fourteenth century in relation to *The Canterbury Tales.*'

'Most definitely,' Ben said, nodding.

'Sod off to your eleven o'clocks,' the tutor said, and we did.

26

In all those fashion features about 'What To Wear To Meet Your In-Laws' or 'What To Wear On A Country Weekend Away' I'd like them to toughen up and tackle the genuinely thorny issues, such as 'What To Wear To Meet Your Lost Love's Wife'.

I know I can't attempt this dinner party with anything in my current wardrobe. So slim are the pickings – and not in the sense that anything is small – I decide on a scorched earth policy, bundle most of it up and take it to the nearest charity shop.

The altruistic glow dims in minutes as I stand holding recyclable bin bags in the middle of Age UK. The woman at the counter has grey hair in a bun and glasses round her neck on a string, like a wonderful granny from a Roald Dahl story who'd adopt you if your parents were wiped out in the first chapter in some blackly comic manner.

'Just here?' I say brightly, hoping for a drop-and-skedaddle.

She makes the internationally recognised – and not entirely gracious – outstretched finger wiggle that means 'Give That Here'.

I hand it over, thinking, I didn't know giving things away for free has an audition process. She starts pulling the contents of my bags out in front of me, sniffing a cardigan disdainfully and asking: 'Are you a smoker?'

Before I can answer in the negative, she yelps in distress as if she's found a nobbly dildo the size of a Saharan cactus and says 'We can do without *these* . . .' holding a rogue pair of socks at arm's length, between finger and thumb. Hmm, my slipper-socks with paw-like rubber grips on the soles. I'm sure someone would be grateful for them. Admittedly, with second-hand socks, you'd have to be not so much in reduced circumstances as bin rifling. But talk about no good turn going unpunished. I want to say: 'Who are you, the Duchess of Dry Clean Only?'

Instead I mumble 'howdidtheygetinthere' and continue my shopping with the socks bulging in my coat pockets, vowing that the aged and their forked-tongued representatives can bloody well help themselves in future.

I need an outfit that says 'Grown up and yet still youthful' 'Dressy but laidback' and 'Not slaggy but not retired from active duty either'.

Unsurprisingly, looking for something in my budget that both a) fits and b) conveys six contradictory statements turns out to be difficult. I thought I was a size 12 and I still cling to this belief despite all evidence pointing north. Or in the case of nipples in very tight material, north-west and south-east.

A trek up and down King Street's fashion stores on a busy Saturday afternoon leaves me frazzled and near-tearful. There's only one thing for it, I decide, and call Mindy. She listens to the problem and writes a brisk prescription.

'You've lost perspective and are no longer in the good decision zone. Go somewhere upmarket, like Reiss, find a simple black cocktail dress. Buy one size up if that looks better, shelve your pride. Pay whatever it costs. Wear with any heels you know you can walk in. Boom, done.'

'But I wore black last time I met Ben? And his friend?' I add, hastily.

'He won't remember what you wore unless it was Bernie Clifton's ostrich costume. Trust me.'

I find her instructions simple and effective. I arrive back home on a short-lived high, until I discover that, while the pop-video lighting in the changing rooms made me look like an 'Addicted To Love' girl, in the fading daylight it's a bit more 'Mafia widow who's been hitting the tortellini in her grief'. I could try to improve on this, or I could have a nerve-steadying vodka and Diet Coke while waiting for the taxi. It has a much stronger lure than a frenzy of turd polishing. I recall a Tao of Mindy phrase: 'You can't polish a turd, but you can roll it in glitter.'

I settle for vodka, and more make-up.

I obsess over what Olivia's going to be like. I know she's blonde, or what I glimpsed of Ben's phone wallpaper suggested so. Ben always went for conspicuous 'knock outs'; no reason to think the woman he settled down with will be any different. I imagine her as a sort of Eighth Wonder era Patsy Kensit, dressed like Betty Draper in *Mad Men*. With the conversational skills of Dorothy Parker and the … oh sod it.

The worst has happened already. She's not me. On the menu tonight: Rachel's heart is turned into steak haché, served with an egg on top.

27

Ben and Olivia's house is a Victorian semi with white gables and a glossy royal blue front door, a lollipop bay tree in a square black planter standing sentry. I ring the stiff brass doorbell and wait, listening to the hubbub of lively voices beyond. I get a ripple of anxiety. No Rhys by my side any more. I hadn't appreciated how solitary being single would feel. I wish I'd had two vodkas.

Ben answers, carrying a bottle with a corkscrew wedged in it, cream shirt, slightly mussed hair, looking like something from a Lands' End catalogue. He and Olivia probably go for hearty walks in Aran sweaters and his 'n' hers chocolate moleskin trousers on Sundays, throwing sticks to their rescue puppy, laughing with their heads thrown back.

'Rachel, hi!' He leans in for a chaste peck on the cheek, and I go rigid. 'Can I take your coat?'

I do an awkward dance, handing him the wine I've brought, unwrapping myself, swapping the coat for the return of the bottle.

Over his shoulder, as he's hanging my coat up, Ben says: 'This is Liv. Liv, Rachel.' Blood pounds in my ears.

A petite woman steps forward, smiling, to relieve me of my booze for a second time. I quiver. Perhaps unsurprisingly, after all this angst, she is just an attractive woman. Slight, duckling-blonde short hair, perfect oval face, golden-coloured. I expected some variant on feminine perfection and Olivia looks like she sweats Chanel No. 5, no surprises here.

If I was going to be a cow – and obviously, I'm not, but if I was going to be – physically, she's the tiniest bit safe, as a Ben choice. His university ones were usually dynamic, healthy, strapping, widescreen-smile Carly Simon sorts. That type of mega-wattage vivacious beauty where trying to deny it was like trying to look directly into the sun without squinting.

'Nice to meet you,' she says.

'Nice to meet you too. Thanks for inviting me.'

'Come and say hello to the others and I'll get you a drink.'

As I follow her I see she's wearing a clinging, draped jersey top and tight-but-flared trousers in shades of grey. Not darks-wash-accident grey, of course, the ones called things like moonstone, graphite and slate that hang in sinuous slivers on padded hangers in shops with the ambience of New York nightclubs. The sort I didn't dare enter this afternoon, expecting to be chased out of at the end of a broom. She's so understated and sophisticated, suddenly my try-hard tart frock makes me feel as if I've wandered out of an '80s instant coffee ad.

Olivia leads me into a living room that opens on to a dining room beyond and guides me over to do my hellos with a tall woman with highlighted, vanilla-and-toffee hair. She looks like she'd have been in the Goal Attack tabard in the rival school's netball team and marked you so hard you'd have fallen over in fright. My eyes move to the man next to her, who's shorter, stockier and wearing a salmon-pink shirt that accentuates his tanned flush.

'Lucy, Matt, this is Rachel. And I think you've met Simon…?'

Simon, inspecting the bookshelf, raises a flute glass in greeting and ambles over. He still looks like he's dressed for the office.

'Can I offer you a champagne cocktail, Rachel?' Olivia says.

'You can, and I will accept,' I say, trying to strike the right partyish note and coming off as a cock. 'Your house is lovely, Olivia. I can't believe you've not been here for years.'

This is a proper grown-ups' dwelling, no doubt about it. The oatmeal carpet underneath our feet is thick and soft, church candles are twinkling in a cavernous original fireplace and there are framed black-and-white photographic prints on the walls of Barcelona or Berlin or wherever they went on romantic breaks while courting, wielding the Nikon.

'Oh, we're still at sixes and sevens, we've dimmed the lights to cover it up,' Olivia calls, over her shoulder, as she ducks out to the kitchen.

'Liv is being modest; she trails order in her wake like most people trail devastation,' Ben calls, from somewhere near the oven.

The table beyond is set with coordinated aqua napkins and taper candles, the centrepiece is a moth orchid in a pebble-filled tub. Some ambient-chill-out-dub-whatever drifts out of a Bang & Olufsen stereo. If Ben's still climbing the ranks, Olivia must be quite a high-flier, I decide, taking in the atmosphere of plushy serenity and discreet wealth. I picture my old home in Sale and realise what different circles Ben and I move in. My mind wanders back to the reassurance Rhys would offer at my side but I quickly start to reassess whether it'd be worth it. His hackles would be right up at this advertisers' vision of cliched contentment and I'd be hoping he didn't drink too much and get 'nowty'.

Olivia returns and puts a champagne flute in my hand, raspberries bobbing in the liquid.

'Is this everyone now, Liv?' Lucy asks.

'Yes.'

'OK, so a – toast. Welcome to Manchester, Liv and Ben.'

'Cheers,' I mumble, clinking glasses.

'Cheers Ben!' they call, as he's in the kitchen.

This is everyone? Six of us, two couples, two singles – Simon and I are being set up. It's not merely a rumour: this kind of crashingly unsubtle matchmaking actually happens. Is Simon equally uncomfortable to have me sprung on him? Lucy and Matt are looking at me curiously. I'm going to have to brave this out by pretending it's not happening. My usual modus operandi.

I turn towards Simon in desperation, with a rictus grin.

'How are you?' I ask.

'I've spoken to Natalie and she's definitely up for the interview,' he says, and I'm grateful to have a topic in common.

'Great.'

'I'll get back to you with a date. OK to do it at her house?'

'Ideal.'

'All right if I come along?'

'If it's OK, I'd rather you didn't.'

'Thanks.'

'I'm not being rude—'

'Oh really? Where does this rank on your scale?'

He deadpans and I laugh despite myself.

'If you sit in,' I say, 'she'll be on edge and looking to you

153

for approval all the time and the whole thing will be stilted. I know it's a big story but she's not Barbra Streisand. It'll be fine.'

'I'll think about it,' Simon says, smiling.

'Those are my terms,' I say, smiling back, hoping this isn't too much sass. 'Good luck taking your terms to the nationals.'

Actually the nationals would bite Simon's hand off to the elbow. I feel reasonably sure from what Ben said that Simon's going to keep his sense of humour, and stick with me.

'What do you do for a living?' Matt interrupts.

'I'm a court reporter for the local paper. You?'

'Management consultancy. Mainly blue chip firms.'

I can't think of any follow-up question, so Matt interjects: 'What's the naughtiest thing anyone in the dock's ever done?'

'Er. Naughtier than serial killing?'

'No, bizarre stuff. Funnies.'

'You lawyers probably see more of them than me?' I say to Lucy.

'I'm in litigation, like Liv,' Lucy offers. 'So no. Leylandii and partition walls.'

'Sit in, everyone,' Olivia says, and we all take our seats, Lucy and Matt making a beeline for the middle, Simon and I left with no choice but to flank them, facing each other. Why didn't Ben warn me? It isn't like him. *You don't know what 'like him' is any more,* I remind myself.

Wine flows, I gulp to finish my cocktail, and salads are put in front of us. I try to remember what polite small talk involves and try to make sense of the 'Ben Plus Olivia Equals Lucy and Matt as Friends' equation. Part of the wonder of mine and Ben's previous life was our radar for who our sort of person was and who wasn't. It was as if we arrived at the friendship with a shared phrasebook and moral compass and map, even if the literal one of the university lay-out was less comprehensible. This turn of events tells me either, as Caroline put it, his thing has changed, or he's being a good host and a good husband. I know which I'm hoping for.

'How are you coping up here?' Matt asks Olivia. 'Do you like *Man-chest-ah*?'

Matt says this in a mock Burnage scally voice that sets me slightly on edge.

'I like Harvey Nicks,' Olivia says, to a titter from Lucy. 'I do. It's much more like a little London than I thought it would be.'

This doesn't sound like a ringing commendation to me. Is it positive to praise something as a miniature version of what you're used to? Unless it's a bum, I suppose.

'You know Ben's always gone on about how amazing it was to go to university here...' she continues. *Good for Ben.*

'Didsbury is so fab,' Lucy says.

'It seems to have everything, yeah. We're going to need to look into schools,' Olivia adds, coyly.

'Oh, do you have some news?' Lucy trills, grabbing Olivia's arm.

I chew so hard I bite the insides of my cheeks.

'No, just planning ahead,' Olivia says, casting a look at Ben.

'Awww...' Lucy coos.

I feel infinitely sad and already slightly tipsy, a combination that foreshadows disaster. However, I notice Ben also looks like he needs the Heimlich manoeuvre.

'Let's not get ahead of ourselves,' he says to Olivia. 'A dog will do for now. We're concentrating on settling in right now, that's all,' Ben says, to the table.

'Don't put it off when you don't know how long it will take,' Lucy says. 'We were trying for how long, with Miles?'

'Eighteen months,' Matt supplies.

'And that was going at it pretty much every night,' Lucy adds. I suddenly find the issue of whether this is indeed chicory in my salad absolutely engrossing.

'I read an article in the *Mail* the other day by some fertility specialist,' Lucy continues. 'He said you should have your family completed by thirty-three. How many do you want, Liv?'

'Three. Two girls and a boy.'

Ben exhales, heavily. 'You don't order them from Grattans...'

'And you're what, thirty-one? You have to get started this instant, right now!' Lucy says, banging the table and giggling.

'Not right now, one hopes,' Simon says drily, and I laugh.

'Stop winding her up, Lucy,' Ben says, with tension in his voice that apparently goes completely unnoticed by Lucy.

'Come on, Ben!' Lucy wheedles. 'If the lady wants it, the lady should get it. Titchies are the best fun!'

I have to look round the room at this for confirmation. She did say 'titchies', right?

'Unless you think you're firing blanks?' Matt adds, quite seriously, to a this-isn't-happening face from Ben.

Wow. Any Matt and Lucy child, I think, must be quite a formula. Matt and Lucy *squared*.

'He'll come round,' Olivia says, patting Ben's arm.

Ben looks hunted and takes a swig of his drink.

'What about you, Rachel?' Olivia says, and all eyes swivel towards me. 'Do you want kids some day?'

'Uh.' I have a forkful of green leafy matter stalled halfway to my mouth and I plonk it back down on the edge of my plate, so I don't look like one of the gorillas in the mist with the vegetation being observed by five Dian Fosseys. 'It's not top of my agenda. But, yes. Why not? If I find someone to have them with.'

There's an uncomfortable silence: uncomfortable largely due to their matchmaking. I rattle on: 'And I say, don't worry about fertility specialists. That's their job, to tell you to get on and have babies. I'm sure a liver specialist would tell us never to binge drink and heart consultants would say don't cook with butter.'

Another clanging silence, even louder than the first. Ben smiles encouragingly. No wonder: I've taken his place in the shit.

'You binge drink?' Matt says, flatly, chasing some rocket round his plate.

'Not – uh. I don't down bottles of apple Corky's and urinate on war memorials. I don't regularly stick to two units at one sitting though. That's normal, isn't it?'

'Not if you have children,' Lucy says.

'Of course, sleepless night … and so on,' I offer.

'And Miles is nearly four now, I don't want him to be around us, drunk.'

'Well, I should think not,' I say. 'At the bottle at his age.'

Lucy takes it straight, blinking rapidly. 'He's weaned and on solids. He's *three*.'

'Urm, yeah. I meant …' I trail off.

Lucy turns to Olivia and says: 'Oh my God, I forgot to tell you – we finally got the keys to the villa!'

She starts rummaging in her bag, producing photographs. Lucy hands them to Olivia and Ben and they make noises of interest and approval. It doesn't seem as if the photos are going to circulate any further.

'Wrong crowd for that last gag, I'm afraid,' Simon mutters, topping up my suddenly-nearly-empty wine glass.

'Did I say a bad thing?' I whisper back.

'Absolutely not. I was waiting for the spotlight to swing round to my sperm motility.' He looks down. 'Disaster averted, boys.'

Suddenly I'm back at school, giggling at the back of the classroom. When our laughter subsides, we see the rest of the table are watching us with interest.

28

It's fair to say that Matt and Lucy win the evening's competition, hands down. Every subject – work, family, holidays, home – seems to come with right and wrong answers. They quickly realise my answers are duds and lose interest in me. I've never been skiing, or fretted about the best miles-per-gallon among station wagons, haven't eaten at places with a Michelin star, don't have strong opinions on each party's tax breaks.

It's not so much an air of self-congratulation as a thick smog. Being this acquisitive seems so exhausting. I wonder how this game ends, if they'll finish up in a retirement home competing for who's got the biggest necklace alarm.

I sincerely hope that Lucy and Matt are among the few people Ben and Olivia know up here, and they are therefore making a special effort. All my interactions with Olivia suggest she's a nice enough person, yet around Lucy she seems to become Lucy-ish. Ben is quiet, maybe even subdued.

After the main course has been served, eaten and cleared away, I excuse myself to the bathroom.

'Use the downstairs one. Before the kitchen, on your left,' Olivia says.

It's as immaculate as the rest of their residence, and I have a pang about my own homelessness. It's not Sale any more. It's not Rupa's palace either.

Mid-handwashing with something fragrant from a white china pump dispenser, I'm surprised to overhear a muted conversation between Ben and Olivia. From the clanking, I gather it's taking place over the dishwasher. Something about the tenor of it tells me they think it's private. I guess they haven't worked out their new home's acoustics yet.

After some debate over which way the plates are stacked, Olivia hisses: 'Rachel's sweet.'

I freeze, while reaching for the hand towel.

Ben responds: 'Yeah, she is.'

Pause.

'And pretty,' Olivia adds. Ben makes an equivocal noise. 'Nondescript was a little harsh.'

I actually suck in air at this. I look at myself in the mirror. Nondescript, slightly bloodshot eyes in a nondescript face. I think: you asked for this. You went looking for it, you begged for it, you knew it was coming and here it is, and guess what? You hate it. I start mindlessly washing my hands a second time.

'I never notice anyone other than you, darling, you know that,' Ben says with exaggerated gallantry, and Olivia snorts.

'Simon's keen,' she says. 'That's going nicely, I think.'

'Yeah, Liv, don't force it, will you?'

'I'm not!'

'Rachel's come out of a long-term relationship, she's going to be a bit fragile.'

'They were engaged?'

'Yeah. Seriously,' I hear Ben continue, 'she was with Rhys ages. She was with him when I knew her.'

'Then maybe a fling is exactly what she needs.'

'Why do women always have to interfere?'

29

Two courses down, and the booze has really kicked in. Lucy's giggling has got louder, Matt's anecdotes are more risqué. Simon's relaxed but he can hold his drink, so he's giving nothing away. He watches me as I pick up my napkin, sit down again and refill my glass. I feel so hollow, I want to be full of something – it may as well be drink.

I catch the tail end of a discussion about the best age to get married. (Is it the age Matt and Lucy were wed, by any chance?)

'Are you anti marriage then?' Lucy asks Simon, covering her mouth decorously as she hiccups.

'You're not anti, you just haven't met the right woman, have you, Simon?' Olivia says.

She glances at me – Christ, she's saying this for my benefit.

'I'm not anti marriage per se, I'm anti most marriages,' Simon says. 'I'm anti the reasons people usually get married.'

'True love?' asks Lucy.

'Most people don't get married to the person they love the most, they marry whoever they happen to be with when they turn thirty,' Simon replies. 'Present company excepted, obviously.'

Present company excepted is such an elegantly insulting term, I think, given it clearly means *present company especially*. It's up there with *with all due respect*, meaning *with no respect whatsoever*.

'Listen to this, Simon's saying everyone marries whoever they're with at thirty and love's got nothing to do with it,' Olivia says, tugging on Ben's sleeve as he finishes distributing dessert bowls among us and sits down.

'I didn't say love has nothing to do with it,' Simon folds his arms. 'See, this is the problem discussing this with women. They start shrieking. Do most people think, "this person is my destiny" when they tie the knot, or do they think "I can't be arsed to make the effort to see what else is out there now, the hairline's on the wane or the waistline's on the wax, I feel fond, you'll do?"'

'Even if you have got married thinking that, isn't it all about whether you're going to honour your vows?' Ben asks.

'Hey!' Olivia play-slaps his arm.

'Of course I'm not saying *I did*, I'm saying theoretically here your motives matter less than your intentions.'

'All relationships depend on timing,' I say, careful to look only at Simon.

'Suppose so,' he says.

'Let me get this straight,' Matt says, springing into consultant mode, as if he's been charged too much by a wholesaler for photocopier ink and is hunting for the flaw in the sums. 'What's wrong with settling down without making the effort to "see what else is out there"? How do you know anything better *is* out there?'

Simon shrugs. 'You don't, if you don't look. I want the life I choose, instead of letting a life choose me. That's all I'm saying. Don't do the "right thing" to reward someone for long service, if you've grown out of them. Aim high.'

Matt's eyes all but disappear as he squints. 'Even if you want kids, clock ticking, you throw a stable relationship away...?'

'Stable? Stable is for shelving!' Simon says, revelling in his role as agent provocateur. Lucy and Matt look horrified.

'But this means you believe in The One?' Lucy asks, grasping at straws.

'No, dear, I don't. I'm a hardliner. Or as I like to call it, a grown up.'

'Who's this lady you're pursuing if not The One?' Lucy persists.

'You appear to be confusing a marketing concept for romantic comedies with proven scientific phenomena,' Simon says, and I start laughing, despite myself.

'What are you sniggering at, Woodford?' Ben calls, from the other end of the table, forcing me to look at him fully for the first time since 'nondescript'.

'It's Simon – he's so laser-sighted, *lawyer* snarky.' I wave my hand: 'Don't stop. Sorry. You were saying, "The One".'

'She doesn't exist?' Lucy prompts.

Simon sighs. 'There's a percentage of people on the planet you can be reasonably happy with. The One is in fact one of around six thousand. Then it's down to who you cross paths with, and when. The period in the middle where you're in control of your bladder and bowels. Being a member of the point zero zero zero zero whatever per cent club in six billion is still an accolade. Any woman who doesn't understand that has a poor grasp of mathematics.'

'Or a poor grasp of how lucky she is to be in your six thousand club,' I say.

I'm trying to bait Simon. He takes it as collusion.

'Naturally,' he agrees, and winks.

I catch Lucy looking revolted, interpreting the exchange as a betrayal of womankind. I get the feeling that quite a lot of things have been flying over her head at a distance that wouldn't disturb her hairstyle.

'Let's call time of death on your popularity here, shall we, Simon?' Ben says.

'You're a bunch of cynics,' Simon says. 'This is actually a rallying cry for romance.'

'I don't think what you're describing is romantic,' Ben says, tartly. 'Everyone loses their novelty sooner or later. You have a better chance of happiness with someone you know well than an unattainable alternative you've put on a pedestal and pursued. Love at first sight and all that stuff is crap. It's just the thrill of your imagination working on insufficient information. It's that moment when someone can be anyone. Soon passes. And it's all the worse because you've made disappointment absolutely inevitable.'

My eyes are inexorably drawn to Ben's and he feels it, looking away, quickly.

'Having high standards doesn't mean you're never pleased, it means you're rarely pleased, Benji.' Simon's voice has become slightly brittle. Now Lucy isn't the only one with a vague sense of things whizzing over her head.

I feel pressure to break the ensuing silence.

'Here's what I don't get. A marriage where you're madly in love for as long as it lasts and then go your separate ways is a failed marriage. Yet you can be together for decades and be miserable and it's officially successful, by virtue of staying put. No one would say someone who was widowed had a failed marriage.'

'Because marriage is supposed to be until death do you part. By definition you've failed if you're apart and both still alive,' Ben says, looking at me levelly. 'Or one has killed the other.'

'OK, well … the criteria still shouldn't be so crude. "Successful for a limited period" instead of failed. And maybe "enduring" would be more appropriate than successful for the ones who are together but aren't happy.'

'Oh lord,' Simon says. 'You're one of those people who thinks competitive sports should be banned from sports days, aren't you?'

'I'm one of those people who thinks sports days should be banned altogether.'

'Sure you aren't down on marriage because you're not getting married any more?' Lucy says, artlessly revealing 'nondescript' wasn't the only information about me that got bandied.

This renders me speechless. It's far too much, even for my blood alcohol level.

'I'm not down on marriage,' I say, in a small voice.

'Who's for coffee?' Ben interrupts, brightly.

30

The next day, I have an important and considerably less nerve-shredding social occasion: I'm cooking a roast lunch for my three closest friends. Ordinarily I might regret peeling carrots when I could be getting nicely oiled in a gastropub, yet the dinner party has reminded me how glad I am to have friends who are neither a) Matt or b) Lucy.

Rupa's palace appears well equipped at first, largely due to her pristine range cooker. On investigation it turns out this flat is the equivalent of those ultra-sleek modern hotels with nailed-shut cupboards and nowhere to put your sponge bag. Even my ingredients haul from Tesco Metro on the narrow counter makes the place look like a school's harvest festival. As I sweat over the pans and flap the oven door open and shut and wish the chicken was less my skin tone and more Olivia's, I reflect on how Ben's wife floats around on a velvet cloud, rolling on castors. She didn't break a sweat serving dinner for six last night, and it was all done with such confident élan. When I cook for people, I nervously watch them start chewing, preparing to apologise. And I can't possibly accomplish it without stress. ('Just chuck a rustic bowl of pasta in the middle of the table and invite everyone to dig in, what could be easier?' THE PUB.) I catch sight of the ghost of my hassled face in Rupa's glass splash backs and think how Olivia and I are more like different species than members of the same gender.

Confusingly, Rupa has an extravagant dinner service – white, square, edged in silver leaf – so the table setting is easy, but no utensils, and I left most of mine behind. When Caroline arrives, I have to rush back to stir the carrots with a bread knife and check the chicken's firmness with a chopstick.

'It's fascinating to see a consummate professional at work in their natural habitat,' she says. 'Like a Heston Blumenthal gastronomic laboratory. Look! A foam!'

I catch a pan just as it boils over.

'Ungrateful bitch!'

'Haha. Are we waiting to see if Ivor's wearing that ridiculous train driver hat so you have something to serve the mash in?'

She gives an evil cackle and grabs an olive from the dish on the counter, an unstoned Queen Green disappearing inside the sticky oval of her lip-glossed mouth. You know how everyone wears less constrictive trousers and a greasy ponytail on a Sunday, among their nearest and dearest? Not Caroline.

'Cheers,' Caroline says, holding up her wine and taking a deep swig. 'Oh, it's nice to get out of the house.'

She closes her eyes, leaning back.

'Graeme could've come too,' I say, secretly glad he hasn't. He's always restless, off home turf. He'd be prowling around inspecting the fittings and finding fault. It's not that there's anything wrong with Graeme, as such, and obviously he's a great fit with Caroline. He's just a fit with all the parts of her that are most unlike me. We survey our mutual roles in Caroline's life with a kind of benign befuddlement as to what she sees in the other.

Caroline's eyes snap back open.

'He's so grumpy at the moment. Work's getting on top of him. He spends all his time in the study or walking everywhere with the phone clamped to his head. I saw him at the bottom of the garden, trying to talk to someone when he was meant to be mowing the lawn. I had to get him to stop before we were sifting severed toes out of the grass cuttings.'

'He's very, er, driven,' I nod.

'I know. I wonder if we're ever going to slow down, sometimes. We have the big house, the cars, the holidays. All we share is *Newsnight* and Waitrose Thai-for-two dinners. I'm ready for a change.'

Caroline and Graeme have agreed to start trying for a baby next year. Like the pair of ultra-organised executives they are, they worked out a schedule.

'Well he'll have to slow down if you get pregnant.'

Caroline makes a sceptical 'harrumph' at this.

'Can I ask you something, Rach? Personal?'

I throw the roast potatoes around the dish a few more times, jam them in the oven, pick up my wine and utter a decisive: 'Yes.'

It's nice to be back among people who think they have to check before they ask something personal.

'How was it between you and Rhys, bedroom-wise?'

'Uhm...'

'Don't worry, you don't have to tell me.'

'No, no. Er. OK-ish. Bit routine. Usually Rhys after a night out with the lads, crawling into bed smelling of fags he wasn't supposed to smoke any more, whispering "Would you be adverse to a cocking?". 'Course I'd say "The word is *averse*."'

'Oh, great,' Caroline rolls her eyes.

'We've separated,' I remind her.

'I know! That's what I was eye-rolling about. The split-up couple were doing it more than me and Gray.'

'Caroline, Rhys and I did not split up because of sex, or the lack of it.'

'I know.' She picks at the cuff of her floppy, fine-knit jumper. 'Lately Gray has the sex drive of a panda.'

'Is that a lot? Or not?'

'Well, zoos fly in dates for them from China and it's on the news when they get one of them pregnant. Whaddayouthink?'

'Ah. Right. Well these things ebb and flow, it'll come back.'

She nods, grabs another olive. We're interrupted by the sound of the doorbell. I welcome Mindy and Ivor and pour them a glass each, too.

'To Rachel's new start,' Mindy toasts, and as we clink glasses I'm reminded of a similar toast to Ben and Olivia.

Since meeting Olivia, I've barely dwelt on how much I envy her. Not because I don't envy her, but if I started, I'd never stop. I'd curl in on myself like those magic fish you get as cracker gifts, or corrode like limestone in a hail of acid rain. Although it's a shame she's not got a better sense of humour, since Ben has a good sense of humour all of the time. When Lucy was wittering that her son might have ADHD, Simon said 'Can he sell me some? Street price?' and Ben and I cracked up; Olivia only wrinkled her delightful nose. I think Ben should've held out for delightful nose *and* a funny bone.

Although everyone has to have one more glass of wine than I intended, lunch is eventually ready, even edible, and by putting the serving dishes on the counter we all fit round Rupa's tiny Shaker table.

'Tell us about the date, Mind,' I prompt, once all plates are full.

'It was fun, yeah,' she says. 'We're going to try that new restaurant on Deansgate on Thursday. Jake's doing an MA in international business so we talked shop a lot.'

'Maybe you can give him a Saturday job?' Ivor says.

'At least I've got a date, Ivor, whether he remembers John Major's government or not.'

Ivor grunts at this and helps himself to another potato.

'Ooh, how did the dinner party go?' Caroline asks me.

'Fine, yeah. I'm out of practice at all that show-and-tell malarkey, but I think I muddled my way through.'

'So, come on, what's Ben's wife like?'

'Beautiful…' I say.

'Naturally,' Caroline says.

Yeah not all natural, she looks like she goes down the electric beach to catch those blue rays, I think, before I can squash the thought.

'…And nice. I didn't get to talk to her much, they had some friends there. They were good at doing the talking.'

I briefly relate the baby discussion, among other things.

'Ben's wife asked you if you wanted babies?' Mindy asks.

'Yes.'

'That's offside.'

'Is it?'

'Yeah, you don't say that to someone who's split up with their fiancé, do you? Supposing you had gynae issues or something and that was behind the whole break-up?'

Ivor makes a stifled groan.

'What?' Mindy demands. 'I'm serious. What if Rach had said "My insides are all wrong"? "I've got an incompetent cervix"? What would they have done then?'

I nearly spit my Brussels sprout out.

'They'd wish very much she hadn't said it, like I wish you hadn't?' Ivor says.

'An incompetent cervix is a thing, my aunt had it! When she had my cousin Ruksheen. Had to be in bed for, like, three months. So not worth the trauma, I tell you. Ruksheen's a grotty skank.'

'Amazing,' Ivor says.

'What?'

'Rachel's dinner party to a family member's fanny in one smooth move.'

'Thanks for your concern,' I tell her, once my laughter subsides.

'People take advantage of your sense of humour,' Mindy says, staunchly.

'How're you?' I ask Ivor.

'OK thanks. Katya's finally going, she's handed me her notice. Travelling in South America, off by the end of the month.'

'Ding dong, the vegan witch is dead,' Mindy says, smoothing her peacock-blue skirt over her legs.

'Ah, she's not that bad really,' Ivor says, rubbing an eye.

'Oh Ivor!' Mindy wails. 'How often have we heard Katya this, Katya that? "Katya threw my Peperamis in the bin!" "Katya nailed an African fertility symbol to my wall and made big holes in the plaster!" "Katya made me watch a PETA video about ocelot farming and I couldn't sleep for a week!"'

'I don't think I said it was a week,' Ivor says, glancing at Caroline and myself.

'Now she's going, it's "she's not that bad really". You're such a wuss.'

'All I'm saying is, she's easier to tolerate with an end in sight.'

'That end could've come sooner if—' Mindy breaks off as Ivor mimes a sock-puppet talking movement with one hand.

'Are you going to be seeing more of Ben and his wife then?' Caroline turns to me.

Difficult question. It's time to play the ace.

'Maybe. I've got a date with Simon.'

'Simon that I met?'

'Yep. Lawyer friend of Ben,' I add, for Mindy and Ivor's benefit.

'That's great! What brought about this change of heart?' Caroline asks, almost putting her cutlery down in surprise.

I rather fear anticipation of this reaction is what brought about my change of heart. If everyone's watching what happens with Simon, no one's scrutinising any other parts of my exist- ence. Misdirection. For my next trick, I'll need an assistant.

'Spirit of adventure,' I offer, vaguely.

'This is great, Rach.'

'What's he like?' Mindy asks.

'Yeah, give us the vital stats, what weight can he bench press, who'd play him in his biopic?' Ivor rattles off, looking at Mindy.

'Tall, blond, posh, confident, good at cutting remarks. Uhm, Christian Bale with a bleach job? Rupert Penry Jones for TV?'

'A catch,' Caroline concludes, through a mouthful of roast chicken.

Do I want to catch Simon? I'm pretty sure I don't.

'I know it's soon but you have to seize opportunities,' she adds, after swallowing.

'Yeah, that's what I thought,' thinking, I didn't think that at all. I remember Simon grabbing my elbow as I left, murmuring: 'Can I see you again?' *Yes* seemed the only polite answer. Also, it was hardly unflattering to have someone who gave that 'only going for the best of the best' speech after me, even if I'm hoping most of that dastardly bastard routine was bluster.

'When are you going on this date?'

'Don't know. He asked, said he'd call me. I still think we're a wildly improbable pairing but no harm in confirming it, I suppose.'

'That's the spirit.' Satisfied, Caroline sips from her glass and looks approvingly round the room. 'You know, this place is almost worth the money. Not quite, but almost. Even if Rupa's cupboards are about as bare of essentials as our student dump.'

'Is now the time to ask why the gravy is in a vase?' Ivor says.

31

The embezzling payphone in our student house wasn't the first sign our landlord was a south Manchester Fagin. Our detached des-res in Fallowfield had been advertised as a three bedroom – we were without Ivor, who was on a year out in industry.

At the end of the viewing Caroline asked 'What's in here?', trying the handle of a door downstairs. The landlord looked as nervous as if she was a new bride trying to breach Bluebeard's tower.

'That's Derek's room,' the landlord said, as if every deal came with a Derek. 'He's staying on. That's why the rent's so low.'

The three of us exchanged a look. Not that low.

'Derek.' The landlord rapped with his knuckles. Derek produced himself – a hulking, greasy kind of character, and grunted a hello. He was an astrophysics post-grad, which was supposed to cover why he had a telescope on his windowsill.

We made our excuses and promptly left, and over lattes at the nearest café, agreed there was no way we were moving into a house which came with a loner perma-lodger. Then we got more lattes, and carrot cake, and started discussing how spacious the rooms were, how many damp-smelling terraces we'd trudged round, and that Derek didn't seem that objectionable, if you broadened your mind and held your nose. We called the landlord back and said we'd take it.

Luckily, Derek seemed to lead a largely nocturnal existence and spent most weekends visiting his family in Whitby. Where Dracula landed. No further questions, your honour.

He was away on the night of our first noteworthy social event after we moved in, a Halloween party at the university union. I'd spent the day with a stomach bug, throwing up on an hourly basis, getting a chance to closely examine all the corners our cleaning rota didn't reach in the bathroom. I felt deeply aggrieved that I'd not drunk any alcohol to get in this state, and the bug was about to prevent me trying.

Downstairs, a sexy vampire and a brown-skinned witch in stripy tights, balancing a bumper-sized plastic bottle of scrumpy on her hip, gazed at me as I limped into the hallway to say goodbye.

Caroline put the back of her pleasantly cool, black nail-varnished hand against my forehead.

'Yoor absholutely burwing ug.'

'What?'

She removed her plastic fangs. 'You're absolutely burning up. Want me to stay?'

'No, I'll be OK.'

'We'll have one for you!' Mindy said, hoisting the cider and adjusting the brim of her witch hat.

I felt my gorge rise.

'Fanks,' I said, thickly, as if I was speaking through false teeth too.

An hour or so later, there was a knock.

'Who is it?' I shouted, without opening it.

'A bloody cold cold caller,' came a familiar voice.

I opened the door. Ben was buttoned up to the nose in his coat. He yanked it down to chin level so he could speak. 'How are you then?'

'Phenomenally wank,' I said delicately, standing back to let him in.

I was self-conscious about being seen in my voluminous cotton comfort pyjamas. The somewhat psychedelic pattern depicted farmyard animals with slice-of-melon smiles playing musical instruments.

'Where's your costume?' I asked Ben, to divert his attention.

'Fancy dress is a terrible way to ruin a good party. Funny, everyone there is got up as ghoulish and scary, and here you are looking more like death than any of them.'

'Did you stop by to tell me this?'

'No, I've come to check on you. What've you taken for this flu?'

'Two paracetamol, a while ago.'

Two loose paracetamol I'd found at the bottom of my make-up bag. I had to pick a stray hair off one of them. I felt my gorge rise again.

'Right,' Ben said. 'I'm going for supplies. Save me a space on the sofa.'

'Ben, you don't have to do this.'

'Oh, I know.'

'Here you go,' he said on return, passing over the tablets with a glass of water, as I malingered on the sofa. 'These are the business, but they're strong. You on any other drugs I should know about?'

'Only the pill.'

Ben grimaced. 'I didn't need to know *that*.'

I threw them to the back of my throat, swallowing them without water.

'Jeez,' Ben said.

'I have tons of spit in my mouth,' I explained, pointing.

'Great,' he made a sickly smile.

He up-ended the contents of his shopping bag: mineral water, crisps, fat Coke, crackers, Berocca and more paracetamol. He sat down next to me, started flipping channels.

I gave him a sideways look.

'Don't you mind missing the party?'

'Put it this way. The welcome cocktail was something called "Bitches Brew".'

'Ooh, do you think it was made from real bitches?'

'Hard to tell.'

'Cast your mind back. Did it taste of Georgina Race?'

Ben swatted my head with the TV guide. 'Caroline said when she left you looked like an orphaned marmoset on a Monday morning. I thought, oh shit, I know that look, and then my conscience wouldn't let me stay out.'

'Orphaned marmoset!' I laughed, feeling inordinately touched at his affection.

I settled back into my half of the sofa and we started bickering happily over what to watch, agreeing on *The Breakfast Club*.

'You are her. In a nutshell,' Ben said, after a few minutes, indicating Ally Sheedy, peering out from under the fur on her parka hood.

'Compulsive liar basket case? You're the geek in a jock's body. You're Anthony Michael Hall trapped inside Emilio Estevez.'

'Urgh, what a thought.' Ben paused. 'At least you don't think I'm the jock. Do you know what a girl in halls called me, last year? Bland Ben. *Blen.*'

'What? Why?'

'She said I was...' I saw a slight colour rise in Ben's face '... she said I was "standard issue tailor's dummy" and "pleasant" and got on with everyone and that I was *blah*. BLEN. Being condemned as boring is the worst thing, isn't it? If someone calls you an arsehole you can work on being less of one. If a boring person tries to be interesting... they're probably just being more boring.'

'Utter cow!' I cried. 'I bet you, no, I promise you, she was rejected by some lad who looked like you at school and is taking it out on you. There's nothing wrong with being nice.'

'Nice,' Ben smiled, yet winced.

'Kind, then. Thoughtful. Not a twat. Puts people at their ease. Popular. You are not bland. She doesn't know you well enough to know you're not up yourself about your looks. I think she was mistaking decent for dull.'

I realised I'd said more than intended and kept my gaze on the television.

'Thanks,' he said, sounding gratified, perhaps even faintly surprised.

Ben opened a packet of Hula Hoops, turned the bag towards me in offering. I took one whiff, jumped off the sofa and ran upstairs to the bathroom, trying to stifle the heaving before the bowl was in sight. After I'd brushed my teeth three times, I returned to the living room, pale and wan.

'At least your lungs sound strong,' Ben said. 'Silver linings.'

'Stomach lining, mostly,' I said, and he put a hand over his mouth, the crisps back down on the coffee table and one thumb up.

Half an hour later, despite only Volvic passing my lips, the nausea returned. I didn't have time to get upstairs and bolted through Derek's room and to his en suite, trying not to look at anything that might be lying around. I held my hair out the way and heaved, my body aching from the effort when I'd finished, pulling the handle and slumping against the china cool of the bowl. I dragged myself over to the sink and rinsed my mouth. There was a soft knock at the door and Ben put his head round.

'Better?'

Beyond vanity, I nodded. On the verge of tears in my pathetic physical state, regressing to childhood, I whimpered: 'I don't want to be sick any more, Ben. I'm so tired.'

'I know.'

'I want my mum,' I added, barely kidding.

'What would your mum do?' he asked, not rhetorically.

I lifted and flapped my arms, helplessly. 'Give me a cuddle? Make me hot lemon squash.'

'You'll have to make do with me and Berocca, then.'

Ben came in and put his arms around me. It felt nice to be supported by someone stronger and healthier, as if I might absorb some of it by osmosis. I leaned my head on his shirt. We stood there for a moment. I let him take my weight, completely, forgetting to be self-conscious.

'You make a nice mum,' I mumbled.

'I always hoped one day the woman of my dreams would say those words to me,' he said, ruffling my vomity hair. I would've poked him in the ribs in reprisal, but I lacked the motor skills.

32

The greatest fiction in courtroom dramas is not the number of times lawyers shout 'Objection!' or the pacing up and down with direct, emotive appeals to the jury. It's the whip-crack pace of the dialogue. Forget those flourishes in summing up that turn a case on a sixpence: real court cases are exercises in mind-numbing pedantry, as facts are picked over in necessary but toothcomb detail.

The prosecution lawyer in the cosmetic surgery case has spent the last half hour going over the minutiae of anaesthesia procedures with an embattled nurse. I've got a throbbing headache and a conviction never to book in for body contouring. There are some court cases that have moved so majestically slowly I've been convinced they'll never end, and I'll be briefing my successor before I retire. The judge announces that we'll break early so he can consider the latest written submissions. *Aha*. He wants to flick through a trashy celebrity weekly too.

In the press room, I open my laptop and check my email. Amid messages from colleagues with unpromising subject lines like '*FWD: NSFW: This really made me laugh!!!!!!???????????!!!!*' I see one from Ben Morgan.

My heart goes *thump*.

Then I have a stern word with myself, open it.

'*Hi! Did you have an OK time on Saturday? Sorry for Simon being … Simon. Ben.*'

I reread this several times, then type:

'*Hello! It was very enjoyable, thanks for inviting me. How did you get my email address?*'

A reply arrives inside a minute with '*I hope you're not an investigative reporter*' in the subject line. The message reads '*… it's under all your stories in the paper.*'

I laugh out loud, and reply: '*DOH. Simon's amusing …!*'

Ben responds: '*We weren't trying to set you up, I apologise if it looked that way. A few other people dropped out and we only realised it might be misinterpreted when it was too late.*'

From the conversation I overheard, I feel sure that if this is true it applies only to Ben, not Olivia. It doesn't sound like Simon's told Ben that we're going on a date. Not sure I quite believe it either.

'*It was fine,*' I type. '*And in return I want to invite you and Olivia to my flat warming.*'

Uh? I'm having a flat warming? Nice of my subconscious to tell me.

Ben replies '*Love to! Just tell me when/where. Anyway, back to the grindstone. B.*'

I type a cheery goodbye and reread the conversation. I'm interrupted by Gretton, the smell of cigarettes clinging to his clothes.

He hums to himself as he flicks through a stack of tabloids to see if his stories have been used. As he's not a staffer, most papers put another employee's name on it, or simply the paper's title and 'reporter'. He still gets paid if it's used, which is all he cares about.

'You're chirpy,' I say, suspicious.

'Chirpy chirpy cheep cheep,' Gretton says, tapping his nose. 'Chickens coming home to roost.'

'What *grade* have you been smoking, Pete?'

He produces the *Sport* from his pile of papers, shakes it out theatrically and disappears behind it.

An email arrives from Simon with the details of my interview with Natalie Shale. It has a '*PS — let's go out for that drink when this is done. Business before pleasure and all that.*'

This makes me smile. Simon's canny enough not to wine and dine me before I've closed the deal for him. Closed the deal … he won't try to come home with me on a first date, will he? Doesn't seem likely, yet I've been out of the dating arena for so long, all the rules could've changed. I'm not sure I should be going on a date with someone I can't quite ever see myself wanting to take home, but Caroline says this is what I ought to be doing, and Caroline's sensible.

Zoe walks in, plonking her clingfilm-wrapped butties and paperback down.

'Zoe,' I say, 'will you be OK to take over this lipo case on Friday? I've pretty much done the backgrounder. If there's a verdict, I'll email it to you.'

'No problem,' she says. 'I'll mention it to news desk but I'm sure it'll be fine. Is this to free you up for your interview?'

'Yep.'

'Nice one. Anyone want anything from the café?'

I shake my head and Gretton watches Zoe leave. 'Do you have no pride, Woodford?'

'Uh?'

'She's a story stealer if ever I saw one. Don't expect a joint byline on all that work.'

'Have you ever trusted someone and been repaid for it, Pete?'

He opens and smacks wet lips together, ruminatively. 'I'd have to say no.'

'That should tell you something.'

'Given that I'm ten years older than you, that should tell *you* something.'

'Ten? Fifteen if it's a day!'

33

Natalie Shale's house is a bay-fronted pre-war redbrick semi, the sort that Manchester suburbs specialise in. I press the doorbell and hear a tinny tune bouncing off the walls inside. I stamp my feet and wonder if neighbours are watching from behind their nets. Natalie opens the door and I'm struck again by how exquisite she is, even in her daytime-mum attire of vest top and jogging bottoms.

'Rachel?' she asks, warily, as if there has been a procession of fraudulent Rachel Woodfords at her door this morning. I get a vision of Gretton in a dark wig, hairy legs sticking out under a too tight pencil skirt. Urgh…

'That's me, Simon arranged this…? Thank you so much for offering us the interview.'

'Yes, course, come on in.'

I follow her to the lounge, lower myself on to the sofa and get my notepad out, noticing Natalie already has a Dictaphone on the coffee table.

She notices me eyeing it and asks: 'You don't want to record it too?'

'No, I prefer shorthand. I don't trust tape recorders.'

'Oh.' She glances at the device in confusion, as if it might bite her. 'Simon said I should record it, sorry.'

Why doesn't that surprise me?

'Sure,' I say, and Natalie looks grateful there's not going to be a confrontation.

'The photographer's coming at two,' I remind her. 'Is that OK?'

'Yeah,' she smiles. 'Don't worry, I'll have changed by then. Tea?'

'Thanks. White, no sugar.'

While the kettle boils windily, I look around Natalie's living room and make some mental notes for 'colour' in the article. I could make actual notes, but it feels impolite to be jotting things down about her house while she's dunking the Tetley's. There are photographs of her daughters on almost every available surface. I might be tempted to show off if I'd pushed out children as attractive as her twins. The most recent pictures show them in hers'n'hers OshKosh dungarees, their hair pulled into cloud-like afro bunches. In most of the photos they're giggling, open-mouthed, revealing little goofy milk teeth pegs. A huge football pitch-sized frame over the mantelpiece shows Natalie with the girls, in a formation as if they're sitting in an invisible canoe, hands on each other's shoulders.

It's the sort of barefoot everyone-in-Levi's studio portrait that strives so hard to portray a happy family that it somehow only reminds me of dysfunctional American ones where the strange bumfluff-chinned twitchy son eventually herds everyone into the garage and picks them off with a shotgun.

The television is on at a low murmur, showing some kind of heavily studio-lit, imported US soap. The atmosphere is one of contentment and calm. You'd never guess the trauma the people living here have been through.

'Hope it's not too weak,' Natalie says, returning with a cup. 'Lucas always says I like mine like Horlicks – baby tea, he calls it.'

As she passes it to me I see it has 'World's Best Dad' on it. I wonder if she noticed this, or if she was merely concentrating on making the tea.

'It's fine,' I say, sipping it. I've had many dodgy cups of tea while out on jobs – cracked mug, the smell of stale milk, poorly washed-up vessel handed over by kindly host with failing eyesight, usually accompanied by spectacularly bendy biscuits – and I've made a point of finishing them all. I'm rarely imposing on them because they've had good news, after all.

'Your little girls are so cute,' I say, pointing at a picture.

'Thank you,' Natalie says. 'They're at nursery, it'd be bedlam otherwise. Do you have kids?'

'No.' In case statement of the blunt fact makes me sound like I'm passing judgement on her having kids, I add apologetically: 'Sure I'll get round to it.'

There's a beat of silence while we sip our tea.

'So Simon says we can talk about anything other than the details of the appeal case?' I ask.

'Yeah, that's fine.' Natalie lays her phone down on the coffee table, next to the tape recorder.

I flip to a clean page in my notebook, wondering where I should begin … at the start, when she and Lucas met, or cut straight to the drama and work backwards? Some interviewees need warming up, others have short attention spans.

'There she is!' Natalie squeals girlishly, suggesting she might be the latter sort, craning to look out of the window. 'My friend

Bridie, she's just got back off holiday and I need to talk to her about her cat … sorry, do you mind?'

'No, no,' I say. 'Go ahead.'

I watch Natalie hurtle down the front path and ambush the scatty-haired, sizeable Bridie. She's practically ovoid, clad in a black jumper, and looks a likely customer for Jonathan Cainer's daily zodiac forecasts.

Natalie starts gesticulating, presumably about the moggy, and I think how impressive it is to care about your neighbour's pet when your other half is in prison for a crime he didn't commit. I turn away and try to concentrate on the telly, which is now running adverts. Ambulance chasers and loan sharks that can save you from all the other loan sharks in one affordable monthly payment, and something that makes child's play of slicing vegetables with its multi-function blade.

If I really give this exclusive some welly, I think, and add enough thoughtful flourishes, I might get a press award. Then Natalie can be proud to know that her trauma has sent me to an industry back-slap jolly in Birmingham or London where I can neck warm white wine from Paris goblets, get a round of reluctant applause and fight off unwanted attention from pissed-up sports desk nominees.

Natalie's still talking ten to the dozen. A text message beeps on her clamshell phone, the circular window lighting up electric blue.

A wicked thought occurs, so wicked it surprises me. *Read the text*. Here you are, alone with her phone – why not? Most reporters I know wouldn't hesitate. We use enough backroom bargaining and wiles and wheedling to get into homes in the first place that outrageous nosiness once inside doesn't rate as that big a crime. Some reporters would think it was bad journalism *not* to read the text. Am I one of them?

My mind starts racing. I'd have to delete it, obviously, or she'd realise I've read it. What if it contains urgent information, and I can't relay it without revealing what I've done? Or what if the person who sent it wants to know why she didn't reply, mentions when they sent it, and they work out the timing…?

Oh, stop being such a banana, Rachel, I think. Most texts are about as important as Rhys's regular ones from the pub, sent covertly under the table during quizzes: '*What is year Dirty Dancing came out. Quick.*' Or as much fun as my mum's: '*Have you had smear test yet this year. Wendy at work has been diagnosed with ovarian cancer.*' Cancer, that's something to worry about, not reading a text that's not intended for you.

I put my hand out and then pull it back sharply. What am I thinking? Where are my principles? I look out of the window, where Natalie's still talking. The seconds tick on.

A further thought, the clincher: it's from Simon, asking how it's going. Bound to be. Will he say anything slighting about me? This is someone I'm contemplating dating. Seeing the proof that he can be pitiless could save me a lot of angst. *Sod it*, I think. One slight slip of the standards and I'll be discreet about whatever the text contains. Natalie need never know. Responsible snooping. Checking she's still at a safe distance and absorbed by her neighbour's feline kerfuffle, I flip her phone open and click on the message. A stranger's words sit in my sweaty palm.

'*How are you today, N? I miss you so much. Can't stop thinking about the other night. Xxx PS What are you wearing?*'

Eyes wide, I look out of the window, back to the text, out the window again, trying to make sense of it. Her phone doesn't recognise the sender as a name from her phonebook, only a number.

It's from her husband, I reason, snapping the phone shut and replacing it on the table. Obviously. He must have access to a mobile. Don't some cons smuggle them into jail, hidden in unholy places? Yes, that's right. That's it.

But — it mentions 'the other night'. Lucas hasn't had a 'other night' with his wife since last year. Ah — wrong number! Yes, it's a wrong number. No. That can't be it. The message calls her 'N'.

I glance out of the window again. Natalie's still talking. Panic hits me: I forgot to delete the message. She'll know I read it. I pick up the phone again, open it, hesitate, scribble down the number. One check against Simon's number, then I'll get rid of it. I delete the message and replace the phone on the coffee table, careful to turn it back so it's pointing towards where Natalie was sitting. I gulp down a huge swig of tea, as if she's going to walk back in, inspect the volume in my cup and say: 'That's two millilitres too full.'

I wait, heart beating a pitter-patter, thoughts tumbling over themselves.

'Sorry about that, her cat did a runner while I was feeding him. Total nightmare,' Natalie says, flopping back on the sofa. She checks her phone. My heart goes *kathunk-kathunk-kathunk*.

She switches on the Dictaphone and checks it's running.

'Where do you want to start?'

I clear my throat.

'When the jury read out their guilty verdict, how did you feel?'

34

Natalie's fragile physical appearance belies her steely resolve, the kind required to raise two young children alone and coordinate her husband's campaign for justice, and above all, keep the faith that he is coming home soon. Can she still believe in a system that has, she believes, wrongly convicted her husband? Her reply shows how a former optician's assistant from Bury has had a crash course in the judicial process and the power of positive thinking.

'The courts can make mistakes. The appeal system wouldn't exist otherwise,' she says, 'and Lucas's legal team are confident that the fresh evidence will be enough to get the verdict quashed, and they won't order a retrial.'

In her visits to Lucas, she says, they never discuss the possibility his appeal will fail. 'We talk about the girls, whether I've paid the bills. Boring stuff, but Lucas says it keeps him sane.'

While other family and friends collapsed and openly wept when Lucas's sentence was delivered, Natalie remained composed. What was going through her mind, in those terrible moments? 'I knew I had to be strong for my husband,' she explains. 'He's *innocent, that's all that matters, and the truth will come out. If I broke down, how would that help him? He looks to me for support. He depends on me.'*

I glance up from my notes, feeling light-headed, as if I can't quite get the ground underneath me to lie flat.

If this is the way it looks, and Natalie is having a fling, I wonder if it pre-dates her husband being locked up. Once upon a time, I'd have been appalled at this. But really: only two people really know what's going on in a relationship. *And sometimes, not even that many*, a voice says.

An hour later, I'm running the spellcheck and preparing to send it to news desk. No more than a workmanlike job, not up to competition standard, but I want it finished, done with. I don't want to think about the number that wasn't Simon's.

Ken emails back within twenty minutes. '*Nice read,*' the message says. '*We'll hold it until the week of the appeal. Good pix too.*'

If we were on the phone, I'm sure he'd add 'She's bang tidy!' On email, he's a politician: never get caught out by the reply-instead-of-forward faux pas, never leave electronic record.

The photographer calls me to check the spelling of the twins' names. 'Weird she didn't have any photos of her husband out, wasn't it? She had to go searching for one we could use.'

'Probably too painful for her to look at,' I say, and cut the conversation short.

❤ ❤ ❤

Every job has its small perks and mine comes with the occasional burst of free stand-up comedy or, to give it its formal title, contempt of court. Whenever an unhinged or flamboyant character takes to the stand, word goes round. And it's not just journos – solicitors and court ushers join in with the whisper. 'Get in 2, quick' spreads like wildfire – and suddenly the court fills up with people pretending they have a reason to be there. The favoured pose is sliding into a seat at the back, vaguely scanning the room as if you have an urgent message to deliver to someone you can't immediately locate and don't want to disturb proceedings.

Among the greatest hits have been a streetwalker who flashed a tattooed boob at a judge and told him he 'looked like a client' (Gretton was absent for that one, off for root canal work – I don't know which was more painful for him, the teeth or the missed tit), a man with a multiple personality disorder which caused him to answer every question in a different accent, and a drum'n'bass DJ who solemnly took off his shirt in the dock to reveal a t-shirt saying 'Only God Can Judge Me'. (In front of a dry circuit judge, who lowered his spectacles and said crisply: 'Unfortunately for you, He delegated discretion in sentence to me.')

So on Monday lunchtime, when a gangly lad from a weekly paper pops his head around the press room door and says breathlessly: 'Have you heard…?' I assume that someone's happy-slapped a QC or informed a packed courtroom that they're a high-ranking Scientologist and thus privy to most of the secrets of our puny human universe.

I break off typing up my quotes from the Natalie Shale interview.

'No, what?'

Instead of issuing directions about where it's taking place and charging off again, he comes in and spreads a copy of the *Evening News* on the desk. He thumbs through to the classified adverts.

'Here,' he says, jabbing at an extra large announcement in 16pt font, blocked off in a thick black border.

'*Desperately seeking Dick,*' it reads. '*Zoe Clarke of the Evening News is looking, without success. If you have any information about where she can find Dick, please call –* ' and a mobile number follows. '*She will pay extremely well for information leading to Dick.*'

'Ingenious. What a way with words. Who did this?' I ask.

The gangly lad sniggers, shrugs. 'She's got on someone's wick, obviously.'

'It's really unnecessary,' I say, and all of a sudden I know why Gretton was so unnaturally buoyant. 'How did you know about this?'

'It's all round the office at yours. Someone called with a tip-off.'

I flip through the rest of the paper and see a double page on the liposuction story, which yielded two guilty verdicts for the doctors, though the nurse got off. It uses the backgrounder and it all bears my byline, no Zoe, despite the first eight paragraphs being solely her work. I scan the ad a second time and go in search of Zoe in court, coming up empty until I spy her through the front windows.

'Please don't laugh, I've been piss-ripped all day. I've had heavy breathing calls and I've had enough,' she says, dragging on a fag with the hunger of a former expert who's fallen off the wagon with a thud.

'I'm not going to laugh, I think it's horrible. Have you complained to news desk? It shouldn't have gone in.'

'Yeah, Ken said it made us look like tools and called ad services to have a go about how they should've put their brains in gear when it was booked, but that's all. And what's the point anyway? We all know who's to blame.'

'If it was Gretton, I'm going to kick his whiskery arse into Stockport for you.'

'It's got to be him.'

I nearly say 'Unless you've annoyed anyone else?' and think better of it.

'Very likely.'

'It's nice to speak to someone who doesn't think it's funny.'

'It's not. Gretton's a vindictive sod. And thanks for putting my byline on the lipo case. You should've made it a joint byline, you did loads.'

Zoe looks surprised, mind still elsewhere.

'Sure. The backgrounder was really thorough. You can tell you've done this a while.'

'You're not wrong. Drink with an old lady, later in the week?'

'Yes, please. I'll email you my new number, when I get it.'

'New number?'

'I can't keep this one, every freak in Manchester's calling me.'

I grasp at something to cheer her up. 'Will you come to my flat-warming party next weekend? Only a small do.'

Zoe perks up. 'Yeah.'

Leaving Zoe sparking up again outside, I go looking for Gretton inside. It must be the first time I've been pursuing him around court.

'Can I have a word, please?' I say, tugging on his jacket sleeve as I catch up with him, rounding a corner.

'Woodford?'

'What you did to Zoe was completely over the top and nasty.'

Gretton gives me a vampiric grin. 'She sowed, she reaped.'

'She's good at her job, and younger than you, and female,

196

and that triple whammy is more than your ego can cope with.'

'How come we've never fallen out then?'

'Because I put up with you. Zoe put up a fight instead and you've gone too far with this retaliation.'

'Let me tell you something, you may have been walking around in a daze since your love life went kaput…'

I fold my arms, purse my lips. Impertinent git. I haven't been in a daze. Have I?

'…She's done more than put up a fight, she's on the attack, and people like her need slapping down. You should've seen her at the end of the blobby bird trial, elbowing me out the way to get to the family afterward. Them all giving me daggers… She'd definitely said something.'

'Y'see, right there, Pete. The "blobby bird" trial. Do you ever stop to think how offensive that could be to Zoe?'

'Why? Clarke's not fat. Face like a hobnail boot, but not fat.'

'You don't know anything about her background or history or… Look, this is one of the reasons why civilised people don't go round using phrases like "blobby bird".'

'Belt up, love. Go and work for the council if you want to be PC.'

'This stupid advert is the end of it, OK? No more games. Stay away from Zoe. Promise?'

'If she starts with the—'

'I'll keep her in check in return. Promise me!'

Gretton wrinkles his nose. 'For you, then. I've got no issue with you.'

'Thank you.'

'Your news editor thought it was funny, though.'

'Eh?'

'I rang Baggaley anonymously to tell him it was there and he was roaring, I can tell you.'

Ladies and gentlemen – the line manager in charge of my pastoral care.

'D'ya fancy a quick pint?' Gretton adds, unusually friendly.

I shake my head.

'Got to see a man about a dog, I'm afraid.'

35

I thread my way through the well-shod early afternoon shop-
pers and office workers, catching sight of Rhys outside Holland
& Barrett, looking like a man who could do with some
de-stressing St John's Wort. He's wearing a navy anorak and
a concentrated scowl. I remember pulling on the drawstring
at the hood to tighten it at the neck when I kissed him
goodbye. Only likely to happen now in an attempt to cut off
blood supply.

I expect to feel a nasty pang – I've been churning on this
meeting for twenty-four hours – yet now we're face-to-face,
I don't feel any tumult of emotion, only a resigned sort of
grief. We're just two people who were once very fond of each
other and now don't get along any more.

'Hi,' I say.

'I'd nearly given up. We said one.'

'It's only five past…' I check my watch. 'Ten past. Sorry.
Case overran.' Er. The case of the tardy woman and the glossy
magazine.

Rhys thrusts a canvas holdall at me. 'Here you go.'

'Thanks,' I unzip it and peer inside. Books, a necklace, a teapot I'd forgotten belongs to me. How did I miss all this?

'Why did you leave so much stuff? What am I meant to do with it?' Rhys asks.

'I thought the idea was I left things.'

'Yeah, furniture. I didn't say leave ninety per cent of your crap strewn about the place. Were you making the point that you wanted to get out of there so fast you left tyre marks?'

'No.' I see the ghost of genuine hurt behind Rhys's mask of perpetual annoyance. 'I didn't want to fillet it, that's all. If you want me to take more, I can come back for it.'

Rhys shrugs.

I wonder whether to suggest getting some lunch.

'Why're you off work?'

'Booked a day to go car shopping.'

'You're not keeping the old one?'

'Fancied a change. You know how that feels.'

A pause.

'Your place is in town, then?' Rhys says.

'Yes. Northern Quarter. Come round sometime if you like.'

Rhys makes a face. 'No, ta. What for, Dorito Dippers and *X Factor*?'

'Just, you know. To be civilised.'

'Huh. What's it like?'

'The flat?'

'No, *X Factor*. Yes the flat.'

'It's...' I have absolutely no idea why I think saying it's incredible feels so personally wounding, but it does, and I mumble: 'Alright. Bit cramped.'

'Cramped for one person with no possessions. Must be tiny.'

I need to change the subject. 'Have you eaten?'

'Yeah,' Rhys says, thrusting his chin out.

'OK.'

'No offence, but I'm not going to go for lunch with you like nothing's happened.'

'I didn't mean it like that.'

'I'm sure it would make you feel better.'

'Rhys, come on …'

I glance up at the faces streaming past and the sight of Ben emerging from among them is like being socked in the stomach. We spot each other simultaneously, there's no time to turn my back. He swerves off course to come and say hello, his smile freezing on to his face as he sees who I'm with.

'Afternoon!' I say, trying for casual. Rhys glances over. 'Rhys, you remember Ben from uni? He's moved up to Manchester.'

I think I'm holding it together. Ben, however, looks mortified.

'Hi. Wow, long time.' Ben sticks out his hand.

Rhys shakes it. 'Yeah. How are you?'

'Good. You?'

'Fine.'

Conversationally, it's clear none of us have anything else to offer. Ben glances at the bag in my hand and starts backing off, bumping into passers-by.

'I better run, anyway,' he says. 'On the clock at work. Nice to see you again.'

'Bye,' I say.

'Yeah, bye,' Rhys adds.

Ben rejoins the flow of pedestrian traffic, very much in the fast lane.

'That was awkward,' Rhys says, and I look at him in startled confusion.

'Why?'

'Don't remember him at all.'

36

I'll say one thing for entering your third decade and your life falling apart, it does shift the pounds before a party. As diet plans go, though, it might be a bit extreme. The old red dress I haul out for my flat warming suddenly fits quite well and skims over my 'twin airbags and side impact bars', as my ex-fiancé had it.

It gets screeches of approval when Caroline and Mindy arrive with their other halves, plopping overnight bags inside the door. Caroline asked to stay over as she's booked an induction at a city centre gym for half nine the next morning (nothing changes) and when Mindy found out, she demanded to stay as well.

'Mindy, you live ten minutes' drive away,' I said.

'If she's staying, I want to stay too,' she insisted. 'It'll be like old times!'

'That's what I'm afraid of,' I said, remembering when we stayed up talking until dawn in our halls. These days, I need my sleep. Mindy settled the issue by saying there was easily room for three in Rupa's bed, and I couldn't deny that.

'Rach, this is Jake,' Mindy says, as a slight, dark-haired, nervous-looking man follows the done-up-to-the-nines Mindy into the flat. I don't like to think we look old, but he does look young.

'Nice to meet you,' I say. He blushes. Yep, *very* young.

Mindy does a pirouette in a black sequin dress. 'Does this say Studio 54 – or "fifty quid for him to watch"?'

Before I can answer, Ivor butts in. 'You could never look that cheap, Mind.'

She puts her tongue in her cheek and turns to him. 'Wait for it.'

'It says "a hundred pounds for him to watch, plus dry cleaning, and not on the face".'

'Zing!' Mindy says.

Ivor holds up clanking bags to me. 'Where?'

'Over there,' I say, pointing to the pink lady fridge.

'You're trolleyed already, aren't you, Rach? Is that boozer's flush I see?' Graeme says.

'It's rouge,' I say. 'Going for the Palace of Versailles look.'

The only way to deal with Graeme is to play along. Or at least, that's the only way to deal with him when he's married to one of your best friends.

Graeme peers into the sink.

'What the devil's going on here?'

I've put the plug in and filled it with white flowers, peonies, lilac and roses, their stems coiled and bent under the waterline. I saw this piece of stylistic flash at the gathering of a fashion writer once and always wanted to copy it. It wasn't on the cards when I lived with Rhys. He'd have demanded to know where he should put the dregs of his lager and, most likely, I'd have told him.

'Did you run out of vases?' Graeme asks.

'Gray,' Caroline says. 'Stop being a wind-up merchant.'

'Vases are for gravy,' Ivor says.

Graeme looks nonplussed.

'You've done a great job,' Caroline says, looking round and, if I do say so myself, I really have. I've run 'landing strips' of tea lights in clear glass holders along every straight line and there are vertical explosions of white gladioli in glass tanks dotted around the room. I was never much of a fan of gladioli when I lived in Sale, but there's something about their imperious legginess that suits this apartment.

'Funeral parlour minus the corpse,' Graeme says, with what he imagines is his roguish twinkle that exonerates all sins.

'One could be arranged,' Caroline says, crossing her arms.

'So,' Graeme fixes me with a beady look, 'Our Lady of the Ruinously Expensive Tastes, what's your rent here?'

'None of your business,' I say, hopefully sounding sweet.

'I'm only thinking of you. You're going back into the housing market with a single income, and six months here is a chunk of your deposit gone, I'll bet.'

I look to Caroline to silence him, but she's already stalked off to get a drink.

'I can't buy yet.'

'Why not?'

'Because I've split up with someone I spent half my life with and I don't know what I want or where I want to live.'

'You'll always need a roof over your head, won't you? You're not going to join a Bedouin tribe?'

'You can't always do what makes absolute practical sense... I've got a drink, Caro, you're alright.'

She nods, hands Graeme a glass, sips from her own, eyes downcast.

'Living for the day is all very well in your twenties, you've got to start planning for the future sometime,' Graeme continues. I know what he means is, no one else is going to do it for you now. 'Things don't fall into place by accident.'

'Maybe.'

As he launches into another monologue, I interrupt: 'Graeme. Par-tee. Noun, two syllables, a social gathering for the purpose of pleasure.'

❤ ❤ ❤

Ben, Olivia and Simon arrive while I'm busy mopping up a spilled drink and Caroline lets them in.

She leads them over to the kitchen, and as I join them Simon's saying to her: '… Had cocktails at a bar on Canal Street, or should I say Anal Treat. Ben said it was mixed straight-and-gay, then the only woman in the place had an Adam's apple like a tennis ball. They were all the sort who could select scatter cushions, I'm telling you.'

Never mind Adam's apples, I just hope Simon's tongue is in his cheek most of the time.

'We brought you a homophobe, and this,' Ben says to me, as Olivia hands over a Peace Lily in a gold lacquered pot, 'to help warm your flat.'

Ben's wearing washed-out-to-look-old-but-new grey jeans and a black sweater. As ever: *phew*. Olivia's in a delicate grey wrap dress. Between the two of them, they must *love* grey. He leans in and does that double kiss thing again. I'm better prepared for it this time but I still get flustered, glad of the distraction the plant affords.

'This is amazing,' Ben says to Olivia, looking at the flat, putting an arm around her. 'Isn't it, Liv?'

'Your house is even nicer and your house is really yours,' I say to Olivia, with feeling, and she beams.

37

I'd forgotten that approximately four per cent of parties, like four per cent of nightclubbing experiences, are truly superb, which is why you waste time, money, bandage-like undergarments and hopes on the other ninety-six per cent. And astonishingly, odds-defyingly, my flat warming has fallen into the magical minority. Conversation's buzzing, the drinks flow, the soundtrack works, the décor's admired, circulating happens effortlessly, my domestic-slut choices of snack (square crisps, round crisps, the ones that resemble tiny rashers of bacon) have been received well, or at least, eaten.

Zoe appears to be having a whale of a time, laughing non-stop with the *MEN* crowd, Gretton's advert forgotten.

I feel as if I've been climbing a hill for a very long time and suddenly the sun's broken through and I've found a spot to sit on my cagoule and admire the vista. I've been missing Rhys like a phantom itch in a lost limb but for the first time I don't miss him at all. Time for another drink.

As the night wears on, Mindy takes control of the music, which makes things more raucous. Jake waves to me as he leaves, having explained he has to be up to revise in the morning;

Ivor rolls his eyes behind his back. Caroline is deep in conversation with Olivia. I find myself next to the panoramic window, with Ben and Simon.

'Natalie said the interview went well,' Simon says.

'Good, I'm glad,' I say, dismissing a stab of discomfort. 'I thought so.'

'And when do I get to take you to dinner?'

Ben does a double-take.

'Whenever you like,' I say.

Ben does what I suppose must be a triple-take.

'Do you like Italian food?' Simon asks.

'Sure. Food in general, really.'

'Rachel's learning Italian,' Ben says.

'I know some Italian, stayed in Pisa on an exchange trip,' Simon says. '*Parli bene?*'

'Uh … *non.*'

'*Non?*'

Oh shit. Shit! Subject change, quick.

'I was reading these tips about icebreakers today,' I blather. 'Party prep. Can I try one out on you two? OK. Your most embarrassing incidents in the last year. Go.'

'Last week. My Latvian cleaning lady caught me in the nuddy,' Simon says.

'Seriously?'

'I grabbed the nearest thing to hand that was large enough to cover my modesty.'

'Which was?'

'My payslip.'

'Tosser!' I laugh despite myself, which is becoming the form with Simon.

I see Ben looking at both of us with mild concern, no doubt trying to figure out the dating thing. When he comes to a conclusion, I'd be grateful if he could explain it to me.

'There's one he prepared earlier,' Ben says.

'Yours?' I ask Ben.

'Apart from totally forgetting your name when I bumped into you again after ten years? Let me think...'

'You didn't?' My kneecaps feel as if they're not screwed on right.

'Of course I didn't, you arse.'

Ben's disbelieving expression reads *how could you fall for that?*

Because the idea of you having erased me, clicked and dragged me to the mental trash can icon like a deleted file, is the stuff of anxiety nightmares, right up there with the one where I'm scuttling the streets at dawn, naked, hiding behind milk floats.

'It was offering an albino girl my seat on the tram. I only saw her from behind, I thought she was 72, not 22.' Ben bites his lip at the memory, Simon laughs, I wince.

'Lack of pigmentation can be heavy on the legs,' Simon says.

'Hey, you meant well,' I say.

'Yeah. *Simon.*' Ben pushes a hand in a pocket as he drinks.

It strikes me that Ben and Simon are competing. What for? My attention? Surely not. Not Ben, anyway. He's married. Am I flirting by having a laugh with them? I imagine Olivia on the way home, saying acidly: 'She certainly puts the "ho" in hospitality.'

'More drinks?' Simon asks, and departs to the kitchen.

I rebalance myself on my chafing heels and clear my throat to make some explanation about the Simon date.

'Oh my God, blast from the past. Teenage Fanclub?' Ben asks, tuning into the music amid the chatter. 'You would've laughed at mine and Liv's first dance.'

Probably not *laughed*, I think.

'Why do you say that?'

'In the first big compromise of married life, I let her have what she wanted.'

He mouths 'Coldplay' to me and grimaces.

'Oh, well. I was wedding planning myself not so long ago. Glad you resolved the DJ/live band divide. It was the Gaza Strip for me and Rhys.'

I discover a yearning, of some considerable proportions, to tell Ben what happened. Talk about my real life – not the sort of things you discuss as bullshit icebreakers – with a real friend.

'The thought of getting married brought everything to a head for us,' I say, and Ben nods. 'The way they call it the happiest day of your life – well, it cuts both ways. If you're not happy, it's hard not to notice.'

'Was it a sudden thing? Or had you been unhappy for a while?'

'Hmm. Well. We muddled through our twenties. We had the pressure valves of his band and my friends. But your thirties – it's decision time, the wedding, kids. I realised we weren't happy enough to make the next stage work. Does that make sense?'

'Some,' Ben nods again. 'You seem to be coping really well.'

'On and off,' I say.

He gives me a sad, sweet smile, and looks at the floor.

'Which Coldplay song was it?' I ask, trying to lighten the mood. 'Oh no, hang on, let me guess. Does it go, "Dum dum dum da dum dum ... *Sorry, all our operators are busy at the moment. Please keep holding, your call is important to us.*"'

Ben's eyes crinkle up appealingly as he laughs. 'You've not changed! So *arsey...*'

'You egged me on, you have to admit.'

'Egged Rachel on how?' Olivia says, as she and Simon join us.

'She was cruelly mocking our bedwetter indie choice of music for the first dance,' Ben says.

'No! *You* said—' I can't repeat the fact that Ben was mocking it first, that's even more incendiary. I know this insult is going to be taken in entirely different spirit by Olivia. *Thanks Ben.* 'I like some Coldplay...' I finish, lamely.

'Yeah, right!' Ben says, making it worse.

'What would you have as your first dance?' Olivia asks me, sharply.

Ben glares at her, presumably to communicate that you don't ask someone who recently broken off an engagement what their first dance would have been.

'Rhys said he wanted "What Have I Done To Deserve This?" by the Pet Shop Boys. So I dodged a bullet there.'

'But what would you choose?' Olivia persists.

'Liv...' Ben's dismayed, failing to understand why she's being so insensitive, whereas Olivia and I understand each other perfectly.

'The way things are going, it'll probably have to be Etta James, "At Last". And some sort of young volunteer helping me and my bridegroom get out of our seats.' No laugh. 'We'd chosen "May You Never" by John Martyn for our first dance,' I concede.

Ben nods, impressed: 'Lovely choice.'

'Never heard of it,' Olivia snaps.

Ah well, it must be rubbish then.

'Slightly, just slightly too fast tempo?' Ben says. 'I'd go for "Couldn't Love You More", of his.'

I nod back. Not much to say to that, other than for my pupils to dilate and to continue drinking until my liver resembles a twenty-ounce, pepper-rubbed sirloin.

'Why didn't you ask for it then?' Olivia says to him, waspishly.

'I wanted you to have what you wanted,' Ben says.

'I think you should have something you love as your first dance, not something cool,' Olivia says in my direction, pointedly, not ready to forgive me.

'No one could accuse you of choosing Coldplay to be cool,' Ben laughs. He's going to be in *so* much trouble when they get in, and he doesn't even know it. Olivia folds her arms and doesn't take her eyes off me. I stare at the ice in my drink.

'Now, I know this,' Simon says, cocking an ear to the party soundtrack. '"Unfinished Symphony".'

'"Unfinished Sympathy",' I correct him.

'That's what I said.'

38

'Which side do you normally sleep?' Caroline asks, once we've put a severely impaired Ivor to bed on the sofa. When taxi time arrived, he was slumped in some sort of cocktail coma and we took a call that it was best to accommodate him. We tucked him up with a towel underneath him, a washing-up bowl at his side and numerous tea towels round his head. He had a deathly pallor and his hands crossed on his chest, like an Egyptian funeral for a pharaoh who owned shit things.

'There isn't a normally yet. I haven't been here long enough.' What I really mean is, there isn't a side to choose now the bulwark of Rhys's bulk is absent.

'You in the middle, then,' she says, flicking a corner of the duvet back. 'I'll go here, Mindy the other side.'

Mindy comes back from brushing her teeth, clad in beautiful scarlet Chinese pyjamas. Next to Caroline's black strappy lace-edged floral slip, I'm rather glad I left the toothpaste-stained Velvets t-shirt behind.

'Ivor woke up,' Mindy announces. 'He made a noise like: *BWORK. BWORK. BWOOORK.* Then he ran off to the loo.'

'Anything on the soft furnishings?'

'No, I totally got behind him and pushed him faster than the speed of sick.'

'Good, good.'

We arrange ourselves, then click the bedside lights off.

'How did Rupa get a mattress this big up those stairs?' I ask.

'She had it winched in one of the windows, I think,' Mindy says.

I feel my muscles relax against the springs.

'What's the deal with you and Ben then?' Caroline says.

All the tension returns. And then some.

'What do you mean?' I try to convey total amazement to Caroline while horizontal and invisible to her, sure she must be able to feel the heat of the guilty sweat I've broken out into.

'Weeelllll ...' Caroline says. 'It's a weird one.'

'What is?' I am ramrod straight, like an exclamation mark between their brackets. I will Deny Everything. Forever.

'When that light bulb went and you were standing on that chair changing it with Simon holding on to your legs, I saw Ben give you two a real *look*.'

'That's because we were driving a coach and horses through health and safety regs.'

Silence. Feeble jokes are not going to work here.

'It was very intense, very serious. And when Simon helped you down and managed to grope your arse in the process, I swear Ben almost winced.'

'He's not Simon's biggest fan. I don't think he thinks it's a good idea we're going on a date,' I add, hoping I've done enough to close the subject.

'Yeah. This is the thing. If I didn't know better, I'd have said it was simply plain old violent male jealousy,' Caroline says. 'Why doesn't he want you to date Simon, exactly?'

'Lucky you do know better,' I say. 'Given Ben's very happily married.'

'If he's happily married, he can't have a thing for you?'

'No.'

'OK. Number one, there is no such thing as a happy marriage—'

'Oh, Caroline!' Mindy wails. 'Enough!'

'I haven't finished.'

'I know you haven't, because I still have a shred of hope left,' Mindy says.

' —There is no such thing as a happy marriage if you mean an invulnerable one. Every relationship has its weaknesses and bad patches.'

'You don't have to be married to know that,' I say.

'I know, I know,' Caroline says, trying to soothe me. 'I'm not running down what you had with Rhys. But he hung around with other blokes in his band all the time. You never had to worry about female friends.'

'I still don't see what you're getting at.'

'That if I'm right and Ben's got a soft spot for you, you need to be wary. You don't want to cause trouble by unintentionally encouraging it. Weren't you quite close at uni? Did you ever suspect anything then?'

'No! And Ben would *never* have an affair.' At last I'm able to say something with perfect certainty.

'How do you know?'

'I know. Honestly, I know it like I know my own name. There's no way Ben would ever do that. He's totally honourable. I wouldn't sleep with a married man either. I hope you don't think I would do that.'

'Nooooo,' Caroline says, with no idea what agonies this conversation is causing me. 'But I think you might find yourself in the middle of something before you know you've started. You two were lit up like Christmas trees when you were talking to each other. No one has a crafty fag behind the bike sheds expecting to get lung cancer.'

'I'm not smiling at Olivia, inviting her to parties and moving in on her husband!'

'I'm not saying you're moving in on him,' Caroline says.

'Look,' I continue, with a dry mouth that isn't all down to booze dehydration, 'Ben and Olivia are married, Ben's not interested in me in that way, I'm not out to get him and I'm going on a date with Simon. And that's that.'

'I'm not so sure everything's great with Ben and Olivia. I get the impression it's been a strain moving up here. She's miles away from all her family and friends and I think she misses her old job,' Caroline says.

Pause.

'If you want my advice, Rach, the time you need to worry is if he ever says things at home are complicated,' Mindy says. 'It's *never* complicated. "It's complicated" only ever means, "Well yeah there's someone else but I want to do you too."'

'What they actually mean is: it's not as complicated as I'd like it to be,' Caroline says, laughing.

I'm not laughing.

'Oh, sorry, I didn't mean to wind you up,' Caroline says. 'Most likely if Ben's feeling anything it's nostalgia for being twenty-one. I mean, if you'd been right for each other, it would have happened then.'

'True,' I squeak, grateful for the cover of darkness.

'We all get a bad attack of the what-ifs from time to time.'

'Yeah.'

We say our goodnights. Caroline and Mindy drift into sleep. I'm wide awake, mind racing.

39

If you were cool, Friday night meant clubbing somewhere a bit druggy and dancey, or if you preferred beer and guitars, it was 5th Avenue or 42nd Street. If you were a significantly less cool student, you went to a meat market shark pit where they banned jeans and trainers and played music that was in the charts. And if you were truly tragic, you went to the halls disco and drank cider out of plastic receptacles, danced around a room that doubled as a canteen by day and staggered into the takeaways opposite at half two.

Being skint is a great leveller, however, and by the second year, with the expense of 'living out' biting, a lot of people we knew collided at the latter venue. Among the dozen or so that had gathered one particular night were Ivor, back on a weekend from his placement, and Ben and his latest girlfriend, Emily. They'd been together for a few months – good going for Ben.

She was cool in a way I could never hope to be: hi-top trainers, hacked-off denim mini, two-tone peroxide hair piled atop her head. The look was predatory-sexy and yet conventionally pretty in an 'I don't need to labour the point; it's so obvious, I can work against it' way. He always went for hues of blonde on the colour wheel, I noted. I hadn't had much of a chance to get to know her and I was disappointed that they sat at the far end of the table, merely waving their hellos. If I wanted to get to know Ben's girlfriends, I had to strike while the iron was hot. None of them lasted much beyond a term. Whoever got Ben to settle down one day was going to have her work cut out, I thought.

When it was Ben's turn to get a round, it occurred to me it would be an opportunity to chat. I pushed my chair out and went over to give him a hand.

As I approached the bar, I saw a gaggle of rugger buggers had struck up conversation with him. Ben played football and had an XY chromosome and therefore existed as a human being rather than a heckling target.

'Oh, hello. Do you know what we call you?' said one of the rugby gang, as I joined them. 'Ben does. Hey, Ben! Tell Rachel what we call her.'

Ben looked deeply uncomfortable. I frowned at him.

'Rachel *You Would* Ford. Ahahahhahaha!'

Ben muttered: 'I bloody wouldn't.'

Rather like the truth or dare 'sister' day, I wasn't entirely sure what to make of this denial. Ben and I ran relays between the bar and the table, two or three pints at a time, passing at the midway point.

I felt the group's eyes on me as I retreated and briefly wished I hadn't worn my new black cords that were a little tight on the rear. As I carried the second lot of glasses back to where we were sitting, I felt a hard – frankly, painful – pinch to the arse, and whipped round.

'Oi!'

'It was him.' They all pointed at each other, arms crossed over, comedy skit style.

There wasn't a lot I could do with full hands, so I settled for giving them serious stink-eye. When I went back for more drinks, I made the point that I was refusing to be cowed by casting a deliberately contemptuous look in the direction of my antagonists. Mistake: this only caused another ripple of amusement.

'Don't take this the wrong way but we want to see the back of you,' said one particularly unpleasant-looking specimen, who was short, squat and acne-covered. I could see he was making up for insecurity about his deficiencies by behaving even more badly than the rest of them.

'Drop dead. Try it again and I'll smack you.'

Rachel against ten rugby players was a prospect unlikely to make them skid their pants in fright, but I still felt I had to assert myself.

'I won't try that again,' said hobbit rugby boy. 'Can I check, is this not allowed either?'

He reached out and squeezed my left breast, as if it was the horn on a vintage car. The rugby boys started braying with laughter.

'Hey!' I shouted. 'You arsehole!'

'Sorry, sorry, that was wrong,' he said. 'It was actually this right one that caught my eye.'

He performed the same indignity on my other breast and I went to slap him, hard. He caught my wrist before my palm connected with his lumpy cheek. I'd seen this move in bad soap operas and didn't think anyone had fast enough reactions in real life. He had a horrible, clammy claw-of-a-vice grip. I couldn't wrest myself free and started to feel panicky.

'Gerroff me!' I shrieked, to more raucous laughter. I could still feel the imprint of his nastily rough fingers. I'd lost control and felt my lungs constrict.

I was suddenly aware of a presence at my side. My wrist was abruptly released. I turned in time to see Ben lunging towards the spotty groper, his fist connecting hard with his jaw in a wet-sounding crunch.

'Ow!' he cried. 'I—'

He didn't get a chance to say anything else as Ben punched him again, quite ferociously, this time knocking him off balance and sending him sprawling to the floor. I momentarily worried that his friends might defend him and square up to Ben. Instead they stepped back and watched him flailing. Nice guys.

'Apologise!' Ben shouted. Actual real violence had taken place and I felt like I was going to throw up. This was the halls bar, not some terrifying pub in Moss Side.

'Sorry,' said spotty man, rubbing his cheek and looking wary of getting another right hook.

'Not to me, to her!'

'Sorry,' he sulked, casting a very quick look up in my direction.

'*Idiot*,' Ben said, injecting the word with great feeling. He picked up the last two pints and I followed him back to our table.

As we walked away, spotty man shouted, at a volume that brought the whole bar to a standstill – or the small part of the bar that wasn't already watching: 'Ben, I didn't know she was your girlfriend!' Pause. 'I DIDN'T KNOW SHE WAS YOUR GIRLFRIEND!'

I cringed. I was absolutely certain Ben cringed. When we reached our group, everyone demanded to know what had happened.

'They were being idiots,' Ben muttered, taking his seat next to Emily again.

'He indecently assaulted me!' I wailed, covering my self-consciousness with theatrics.

'How do you mean?' Caroline asked.

'He grabbed my baps,' I said, feeling I had to explain that Ben's reaction was within the range of reasonable response.

'And you smacked him?' Caroline said to Ben in awe, her crush clearly going nuclear.

'Congratulations,' Ivor said. 'I've been hoping someone would do that since I met them.'

'Yeah, cheers, that was heroic,' I said, thanking Ben for the first time. He didn't seem to want to look at me, or anyone else for that matter, draining his pint in great gulps.

'I didn't know you were hard!' Mindy said. 'I might have to secretly fancy you from now on.'

'I'm not hard, my knuckles are killing me,' Ben said, putting his glass down and rubbing his hand. 'I don't know if I did it right.'

'What a great fella you've got,' cooed another girl in our group to Emily. It was then that I noticed the stunned expression she was wearing. It was as if she'd been punched. *She must've been so worried he was about to get a pasting,* I thought. Even though I hadn't asked for my secondary sexual characteristics to be mauled, or for Ben to step in and defend them, I felt peculiarly guilty and anxious.

A week later, word reached me that Ben and Emily had broken up.

40

Ivor is awake when Mindy and I drag ourselves out of bed, Caroline having disturbed him on her way to the gym. He's sitting up on the sofa, bespectacled and bare-chested, drawing the coverlet around him when we emerge.

'Are you hoping we'll admire your buffness and forget the sickage?' I say.

'My t-shirt was somewhat soiled,' Ivor says. 'Christ, was I very bad?'

'Was he very bad, Rach?' Mindy turns to me, sarcastic, hand on hip. '*Was he very bad?*'

I scratch my head, yawn. 'How do I put this? Bonfire of the dignities, Johnson.'

I make cups of sugary tea and when I deliver Mindy and Ivor's, she's climbed under the covers next to him.

'I hear you were trying to show the twenty-three year olds how it's done?' I say, returning with mine, settling into an armchair.

'White Russians,' Ivor says, blowing on his tea. 'They were more like Beige Russians with all the Kahlua. I feel like dungy hell. My tongue's like a Ryvita.'

'I take it Jake won?'

'Oh no,' Ivor says. 'I won.' He gestures at his half-dressed, bedraggled form. 'This is what success smells like, ladies. The cologne of victory. Inhale deeply.'

Mindy and I laugh.

'Think I was drinking to forget,' he says, putting his tea down and rubbing his eyes under his glasses, making them flip up and down like a music hall act. Ivor without glasses always looks wrong. 'Major misdemeanour, the night before last.'

'Did you snap when a Belgian teenager levelled their troll before you did on *World Of Warcraft*?' I ask.

'Nah...' He rubs his head. 'It was Katya.'

Mindy's head, resting in the crook of his arm, snaps up. 'You haven't let her extend her notice? Ivor, what is wrong with you?'

'No, she's still leaving.'

'So?' I say.

'We got smashed on her homemade damson wine.'

Ivor gives me a mischievous, bashful smile that I think I interpret correctly.

'You didn't make her eat meat, did you?' Mindy says, into his armpit.

Ivor starts laughing and then winces. 'Don't say funny things, it hurts.'

'Why is that funny?'

'It's funny in the context of what we did do.'

There's a pause, then Mindy moves away from Ivor as if propelled by the blast of her own verbal explosion.

'*WHAT?!*'

Ivor's startled by the force of the reaction and for a second, speechless.

'You shagged her?' Mindy demands, rounding on him.

'Uh. A bit.'

'This isn't funny, Ivor! This is gross!'

'We were drunk. It was a one-off. I'm not going to let her stay on or anything.'

'This isn't about that, this is about you doing *that* with *her*. When you hate her!'

'She's not that bad...' Ivor mumbles.

'You never stop complaining about her! And at the first opportunity, you get into bed with her? What does that say about you?'

'Hardly the first opportunity. She's always making fruit wine.'

'When we said to show Katya you had some balls, we didn't mean LITERALLY!'

I take a gulp of tea before I laugh, as I can see Mindy is far from seeing any humour in the situation. Actually, Ivor isn't laughing now either, face flushed in shame, or anger. Or both.

'Oh right, so I have to take lessons on this from Miss Superficiality 2012, do I?'

'What's that supposed to mean?'

'It means are your vacuous fops superior to Katya? Should I have met her through the personal ads and overlooked her annoying qualities if she was photogenic enough?'

Ivor's got a point there. He glances over for my support, but no way am I getting in the middle of something that's rapidly turning so unpleasant.

'That's what normal people do,' Mindy shouts, bearing down like the fiery bitch of doom in her red pyjamas. 'They date! They don't take advantage of drunk people who have to pay them rent. What're you going to do, let her have the last month free in return?'

'Mindy—' I say, nervously.

'I took advantage of her?! Are you seriously implying that this was in some way *rapey*?' Ivor shouts.

'I'm saying it's the sordidness thing I've heard in a long time.'

Ivor stands up, clad only in his boxers, modesty forgotten.

'There's no such word as sordidness. You AIRHEAD.'

'Go to hell!' Mindy screeches, bursting into tears and running back to the bedroom.

Ivor drops back onto the sofa, mouth open.

'Jesus,' he says, eventually, hand on head. 'What the fuck was that?'

'Low blood sugar?'

'I'm not proud of what I did, but was it that bad? She's behaving as if it's exploitation. If she thinks I'd …' Ivor makes an incredulity noise. 'I don't want to spend my time around anyone who thinks I'm capable of that. She can go to hell too.'

'We need a fry-up, and to calm down. Mindy's emotional, that's all.'

I'm glad Ivor doesn't ask me why she's emotional. I don't quite know.

'And what would she say if I was seeing twenty-three year olds? What is it about her shining example of a life that gives her the right to call me the turd?'

'Let's have another cup of tea—'

'No, I'm going, Rachel,' he says, fumbling for his t-shirt on the floor. 'Sorry, it's not your fault.'

'OK.'

I go to find Mindy – face down on the bed, head buried in a pillow.

'Hey,' I say, patting her hip. 'Ivor's going. I think we're all grouchy after last night's excess.'

Mindy sits up, hair askew. 'Tell Sex Pest Specs Pecs I said bye.'

I push the door shut, fast. 'Uh. Yeah. Might not. What's the matter?'

She sniffs, says nothing.

'Are things not going well with Jake?'

Mindy gives a small shrug.

'Do you want to talk about it?'

She shakes her head.

'Do you want a massive full English?'

She shakes her head again.

'I'll go see Ivor out then.'

When I get to the door, Mindy says: 'Rachel. I might have a part English. When he's gone.'

The front door bangs.

'Oops,' I say.

'Was I too hard on him?'

I put my head on one side and open my mouth to assemble a diplomatic answer that isn't *Well, you scared the shit out of me, and I was only a blameless bystander.*

'Do you know what, I don't actually care!' Mindy yelps. 'What he's done is—'

'What people do,' I interrupt. 'Not that I'm saying it was a great decision.'

'Yeah, people, as in letchy men with no standards. Whatever else, I never thought Ivor was the kind who'd jump on anything that passed. And *Katya*. She wears Crocs. With socks. Crocs with socks! I think I've seen her in Reebok pool slides like they're proper shoes, too. How would you even get rigid enough to do the deed?'

'Perhaps he's lonely.'

'Why would he be lonely? He's got us.'

'As great as I definitely think we are, I don't think we fulfil all of his needs. He hasn't gone out with anyone for a while. Since whatsername, who moved to Copenhagen.'

'Hannah,' Mindy sniffs, wipes her eyes. 'Split ends, bad table manners. Uhm, hello, tapas "sharer" plates doesn't mean you scarf all my boquerones. No loss.'

I sit down on the bed next to her. 'What's this really about?'

'It's about what it's about.'

'OK.'

A pause.

'Oh, I don't know. Jake's nice, but. You go through ticking all the boxes and find your ideal match and it's not ideal. You wouldn't choose your friends that way. Look at me, you and Caro. Totally different. She went to see Simon and Garfunkels at Hyde Park.'

'Garfunkel. Yes. See what you mean.' Perhaps not the time to suggest Mindy could also widen the search to include men who are not what she terms 'hard tens'.

'Everyone's always saying your thirties are when it all makes sense, you know, you read interviews with actresses and they're like *Oh I'd never want to go back to my twenties they were so turbulent, and now I've got this … tremendous sense of calm and I know what clothes suit me, classic pieces*, blah blah and it's bullshit. Your twenties are a starter of You Don't Have To Have Worked It Out Yet. And your thirties are more the big stodgy main course of Maybe This Is How It's Going To Be. I haven't met anyone worth having a proper relationship with yet. And I'm thirty-one. What's to say anything's going to change by forty-one?'

'Oh come on, you're in your prime and you've got plenty of time to meet someone.' Hypocrisy: I don't recall this line working on me.

'I'm serious, Rachel. What if it doesn't happen for me? It's as if everyone grew up and moved on and got more serious and I didn't. That's probably why I'm seeing twenty-three year olds. It's where I'm stuck.'

'Yeah. I know that feeling of knowing you aren't happy and not knowing what to do about it.'

'But at least you committed. You were with Rhys for thirteen years. You were engaged.'

'Being with the wrong person is lonelier than being on your own. Or it's as lonely, in a different way, trust me. I wasn't dating, or looking, like you. I have to wonder if I wasted all the time I had to find the right person, waiting for me and Rhys to work.'

'Honestly?' Mindy says. 'We didn't know. You seemed OK.'

'I'm crap at knowing how I feel, Mind. It's like I don't even let myself in on the secret.'

Pause.

'At least you do a job that you had to apply for. Ivor thinks I'm some thick businessman's daughter, a spoilt Injun princess who got everything given to her. I'm not Rupa!'

'He doesn't think that.'

'You heard him. "Airhead".'

'He was lashing back, he didn't mean it.'

'He did. People say what they really think in arguments.'

'They say what they think will hurt the most.'

A pause. 'I need Ivor to be a good person, Rachel. If he's a shit too, then I give up. I really do.'

'He is good. He did something you don't like, is all, and sounds like he doesn't like it much either, in the cold light of day.'

Mindy rests her head on my shoulder and I put my arm around her. 'And maybe, when you've both made up, if you wanted to be very petty, you could point out to Ivor that, while your phrasing was a little off, "sordidness" is a word.'

Mindy pulls away, perks up.

'It is? Ha. In your FACE, Johnson.'

41

In the falling dusk, my heels go *clip clop clip clop* on the pavement, and when I check the time and break into a canter, *clipclopclipclopclipclop*. I've discovered the great thing about living in the city centre is you can walk everywhere and the crap thing about living in the city centre is you have to walk everywhere.

I feel nervous at this date with Simon but I can't honestly say any nerves come from thinking I might be about to fall head over heels in love, or even head over shreddies into bed. He's attractive, I can see that. My appreciation is very much of the objective, unfelt, other-ladies-must-like-him variety though. But Caroline's right, I'm better off behaving like a single person and doing some dating straight away, rather than leaving this step another year. If I feel out of the loop now, well, that's only going to get worse.

Sometimes I think I need a bossy life sat-nav clipped to my belt. '*At the first opportunity, make a U turn …*'

I reach the corner near the restaurant and slow down, instinctively smoothing the back of my dress to make sure it isn't caught in my knickers. After hobbling here with the bandy gait of a *Monty Python* man in fishwife drag, I try for a more fluid swingy motion, one foot directly in front of another.

I read somewhere that the footprints of a debutante in sand are one long line, not side by side. I ignore the shooting pain in my left heel that tells me Manchester pavements aren't the beach and I'm no book-balancing beauty. I try to paint a beatific sailed-here-on-a-scented-breeze expression on to my features.

After saying I was free and easy where we dined, I had a late-dawning realisation that I didn't want to go anywhere frighteningly exorbitant with Simon and ratchet up expectation. I suggested an Italian place near the Printworks that's really an enhanced Pizza Express and expected him to argue to prove he was discerning, but he agreed straight away. Must be in the English gent code that you don't quibble with a lady's choice. Or he liked the realistic pricing.

I see Simon's stood outside, it obviously also being in the English gent code that you don't enter the venue without the lady. He could've heard me coming: I was clattering down the street like a dog that needs its toenails clipping.

He greets me with: 'Good evening. You look fantastic. Shall we?'

I don't look anywhere near as crisply-pressed and collected and plausibly first date-ish as him – white shirt, and what could, distressingly, be chinos – but I appreciate the sentiment, and agree we shall.

We're shown to the sofa in the waiting area, by a gigantic potted palm. The restaurant is a symphony of the tinkle of glassware and cutlery on china and chatter. Black-clad waiting staff flit about in the choreography of attentive service. This is where the rest of society has been spending its Saturday nights, not propped up in bed with a 3-for-2 deal paperback by ten p.m., while their partner heckles *Match of the Day*.

Simon's handed the wine list and, as he's flipping authoritatively through the faux-parchment pages, says: 'How well do you know Ben, then?'

Not Simon too.

'What do you mean?'

'Are you exes, or what?'

'No. Old friends. Why?'

'That's what he said. Yet I got a tetchy lecture about looking after you, blah blah … as if I was the big bad wolf trying to get into your basket.'

I'm touched by this, and surprised. I try not to show it.

'He's got a little sister. It's a common syndrome – big brothers are always protective of female friends by extension.'

'Right. So you've never climbed aboard?'

'What?'

He's asking the thing no one else would ever ask as his first question? If I was in a childhood comic book, cartoon Rachel would have a mouth like a cat's bum and the thought bubble caption 'GUMPF'.

'You've never *hopped on* our Benji?'

My shock gives way to laughter at the audacity of the inquiry. I should say: 'Look at me, look at Ben. Look at Olivia. Look likely?'

The waiter announces our table is ready.

Simon stands up and does up a button on his jacket, as if we're being led to the podium at an awards ceremony, wine list clamped under his arm like a clipboard. 'After you.'

When we've been handed the menus, I lean across the table and hiss: 'No, I haven't. I can't believe you're asking that. He's your friend. Haven't you asked him?'

'Always question people separately.'

'Ah, of course. Perhaps you'd rather do this in the custody suite of Bootle Street nick?'

'It's not got mood lighting,' Simon smiles. 'I like to know what's what.'

'So I see.'

'Actually ...' Simon now looks uncomfortable, which is novel '... the last woman I fell for was married. It's made me cautious of complications, shall we say.'

'What happened?'

He acts as if he hasn't heard me, picking imaginary lint off his sleeve.

'I didn't mean to get on to this before we'd ordered the wine.'

'Let's go with it. I don't know all the modern dating guidelines anyway.'

'I was keen. She turned out to be married. Husband found out. She stayed with him. Anecdote ends.'

'I can promise you I'm not married.'

'This much I know. No other huge terrible secret weighing on you that you'd like to declare?'

'Only that I know nothing about wine.'

'Allow me,' Simon says, back in his element. 'What main course are you having? Meat or fish? You're not a troublemaker, are you?'

'Troublemaker?'

'Vegetarian, pescatarian, humanitarian. Any other euphemisms for pleasure-intolerant.'

'I won't eat anything with a face,' I say, pretend-pious.

'Oh, don't worry. Everything I'm going to order has had its face sliced off.'

♥ ♥ ♥

I'd worried that the adversarial nature of conversation with Simon could be difficult once I was his date. I needn't have. He keeps things bouncing along with a stream of polite questions. He tells me about colourful clients, I tell him about colourful court cases. We trade tales about barristers and judges we're mutually acquainted with. He moans about intrusive, slapdash reporters, I complain about standoffish, unnecessarily secretive solicitors to even things up.

He seems genuinely interested and amused, and after a while I notice how much I'm enjoying being listened to. His attentiveness is slightly intoxicating, though not as intoxicating as the heavy red he chose.

Rhys would sit here grunting, eyes flicking towards the exits, foot tapping a rhythm on the floor, impatience greeting my every utterance. Band practice aside, he liked to move in an established pattern between three points on a triangle – home, work, pub – and any deviation left him agitated, almost resentful.

While I appreciate the contrast, it gradually dawns on me that while Rhys was rough going, Simon is all planed, slippery surfaces. There's nothing to throw a grappling hook into and actually make some headway in getting to know him. There's one moment his composure unexpectedly wobbles, when I mention a colleague of his who gets all the females in crown court swooning.

Simon snaps 'Really?' as if this is incomprehensible and promptly changes the subject. I vaguely wonder if he's the jealous type.

The discussion turns towards a couple in the same department at Simon's firm, and how the employees get drawn into their domestics.

'I've always thought it's a bad idea to be in the same line of work. Too much shop talk, and rivalry.'

'Ben and Olivia seem to do all right,' I say.

'They have their moments.'

'Do they?' I'm not entirely sure what he means and try to conceal my curiosity.

Simon pours out the last inches of the wine. 'Liv wears the trousers, no question. I think moving up here's the first time Ben's asserted himself and she's still getting used to it. I told him, never marry a woman with that much more money than you. She's going to think she's the manager in the marriage. And lo and behold...'

'Does Olivia earn that much more?'

'It's not what she earns, it's the money she's from. Her dad sold his haulage firm and retired when he was forty or so. Olivia doesn't have to work.'

Goodness, all those gifts and rich too.

'Perhaps she likes her independence,' I say.

'Oh yes. Don't get me wrong. Totty breaking the glass ceiling is a fine thing.'

'Most of what you say is ironic, right?'

'I'm only sexist insofar as blaming womankind alone for James Blunt's success. Nightcap?' Simon asks, beckoning the waitress for the bill.

'I'd like to get this,' I say, decisively, also gesturing for the bill.

'That's good to know.'

The waitress assesses the balance of power and the bill is handed to Simon on a saucer. He slips his card on top and hands it straight back.

When Simon said he 'knew a place', I pictured a plush gentle-men's club with wingback chairs and burgundy Regency stripe wallpaper and crackling fires. Simon would flash membership ID, or give the liveried doorman a Masonic handshake, and the gates would swing open.

Instead we duck down a barely-lit backstreet to a scuzzy den for the kind of career drinkers who can sniff out a late licence with nose aloft, like a Bisto kid.

'Mind. *The yack*,' Simon says, in a tube station announcer voice, his hand gripping my elbow to guide me round a dustbin lid-sized puddle of puke near the door. The venue is marked only by a illuminated white sign advertising a brand of beer. Nearby there's a gaggle of unsavoury characters who instinctively turn their backs on us in case we gather too much detail for the photo-fit.

'Know how to show a girl a good time, don't you? Do you meet clients here?'

'Ah, come on now. The Rachel I'm getting to know doesn't need lacy doilies under her drinks.'

He holds the door open for me. I get an unexpected stirring of attraction towards him, simultaneously noticing how tall he is and how well on the way to drunk I am, and that I like it that he has surprises.

The grimy exterior gives way to a grimier interior, a basement with bar stools and a big Wurlitzer-style jukebox, like a super-sized garish toy or leftover *Doctor Who* prop. The lighting is set to 'gloaming', the air perfumed with an unmistakable acidic base note of unclean latrine.

'Vodka tonic's your drink, isn't it?'

'Thanks,' I nod, though it isn't, it's Caroline's drink, and I don't know if this is significant. I find a booth. He puts the drinks down and slides into the seat opposite, trousers squeaking on its vinyl cover.

'This surely isn't a Simon-ish place,' I say. 'You're throwing me a curve ball to see if I can catch it.'

'After one date, or...' he pulls back a cuff to check what appears to be a Breitling watch, which rather underlines my point – he'll probably get his arm snapped like a pool cue for it – '...two-thirds of one date, how would you know what a Simon-ish place is like?'

'Come on, of course it isn't.' I pause. 'What was all that stuff about the hypocrisy of marriage at Ben and Olivia's dinner party, then?'

Simon smirks. 'I wondered when this would come up.'

'I'm not asking because I'm bothered,' I say, curtly, with a smile.

'Why, then?'

'Most guests just try to avoid giving offence like that.'

'Is saying most people are giving up when they settle down that controversial? I bet they agreed with me. I'd question how

240

brutally honest anyone could be on that subject, with their spouse sat beside them.'

'You weren't thinking of anyone in particular?'

Simon raises his eyebrow. 'I'm taking my own advice and going no comment. How about you tell me something about this engagement you broke off?'

'Do I have to?'

'Well, it's usual to find out something personal about each other on a first date, and so far I know that you're not fond of beetroot.'

'There's not much to tell. We were together a long time, we were engaged, it became obvious neither of us was that keen on getting wed and I was the one to say so.'

'He didn't want it to end?'

'No.'

'Any chance of a reconciliation?'

'Doubt it.'

Despite my best efforts, my voice has thickened.

'How long were you together?'

'Thirteen years.'

'Ouch. I guessed it was a while.'

I'm sure that Ben will have told Simon this, yet I humour him by asking why.

'You have the hunted, wary look of the serial monogamist who's unexpectedly stumbled back into the singles jungle and forgotten she needs a machete.'

I laugh.

'It's harder for women,' Simon says. 'Single blokes in their thirties look choosy; women worry they look like victims of that choosiness.'

I gasp, and Simon adds: 'Even when it's entirely unwarranted. Anyway, there's worse things. Like Matt and Lucy. What a chore they were.'

I laugh, nodding vigorously.

'So was Ben quite the boy at university?' he continues.

'He had a few girlfriends, yeah.'

'Surprised you weren't among them.'

'Why?' Nervous again. I hope he's not going to do a 'trip to The Cheese Shop' line and order a whole truckle of cheddar by implying I'm irresistible. I doubt it would be sincere.

Simon shrugs, necks the last of his neat vodka.

'You're cute and you two appear simpatico, somehow.'

'Like I said, thirteen years. I wasn't single,' I say.

'Doesn't always stop people.'

'Are you looking for, what do they call it, watercooler conversation?'

Simon laughs. 'God, the ladies at work are nauseating about him.'

'Yup, that sounds like the Ben Effect,' I laugh, hopefully lightly. 'Why did you ask me out?' I say, to turn the topic, and as soon as the question's left my mouth I rue it. 'I mean, I didn't think I'd be your type.'

'And what did you think my type would be?'

'Uh. Zara Phillips? Someone horsey but dirty who you can still take home to Mummy.'

Simon laughs heartily at this. 'You've got me pegged as some upper-crust idiot, haven't you? Don't be so quick to pigeonhole.'

'Hah, like you haven't done the same in reverse?'

'Absolutely not. I like people with some mystery.' Simon rolls his empty glass between his palms.

'I have mystery?'

'Oh yes. There's definitely something you're not telling.'

For once, a glib comeback doesn't spring to my lips.

Two drinks down in the dive bar and the landscape starts to tilt. I don't want to lose control and I don't meet any resistance from Simon when I say it's time I went home.

He insists on walking me back to my flat and mentions how he can just as easily catch his cab from there, in case I think he's trying it on.

I like the city late at night, the blasts of music and the splashes of light cast from bars that are still open, shoals of brightly-dressed clubbers, the beeping taxis and the greasy, savoury smell of meat and onions from the burger vans. We walk briskly, looping round the groups of people who intermittently block the pavement, arriving outside my flat in jump-cut drunken time. On the way out, the same distance apparently took three times as long to cover.

'Night then. Thanks for a lovely evening,' I say, amazed to find I haven't consumed enough alcohol to stop this being awkward. Damn fresh air.

'Come here,' Simon says, in a low voice, pulling me towards him, and I think how very Simon it is to issue commands instead of endearments.

He kisses the way I'd have predicted he'd kiss, if I'd given it any thought beforehand: firm, almost pushy, as if one of us is going to be declared winner when we break apart. It's not unpleasant, but it's not going to involve tongues, I decide, pulling back. I thought the first person I kissed after Rhys would feel like a watershed, but it feels — what's the word? Prosaic. Like the intervening thirteen years never happened.

'What's the verdict then, Court Reporter-ette? Can I see more of you?' he says, quietly, and overtly suggestively.

I'm flattered, and drunk. And surprisingly lost. Part of me wants to say yes. Most of me knows it isn't what I want, it's just what's here.

'Er — Simon.'

'Er — Simon,' he mimics, getting louder. 'Uh oh.'

'I've really enjoyed myself. Even more than I thought I would.'

'The strength of the compliment depends on how much you thought you would, doesn't it?'

I wonder if there's a stage of refreshment where Simon's less articulate and argumentative. He must've honed these skills doing daily battle with members of the Crown Prosecution Service.

'It's a bit too soon for me after Rhys and everything. Can we be friends for now? I don't know my own mind and it's not fair to inflict myself on anyone.'

'Fine. Well, obviously I'd rather we were going at it gang-busters, but whatever you want.'

I laugh, feeling a twinge of relief at avoiding intimacies with a man who uses the phrase 'going at it gangbusters'.

'Thanks.'

A pause. 'Night then,' I say.

'Night.'

I dig my key out of my handbag. As I walk off, Simon calls back: 'Know why I'm all right with this, Rachel?'

I shake my head, glancing around.

'Because you're worth waiting for,' he says, raising a hand. 'Night.'

As I make three attempts to get the key in the lock on my door, I wonder if that was an assumption rather than a compliment.

After a lot of – well, some – internal debate about whether it's appropriate, I email Ben to tell him how it went with Simon. I don't want him to think I'm some pasta-guzzling tease.

I send: '*Hi – Bit of a weird one, had really nice time with Simon but not sure if going to see him again. Bit soon, etc. Hope you & Olivia not going to feel put in the middle.*'

I come back from a break in court to find the reply: '*Well… we do ask that you marry him to make any future dinner-party seating plans easier for us. Is that so much to ask?*'

I giggle like a moron at this, then see the PS: '*I'm trying to be healthy during my lunch hour and going for sandwich/walk in Platt Fields at one to get away from the office… want to join & have a chat? No problem if not, I'm not much of an agony aunt.*'

I respond instantly in the affirmative and hop on a bus, Platt Fields not being as wildly convenient as I'll insist it is if he asks. A change is as good as a rest and all that.

When I get to the park entrance, I see Ben is clutching brown paper bags, kneeling down, talking to a little girl in a dark duffle coat. A harassed forty-something woman joins them and as I approach, Ben says, in a slightly kids' TV voice: 'Here's my friend! Rachel, hi.'

'Hello!' I say, trying for jolly, unsure as to whether to pitch my response to the adults or the child.

As we move away, Ben mutters under his breath: 'Speak to someone's lost kid these days, you're more likely to get arrested than thanked. Was I glad to see you.'

'Unless they think we're a Brady-Hindley double act?' I say.

Ben laughs: 'I'd forgotten what I'd been missing with your sick sense of humour.' Before I know whether to mind being forgotten or pleased at being miss-able, he adds: 'Did you bring food?'

I realise that in my haste, I didn't.

'I bought you this. You still eat ham and pickle?'

He hands me one of the brown paper bags. I peer inside at a ciabatta sandwich, wrapped in a napkin. 'Thanks!'

I'd never think to go and look at nature in the middle of a day at the courtroom coal-face and yet I'm instantly struck by the springtime loveliness of the park, the light glinting on the lake.

'So … Simon and Rachel a non-starter?' Ben says.

He gives me a mouth-full-of-food grin, as we gnaw the edges of our ciabatta sandwiches. I always think these things seem like a good idea and in practice are like chewing bricks, covered in brick dust. I give up and start pulling bits of ham out of the bread, inside the bag, so Ben doesn't see me looking like I dipped my face in a bag of flour.

'We went for dinner and it was surprisingly enjoyable …'

As I tail off, considering how to phrase this, Ben suddenly looks like a pubescent boy being forced to listen to the story of his own conception. 'Oh-kay … There isn't going to be, an, er, PG-13 …'

Looking at his fraught expression, I can't resist continuing: 'Afraid so, because when a man and woman like each other *very* much they have a sort of special cuddle…'

'Argh, stop there! God, the thought of Simon banging the headboard shouting "Bravo! I have reached my conclusion! Preparing to disengage member in three, two, one…"' Ben shudders. 'Find another confidante for this stuff.'

'Kidding!' I say, through the considerable yet slightly tense laughter. 'It was *dinner á deux, home un une.*'

Ben makes a forehead-wiping gesture with his napkin.

'Simon was more enigmatic on the point, of course. Oh she's *rilly something*, Ben.' He pulls a Roger-Moore-eyebrow Simon face that turns into a *yuck* Ben face.

We laugh.

'I don't know if we're a good fit, I guess,' I say. 'He's very clever and witty and scathing and so on. I think we're very different. I'm sure he'd be a challenge. He scares me a bit to be honest with you.'

'Hmm, I'm not entirely sorry you say this.'

I think of Caroline's observation from my flat warming. This frank admission from Ben makes it more likely that his motives are above board. I feel relief, and the smallest tinge of what might be disappointment.

'No?'

Ben shakes his head while chewing and swallowing. 'I get on with him, I don't really trust him. I couldn't in all conscience advise a friend to date him.'

A friend. I am a friend again.

'Liv thinks I'm being ridiculous and you two would be great, though, so what do I know.'

Hopefully a lot more than her when it comes to me, but I don't say so.

'I was slightly surprised you agreed to a date at all, if I'm honest,' Ben continues.

I extract another piece of ham. 'When's the right time to start seeing people again after thirteen years? How do you know for sure who the right person to see is? Caroline said I had to give it a go and I thought she was right.'

'You ought to trust your own instincts more. Caroline's great but Caroline's choices are Caroline's choices, not yours.'

I'm touched by this, so touched I blurt: 'That's very thoughtful. You're what they call "just gay enough".'

Ben shakes his head and says through a mouthful of bread: 'And I was being supportive. Anyone ever tell you you're a heartless witch?'

'Yeah, some bloke at uni once.' I wave my hand, dismissively.

Too far. Ben swallows with a hard gulp, a thin smile settling afterwards. Despite the rehabilitation, a twinge from the old injury, reminding us not to overdo it, not to put too much weight on it yet.

What are Ben and I to each other? There's no word for it. Not exes and, despite what he said and what I want to believe, not exactly friends either. No wonder other people have asked for a description. I yearn to broach the topic. But it would ruin everything.

'Second date with Simon unlikely then?' Ben asks, as much for anything to say, I think.

'Unlikely. Not impossible.'

'I'll tell Liv it's a "definite maybe". That'll keep her off your back and won't insult Simon if he asks her.'

'Good idea,' I say, gratefully. 'He's got some interesting opinions, I'll give him that.'

'Hah. Such as the dinner party thing about how we'd all
married the wrong people? Yeah, he doesn't have much respect
for other people's relationships in general, from what I can
glean,' Ben says.

'I think I know what you're referring to. If you mean his
past that is. He mentioned it.'

'Oh. What did he say?'

'That he'd had a thing for a married woman and she'd gone
back to her husband.'

Ben nods. 'He told me that too. He knows my views. Even
if he had a grand passion for her, he shouldn't have had a go.'

See, Caroline, I think. *This is Ben. He might've enjoyed success
in the arena, but he does not condone, or emulate, skirt stoats.*

'But he's your mate?'

Ben shrugs. 'He's known Liv since uni and he's been good
to me at work. I don't want to date him.' He frowns. 'I feel
bad if I've put you off. Keep your wits about you, and you
never know. You could be the making of him. I don't quite see
what's in it for you, that's all.'

'Not dying old and alone?'

Ben laughs. 'As if. Can I ask your opinion about something
in return?'

'Sure.'

'Liv wants to move back to London in a year's time.'

'Oh.' *I'm not going to offer unbiased advice. This is a horse kick
to the heart.*

'If I agree to it, our money won't stretch to a house like the
one we have here, down there. She wants me to let her parents

buy us a giant place, near them. They've offered to get their little girl back down south, I think. I've refused. Am I being unreasonable?'

'Your reasons are …?'

'Aside from the fact they're set on God-awful-ming in Surrey, it's too much. I don't want to be in hock to my in-laws for a fortune. Don't get me wrong, they're nice people. But I don't want to be owned. I knew they were pretty formidable before we got married. This piece of incredibly well-timed generosity makes me think I underestimated them.'

'The money isn't available to you to buy up here?'

'Oh no,' Ben smiles, grimly. 'Not that I'd take it, but no. That's not the deal.'

'And Olivia's thoughts?'

'She thinks I'm selfish. I'm endangering the happiness of my wife and security of our future children on an abstract whim. She says it's money she'll inherit eventually anyway. She'd be off tomorrow. She says she's tried the north for me and doesn't like it, experiment over, obligation fulfilled. Whereas this is the best I've felt in ages.'

Pathetic, given I am irrelevant, but: this last remark makes me want to hug him.

'Difficult.'

I'm conscious that whatever I say may be repeated to Olivia, and this is none of my business. Only a few minutes ago, I was hearing how my judgement is better than Caroline's, and yet this feels uncannily like the very thing Caroline warned me about. Ben has no one else to talk to up here, I reassure myself. This is fine. This is two old friends, chatting. Despite 'friends' not quite covering it.

'I can see why you feel the way you do. There could be a compromise, where you pay them back in a certain number of years?'

'We're talking the kind of sum I could never fully pay back, Rachel. Repayment's not the plan. Once we're in there, it'll be about filling the rooms...'

He breaks off. The kids issue. I'm definitely not asking about that.

'I think you're right to want to keep your autonomy,' I say. 'As for security, it's not as if Didsbury's a Soweto shanty town, is it?'

Ben shakes his head. 'No.'

'Olivia will come round, once Manchester improves on her,' I add.

Ben raises his eyebrows and looks off into the middle distance, makes an equivocal 'Hmm' noise.

I sense there's much more he could say but that he already feels disloyal.

There's a heavy pause.

'What're Simon's family like?' I ask, my turn to find something to say.

'You don't know about that?'

'No?'

'His parents died in a car accident when he was about seven or eight. His aunt and uncle were made his guardians but they weren't exactly the nurturing types and packed him off to boarding school. I think it was paid for by the life insurance.'

'Oh, no. That's terrible.' I'm terrible. I cringe at the memory of myself mouthing off about 'Mummy'. 'I've said things about him being a toff...'

Ben shrugs.

'You weren't to know.'

The sun's gone behind a cloud. I stare over the flat, tarmac-like expanse of water, whipped into shallow ripples by the wind. 'That's why I shouldn't have said it.'

The mood has dipped. I tear a bit of leftover bread off.

'Can I share this with the ducks?'

'Be my guest.'

There's a flurry of bottle-green, cream, black and yellow as the birds descend on fragments of soggy ciabatta.

'What about the weedy one who keeps getting missed out?' Ben asks.

'Where?'

'There! At the back. Poor beggar.'

I hand Ben a large lump of ciabatta and he smiles at me – not any old smile, a slightly poignant, Sunday afternoon matinee, yellow-filter-on-the-lens *would you look at the pair of us* soppy-inducing smile. He starts lobbing bread chunks with more over-arm throw vigour than me.

'Got him! There you are, mate. Life isn't as unfair as you thought.'

'Hoo hoo, yeah it is,' I say.

Ben gives me a sideways glance. I feel 'A Moment' developing.

'Course what we're actually doing is killing fish,' I say. 'Apparently the leftover bread rots and then there's too much nitrogen in the water, or somesuch.'

'Oh, Captain Bringdown,' Ben says. 'And there I was, thinking this was nice.'

44

As I hang on a ceiling strap on the bus, I'm lost in thought about orphan Simon, newly worthy of tenderness and sympathy, despite the shenanigans with the married woman. Although I trust Ben implicitly, I can't help wonder about Simon's version of events. I think about the pass I've given Natalie Shale and my debate with Caroline, and suspect I ought to toughen up and *take a line* on things, as Rhys would say.

My mobile chirps with muffled birdsong in the recesses of my bag. I balance it on my hip and hastily dig the phone out. It's Ken. Not a good sign.

'Hello?'

'Woodford?'

'How are you finding Zoe Clarke?'

'Finding her? To work with?'

'No, by candle light. YES TO WORK WITH.'

'Erm, she's …' I block out the traffic and chatter around me with an index finger jabbed in my free ear '… she's excellent. She's a great reporter and she hasn't needed any hand-holding.

254

She's backed me up and I know if I trust her to cover some-thing she'll always come back with the story.'

'Right. I've had a word with the editor and we like her strike rate in court.'

Uh oh ... have I talked myself out of my job?

'So, we want to try a new arrangement, as an experiment ...'

My muscles start to bunch. Argument will be futile. Once Ken has made up his mind, especially when he's rushed the legislation past the editor, he's unstoppable. You'd have a better chance of knocking a hurtling oil tanker off its path by sticking your leg out.

'We're going to put her in court full time ...'

This isn't happening. I'm not about to find out that I'm going back to the office as a general reporter, with council meetings and death knocks and late shifts. No. I refuse. I'll leave. Oh yeah ... *and then who'll pay for that stupid fancy flat that's overstretching you as it is?*

'...As your deputy. Free you up to spend more time on backgrounders like the Natalie Shale piece. We liked that a lot too. Good straight piece. Didn't ladle it on.'

I stutter: 'Oh, right, thanks ...'

'Starting next week?' Ken asks.

'No problem.'

He hangs up without saying goodbye, Ken Baggaley being the only person outside movies to actually do this.

The bus doors open with a hydraulic hiss and I step out, taking deep lungfuls of carbon monoxide–laden Manchester city centre air and letting the panicky despair of moments ago start to dissipate.

A deputy. I'd have the time to get my teeth into the bigger stories, possibly rediscover a passion for the job. I knew the Natalie Shale exclusive was a feather in my cap. I didn't anticipate getting an effective promotion out of it. I smile to myself as I start walking towards work.

Caroline implied getting friendly with Ben again could bring bad things to my door. So far, it's brought only good.

❤ ❤ ❤

I'd like to go somewhere upmarket to celebrate our joint promotion, but my rent's really biting. Even with a pay hike, I doubt Zoe's high rolling, so we end up in The Castle, cursing our predictability. Zoe goes to get the drinks while I inspect a pun-laden leaflet about Thursday's Curry Club: '*Tikka The Night Off Cooking!*' She returns with two fishbowl-sized glasses of white wine and I propose a toast to collaborating in court.

'To teamwork,' I say, raising my glass for Zoe to clink. 'And to Pete Gretton, who gave us something in common from day one – an enemy.'

We slurp.

'You know all this is thanks to you, Rachel.'

'Don't be silly, it's thanks to you being shit hot at a tender age.'

'Seriously, though. I remember that first day when I didn't know what I was doing. I appreciate you having the patience.'

We sink into gossipy shop talk and when we're on the second round, I decide I can afford to unburden myself a little bit.

'Zoe, can you keep a secret?'

'Ooh, I love secrets. Course.'

'When I was interviewing Natalie, I read a text on her phone. I thought it might be about me. I went on a date with her solicitor. Not that it's an excuse.'

'And?' Zoe's slate-grey eyes widen.

'And it was from a ... lover. I think.'

'*Shiiiiit*. Her husband's in prison and she's getting up to stuff. Winnie Mandela badness.'

'I wondered if it was the bloke I was seeing. It wasn't his number.'

'You took down the number?'

I squirm. 'Yeah. Only to check it against Simon's.'

'Didn't you call it?'

'Not like I'm going to learn much from a random voice.'

'Got the number?'

'Why, what're you going to do?'

'Basically, call him without saying who I am.'

'And ask what – "Are you the man who's having it off with Natalie?"'

'Nope.'

'A call where you don't tell him anything or ask him anything? Sounds like an exercise in futility.'

'We'll see.'

'You promise me this is no risk?'

'No risk at all. Trust me.'

I fumble my notebook out of my bag, flip it open. A fairly loud internal voice tells me I'd be thinking better of this if I hadn't had the best part of a bottle of wine on an empty stomach. There's the number, scribbled on the inside of the cardboard cover, next to the words 'GOOD PLUMBER', in case Gretton started copying anonymous numbers over my shoulder on the off-chance they were Natalie's.

'Read it out,' Zoe says, biro poised above the back of her hand. I dictate the numbers and she scrawls them down, dragging her skin with smudgy blue ink.

'Right, follow me.' Zoe slides off her stool, scanning the pub for a payphone. I drape my coat over my seat, shoulder my bag and follow her. She feeds in coins and dials the number while I act as lookout, though I'm not sure for what.

Zoe makes a 'mad excitement' face while it rings through, as if she's desperate for the loo. The manageress casts a suspicious glance in our direction. I haven't felt like this since I was fifteen and playing truant in HMV.

'Hello, is that Liz?' Zoe asks the receiver. 'Oh, I'm sorry. Wrong number.'

She hangs up. 'It's a man.'

'I don't think this qualifies us for the Woodward and Bernstein investigative medal.'

'Patience,' she chides, and I wonder when Zoe became my mentor.

She dials the number again.

'What are you doing?' I mouth, and she puts her finger to her lips.

This time she doesn't speak, and hangs up. 'Bingo.'

'What?'

'Not many people answer a wrong number a second time. I got his answerphone.'

'And?'

'And, Natalie Shale is bonking someone called Jonathan Grant, who can't get to his phone right now, the lying sod. All we have to do is find out who this Jonathan is,' Zoe chatters. 'Electoral roll might help. I tell you what, he sounded posh, not like some gangland hardnut … you OK?'

'Zoe, I think I know who he is,' I say.

'*Fuck*. Who?'

'He's Lucas Shale's last solicitor.'

We stare at each other, Zoe agape.

'Fuckin' aye!' shouts a lad nearby, as a fruit machine spits out pound coins like gunfire.

45

'I need to think clearly,' I say, reinforcing this statement by lifting a third full wine glass to my lips, and Zoe nods gravely.

'On the one hand, this is clearly a story,' I announce, needlessly.

Zoe holds her inked skin up. 'On this hand. It's a cracking story.' Her eyes sparkle, suddenly much brighter and clearer. 'You are a flipping legend.'

Despite the sensation of having peered under a rock and found a creepy-crawly, I feel my head swell slightly. At least I'm showing Zoe a good time.

'Not down to any journalistic nous. But thanks.'

'On the other hand...?'

'On the other hand, Natalie Shale will be hounded. Lucas's appeal could be jeopardised by all the publicity. Imagine being locked up for something you didn't do, and finding out something like this? Jonathan Grant will most likely lose his job. I don't know exactly how it works in law. I think once you've done something this unprofessional, you get struck off.'

'True. She decided to start shagging her husband's brief, and vice versa. That's not your responsibility.'

'I know, but I wouldn't have found out about it if I hadn't snooped while I was a guest in her house.'

'Where was she when you were looking at her phone?'

'Outside talking to a neighbour.'

'But you've got to remember, this is massive,' Zoe says. 'This is the story they'd talk about in your leaving speech. You could always call Natalie and see if she'll talk to you about it.'

'Somehow I don't think that's even slightly likely, and I can't test the water without creating a big fuss. I'm friends with her husband's current solicitor.' More than friends, perhaps. 'It'd end up with them freaking out and demanding I spike my interview, I guarantee it.'

Zoe gnaws her lip.

'If I hadn't called that number, you wouldn't have to worry about this.'

'S'alright,' I say, tipsily. 'I'm gonna go to the loo, and by the time I come back, I'll know the answer.'

As I yank paper towels out of the dispenser with excessive force, a drunken thought worms its way into my mind, a worm in the rotten apple I have for a head. Leave Natalie to her affair, leave them all alone, because who am I to say how she's found happiness, anyway? Lucas could've been a tyrant of a husband, for all I know. Jonathan may have swept her off her size three feet. It could all be over by the time Lucas is released. It might've been a 'moment of madness' she regrets, as politicians have it. What truly matters to me isn't the morality of what they're doing, or a front page splash. It's a man in south Manchester. I want to do whatever would make him proud, even if he'll never know a thing about it. Is there a way to break this story and not anger Simon or alienate Ben? Would I take it if there was, turn Natalie over and head off into the sunset? I ball the paper towels, aim a throw for the bin, and miss.

I rejoin an expectant Zoe at the table.

'Well?' she says.

'Well, there was no thunderbolt. Which is frustrating as I usually have all my epiphanies in the bogs at The Castle.'

Zoe laughs. I feel pissed.

It's time to stop pretending when I know what I'm going to do. 'No, I'm going to leave it be, Zoe,' I say. 'Not the boldest decision I ever made, but I'll be able to sleep at night.'

'Really?' Zoe says.

'Really. Nothing good can come of what I did. It was wrong. Every instinct I have is telling me to steer clear.'

'I think you've probably made the right decision.'

'Do you know what, I'm absolutely sure it's the right one. I can feel it.'

'God, can you imagine what Gretton would do if he had this in his sticky mitts?' Zoe giggles. 'He'd die and go to heaven.'

'Gretton's not going to heaven, he's off to the hot place,' I say. 'Speaking of hot, fancy soaking all of this up with a curry?'

46

I marked my twenty-first with an Indian meal at a restaurant in Rusholme. It was our favourite on the curry mile: the waiters recognised us, made a fuss of us and brought us free kulfi along with mints and the platter of plastic-sheathed tubes of hot, artificial lemon-scented flannels.

When I booked I explained the occasion, and on arrival we saw they'd kindly draped the table with streamers that ended up getting dragged through the mango chutney. It wasn't much of a celebration, as twenty-firsts go, but we were on the verge of our finals and everyone was a little weary, tense and spent up.

As Ben didn't know my friends all that well he brought his latest girlfriend, Pippa, who I'd been told had nursed a thing for him for a long time before they got together. I wondered if he was in love too. I'd heard a male friend of Ben's admiringly describe her as 'the whole package'. He pinned down exactly what made me uncomfortable about petite Pippa. Ben had been with many honeys but never such a *nice* one. River of Caramac-coloured hair, proportions like a porn Thumbelina and worst of all, the inner to go with the outer.

'You look beautiful,' she said to me earnestly, in her soft Dublin lilt, which made it sound even more earnest.

'Thank you!'

I didn't. I'd spent an hour creating a Shirley Temple do with curling tongs. I imagined loose, glossy ringlets, the type which bounce like telephone wire in the adverts. Instead I looked slightly manic, like the mugshot of a disgraced American prom queen who'd got caught consorting with the king in the parking lot.

As Rhys took charge of dispensing the Cobras, Caroline wanted to know what he'd bought me for my birthday.

'Typical girl things. Perfume, underwear. The grundies are for me, though.'

'You're a cross-dresser?' Caroline asked, heaping a sliver of poppadom with pink onion.

'I'll appreciate her in it. You should see the stuff she usually wears ... like a St Trinian.'

'Shut up,' I barked, covering my mouth to avoid spraying the table with shards of deep-fried appetiser.

'Some men like that,' Caroline said.

'Not sturdy stuff, like you're doing PE.'

'Rhys!'

'Ooh, I think you'll find they do,' Caroline said, drizzling with a zig-zag of mint sauce from a teaspoon.

'One of my boyfriends made me do role play where I had to call him the Maharaja,' Mindy offered, and we all politely ignored her.

'She's even got pants with pictures of cartoon characters on them,' Rhys continued. 'What's that woolly thing from Sesame Street with a hat called?'

Face on fire, without the help of a vindaloo, I kicked Rhys hard under the table.

'Ow, fuck! That hurt!'

I glanced at Ben to check if he'd heard any of this. He pretended to be engrossed in the menu for my sake, which made me even more embarrassed.

'Oscar the Grouch,' Caroline offered.

'Grouchy? She's chipped bone,' Rhys said.

'No – the cartoon creature.'

Adjusting my dress on my return from a loo trip, I noticed Ben was absent from the table. I spotted him outside, back leaning against the window. The drink was flowing at the table. Everyone was still picking at dun-coloured jalfrezis, dhansaks, kormas and anthills of clove-studded, primrose yellow rice. I squeezed unnoticed through the dining room and out the door.

'What's going on here?'

Ben started at the sound of my voice.

'I needed some air. What're you doing out here?'

I clutched my rounded belly, under the lace of my dress. 'I reached a tandoori grill event horizon.'

He smiled.

A car with a pimped-out exhaust hurtled past, dickhead music blasting from its four wound-down windows. We said nothing until the noise faded, shivering slightly in the northern England early evening. The air smelled of wood-smoke and the spicy chicken wings shack doing brisk business next door.

'Twenty-one, eh, Ron? Knocking on.'

'Hah. Yeah.'

'Got a plan? Everything mapped out? Career, marriage, kids, that sort of thing?'

'Not really.'

'But you're definitely going back to Sheffield?'

'Well yes, since the journalism course will have me.'

I was vaguely surprised at the question. Since I'd applied, been accepted, and wittered about it at great length, what else would I do?

'What about you? You going to end the Great World Tour in Ireland?' I asked.

Ben and his friend Mark had been planning a six-month globetrot since they were about fifteen. Ben's redoubtable work ethic meant he was sitting on some serious savings. They'd recently bought the tickets and Ben had excitedly shown me their route on a map of Asia spread out on a table in the refectory.

His imminent departure was forcing me to face a thought I'd been trying to avoid: how were we going to stay in touch, in the sense of actually being involved in each other's lives, beyond the odd postcard? Would his serious girlfriends be OK with me? Would Rhys start to make jokes about my Other Man that would make us all uncomfortable?

Ben and I had been this exclusive club of two, both tacitly understanding it was one no one else could join. This exclusivity would likely prove our undoing. With all firm good intentions, I couldn't quite see it working across a geographical distance as well as gender divide. If anybody had asked if Ben and I were going to stay mates, I'd have said yes, but if you took me to an interrogation room and shone a lamp in my face and demanded to know *the goddamn truth*, I was pretty sure how the odds were stacked. There'd be no 'going out for a session and crashing at his' once time had elapsed and suspicious significant others had to sign it all off. Letters and phone calls would entail offers to visit that both of us would find awkward to keep pretending we would make, so contact would gradually dry up. In the face of various practicalities, multiplied by years, friendship would dwindle away and, worst of all, we'd want to forget and let it happen, because it would be easier that way.

'Do you think I should move to Ireland?' he asked.

'Pippa seems lovely,' I said, truthfully.

We both glanced into the restaurant to see an animated Rhys twisting a balloon into a comedy shape to entertain a giggly Pippa.

'That's not an answer.'

'Only you know if you should, Ben.'

'This is true. I don't know.'

Say something meaningful, I thought. Tell him we're going to stay friends and distance doesn't matter.

'Out of all my friends back home I was the one who never stressed about anything,' Ben said. 'I thought it would all fall into place. I've changed my mind. Do nothing, and nothing happens. Life is about decisions. You either make them or they're made for you, but you can't avoid them.'

'You don't have to do anything you don't want to.'

His sadness was almost palpable, like moisture in the air before it rains. Although this was Manchester, it probably was about to rain anyway. With Ben in a low mood, I wished the evening could've been better.

'Sorry about Rhys, earlier. He goes too far sometimes,' I said.

There was a gap where I expected Ben to demur, and he didn't.

'Why do you take it?'

My stomach flipped, full as it was. 'What?'

Ben didn't criticise Rhys. If I ever recounted disagreements we'd had, Ben invariably saw Rhys's side. I feigned annoyance, but it was reassuring, considerate. The same way sensitive friends know not to join in when you're slagging off your family.

'You don't seem very equal, to me. You can be so confident, but that disappears when you're around him. It doesn't make sense.'

My embarrassment curdled into irritation. What the hell? It's my *birthday*.

'I give as good as I get – I don't pick fights in public, that's all. Look, you might be feeling down but don't take it out on us.'

The 'us' was deliberate. We stand united, even when Rhys is making a balloon poodle for another woman. Ben frowned and said nothing, staring determinedly ahead. I'd never seen him like this before. I wondered if I knew him quite as well as I thought I did.

Eventually he said: 'To be fair, it's pretty weird to have Oscar the Grouch in the garbage can on your crotch. What's the message? "Here's my junk"?'

The tension eased. I took the olive branch.

'It was Fozzie Bear.'

'Ah, Fozzie. He makes much more sense when wooing is in mind. I take it all back.'

'They say "Wocka Wocka Wocka" on the rear.'

'Hmm. All I can say is, if you were my girlfriend, I'd certainly be desperate for you to take them off,' Ben said, smiling that disarming smile at last, though this uncharacteristically flirtatious remark had already disarmed me.

'We'd better go back in,' I said, nervily.

As the warm smell of spices and twang of sitars hit us, a ragged chorus of 'Happy Birthday' started up. Two waiters appeared with a whipped-cream-topped sundae, a smattering of candles sticking out of it. As Ben returned to Pippa's side and everyone started clapping, I blew my candles out, took a small bow and returned to my seat.

Rhys got to his feet, holding his pint of Cobra. 'If I could say a few words—'

'Rhys,' I said. 'What ... um?'

'I know this is a bit formal for a twenty-first, but you all graduate soon so it might be the last time I go out to dinner with you. I wanted to say, not only is Rachel the greatest girl-friend in the world ...' He paused here for the obligatory ripple of sighs that went round the female members of the party. Greatest girlfriend? He thought that? '... Since I started visiting Rach in Manchester three years ago, you've made me feel that you're my friends too. I want to say how much I've appreciated it. I even hear that Ben went above and beyond once and smacked a bloke who deserved it, on my behalf.'

Pippa yelped with admiration and put an arm round him, a welcome correction to the lingering fear that the incident had worked an opposite effect on a previous girlfriend. Ben only looked startled.

'You're a great bloke. And there I was, thinking I hated students and southerners and southern students most of all. You should be my Kryptonite.'

Laughter. Rhys tipped his glass towards Ben and Ben raised his in return, still looking slightly stunned and blank.

'To my girl Rachel. Happy twenty-first and cheers.'

'Cheers,' I mumbled, and we raised our glasses and clinked, drank.

I felt an adoring-envious hum from the hive mind of the group: *isn't she lucky, isn't he nice, isn't this lovely.* I was lucky. Rhys grinned and winked at me as he sat down, the Fozzie Bear crime expunged from the record. I grinned back, grateful, amazed and a little overcome. If you clicked the shutter on life's great camera at that second, I was on the brink of it all and I had everything I wanted: devoted boy, great friends, future plans, garlic naan.

Yet something wasn't right. Someone who mattered was unhappy. As the discussion over the bill and where to go next began, I looked around the table at the contented faces, committing the tableau to memory. I forced myself to include Ben in the visual sweep. He was frowning, deeply, at the rubble of a near-untouched lamb bhuna.

I thought about the truism that you never know you'll miss things until they're gone. I missed Ben's optimism. Clearly, it had left university before he had.

47

I check my watch as I scurry into the cinema and find that, thanks to some kind of Greenwich Mean Time prank, the clock has leapt forward by ten minutes somewhere between Sackville Street and here. Another drawback of living in the city centre and walking everywhere is you don't get to blame the traffic.

Caroline taps me on the shoulder, folds her arms.

'Save it,' she says, as I embark on my excuse. 'You can pay for my pick'n'mix by way of apology.'

We've taken our Friday night date into town as Graeme's got off the red eye from somewhere this morning and needs to sleep. Caroline said she'd drink too much if we stayed in at mine and she has the in-laws arriving the next day.

She marches across the lobby of the Odeon, towering and lean in indigo denim, and starts trowelling penny dreadfuls into a paper bag. I get a gallon of sugar-free fizzy drink and we troop into the auditorium. It's barely a third full, the screen blank.

'Why hasn't it started?' I ask, adjusting my fingers on the damp weight of my cardboard bucket of liquid.

'Because I told you it started half an hour earlier than it does. Let's sit over there.'

I open my mouth to object and realise the end has justified the means. Following Caroline, we settle down into the seats.

'How did the date with Simon go, last week?' she says, folding a red liquorice bootlace into her mouth.

'Good. It was a laugh. Dinner, goodnight kiss. Nothing more.'

Caroline chews, with difficulty, given she's eating something more plastic than foodstuff.

'Great!' she says, gummed up. 'When are you seeing him again?'

'Um – not sure.'

'Is he playing hard to get?'

'I'm taking things slowly. I don't want to rush into anything.'

'Rushing into another nice dinner? Woah, nelly.'

'You know what I mean. I don't know how I feel yet.'

'But you like him?' she asks.

'*Yeeeees*. He's entertaining. If frightening and eccentric.'

'You need an eccentric. You're an eccentric.'

'No I'm not!'

'Of course you don't think you're an eccentric. No one does. Like no one thinks they have bad taste.'

'I have bad taste?'

'*No.*'

I take a noisy suck on my drink, swish the ice around with the straw.

'Olivia says Simon's asked Ben about you, seems very keen,' Caroline says.

The fact Caroline's used the very words I overheard from Olivia at the dinner party makes me think it's a direct quote. Olivia must know Caroline will tell me this, so I partially discount it as propaganda. What I'm much more interested in is that Caroline's seen Olivia. I feel an awful gut-spasm of insecurity.

'You've seen Olivia?'

'We went late-night shopping. She wanted a fascinator for a wedding so I took her along to Selfridges.'

'How did you even have her number, or vice versa?'

I know this is a Jealous Person's Question. *Which bus did you catch? Did you have a drink afterwards? Tell me girl, where did you sleep last night?*

'We exchanged numbers at the party at yours. Like I said, I think she's short of friends up here. We should do a girls' lunch with her.'

'Hmm,' I say, remembering the venom-tipped arrows she fired from her eyes during the wedding music conversation.

Pause.

'She says Ben's being a bit distant,' Caroline adds.

'Right.'

There's a pause that turns into a 'insert explanation here' pause.

'He's not talking to me about anything, if that's what you think.'

'You haven't seen him?'

I get the distinct impression Caroline already knows the answer.

'We went for a lunchtime sandwich. Simon was the main topic of conversation.'

'Olivia asked me about you two at university, what you were like.'

'Did she? What did you say?'

I cover my nerves by rummaging in her pick'n'mix bag, coming out with a white mouse filled with radioactive pink goo.

'That you were friends.'

'She already knew that.'

'I know. I wonder what's causing her to question it.'

I slip the mouse into my mouth. 'Are you telling me she was seriously concerned?'

'Nooo …' Caroline relents, fishing in the sweet bag. 'I think she was merely curious about Ben's past, like any partner.'

'There you are then.'

'They're seeing things very differently since they moved up here. It was meant to be for good and now they're divided on whether to stay. He's being very unsympathetic about her missing her family and wanting to plan a longer-term future down south, Olivia says.'

'Why move up, if she's only going to lobby to go back down again?' I say, warily.

'If they have kids, of course she's going to want to be around her mum.'

'Doesn't sound like Ben though. He's so easygoing.'

'Isn't anyone, with someone other than their other half?' Caroline looks distinctly irritable as she throws a handful of cola bottles to the back of her mouth.

'Hmm,' I say. I sense non-committal noises are my friend here, and having opinions, and expressing them, are not.

'By the way, when I asked Ivor and Mindy out tonight, they both said the same thing. "Not if you've asked Ivor-slash-Mindy",' Caroline says. 'They're still at each other's throats over Katya? I do think Mindy should think before she speaks sometimes.'

'Yeah, that row was rococo. Mindy went batshit insane. I thought it was hangover-rage but doesn't sound like they've made it up. Ivor says he's mortally insulted and is making threats he's not going to come out with us as a four again. We need to put them in the same room, let them slug this out. They're both as stubborn as each other.'

'I have a theory,' Caroline says.

'Which is?'

The lights dim and the adverts begin. An hour-and-a-half of slapstick hilarity later, I forget to repeat the question.

48

I can't convince Caroline to stay out for a drink – 'Gray's parents can spot a hangover at thirty paces, and the thought of putting up with them makes me want to drink a lot, a dangerous combination' – so she goes for her tram and I make my way back to the flat, wondering what I'm going to do with the rest of the weekend. Your life should get fuller as you get older, the canvas become more crowded, a Renoir café instead of one of Lowry's industrial wastelands. Instead here I am, thirties in progress, and I probably had more of an agenda when I was a teenager.

The deal when I was with Rhys was Fridays with the friends, Saturdays with him, after band practice. We'd go to a neighbourhood restaurant, or pub, or most often, spend an evening in with Rhys cooking something blokey with fresh chillies, both of us slamming down too many bottles of wine. It's not as if the loss of our coupledom has blown a hole in the middle of my social life, but being together is enough of an alibi for society about how you're spending your time. I'm considering booking a weekend on my own in Paris for the date of the would've-been wedding. City of Love … maybe not. I'll probably see a

276

kissing couple like the ones from that famous wartime photo and have to be fished out of the Seine.

My phone starts ringing and I hope Caroline's thought better of the abstinence and doubled back. I see the caller's Simon and before I can stop myself, I start smiling in anticipation.

He doesn't bother with hello.

'Do I have to send a barbershop quartet round to court singing "Take A Chance On Me", then?'

'Hello, Simon. What would you do that for?'

'To have a hope of a second date.'

'Hah! That would extinguish all hope forever.'

'There is some hope, then?'

'Never say never.'

'Friends, then? Can men and women be friends or does sex always get in the way, and other clichés?'

A gang of blokes with untucked shirts in every shade of the Ted Baker rainbow pass by, giving an obligatory 'you're a woman!' roar. I'm glad it prevents me from having to make an answer.

'Have I disturbed your book group?' Simon asks.

'I'm walking back from the cinema.'

'On your own? I'll have to talk to you until you arrive home safely, then.'

'Very kind.'

'Can I check, has Ben been sticking his oar in, by any chance?'

I swap the phone to my other ear. 'Eh?'

'I thought Ben might've talked to you about me. Maybe I'm wrong. If he has, though, I'd rather you judged me for yourself.'

'Why would it be a problem if I had talked to him?'

'He's quite protective when it comes to you, remember.'

'Ben's not going to, erm, brief against you though?' *Except that's what he has done, I guess.*

'When he asked how the date went, I felt like he was on the porch in his rocking chair, with a shotgun. You *sure* you two have never collided without clothes on?'

This throws me and annoys me in equal measure. Dig, dig, dig. Ben seems to be looming far too large in our conversations, and I can't work out why. I consider mentioning Simon's continuing stirring to Ben. Only that would mean us both admitting there's a pot to stir. No chance. *Always question people separately.* I can see why they're going to make him a partner.

'I'm sure, Simon, I think I'd remember. Why the obsession on this point when you've been given an answer?'

'I'm a lawyer, Rachel. We keep going until we get an answer we believe.'

'That's funny, the lawyers I know take the answer they think will fly with the duty sergeant.'

'You're very good at the art of deflection yourself, aren't you?'

'Why are our conversations more like a battle of wits?'

'You tell me.'

'Hah. Well ... I'm home now, thanks for the company.'

'Have a lovely evening,' Simon replies, smoothly.

I'm three streets away from my flat, but the talking had gone as far as I wanted it to.

49

I wake up groggy on Sunday morning, rays of feeble sunshine on my face. Rupa's billowing voile magenta curtains that pool on the floor are incredible in every respect apart from the 'keeping the light out' bit.

I spent a hectic Saturday night watching DVDs and drinking wine alone with no co-drinker to help hide how much I've had. I've slept so long my bones have gone floppy. I briefly imagine it's dawn because of the birdsong, before gradually realising it's the tweeting and chirruping of my phone, submerged under discarded clothing. I get out of bed, sweeping my hair out of my face and cursing whoever thinks it's acceptable to disturb me.

It stops as I pick it up. I check the missed call ID. Pete Gretton. What the hell does he want? I can't remember why we ever exchanged mobile numbers but I'm sure it was on the tacit understanding he'd never use it. I notice he's called four times already. No message. As I'm contemplating the size of the flea in the ear I'm going to give him tomorrow, he rings again. I answer it in a snap of annoyance.

'What, Pete?'

'Woken you up?' he asks, uninterestedly.

'Yes, you did.'

'Have you seen the Sundays?'

'Obviously not if I'm still in bed.' Oh yuck, I mentioned being in bed to Gretton.

'Go and get the *Mail*.'

'Why?'

'I'm not going to tell you. Go and get it and call me back.'

'Listen, this is shitting me up. What are you on about, Pete?'

'Go and get it.'

Heart beating a little faster than I've told it to, I pull a jumper over my pyjama top and cast around for some shoes.

I decide on the way to the newsagents that I won't read it in the shop so I can absorb whatever blow this is in privacy. The person in front of me buys scratch cards and Benson & Hedges and spends an excruciating amount of time counting out their change. I almost run back to the flat, slam the door behind me, throw the paper on the floor and kneel over it. The pages stick together as I scrabble through them. Some grotesque latest twist in the lipo story, perhaps.

I turn to a double page spread, headlined: *'The Armed Robber, His Wife, His Lawyer – Her Lover.'*

There are some long lens shots of Natalie Shale in a fedora, pulled low like a pop star exiting a hotel, arriving at a house that isn't her own. The door's held open by a thin, rakish figure that I recognise as Jonathan Grant, the twenty-something solic-itor who's often swaggered around court full of self-consequence, flirting with female QCs. There's Lucas Shale's arrest mugshot, and a photo of Natalie stood demurely behind Grant as he addresses a gaggle of press outside the court.

I can barely concentrate on the story long enough to do anything more than pick up the odd phrase. '*Secret trysts at Grant's £350,000 lovenest in Chorlton-cum-Hardy...*' '*In public, Natalie Shale was a devoted wife and mother, who protested her husband's innocence, in private, friends say she was "increasingly desperate" and Grant provided a shoulder to cry on...*' '*The 27-year-old is regarded as a rising star at his firm...*'

Then I spot it. The fact that makes something this bad a hundred times worse. The first name on the story is a well-known Mail staffer. But there's a second name in the byline.

I spend longer than is respectable for someone with no formally recognised learning difficulties wondering if there's another Zoe Clarke.

At a loss for what else to do, I call Gretton back.

'Seen it?' he says.

'Yes.'

'I feel for you, Woodford, I really do. What she's done to you is a fucking disgrace. I presume this is something you've been sitting on and she's nicked it?'

'No.' I feel feverish and dizzy. Gretton's not going to be the only one who thinks I'm involved. Not by a long way.

'How's she got this then?'

'I don't know.'

'Well, she's certainly stolen your thunder and shat in your trifle.'

'I can't believe it... I don't believe she's done this. It could ruin Lucas Shale's appeal... Jonathan Grant is going to lose his job...'

'To give Clarke her dues, she had some brass balls to negotiate herself a job off the back of it.'

'What?'

'I hear she called in last thing on Friday saying she wouldn't be back.'

'She left on Friday? Why did no one tell me?'

'I tried to call, you had your phone turned off. I left a message.'

The film, with Caroline. After I finished talking to Simon, I noticed I had a voicemail and decided it could wait. Gah.

'She didn't say why she was going,' Gretton continues, and I realise he's enjoying himself hugely. 'She told them she didn't have to work notice according to her contract, gave them the old back-to-front victory sign. I expect you were going to get the bad news on Monday.'

My phone starts beeping with another call. I have a good idea who it might be. I say goodbye to Gretton.

'Have you seen the *Mail*?' Ken asks.

'Yes,' I squeak. I wish I'd had longer to work out how to play this.

'Then the explanation you're about to give me better be nothing short of fucking miraculous.'

'I don't know what's going on.'

'Not going to fly!' he bellows so loudly I have to move the phone away from my ear. 'Not going to so much as taxi along the tarmac! Try again! You have the only interview with this woman and your friend in court takes this line to the nationals! You're seriously telling me this is a coincidence? Do you think I was delivered with this morning's milk? Is it my fucking *silver top* that's confused you?'

When Ken starts delving into his rhetorical repertoire, you know you're in deep shit.

'I had nothing to do with this at all, I swear.'

'Then how'd she get the story?'

'I don't know.'

'If you value being in employment, try harder.'

'There were rumours.' I'm desperately trying to think three steps ahead, with blood pounding in my ears and the phone slippery. 'Gossip round court a while back that Natalie and her lawyer seemed too close, and maybe that was why he was moved off the Shale case. That was all. Zoe took a chance and it paid off.'

'I'd say it paid off, yeah. Based on nothing more than a hunch, she went to the *Mail* and never once mentioned what she was doing to you?'

'I'm guessing she kept it from me because she knew it would ruin my story and I'd warn you.' *That's better, that's good, Rachel.* No one knows about the text. Oh God, what if Zoe's told people about what I did and Ken's merely seeing whether I own up? *Fuck, fuck.*

'Why didn't you take the rumour seriously?'

'None of us did.'

'Apart from the new girl?'

'Seems so,' I say, limply.

'Here's what I think. I think Natalie Shale confessed she was doing the lawyer in some girly confidential with you, and instead of bringing the story to us you gossiped to a junior reporter, who for all her backstabbing double-dealing has still behaved more like something resembling a fucking journalist.'

'Why would Natalie Shale tell me? That interview I did with her was all about getting good PR. She wouldn't want this in the papers.'

'And this has well and truly shafted our exclusive, hasn't it?'

'Yes,' I concede, miserably.

As the initial shock recedes ever so slightly and the truth of this turn of events sets in, a significant degree of humiliation takes its place. To think I trusted Zoe. To think she play-acted agreeing with my decision to drop it. Zoe was probably contemptuous of me all along, while I played the experienced old hand.

'I'm going to have to explain this to the editor and you've given me precisely fuck all to work with,' Ken continues. 'I've got plenty more to say to you and if you know what's good for you, you're going to find more to say to me. See me first thing tomorrow.' He hangs up on me. At least that's business as usual.

I pace the length of the flat trying to get a grip, think straight. OK, OK. Breathe in, then out. 'First thing tomorrow' – I'm probably going to keep my job. If Ken was going to sack me he'd want longer to confer with the editor and check it was feasible without risk of tribunal. But if Zoe tells anyone about the text, all bets are off.

Bottom line: what I did is illegal. I struggle to remember my long-ago training in journalism law. I think it goes, you're allowed to look at the top page of a document left near you, but turn the pages to look inside and it constitutes trespass. Picking up a phone and opening a text would certainly qualify, should Natalie want to sue. Loads of reporters have crossed similar lines, I know some of them have pocketed photos. The difference is being caught doing it. Ken Baggaley would have no qualms about hanging me out to dry, I'm sure, as punishment for the real crime of giving the story away.

Blurry with rage, I call Zoe, punching at her number in my address book, marching up and down as I wait for it to connect. *This number is no longer in service.* I recall she kept saying she was going to change it after the personal advert hassle, but hadn't got round to it – what fortunate timing to get organised this weekend.

Before I can talk myself out of it, I scroll through the numbers on my phone and call Simon.

'Yes?' he says. He sounds haughty and inscrutable, but then Simon generally does. He's with someone, perhaps.

'Simon, you need to see the *Mail*, the stuff about Natalie. I promise you that I had nothing to do with it—'

'I've seen it.'

'You have?' Oh dear God, thank you, he's seen it and it sounds like he's not lost it. 'Simon, I—'

'I've talked about work enough this weekend. Meet me in St Ann's Square, one p.m. tomorrow.'

'Sure, I'll be there.'

I hear the *beep-beep-beep* that indicates he's rung off. Definitely with someone from work, that's why he was so abrupt. I hope.

After some more pacing, hair-pulling and cursing, I call Caroline, which results in an unsatisfactory conversation taking place, at her end, on a golf course with Graeme's parents. It might be distraction due to the game, but she doesn't seem to understand why this makes me look – and feel – so bad.

'If nobody can prove you told Zoe about it, then it's on her, surely?'

'They suspect I did.'

'They can suspect all they want, Rach, they need proof and if you tough it out you'll survive, I'm sure.'

'What if I they already know and they're testing me to see if I own up?'

'Then you're screwed either way, so still say nothing.'

'I suppose.' This thought isn't remotely comforting.

I hear Graeme in the background, calling 'Cee, hurry up, we're turning to stone here.'

'I've got to go,' she says. 'Have you spoken to Simon?'

'For about three seconds. He wants to meet up tomorrow to talk about it.'

'Yes, *alright* Gray – I've got to go. Let me know how it goes with your boss.'

When my phone rings an hour later, I practically sprout wings and flap across the room to answer it, hoping Ben's going to give me the inside track on what's gone on. It's Rhys. For the first time since I left, the thought of him provokes annoyance rather than guilt. I haven't got the strength to be made to feel bad about anything else right now. I'm guessing this is more logistics and unfinished house clearance.

'Hi. What's up?'

'I wanted to talk to you,' Rhys says.

'OK, if it's a kicking, I should warn you you're going to have to take a ticket and wait till your number's called.'

'Jeez, what's up with you? You sound like you're on the brink.'

'I am.'

A pause while Rhys sounds like he's weighing things up. When he speaks again, his tone is the most conciliatory I've heard in a long time. 'Actually, I was ringing to see if you'd be up for going for a drink. I've got a gig in town next week, thought we could meet up first. Draw a line under a lot of aggro. Sounds like you're too busy though.'

'No,' I say, weary. 'No. I'd like to. I've got to sort a few work things out. Let me know, OK?'

'Sure. Er … take care of yourself.'

'I will. Thanks.'

After our goodbyes I find myself missing Rhys, badly. I miss how he would've sworn like a plasterer with a stubbed toe about this, given me a hug and made a crack about how I wouldn't need their poxy job if I fired out babies instead.

He sounded different. Less angry. That was the first exchange where it seemed like he might want to talk like civilised adults rather than entrenched opponents in a never-ending civil war. I'm happy to hear him sounding happier and I'd like very much to be friends, as much as that's realistic. Only I feel like a fraud at the arrangement, as 'some time next week', when I've weathered the storm tomorrow, only exists as some fantasy CS-Lewis-like land right now, where I may have the legs of a magical goat.

50

I attempt to stride purposefully through the early morning buzz of the open-plan office, internally repeating the mantra 'no one's bothered, yesterday's news'. Only 'yesterday's news' doesn't count when it broke on a Sunday and today is Monday, the first opportunity to discuss it, and it's this juicy.

Everyone looks over, and I could swear an expectant hush falls as I approach Ken, who's busy hectoring a colleague on news desk. I stand and wait, before Vicky nods her head at me and he turns, fixing me with a cockatrice stare.

He heaves himself out of the swivel chair and stalks over to his office as I slope behind him, feeling multiple pairs of eyes bore into my back as I go.

'Shut the door,' he says, dropping into the chair behind his desk. I push it closed and stay standing.

'I'm going to allow for having caught you on the hop yesterday. Today, I'd like the truth.'

I open my mouth to reply, and Ken cuts me off: 'And I strongly advise you think before you speak, if you don't want to see out your journalistic career spellchecking the letters page of Oxfordshire's *Banbury Cake*.'

I teeter on a ledge. On the edge of a ledge. Caroline's words about holding fast ring in my ears. I lick dry lips.

'Natalie Shale never discussed any affair with me when I interviewed her. The name of that solicitor never even came up and he wasn't my contact. Zoe's worked off her own back and messed my story up. That's all I know and I can't defend or explain something I knew nothing about, even if it looks dodgy because Zoe and I worked together and I interviewed Natalie.'

I expect Ken to start screaming and shouting. Instead he simply nods.

'That's no more than I expected, unfortunately.'

'It's the truth.'

'Is it?'

'Yes.'

'All right, let me give you some home truths. There are two reasons you've still got a job, Rachel Woodford. One, I can't sack you without proof you're lying. Believe me, I've looked into it, because I can't stand liars, or reporters who don't have any loyalty to their paper, and you qualify on both fronts from what I can tell. Should I get any proof, things will change. Two, I haven't got anyone to stick in court in your place. For now. In the meantime, you can send me a list at the end of every week telling me what stories you're working on, and that includes ones you can't stand up. So if there's a fanciful rumour doing the rounds that a defendant's wife is shagging her husband's lawyer, I strongly advise you include it. I'll decide what's worth pursuing. And if I see a line like that turn up elsewhere and someone *we have in court full time hasn't fucking brought it to us*, I'll want to know what we're paying you for.'

Ken pauses to let the slug-sized bulging vein in his neck shrink slightly.

'You're going to go back to Shale and ask for an interview about the latest twist in the saga, and use all your persuasive powers, knowing that you're not likely to be getting entered for any awards here for a good long time, or so much as invited to the Christmas party, without doing some mop and bucket work on this massive fucking mess. Do you understand me?'

'Yes.'

'Then get out of my sight.'

I spin round and open the door to face a newsroom that lip-read every word as it was enunciated clearly on the other side of a glass partition. Once they've ascertained I'm not crying, they look away again and pretend not to notice me. As unpleasant as being put on school report is, that could've been worse. Asking to interview Natalie is futile, Ken knows that and he knows I can't say so. I have about as much chance of success as I would in winning the Burghley Horse Trials on a Shopmobility scooter. I will pretend I tried when everything has calmed down. Or, I'll ask Simon.

As I'm about to win my freedom, Vicky beckons me over: 'Rachel!'

I have less than no desire to talk to her but I can't afford to make any more enemies.

'What did Ken say?' she says, casting a glance to make sure he hasn't emerged from his office.

'He's not pleased,' I say, flatly. 'He's not the only one.'

'I told him Zoe Clarke might do something like this,' she says.

Of course you did, you Zara-clad Nostradamus. 'Did you?'

'Yeah. There was all that hassle where she told some weekly paper she was a senior, when she hadn't even done her NCTJ. They sent us a letter about her and she denied it.' I open my mouth to ask more, but the story's pretty much all there, and Vicky's on a roll. 'And then there was what she did to you over that cosmetic surgery thing.'

'What?'

'That lipo case. She covered the verdict for you, didn't she? She sent it through with her name on it. I saw it and said to Ken "how's she written something this size in an hour?" and we realised she'd put her name on your backgrounder. He gave her a rollocking and took her name off it completely. Didn't you know?'

'No.'

'No, I suppose not, why would you? Not like she was going to tell you.'

'I wish you'd told me,' I say, stiffly. 'I would've been more on my guard around her.'

'Oh, yeah . . . well, like I said, Ken sorted it. I didn't want to bitch.'

I stifle a mirthless laugh at this. For a crazy moment I think Vicky's going to say something authentically supportive, then she checks the time on Sky News and says, 'Doesn't that drugs five-hander start this morning?'

Meaning: you can't afford to drop even one more ball.

Don't I know it.

She turns away to her screen, to indicate my audience is over.

'Yeah, I'm on my way,' I say, to her back.

I had forgotten about it, and break into an undignified run once I'm out of sight of the office.

51

After a morning of taking notes in shorthand so shaky and frac-
tured it looks as if I'm recovering from a stroke, I dodge Gretton
and edge my way out of the court and into the fresh air. I head
towards St Ann's Square with my stomach on spin cycle.

Every step I take, my apprehension mounts. Now Simon's
at the top of my in-tray, as it were, I have more time to consider
his feelings, and my conclusions aren't good. Belatedly, I'm
remembering how wary he was of journalists, how badly this
must have blown up in his face as well as mine. I start to wonder
whether the urbane, unruffled Simon persona will remain intact,
as I'd hoped. I got scant clues from our exchange on the phone.

I have my answer as soon as I spot Simon pacing up and
down by the fountain, craning to see me in the crowd. His
homicidal intentions are plain.

'Hi.' My attempt at a confident tone quavers and Simon
almost bares his teeth at me. It's only then I see Ben next to
him, frowning. This is too much. In fact, Simon's more than
enough by himself. I can't deal with Ben lambasting me as well.
I couldn't deal with that on its own.

'Are you here to hold his coat?' I blurt.

'I'm here to make sure he doesn't go over the top,' Ben says, looking wounded. 'How are you?'

I'm so surprised at him asking the question that's been on the tip of nobody's tongue, I don't know what to say.

'Is it true that one of the people involved in the *Mail* story is a colleague of yours in court?' Simon says.

'Yes. Zoe. Was a colleague, she's at the *Mail* now.'

'What happened?'

'I don't know, Simon. Honestly, I'm as shocked as you are.'

'That's the best you can do? What's that, your Out of Office Autodenial? Rachel's taken annual leave of her senses?'

I try to look like I'm coping. Panic rises up through my chest and throat.

'It's not an excuse, it's the truth. This has ruined our interview…'

'Oh, *you reckon*?'

'…Why would I destroy my own story?'

'A bluff. You probably gave her the tip-off and you're splitting the money while you keep your job here and your hands clean. How am I doing, eh? Bit more like it?'

An elderly couple sitting nearby eating messy egg mayonnaise sandwiches start listening in.

'I wouldn't do that,' I say. 'Does this seem anything like a plan going as planned to you? How brazen do you think I am?'

'You don't want me to answer that. How did your colleague know about this affair?'

I squirm.

'I don't know.' Pause. 'Did you know about it?'

293

Simon's face twists. 'That's irrelevant.'

'If it was a rumour, lots of people could've passed it to Zoe.'

'Do you honestly think I'm a big enough spazz to believe you had nothing to do with this?'

I appeal for mercy, knowing it's pointless. 'Simon, I'm as upset as you are and I'm in a heap of shit at work.'

'*You're* in shit?!'

Egg sandwich couple are dropping cress all over themselves, eyes wide. Ben shushes Simon, which is like trying to put out a house fire with handfuls of mist.

'…Jonathan Grant has been suspended. I'm being blamed for the bright idea of getting the media involved and, guess what, I'm not going to be made partner any time soon. The appeal could be fucked. Natalie Shale and her kids are in hiding because of the scumbags camped on her drive. Tell me, who gives a shit what kind of day you're having?'

'This looks terrible, I can see that, but I can't control what my colleagues do.'

'I had doubts about you from the start. Ben vouched for you,' he casts an accusing look at Ben, 'but I should've trusted my instincts.'

If Simon's pulling no punches, I have to stand up for myself. I look from him to Ben and back.

'Such misgivings that you asked me out on a date?'

Simon looks as if he wants to grab me by the throat. 'And what was that about on your side, I wonder? It was research, mentioning Jonathan to see if I'd bite. Then it was job done, all batting eyelashes and "I'm not over my fiancé…"'

'Simon, come on,' Ben interjects, embarrassed on my behalf.

'Strange that when I called you on the Friday, when the

story was in the bag, you couldn't get me off the phone fast enough,' Simon continues.

'What do you mean? We talked.'

'For a few minutes, before you said you were home.'

'Yes.'

'Were you?'

'Yes.'

'I called your landline and let it ring for a minute to say goodnight and check you got in OK. Thought you'd appreciate the gesture. You never answered.'

Simon's nostrils flare, he's triumphant.

'Oh my God, what is this?' I splutter. 'The only reason I mentioned Jonathan was because he's the showy lawyer everyone fancies. It was a coincidence. We talked about loads of people from work that night. And the only reason I remember mentioning him at all is because you went funny. And I said I was home because I was nearly at my block of flats. I hadn't got the lift and literally put my key in the door and I had no idea you'd care either way.'

'Billy Bullshit. I thought you had some kind of ulterior motive in getting involved with me and, again, I ignored my instincts. Good to see you prove that you can tell a barefaced lie when it's expedient, though.'

I make a 'I give up' gesture. 'I don't know what you want from me or what I can say.'

My righteous exasperation is entirely play-acting. If Natalie and Jonathan figure out I was there when he sent that text she never received, this is all over. Job, home, professional respect … friendship with Ben. And it'd remove the very small margin of doubt that's stopping Simon tearing me limb from limb. I'm practically shaking.

'What I want is the truth about what you've done, but that's too much to ask from you, isn't it?'

I make a silent pact that at some point I'm going to tell Ben, at least, the truth about this.

'I swear I had nothing to do with Zoe selling this story.'

'Nothing to do with her selling it, or nothing to do with it?'

Lawyers. I hesitate.

'Nothing to do with it whatsoever.'

'Alright, she's answered you,' Ben says. 'Let's call a truce and get back to the office.'

'Stay out of this,' he barks, rudely.

'No,' Ben says, and I watch two men fighting over me in a way that's considerably less enjoyable than it's made to appear onscreen. 'Stop using her as a punch bag. It's not her fault this woman and Jon got involved, and it's not her fault someone's written about it.'

'What is it with you two?' Simon says, looking from Ben to me, feigning amazement. 'Did she keep the negatives after you broke up, or what?'

Ben ignores this. 'I know Rachel well enough to know she wouldn't stitch you up. If she'd turned you over and didn't give a shit she wouldn't be here right now, would she?'

'Maybe it's for your benefit?' Simon says, with a very unpleasant curl of the lip.

'When she didn't know I'd be here?' Ben says. *Thank you, Ben.* 'When you've calmed down you might realise she doesn't deserve this much abuse.'

The attack-dog glint in Simon's eyes finally starts to fade. I allow myself to breathe and Simon senses this, drawing himself up to his full height and going in for the kill.

'You're a liar. A despicable, miserable, weak little liar who's sold everyone out and doesn't even have the guts to admit it.'

'Jesus, enough!' Ben cries.

Unperturbed, Simon continues: 'I'd think more of you if you stood here and said you'd done it and you didn't care. If I ever see you again it will be a lifetime too soon.'

My shoulders drop, and I know now I couldn't make many intelligible noises even if I wanted to. I fight the liquid back from my eyes, concentrate on keeping my breathing steady, clench my jaw.

'OK,' Ben says, possibly seeing this imminent loss of control and stepping between us. 'Enough, Simon.'

When he's satisfied Simon's verbal onslaught is at an end, he steps out of the way again.

'Come on.' He puts a hand on Simon's arm. 'Let's go.'

Simon shakes him off.

I make a last attempt to steady my voice and gasp out: 'Tell me if there's anything I can do to help put this right…'

'Are you joking?' Simon spits. 'Because it's about as funny as being told the cancer's spread to the bones.'

'No.'

'You're actually trying to make *more* for yourself out of this?'

'That's not what I—'

Simon looks towards Ben. 'Whatever she's got on you, I'd cut her loose.'

He strides off. I definitely can't speak. I blink at Ben. He stares back.

'He's taken this very personally,' Ben says. 'As you might've picked up.'

'Ben, this has been a total nightmare, I never meant…' I try to swallow what's rising up. My next attempt at speech breaks into speaking-sobbing; it could also be described as a kind of adenoidal howling. 'I never knew this was going to happen. I worked with Zoe and she was my friend, I never thought she'd do something like this...'

Ben glances left and right, as if we're in the middle of a drugs deal, and to my total surprise gathers me into a hug. As unexpected as it is, it's also incredibly welcome, not least as it stops St Ann's Square's curious population staring at me. Foremost among them are egg and cress couple, who think they've stumbled on some modern guerilla street theatre, a kind of am-dram 'pop up'. And I'd rather Ben hugged me than looked at me, too; I'm not doing soft-focus Julia-Roberts-esque 'startled nymph' crying.

'I know you didn't mean this to happen,' he says, shushing me.

'You're the only one who does,' I say snottily, into the thick material of his coat.

'Don't take Simon's biblical fury too seriously. He's had a torrid weekend. Journalists called Natalie on Saturday to see if she wanted to "put her side of it" and she completely lost it, rang Simon screaming and crying, a neighbour had to take the kids...'

Bridie, I think. It would've been nice hippy-dippy Bridie with the runaway cat. I feel like utter shit.

'Did he call you?' I ask, looking up. I don't know why I want to know.

'He did, actually. I assured him you wouldn't have had anything to do with it. I was forbidden to call you. I thought it was easier if we didn't talk so he couldn't catch us out on it. He doesn't need more fuel for his conspiracy theories. How bad's it been at work?'

'As bad as it can be without being sacked.'

I wipe at my face with my coat sleeve and my head drops onto Ben's shoulder again. He puts his hand on the back of my head.

'Hush, come on, it'll be forgotten soon enough...'

He moves his hand a fraction and I think he's moving it away. No. Wait. He's − stroking my hair? I go tense, hold my breath. Perhaps he feels this as, simultaneously, we break apart.

'Sorry, sorry, I'm such a mess,' I mumble, scouring at my running mascara again with the hem of my sleeve.

'I'm sorry, Rachel. Here I was thinking I was being helpful putting you and Simon in touch,' Ben says, a notch louder than necessary, returning us to more formality.

'You were!' I protest. 'I'm the one who should apologise.'

'I'd suggest a stiff drink,' Ben says. 'But I don't think being seen going to the pub with you today would be − erm − politically astute. You understand?'

I nod, manage a weak smile.

'Tomorrow's chip paper. Today's, in fact. It's at the bottom of litter trays already. Chin up.'

I nod again.

'You were let down by someone you trusted. Happens to us all,' he says.

52

We weren't yet graduates, but the small matter of the graduation ball loomed. The Chem Soc one in the faded grandeur of the Palace Hotel had emerged as the front-runner and we'd bought tickets en masse. Taking a date, if you had one, seemed more important than usual and, after his effusive words at my twenty-first, I'd asked Rhys to come.

His hired penguin suit was hanging on my wardrobe door in its polythene dry cleaner's shroud, next to my bell-skirted prom dress. I'd reminded him constantly as the ball drew nearer. Nevertheless, the call I'd somehow expected came the day before. I was in splendid isolation, Caroline and Mindy each having gone home to drop off the first wave of their possessions, Ivor back in halls for his third year, Derek thankfully apparently attending to sociopathic business elsewhere.

'Rach. That thing, the party—'

'My graduation ball?'

'Yeah. I can't go. We've got a gig and I've got to do it.'

'Rhys!' I cried. 'When was that booked?'

'Sorry, babe. It's a last-minute thing. I can't duck out, Drugs Ed would have my bollocks.'

I'd lost a competition with Drugs Ed. Unless it was a competition to see who could take the most drugs, this was a poor state of affairs.

'This is really important to me. You promised!'

'Ah come on, there'll be other parties.'

His insistence on dismissing it as a 'party' riled me. This was a landmark, the last hurrah of studenthood, when I said goodbye to Manchester and the life and friends I'd made here.

In truth, things had already been slipping, slightly. Ben's words at my twenty-first had played on my mind too. Doubt had crept in and been allowed to stay. Rhys's eagerness to run my life started to feel less like support, more like control. His superior knowledge on every subject had become less impressive and more supercilious. His avowed loathing of 'student nob heads' increasingly kept him at home at weekends, though I'd pointed out he was coming to Manchester for my company, not the entire undergraduate population's.

When I went to Sheffield instead, I landed among his band mates in the same old pub, wondering why I'd not noticed before that they never took an interest in anything I had to say. And as wonderful as the twenty-first speech was, something about it had niggled me. I'd eventually identified it as the 'greatest girlfriend' terminology. He liked to tell me his make of shoes and guitar were the greatest in the world too. I was a treasured Rhys possession, evidence of his taste, with about as much of a valued opinion as the Chucks and the Les Paul. Rhys had assumed, without me ever recollecting making a decision, we were moving in together after I left university. *Life is about decisions*, I thought. Mine were being made for me.

I'd known Rhys would pull out of the ball because the only reason to do it was to please me. There was no stake in it now: I was coming home, coming back to him. It was a time of endings and new beginnings. I'd started to think treacherous, revolutionary thoughts.

'Do you know how much trouble I've gone to? I spent a bomb at Moss Bros.'

'I'll pay you back.'

'It's not about the money, is it?'

'What is it about then?'

'I want you there.'

'Yeah, well. I want doesn't always get, Princess Rachel.'

'Great, thanks. This should come before the band. There'll be other gigs, I only get one grad ball.'

'Oh, come on. There's more to life than your little world, you know. It's not as if you'd notice whether I was there or not, after the first half hour of Nasty Spew-mantes.'

'Why do you always make anything that matters to me sound stupid?'

'I might've known I couldn't get out of this without a huge barney.'

'Get out of this?'

Rhys sighed. 'Anyway. When you're back I've got a flat for us to go and see in Crookes.'

'I never said I wanted to get a flat together.'

'Eh? Didn't you?'

'You never *asked*. You take me for granted. I feel like I'm a junior partner, or an apprentice. Not an equal.'

'Well, act more mature and then I'll treat you that way, babe.'

I seethed. I boiled. I said: 'Do you know what, Rhys? I think it's best if we say we've run our course.'

A bewildered silence.

'You're binning me because I won't come to this party?'

'It's not a bloody party, it's my graduation ball. I'm "binning" you because I'm not a teenager any more and I'm not going to be steamrollered.'

'You really want to finish?'

'Yes.'

Rhys had been playing it cool in this confrontation and clearly didn't see any reason to change tack. 'Seems an overreaction.'

'It's how I feel.'

'Right then. That's that then.'

Another silence.

'Bye, Rhys!' I slapped the receiver down.

After a moment's hesitation I dialled another number on the landlord's payphone, listening to the heavy chink as my 50p fell into the pirate's booty pile of silver inside. We tried to chisel it open one night when we were drunk, with no success.

'Ben, what's happening? Want to go and get hammered?'

'I've said I'll play pool with the house-mates. Wanna come?'

'I'd be crap company tonight.'

'Thanks for asking me out, then!'

I started laughing. 'I meant, I was thinking of a quiet one-to-one.'

'Sod pool then, quiet sounds good.'

'I don't want to ruin a house night out.'

'Nah, we're going to the ball tomorrow. We'll see plenty of each other there.'

'OK then. The Woodstock? For old times' sake?'

'Can you have old times at twenty-one?' Ben asked, sounding pleased.

I got to The Woodstock first, bought a round and found a picnic table in the beer garden. I started drinking too quickly in the muggy heat, enjoying the feel of the grass tickling my bare legs in my summer dress and sandals. I knew the worst way to deal with breaking up with Rhys was by waking up to the reality of it tomorrow with a blinding hangover, but that absolutely wasn't going to stop me for a second.

I wondered what Ben was going to say. I didn't want him to declare open season, to say *I told you so*, to reveal he'd thought it needed doing for the last three years. Mind you, I didn't want him to exclaim *you idiot* either. In fact, I didn't know what I wanted him to say. He appeared on the other side of the lawn, holding another two drinks, grinning broadly when he saw we'd doubled up. I smiled back. In Ben's company, I was going to feel fine. This wasn't what you were supposed to do when you'd dumped your long-term boyfriend, was it? Where was the chocolate binge, the recriminations, Gloria Gaynor? It was as if without the echo chamber of my female friends around, I was free to invent new protocol.

'Shall we park the finals talk? Is that what's making you anti-social?' Ben asked, after the greeting. 'If so, you've got nothing to worry about. You're the essay queen.'

Princess Rachel crowned as essay queen. I wasn't sure I liked the way the men in my life saw me.

'Mmm...' I lifted and dropped my shoulders to indicate *maybe*, not yet able to get the words out.

Ben rubbed the condensation off his pint glass with his index finger. I fiddled with the stem of my wine glass, enjoying the feeling of the first half glass-full hitting home.

'How's Pippa?'

'Not sure. We split up.'

I was taken aback. I thought Pippa was going to be the game changer.

'Oh, God. Sorry to hear that. How come?'

'When I really thought about it, I knew I wasn't going to be flying back and forth to Ireland when I got back from my trip. Seemed fairer to finish it.'

'How did she take it?'

Ben shook his head. 'Not brilliantly. Still. Better done now rather than later.'

'I'm sorry. You two were good together.'

Wow. He'd not taken the option on Pippa. She was the kind of uni-pull most boys parade around their home town like the Champion's League Cup. For a second, my imagination spooled forward to the Cleopatra-esque, peerless goddess who'd see Ben finally commit.

'Still – now you're clear to hit on Polly-Annas from Richmond-upon-Thames,' I added.

'Who?'

'Rich girl "gappers" at Thailand's Full Moon parties, discovering a world beyond materialism while spending daddy's dollars.'

'Ah. Them.' Ben shrugged and put a hand on the back of his head.

'So we're both enjoying the single life,' I said.

'I wouldn't say enjoying, especially.'

I paused to let the penny drop.

'Did you say "we"?'

'Yep. I finished with Rhys.'

Ben looked as if he was waiting for me to say *Aha, not really, had you fooled*. He stared in astonishment, mouth open. 'You did? When?'

'On the phone, earlier. He piked out of the graduation ball for no good reason. We've been arguing a lot lately. I lost it and told him it was over. In a shouty sort of way.'

I knew why I exaggerated. I wanted to make the point I could stick up for myself.

'For good?'

'Pretty much.'

'I'm sorry,' Ben said, eyes downcast.

'No worries,' I said.

I dodged further questions by swerving into superficial chatter. I looked and sounded like myself. Inside I was wondering who I was now I wasn't Rhys's Rachel. *Rhys and Rachel, Rachel and Rhys*. Ben looked like his mind was ticking over too, his view of me undergoing some adjustment. I wasn't sure if I was imagining we held each other's gaze for longer, in the gaps between speech, or if it was the potent combination of dehydration, nostalgia and pub quality Pinot Grigio.

'If I'm single I'll have more time to visit friends at the other end of the country,' I said, halfway through the evening, once the sun had gone down and the lamps had gone on.

'Yeah, that once-a-year get together's going to be a *blast*,' Ben said, with a sour edge.

'Ow. We might manage more than one,' I said, nudging him.

'Two?'

'Why so negative?'

'Not the same as this though, is it?'

'Nothing will be. University's like this little world, a bubble of time separate from everything before and everything after.'

53

Ben walked me home that night through quiet, suburban tree-lined streets, the sodium orange glow of the streetlights buried among their leaves. The air still and thick, even late at night, as if we were in the Med. It was as though Manchester itself was laying on a farewell party for us and had ordered in special weather. We reached my front gate.

'Urgh, I don't want to go in,' I whispered to Ben. 'I don't know whether creepy Derek's left or not. He's locked his door. He'll probably start bumping around and growling at three a.m.'

'You're on your own? The girls have gone?'

'They're only coming back for the ball tomorrow.'

We looked at the house. An interior light was switched off somewhere and it plunged into darkness.

'Brrr,' I said to Ben.

'If you're that bothered about Derek, I can crash here,' Ben said.

'Yeah?'

'Yeah. Have you got sofa cushions, a spare blanket?'

'I've got a sleeping bag, somewhere.'

'I'll kip on your floor, then.'

'You would? Really?'

'As long as you don't snore.'

'Great!'

Ben pretended to be grudging and I grinned like a fool. The house looked strange, a husk stripped bare of our décor and emptied of Mindy's multi-coloured swap shop heap of shoes in the hallway. It was our End Times. Though Derek would probably live on, like the cockroach after a nuclear war.

'I think I have a bottle of Pernod with a gummy screw-top if you want a nightcap?' I said.

'Pernod? I'm good, thanks. Ball tomorrow. Probably shouldn't encourage a filthy hangover.'

'Agreed.'

I got ready for bed in the upstairs bathroom, changing into my animal pyjamas and brushing my teeth. I contemplated my nightie but it was far too short and anyway, I consoled myself, Ben had seen me in these horrors before. I got a wave of self-loathing at being clad in something so silly, sharing my bedroom with someone so good-looking. Child's mittens, cartoon pants, toddler PJs. *If you were my girlfriend, I'd be desperate for you to take them off.* I cringed, rinsed, spat.

On my return to the bedroom, I crossed my arms and hurtled towards the covers, eager not to be seen. Ben had arranged a makeshift bunk-down. Increasingly, the wine ebbing away, the situation felt more intimate than I'd anticipated.

'Can I borrow something to sleep in?'

I swerved off course and rummaged in my chest of drawers. I could only come up with a size XL grey t-shirt, creased from the cardboard insert, with a real ale festival advertised across its not inconsiderable width. I shook it out to its full proportions.

'I won this in a pub quiz and haven't got round to throwing it away.'

'What did the losers get?'

'OK, sleep in your clothes then.'

I threw it at him. He caught it.

'No, no, beggars can't be choosers. They have to be' – he studied the back of the shirt – 'hog wild for the hops.'

I switched the main light off. The room was lit by my rocket-shaped red lava lamp.

'You gonna leave that on?' Ben asked.

'Usually, is that OK?'

'Sure. *Rooxxxaannnnee...*'

I giggled, watched the globules of scarlet goo lazily separating, colliding and bouncing in the Martian water.

'Shut your eyes then, I'm not changed.'

I obliged, slapping a pillow over my eyes so there could be no doubt I had, and heard the soft noises of clothes dropping on the carpet, the clink of a buckle, the sound of him pulling the t-shirt over his head. It was proof of our intensely platonic nature we could do this. I had a strong tingly impulse to look because, you know, it was only human.

'Are you decent?'

I crawled across the bed and looked down. Ben was cocooned up to the armpits in navy blue nylon.

'How is it?' I asked.

'Like lying on the floor, Ron.' He shifted around.

'We can swap if you want.'

'No need.'

I wriggled over so I was lying on the edge of the bed, as

near to him as possible.

'What a weird day,' I sighed. 'I'm single. Best get used to it.'

'Mmm.'

Pause. 'Hey, d'you know, I'm absolutely terrified about being single again.'

I expected an avalanche of *you'll be fine* platitudes and they didn't come.

'You're so good at falling in and out of relationships. And then look at me,' I said.

Still nothing from Ben.

'I mean, you were prepared to let Pippa go,' I blundered on.

'What does that mean?'

'Nothing, only, Pippa's beautiful and bright and has that amazing Irish accent going for her, and she still got dumped. What are the chances of anyone persisting with me?'

Ben said, noticeably coldly: 'I'm not following your logic, sorry. Different woman has different situation shock?'

'She's amazing. I'm less amazing. I'm hardly going to fare any better.'

'What are you on about?'

'And,' I had a sense this was a very stupid thing to say and I'd regret it in sobriety, but the words were already tumbling out of my mouth, 'back when we did that kiss in the Och Aye The No pub, you said yourself it was like snogging a sister. Shit. I'm going to be useless.'

A creaking silence ensued. What did I want or expect Ben to say? I knew I was being unfair and embarrassing us both. Nevertheless I suddenly craved the ego boost of a demonstrably attractive person of the opposite sex confirming I wasn't at least revolting.

'Stop pushing,' he said, flatly.

'What?'

'Stop pushing me and fishing for compliments.'

'I'm not!' *I wasn't. Was I? Oh. Yes, I was.*

Another funny pause.

'There's no need for the low self-esteem schtick.'

'Easy for you to say.'

'Why?' Ben had an edge to his voice. I guessed I must've said something to particularly offend to him in all of this, I couldn't put my finger on quite what it was. Perhaps it wasn't very tactful of me to bring up Pippa when it was still raw.

'You have naturally high self-esteem. The same way some people have good teeth or congenitally raised cholesterol.'

Ben sighed, exasperated.

'I don't understand you, sometimes. But I don't think you understand me ever.'

I wondered why we were talking at cross purposes and when we were going to chat easily about how I would be fine as a single girl.

'I'm being dumb,' I said, and Ben grunted in assent. 'But if you do have any hunting tips that I could apply to northern boys and enjoy the same success you've had with southern girls, I'd appreciate them.'

'I'm not gonna do that.'

'Why not? Selfish! From the Don Juan of Withington.'

'What do you mean by that? I have no standards? I'm a slag?'

'No! You're just very popular with the laydeez. Hey, if you won't help me score – fine.'

'Ron, you're a girl. You won't have any trouble.'

'Yeah,' I sighed. 'It's meeting the good 'uns, isn't it.'

'You'll be fine,' he said, again.

'If I *do* do any wildly off-putting stuff to a potential mate, as my best male friend, I'm counting on you to tell me.'

'Do you actually want me to answer these questions? If you keep asking me them, I will. Final warning.'

'Which questions?'

'Questions about that kiss, my ex-girlfriend and you being on the pull.'

'Yeah, I guess I did ask those questions,' I said, suddenly all bold and casual and more than a little bit frightened. His irritation made me wonder if he was about to say I'd effectively tasked him with being the one to tell me I ponged like a rabbit hutch.

A very noisy silence.

'Right, I'm sorry if this makes you uncomfortable. There's only so much I can take,' Ben said. 'Did I say kissing you was like kissing a sister? Yes I did, because we were being goaded into getting off with each other. Was it like kissing a sister? No, it was bloody amazing, like kissing someone you fancy very very badly usually is ...'

I physically started at this, a whole body twitch, my heart going at a woodpecker-on-speed bpm. Did he say fancy? No – he couldn't have. I'd misheard.

'...Was Pippa nice? Yes, she was, she wasn't the problem. You were the problem. I split up with her for the same reason I have with everyone in the last three years. Men who are hopelessly hung up on someone else tend to make crap boyfriends ...'

I was in a cold sweat. 'I couldn't believe what I was hearing' is usually hyperbole, yet here it was entirely apt. My ears took delivery but my brain wouldn't sign for the parcel. I kept thinking he'd drop a hot girl name in like Beth or Freya and

I'd go 'Ohhhh I thought,' and then have to kill myself when he realised what I'd thought.

'...Will you be OK finding someone else? You're the cleverest, funniest, nicest, most beautiful, if occasionally most infuriating, woman I've ever met, so, yes, I'm sure you'll have tons of blokes after you. But given I'm in love with you, the thought of you with anyone else makes me want to kill, so forgive me for not encouraging you with handy hints and tips on how to take men home who *aren't me*.'

My chest rose and fell with shock. I couldn't speak. And if I had been able to speak, I wouldn't have known what to say. *Love.* He said love.

'What was the last one? "Do you have any off-putting habits?" Being with someone else was the only one that bothered me. However, it at least allowed me the fantasy that was why you weren't with me. Now that's gone too. There. We're done.'

My fingers were grasping the bed as if the furniture was suddenly tilting at an angle.

Ben added: 'I'm sorry if you now feel massively weird. Tell me if you'd rather I went. I'd understand.'

'It's OK,' I said in a strangled voice.

Pause.

'Fuck, great timing, Ben, staying in her bedroom,' he said, with a rueful, humourless laugh. 'And look, you don't have to break it to me that you don't see me that way. I know you don't, trust me. This is my problem. We'll just have one helluva awkward cup of tea in the morning and say our farewells.'

Tomorrow morning. I was having trouble imagining a world beyond this bedroom, one that would keep turning and bring daylight and other days. And *farewells*?

'Did you really not know?' he asked.

'Nope,' I squeaked.

'Oh God. I always thought you had some clue, even if you didn't know how much.'

He tailed off, waited for more, and when I didn't say anything, continued: 'Christ, please at least say "Ewww, gross". The silence is killing me.'

'It's not gross,' I said, trying to find words in the psychological tumult.

Where were the words I needed? Ben's words had made me to face up to feelings I'd been ignoring, twisting out of shape and denying for the last three years. It was like not giving a plant enough light to grow properly, only very rarely watering it, but the seed in the soil still being there.

He felt and thought those incredible things about me? 'Likewise' 'Why' or 'Good God Merciful Jesus Hooray!' didn't do the moment justice.

Uncharacteristically, I made a snap decision. I pulled my voluminous pyjama top off over my head. I wriggled the trousers down, kicking them off my feet with a swimmer's paddling motion. I balled up the body-heat-warm nest of fabric and threw it out of the bed. I thought this would be enough to make my intentions clear, but Ben didn't react at all.

'Ben.'

'Yeah?'

'Do you want to get into bed?'

'Floor's not that bad, thanks. And also – no.'

'No. *Into* bed. *With* me.' Then I added, like the silver-tongued, erotic adventuress of the age: 'I took my pyjamas off.'

A stunned pause.

'…Are you sure?' he said, quietly, into the crimson gloom.

'Very sure.'

This was when the scene should've rippled into a woozy sexy slo-mo with a boom-chicka-wah-wah bassy soundtrack. Instead what actually happened is, Ben got caught in the sleeping bag, needing less haste and more speed to achieve a t-shirt-less exit from a well-made camping accessory my dad got from Millets.

'Bollocks,' he muttered, trying to push it down and getting caught.

'Unzip it,' I giggled. 'I'd help you, but I'm nekkid.'

'You don't need to mention that again, I'm on my way,' Ben said, and I giggled some more.

There was something absolutely brilliant about being in this situation and being friends already. Suddenly it wasn't: *how strange to be doing this*, it was *how strange we've never done this before*.

Ben wriggled free, climbed into bed. When we'd successfully grappled with his boxers (Rachel starts, makes a poor effort, Ben takes over, result still delightful) suddenly there was skin on skin, all over the place, all of Ben and all of Rachel pressed against each other. It felt strange, but very-very-good-strange. Rhys was solid but reassuringly soft round the edges, and hairy; Ben was a lean, football-playing, smooth and muscled contrast. I didn't know bodies could have that little fat on them and still function. I thought a physique like his might make me feel like a chonker but it actually made me feel womanly, even more like myself, somehow.

We got tangled in the sheet and it was soon thrown aside completely. While admittedly he was seeing me by a light that could've probably made the elderly dean of the university look fairly sexy, Ben evidently had no issue with the full unedited version of my appearance. He was confident, and I understood why. It was obvious it wasn't his first rodeo and I very much hoped I was meeting and/or exceeding expectations – my experience no more than a string of times with a clumsy sixth-form boyfriend, and Rhys.

Only now I discovered there was a kind of intense desire that bordered on nausea. I finally understood what everyone was going on about. Who knew that the outer frontier of lust was the urge to regurg?

And although I was outclassed in the company, I didn't fret it might not be mutual: when I murmured a sweet nothing along those lines, minus any implication I might actually vomit on him, Ben replied forcefully: 'I've never wanted *anyone or anything* like I want you', proceeding to kiss me so hard I thought my mouth might suffer minor lacerations. *Nnnngggg*.

Then, at the point where it went from something we were about to do to something we were definitely doing, he gasped, buried his face in my neck and said my name. My real, actual name. Another first.

54

The first words afterwards, when our breathing returned to something like normal. They mattered. They should come from me.

'I love you,' I said. I knew this to be fact and yet there it was, a surprise to hear it spoken. The process of falling in love had been gradual but the realisation that's where I was arrived fully formed. While I was avoiding it, it felt complex. Once confronted, it was extremely simple.

'*Do* you?' Ben said, moving onto his side to look at me intently.

'Absolutely.'

'God, I can't believe it.'

How can you not believe anyone loving you, I thought. Ben seemed custom-designed to be loved. We were glazed with sweat and I felt almost narcotically elated. The noise of some late-night drunks coming home drifted in through the partially open window. I belatedly remembered Derek, and discovered I didn't care if he was squatting down there in a tin foil hat, with recording equipment and a broadcasting licence.

'Of course I do,' I said.

'Uhm, Rachel...'

'Yes?' It was still so oddly thrilling to hear my name in his mouth. I propped myself up on my elbow and kissed his cheek. He moved my arm and placed it over his bare, taut middle. I lay back down against his shoulder.

'It's not exactly an *of course*? I mean, it's taken us a while to get here.'

'Yeah, it has.'

'Did nothing in my love-struck dipshit devotion find me out, then?'

I laughed and squeezed him.

'No. Though I was pleased you hit someone for me.'

'Ohhh, don't mention that...' Ben put a palm to his forehead.

'Why? It was ace.'

'I felt like I'd tapped a glass with a fork and gone "Excuse me everyone, announcement, I've got a thing for this girl the size of Old Trafford. Everyone clear on that? OK, good, carry on with your evenings, and it's advisable for all patrons not to approach her rack."'

'I didn't think that.'

'Well, Emily did. She said, that night: "I'm not finishing with you because you hit someone for her, I'm finishing with you because of the look I caught on your face when she was getting molested."'

'Really? God. Sorry.'

'Not your fault. I'd have beaten him to the ground if he'd been holding newborn twins. She knew it. I thought everyone knew it. Incredible you didn't.'

'Hah. I was stood further away. And being molested. Sorry again.'

He ran his hand up and down my arm.

'I've been dreading saying goodbye.'

'Me too.'

'I was going to say something to you tomorrow. At the ball.'

'You were?' I looked up at him. 'What were you going to say?'

'Just, this is how I feel, you should know in case it makes any difference. Script by Jack Daniel's. Shame by Calvin Klein.'

'Shame?'

'I didn't know you'd be single, did I? The fact you weren't is all that's held me back from making a fool of myself for three years. It was my last chance and I was going to make an exception.'

I squeezed him again.

'I had no idea. Your fantastical carousel of gorgeous girlfriends looked nothing like me. Mostly blondes. *Confident* blondes at that.'

'Why the hell would I want to be with girls that reminded me of you if I couldn't have you?'

He said this so starkly that I got a guilt pang greater than the ego boost. Ennui outside curry houses aside, I hadn't sensed our relationship causing him any pain.

'Sorry if I'm being a bit full on,' he said. 'I've been hoping against hope for three years. I don't quite believe this is real.'

'That felt pretty real to me.' For once, Ben didn't laugh at my flippancy.

We lay in silence. I wanted to say extravagant things about how great I thought Ben was, how great *that* was, but while my mind was flooded, it was also blank. I was still busy feeling rather than thinking. Ben loved me. I loved him. We'd made love. Paradigms had shifted and my pyjamas were on the floor.

'What now?' Ben asked.

'How d'you mean?'

'Do you want to keep seeing each other?'

'Are you kidding? Of course I do,' I said.

'You're going back to Sheffield to do this journalism course.'

'Yes.'

'And I'm out of the country for six months.'

'Yes.'

'You could fly out and meet us? In the holidays or whatever?' Ben asked.

'That sounds great. My local says they'll give me the job back though. I kind of need the money.'

'Your local? Rhys's regular?'

'Yes. But that doesn't matter.'

'I don't like the thought of it.'

Ben frowned. I could virtually hear his brow knit.

'Do you think I'm so easily swayed that if I pull his Stella from time to time, I'll end up going back out with him?' I said. 'Salted, dry roasted, or me?'

Ben didn't laugh.

'Thanks for the vote of confidence,' I said, mock-offended.

Joking aside, I felt us running at two different speeds. I was content to lie there in the post-coital haze and enjoy being close. He needed some answers, I hadn't started thinking about the questions.

'I can't cancel my travelling. The tickets are booked. I can't let Mark down, he'd be gutted.'

'I know. And you've wanted to go for so long, you have to go. I'm not asking you not to go.'

'I know,' Ben said, but rather darkly.

I lay there and tried to work out where we stood. He had a point. The next year or so was going to be tricky to navigate. It didn't seem as insurmountable to me as it did to him. The main thing was, we both knew how each other felt now. The miracle had happened. The rest was admin.

Ben reached down and touched my hand.

'Come away with me. Just do it. Delay your place on the course. Book the tickets.'

'I can't. For one thing, I can't afford it.'

'I'll pay. I've got savings.'

'I couldn't let you do that.'

'Yes, you can. What's mine is yours. A lend, if you'd feel better.'

'I bet Mark would love being gooseberry on his trip of a lifetime!' I laughed.

'Is that what you're bothered about? Mark's feelings? Or is this about yours?'

'Eh?'

'You're going to be doing lock-ins in the Piss Up & Parrot with Rhys while I'm in Kanchanaburi. When I get back, you'll be in college in the week and working at the weekends. How are we going to see each other?'

'I know it's going to be difficult – but we'll get through it. Even if I had to wait a year to be with you properly, I'd do it.'

There was a long, long pause where I nearly checked to see he was still alive. I hoped he was absorbing the size of the intended compliment. He sat up.

'A year? You're honestly saying it's OK if we don't see each other much for the next year?'

322

'I didn't say it's OK, I said I'd wait. If that was what it took.'

'Do you really feel the same way about me as I do about you?'

'Yes, I do!'

'I've got to be honest, I don't even think you and Rhys are over. Sounded more like a lovers' tiff than a break-up.'

'Don't be crazy, Ben. If I wanted to be with Rhys instead, why am I in bed with you?'

'Were you going to say anything to me, before we left?'

'Uhm.' *No. With huge, huge regret: no.* For the first time in my life, I was confronting a character fail, with nowhere to hide. Yes, I was in love with him. No, I wasn't going to risk telling him, what with my presumption of near-certain failure of reciprocation. I was going to pretend to myself I didn't and let him go. I couldn't resolve this contradiction without it saying something about me. That, my friends, is a coward. 'I didn't plan anything, but...'

'That's a no.'

'I didn't know you felt the same way!'

'How would you know until you ask?'

'I didn't want to risk losing you as a friend.'

'I think we both know that tomorrow would've been the end of things as we know it, either way.'

This was true, and I had no answer for Ben. How do you explain to someone so many degrees more brave and cool than you that such strength of feeling and total gutlessness can co-exist?

'Do you still love Rhys? You must do. It only ended today.'

'I don't know,' I said. 'You can't press an off switch. Whatever I feel, it doesn't mean I'm *in* love with him and want to be with him.'

Another long pause, where I worked out what to say next. I felt we'd mounted the kerb and some grabbing of the steering wheel was required to get us back on course. My policy of speaking the first words to come into my head hadn't been the charm so far.

'Fuck!' Ben suddenly exclaimed.

He jumped from the bed as if he'd had a bolt gun to the backside. I experienced a moment's cognitive dissonance of *bad thing happening/good view though*. I realised he was looking for his clothes, pulling his underwear on with a snap of elastic, dragging his jeans up his legs.

'What's going on? Ben?' I sat up, not so confident in my nakedness now. I grabbed a pillow and held it against myself.

'I'm sorry but I've got to go,' he said, some words muffled as he momentarily disappeared inside the neck of his t-shirt. 'I shouldn't have … I couldn't turn you down. Shit—'

'Don't go! Ben? I don't understand! We'll work this out. I'll come travelling, if that's what you want …'

He stopped, looked at me.

'It's not about you doing what I want. You've got to decide what *you* want, and not because uni's over and we're drunk and we've slept together and you've had a fight with Rhys. I feel too much for you for that. I have to go.'

'That's not why this has happened!'

He bent to pull his shoes on and straightened back up.

'You've done me and you're doing one?' I said, trying as a last ditch to appeal to the international code of the non-bastard.

'It's not like that. I can't make your mind up for you about what happens next. I know that's what you're used to.'

'What I want to happen next is for you not to leave.'

'I can't – it's not your fault – but I can't...' he stopped and cleared his throat. '...Be this close with you, thinking it's a one-off.'

He grabbed at his wallet and keys on my desk and I watched in disbelief as he charged towards the bedroom door. I grabbed the sheet from the floor, wrapped it around myself like a short-arsed Greek statue and gave chase. The time it took to pick it up lost me the time needed to catch up with him.

'Ben, please! Don't go!' I called, barrelling down the stairs.

He did go and I was left on the threshold of the house, calling his name.

I heard movement in Derek's room, and fled back upstairs, hyperventilating, trying to figure out how the hell the best of times became the worst of times.

55

I try to force my overloaded mind to take in the complexities of the drugs trial, making copious notes in an attempt to tether my wandering imagination to verifiable facts. When it breaks for a mid-afternoon conference between counsel, I head to the press room, only to have my path blocked by a pinker-round-the-edges-than-usual Gretton.

'Did you see her?'

'Who?'

'Clarke! She'd left a Dictaphone in the press room. Said she had to come and get things from her flat so she might as well pick it up. Brass balls, I told you.'

Avoiding me wasn't worth the cost of a Dictaphone. You're a class act, Zoe. I whip round and scan the court. The defendant's friends and family eye me suspiciously in return.

'She was off to Piccadilly,' Gretton says to me, looking at his watch. 'I heard her tell someone on the phone that she was on the quarter to train. If you get a move on ...'

I look at Gretton. We both know I'm being shamelessly baited, and that I'm going to take the bait. I check my watch.

'I'll cover anything in your case if it restarts while you're away. Scout's honour.'

Gretton makes the three-fingers-to-forehead gesture. For once, I believe him.

I pelt out the door and through town, weaving through the afternoon crowds, climbing the slope to Piccadilly in a running-late-commuter's half-trot, half-gallop, with small bursts of ungainly sprinting. I get to the station with rasping lungs and a stitch in my side. *Oof.* This is the kind of unfitness you remember from cross-country at school. Scanning the departures board I see a likely candidate for Zoe's train. It looks like it's already in. If she's passed the ticket inspectors, I'm buggered. I check my watch again. She's no doubt ensconced in a first-class carriage, enjoying the fruits of her ill-gotten gains. Ah well. At least I tried. For my own self-respect, such as it is.

I turn back to retrace my steps. With a jolt, I see a head of spirally hair bobbing about, a few yards away by Costa Coffee. *Ah hah!* I don't give myself the time to feel nervous.

'Zoe!' I say, marching up to her.

She glances at me in surprise, but not shock, or much fear, standing the flowery vinyl trolley case she's been dragging upright.

'Hi, Rachel.' A tone of polite but terse resignation, as if I'm a battleaxe from three doors down who's always buttonholing her about starting a Neighbourhood Watch scheme.

I take a deep breath.

'One question – how could you?'

'Oh, look, I'm sorry, I really am. The *Mail* wasn't going to run it this soon but something else fell through at the last minute and as they had it all ready to go … I did want to warn you.'

'I can tell that by the way you tried to get in touch so many times on Saturday night. What exactly were you going to say to me? Sorry I've completely fucked you over but the opportunity for me was too good?'

Zoe makes a noise that's either a sigh or huff of exasperation. 'You weren't going to use it and it's a great story, you said so yourself.'

I hope there aren't any colleagues milling about nearby, or this showdown will be the very definition of a pyrrhic victory.

'So great it's going to get me sacked.'

'They're not blaming you, are they?' Zoe says, all innocence. 'I didn't tell anyone about you reading the text, I swear.'

'Cheers a bloody ton,' I spit, even though I'm relieved. 'Don't you even care what you've done to Natalie? Or Jonathan?'

'The criminal's cheating wife and her leg-over? Not really, no.'

'Well, I hope your twenty-five grand a year staff job on a national is worth all the people you've trampled over to get to it. Pleasure knowing you.'

'You were really nice to me, I'm sorry it's all turned out like this.'

'Yeah, I'm really sorry I was nice to you too.'

I failed to notice until now that Zoe has the dead eyes of a rag doll, tossed on a skip.

'I know you didn't ask for this but it's not like you haven't played a part.'

'*Excuse me?*'

'Why did you look at the text, Rachel? Why did you write the number down? Your instincts were right and you wanted to follow it up but you didn't want the hassle, so you gave it to me.'

'That's what you've conjured to make yourself feel better

about this? I subconsciously wanted you to do this all along?'

Though even as I say it, I wonder.

'It's a weird thing to do with a story you're not interested in. I can see why you're annoyed, but you're in a little bit of denial.'

I feel my blood pressure soar like a kite. She hasn't even got the decency to behave like a guilty person. Have I swapped roles with Simon?

'I wasn't tipping you off. I was talking to you because I thought I could trust you.'

A sullen pause, as she wills me to get out of her face. 'All I've done is use something you didn't want. It was litter picking.'

'If that's all you've done, why didn't you ask me?'

'You'd have got stressed out like you are now, worrying about whether it was fair on the people involved. Sorry, I don't give a shit about that. I want to get on. It's not for us to play God and decide what is and isn't news…'

I let out a twisted shriek. 'This is priceless! What, you're some sort of campaigner for truth and free speech now?'

'I'm a journalist. This is what we do. Maybe you should go do something different if you disapprove of it so much.'

She may as well have gripped my shoulder and aimed a blow right below my bellybutton. It's one thing to be told I'm a disgrace to my profession by Ken Baggaley. To hear it from someone who was in college about five minutes ago…

'There's good ones and there's bad ones. From what I can see, you're no different to the Grettons of this world and the way you treat people will come back to haunt you.'

'You're overreacting.'

'When my job's hanging by a thread? Most people in my situation would rip your face off and wear it like a mask.'

'They can't sack you for something I've done!'

'Of course they can, Zoe, but don't even begin to pretend you weighed up the impact on me or anybody else before you did this. You took what you wanted and left others to pay for it.'

She stays silent.

'I've got one last question,' I say. 'Is your mum fat?'

Zoe sounds less confident. 'What?'

'It's not difficult – is your mum overweight?'

'I don't know what you're talking about.'

'Thought not. Hard to keep track, I imagine.'

Some sort of shame finally flares in her face and I think, this is as good as I'm going to get. I turn on my heel and leave her there, with her sweetly silly luggage and her endearingly scruffy hair and her heart made of swinging brick, waiting for my own heartbeat to return to normal as I walk down the hill, into the mouth of the city, back to work.

I want to get on. Not only was my relationship a failure, my performance at my job is by this calculation, too. I allow myself five minutes of feeling like an utter loser, then consider what I've lost. I think the part where I was a bad person was when I read the text, and the part where I was an idiot was when I shared it with her. If her exploitation makes me a crap journalist and her an effective one, well, it's a competition I'd rather lose.

'What's the damage, then?' Gretton says as I approach court. He's on his fag break, glowing cigarette in hand, looking like the cat that got the cream. And the fishsticks, and a ball with a bell in it. 'Will she live to fight another day?'

'She will, but not here.'

'I did warn you. I told you: you should watch out as well. Remember?'

'Oh, right.' I squint against the sun. 'I thought you were having a go at me.'

'Paranoid.'

'No, not paranoid enough.'

'Have top brass cooled off?'

I sigh, smile. 'Oh right, you want to know if they're going to send some green newbie instead and you'll get a good month of the best stories to yourself?'

'No,' says Gretton, tapping ash on to the pavement, doing a passable imitation of someone with hurt feelings. 'Actually, I think we work alright together. We know the rules. I hope you stay.'

'I'm touched,' I say. 'I've survived, bloodied but unbowed. Or bloodied and bowed, but in work.'

'It's not your fault you didn't suss her out,' Gretton says, with huge magnanimity. 'I've got a few more miles on the clock. I've seen her type before.'

'I hope I never see her type again.'

'She's burned her bridges. She won't be coming back to regionals or agencies round here, that's for sure. Baggaley's a man to hold a grudge. Nah, it's London or nothing for her. She better stay at the *Mail*.'

'Thanks.' I almost laugh. 'If comfort came any colder, it'd be liquid nitrogen.'

56

A braver, more dynamic, more sensible person might have got up the morning-after-the-night-before, on the day of their graduation ball, and gone straight round to iron out a disagreement with the newly discovered, newly estranged love of their life.

I chewed my nails, changed my top three times, fretted over facing him in broad daylight and recalling things we'd done in the half-dark. I made cups of tea, procrastinated, perfected speeches in my head and wasted time. Then the girls arrived with bagfuls of foam hair curlers, piles of glitter-flecked make-up and bottles of warm pre-mixed Buck's Fizz. I decided to wait until I had some Dutch courage to hand at the ball that evening. It belatedly struck me, in the middle of creating Caroline's sixties-style beehive with choking-hazard quantities of Elnett, that Ben might not go.

It made me pause, mid-backcombing, so that Caroline said: 'What's the matter? I look something out of a John Waters film, don't I?'

I was flying on auto-pilot: pretending to care about my outfit, my hair, smiling for the photos. All I could think about was getting to the Palace Hotel.

On arrival, we had aperitifs in a featureless chintzy ante-room and I desperately scanned the black-jacketed crowd for him, without success. I spotted a few stray friends-of-Ben but couldn't trace their origins, location-wise, and the ballroom, laid for dinner, was simply too large to effectively scope.

By the start of the meal, I was convinced he was a no-show. I began to formulate a plan. When no one was paying me much attention, I'd slip out and into a taxi, go back to his house. As time ticked on, it was all I could do not to hurl the prawn cocktail starter with a wet salmon-coloured splat at the nearest wall, turn over the table and charge down Oxford Road in my stilettos.

Then, when the key lime pie was demolished and the music had started and I was working out how best to make my escape, there he was. Right in the middle of the room, as if he'd dropped from the ceiling on cat burglar wires. Ben in a dinner suit. If you trained a camera on him, you'd get lens flare.

He'd obviously only recently arrived because a girl on his table jumped up and wrapped her arms around him – giving me stomach pain – and a male friend passed him a beer. I could see Ben loosening his bow tie, ruffling his hair and making an explanation for his lateness. I was going to look something of a fool, but I'd waited long enough.

I sprang to my feet and wove my way over to his table.

'Can I talk to you?'

Ben looked up from his friends in surprise, set his drink down. I thought I was about to be chewed out in front of everyone, but bravery paid off. He shrugged a 'Sure.' I took his hand, led him on to the dance floor. It was going to be him making a declaration of undying feelings at the ball, instead, here I was.

I faced him.

'Listen, Ben—'

'I'm trying. You want to talk to me here?'

I thought the dance floor was the only place we could get some privacy, but it had the small drawback of the decibels. Blur's 'To The End' boomed out of the speakers. We were surrounded by people who'd had enough of the cava to be first on their feet, singing along lustily.

'There should've been another question …'

'I'm sorry?' Ben mouthed, turning his head to me.

'Another question. About my feelings. Last night! When you asked if I was still in love with Rhys …' I put my fingers in my ears to block out Damon Albarn and tune in Ben.

'What's that?' he said, squinting in confusion.

'Let's go somewhere quieter!' I bellowed.

'All right.'

'I'm sorry,' I mouthed, succinctly. Finally, Ben lip-read one line at least.

'I want to say something to you too,' he shouted, shaking his head.

A smile. He was *smiling*. For one shining moment, it was going to be OK. I moved closer to grab his hand again and felt his arm loop round my waist. He tucked my hair behind my right ear and swung in to say something, close. I felt the heat of his breath on my neck and I shivered, closed my eyes.

What happened next seemed to go in slow motion, and not in the anticipated, exultant, moving in for a disco-ball light scattered, *reader I married him, roll credits* movie kiss way. I felt Ben pull back. I opened my eyes. He'd seen something over my shoulder and the smile slipped off his face, the arm from my body.

I turned to see Rhys advancing on us, in a tux, beaming from ear to ear. It was Rhys, as an un-Rhys-like, Big Band member imposter. He'd even attempted to tame and flatten his hair into something parted and Rat Pack slick. I looked back to Ben. Rhys reached us.

'Ta dah!' Rhys said, spreading his hands out at either side, like a magician showing me he had nothing up his sleeves.

Ben folded his arms, looked from me to him. Waited. Waited for words that, had they come, would've been barely audible, but still would've been better than nothing.

'Alright mate? Not cutting in, am I?!' Rhys hollered, with a *ha-ha-as-if* intonation.

Ben didn't answer, looked to me, jaw clenched.

'No!' I said, as reflex response, a placeholder while I worked out how the hell to handle this. 'But, uhm … Ben and I were just … We've just …' *Done it and declared ourselves?*

Before I could say anything else, Rhys shouted: 'C'meeeeere babe!' bundling me into a coercive, bear-hug version of a waltz.

'Wait, wait!' I felt like I was drowning, gulping for oxygen in a crush of musty black poly-cotton and Issey Miyake for Men and blind panic. 'Rhys! Stop!'

'Whazza matter?'

When I disentangled myself, Ben was nowhere to be seen. And he was going to stay that way for ten years.

57

Two weeks after the St Ann's Square massacre, I receive an invitation from Ben to go for a post-work drink.

'Dear lord,' Ben says, as I walk up to him outside the Royal Exchange. 'You're only a minute or two late. Allowing for a margin of inaccuracy with my watch, you might even be on time. Have you got any explanation for this?'

'My desire for a drink?' I say.

'I feel like I should fire a confetti cannon.' He gives me a sidelong smile as we set off.

'I have a lot of ground to make up.'

'Don't be daft.'

'You didn't want to go to the film with Olivia and Lucy?'

I'd noticed Ben had felt the need to explain why Olivia couldn't come too. I had my suspicions she might've lined up slightly differently to Ben in the Hurricane Simon vs Wretched Rachel wrestling match.

'You wouldn't get me to the film they're going to unless you strapped me on a gurney and stuck a syringe in my arm. *He's My Man*, or something. *She's That Girl. Where's My Brain?*'

'There's quite an Oscar buzz around *Where's My Brain*!'

'Flies buzzing round it, more like.'

We laugh.

'How about here?' I say on impulse, as we pass a promising doorway, and as soon as we walk inside I know it's a lucky discovery. Battered wooden chairs and tables painted in mismatched colours, guttering tea lights, art college waitresses, framed vintage film posters on the walls – the whole hipster package.

We take a seat underneath *Gentlemen Prefer Blondes* and Ben gets the drinks, Belgian beer in brown glass bottles. He shrugs the discreetly showy-offy grey coat on to his chair and I try not to gaze at how the oily face and greasy hair that afflict the entire office-based population by six p.m. only serve to make Ben look kind of James-Bond-after-high-stakes-baccarat-with-arms-dealers-in-Montenegro. Good bone structure, I think, makes dishevelment look raffish. I spent ten frantic minutes with my make-up bag in the work loos, painting eyes in and lips back on, like decorating a hardboiled egg.

I tentatively inquire after Simon, as Ben rolls up his shirt-sleeves and I ignore his forearms. When did I become a drooling pervert? (*Too late*, I hear Rhys say.)

He replies, curtly: 'You're not the first female he's accused of ruining his life and you won't be the last. Don't give it any more thought.'

I take a sharp breath and prepare to tell Ben the whole truth, the one I couldn't risk telling Simon. This is my high stakes gamble. I knew on the way here I was going to do it and that many people would think it's lunacy. I can hear Caroline's ghostly scream to *Shut. The. Hell. Upppppp* ... Thing is, I don't want Ben to stick up for me because I've lied to him, too. Ben's decision to defend me doesn't mean anything until he has the facts.

'Ben,' I say, 'if I tell you something else about the Natalie Shale affair, will you promise not to go wappy and tell Simon?'

He looks wary.

'Is this some new lid-blowing fact that's going to change everything? I can do without any more surprises.'

'It's the full unexpurgated truth about how Zoe got the story.'

His glass hovers in hand, halfway to his lips. He sets it back down.

'Please tell me you didn't do the splitting the cash thing?'

'No, I wasn't involved in her selling it, like I said.'

'What then? Don't tell me something I don't want to be told.'

'I had absolutely no part in using it as a story or Zoe going to the nationals and if I had known about it, I'd have done everything I could to stop her. Does that help?'

Ben looks undecided.

'Promise you won't tell Simon?' I say.

'It helps your cause that I don't want to get him more wound up. Now you've gone this far you better tell me.'

I explain. Then I hold my breath.

Ben studies my face while he absorbs this information. 'She took it and ran with it behind your back?'

'Yes. I swear.'

'Why didn't you do the story?'

'It wasn't fair. I thought about it. I couldn't be that hard-faced.'

'Yet you're hard-faced enough to read other people's texts and gossip about the contents?'

'I know. Tell me I'm scum, I deserve it.'

Ben exhales.

'Why are you telling me this at all?'

'You were so kind to me and I don't want to lie to you.' *I want your absolution, above all. I can withstand everything else if I have that.* 'I couldn't tell Simon because he would've lost me my job over it and I have rent to pay. It's not right but there it is. I'm so sorry for the trouble it's caused you, Ben. I wanted to do a good job. I can't tell you how ashamed I feel. This is my proper apology, from the heart.'

Ben exhales some more and looks longingly toward the door. For a moment I think he's going to say *I'm outta here, lady.*

'Wooh boy…'

'Will it get irritating if I keep saying sorry?'

'You shouldn't have gone through her phone or told another journalist about it. Intentional or not, you do appear to have been the Big Bang event for a world of shit.'

'I know.'

'However, you could've got a big story out of it. You didn't. Because of the effect it would have on other people's lives, not because it wouldn't benefit yours. True?'

'True.'

'Then what we've identified is a scruple. You officially have a scruple.'

I give a wry, grateful laugh, faith in Ben's generosity once more vindicated: 'Scruple, singular.'

'It's a start.'

The bar's playing Ella Fitzgerald, we still have near-full drinks. I'm more at peace with the universe than I was before we arrived, that's for sure.

'You took a risk telling me that,' he says, considering me

over his glass. 'Can I take a risk in return, with the same complete trust that it goes no further?'

I feel the hairs on the back of my neck prickle. 'Of course.'

'This never, ever makes it to your colleagues, on pain of death. This stays between us, in this place, right now, and never leaves. Promise me, Rachel.'

I'm rapt. 'I promise.'

'You better keep your word, else I'll call Simon and tell him about the text.'

'Absolutely. Understood. Rely on my instincts of self-preservation instead of honour.'

'Safer.' He lowers his voice. 'I heard that, in pillow talk, Natalie told Jonathan she lied to give her husband an alibi.'

My jaw drops. 'Why would he need a false alibi?'

'Why do people usually need false alibis?'

'Lucas Shale's *guilty*?' I stage-whisper back, incredulous.

'I don't know. I honestly don't.'

'But he's going to be cleared on appeal. Everyone thinks he's innocent. I was sure he was innocent.'

Ben shrugs. 'This can't ever reach the ears of the partners. If it's true, it's major, major stuff that Jonathan let the firm carry on representing Shale. Career ending.'

'Hasn't the affair shot his career anyway?'

'No. Only because Natalie wasn't the client. He's had a serious rap on the knuckles and a cosmetic sacking, with the chance of being quietly re-hired in London when it's all blown over.'

'Shit.'

'It's better than being struck off.'

'I guess Natalie and Jonathan aren't still in touch then? If he's going to London?'

Ben shakes his head. 'Doubt it.' Pause. 'Still, makes it less likely they're going to confer about that text and figure out your involvement, eh?'

I cringe. 'That wasn't why I was asking.'

'I know you weren't, only teasing. You don't worry about your interests enough, in my opinion.'

I'd hoped Ben, with his generosity of spirit, might forgive me. How he's finding things to praise, well – I have no idea why he always sees the best in me. There's a reflective pause that elongates into a comfortable, beer-sipping silence. I look at the lights from the candles throwing patterns on the windows, take in the room. A pretty waitress with hair in an unwinding bun, a pencil jammed horizontally through it, gives me a '*Nice couple*' warm look. I return it with a '*If only you knew*' smile.

'It's great we've been able to do this, isn't it?' Ben says, eventually. 'You and me being friends again, I mean. All these years later.'

'It's amazing. Just picked up where we left off,' I say, without thinking.

'Not exactly where we left off,' Ben says, raising an eyebrow.

'No, not exactly ... uh ...'

Conversation stalls. Ella is over. Our now-uncomfortable silence filled with a horrendous emo cover of The Pretenders's 'Brass in Pocket'.

Ben knocks back some of his drink and I expect a brisk subject change. Instead he looks me in the eye.

'Why did you sleep with me? I mean, I did work out why, but I might as well have it confirmed, after all this time.'

His steady, sardonic expression and slight smile unnerves me. I can see he's thinking I don't know how to gift-wrap an ugly truth. Instead I'm thinking of all the things I could say that I'm not going to say to a married man.

'I gave you a reason at the time.' This is meant to be assertive. My voice sounds plaintive.

He shakes his head. 'It's OK, it was a long time ago. I can take it. You wanted to get back at Rhys and you knew you wouldn't have to see me again. No harm done.'

No harm done? *Is he kidding?*

'That's absolutely not true. I was...' my voice nearly cracks '...I really cared about you.'

Ben's not visibly moved by this declaration.

'Mmm. I think with hindsight, Rhys's reappearance at the ball was well timed, for all of us.'

'Ben.' Long, long pent-up emotion swells up like strings in a sentimental film score and I try to curb it. 'That wasn't it. You've got the wrong impression...' How do I hint at so much I can't say? Oh no. Am I going to use those accursed words? It seems I am. '...It's complicated.'

Now I hear the ghost of Mindy: *Shuuuuutt uuuuppppppp...*

'Ultimately I got the right impression though, given you stayed with and got engaged to Rhys?'

Slam. Dunk. I open my mouth and no words come out. To think I thought to be finally asked this would be a release? It's ten years too late and one of us is too married for it to be anything other than punishment.

'I tried to call. I wrote to you. Didn't you get my letter?'

'Ah, yeah. In order to get...' I hear Ben stop, rewind and amend what he was going to say '...past it, I had to kind of cut off. Your letter didn't exactly say anything I didn't know.'

'I was worried in case Abi opened it. You said once she had

342

form for that. I thought it was best to keep it short. It was meant to make you return a call.'

Ben stares down into his glass.

'Sorry if I was brutal. You deserved better, what with us being mates and everything. I wasn't in a good place during that year out. Which was annoying because I was in a lot of good places, literally speaking.'

He tries too late for lightness and I can't join in.

'Sorry,' I offer, inadequately, more inadequately than he can possibly know.

'Oh, God, no need,' he swirls the liquid in his glass, 'I don't mean to sound resentful. I look back now and I'm so embarrassed...'

I wince.

'...You'd had a big fight with Rhys, you must've been all over the place and then I start with all that angst over a one night stand. I mean, whatever your reasons, it was sex, so I could hardly complain, ha. I'm sure you wondered what the hell was going on. It was amazing you humoured me as much as you did. Lot of twenty-one-year-old fuss over nothing, eh? Still, we can look back now and laugh. Well, hoping you don't laugh *that* much...'

This guts me like a sturgeon. 'It wasn't nothing.'

It isn't nothing. To me.

Ben shrugs, smiles. 'I thought Rhys might swing for me, the other day. I wouldn't have blamed him.'

'I never told anyone about what happened.'

'Too ashamed?' Ben pulls a comedy face.

'I wanted it to stay between us.'

'I told someone.'

My heart starts ka-thumping. Oh God, please not Olivia. *Please.*

'Some Australian bloke I met one night in a bar in Sydney, who had to listen to me crap on for hours. He said I'd meet you again some day and you'd be fifteen stone and screaming at four kids and I'd realise I'd had a lucky escape. He wasn't what you'd call a new man.'

'He was right, bar four kids. And one stone,' I joke, lamely, feeling utterly broken.

'He was totally wrong. It's good to lay it all to rest.'

What do I say to this? It's funny he's saying it's nice to see each other when for the first time I can ever remember, I don't want to be with him.

'Ben...'

My phone starts trilling in my bag. I curse myself for not having put it on silent.

I locate it and see it's Caroline.

'Hello? Caro? Is that you? *Bad line*,' I mouth.

Right after I've said it I realise that it isn't a bad line, Caroline's crying.

58

I rap my knuckles on the hollow-sounding wood of Caroline's door and shift my weight from foot to foot. All I could get out of her on the phone was an assurance no one had died. Ben was understanding as I fled from the bar and leapt into a taxi.

Caroline opens the door, and the words 'Are you OK?' wither on my lips.

Her face is streaked with the grey of black mascara mixed with tears, the skin around the neckline of her t-shirt is a hot pink, as if she's been nervously scratching at it.

I move to hug her but she keeps herself at a distance.

'Cheers for coming,' she says flatly, sniffing loudly and walking back into the house. Fumbling to close the door behind me, I follow her and watch her take up the position I assume she was in before I arrived – prone on her side on the tissue-strewn expanse of the leather sofa. I drop down in an armchair opposite, taking in the near empty wine bottle and the half full glass next to it on the coffee table.

'Where's Graeme?'

'Graeme's been having an affair,' she says, the last word

stretched into an odd shape by the tears that bubble up and burst out as she says it.

'Oh God, Caro.' I kneel by the sofa, put my hand on her arm as she sobs. It's awful to see her like this, in contrast with her usual self-possession. It's as disorientating as hearing your parents at it, or catching your grandparents without their teeth in. I can't think of any follow-up other than: 'How did you find out?'

She wipes under her eyes with her thumbs, speaks on the out-breath: 'He left his mobile behind this morning. I know he doesn't like to be separated from it so I took it with me to work, thought I'd drop it off for him at lunchtime. When he'd got the fifteenth missed call in a row from someone coming up as "John" I thought I'd answer and see what "he" wanted.'

Caroline breaks off to steady her voice. I rub her arm, hoping it's comforting rather than annoying.

'Then I walked out of work, called him, came back here and waited for him.' She pauses. 'He actually tried to claim invasion of privacy about the fact I'd been holding on to his phone. Stupid, stupid wanker.'

'Where is he now?'

'Don't know, don't care. I doubt he's at *hers*, because she's married with kids.'

'He works with her?'

'Yeah. He said it was all a stupid mistake and he's relieved I found it. Can you believe the gall? He trotted all the classics out earlier. "We didn't mean it to happen", "We were drunk and a long way from home", "I didn't know how to finish it". Listening to the lament anyone would think he was forced into taking his trousers off at knife-point.'

The done thing here would be to say I didn't expect it of Graeme, of all husbands, yet that wouldn't be quite true. I settle for: 'It's terrible he's done this to you.'

'He tells me I've got to take some of the blame for being "married to my job" and never around when he needed me.'

'What!' I try not to shout. 'He's the same! He's always been proud of how well you've done. He couldn't be with someone who *isn't* like you.'

'Apparently he can, repeatedly, at a variety of locations around the UK and mainland Europe. No wonder he was so concerned with getting that roaming package sorted on his phone. *Roaming package*, hah.'

The more I think about the abandonment excuse, the more I grind my teeth.

'How long's it been going on?'

Caroline reaches for her glass and knocks the contents back in one. 'Couple of months. Assuming he was telling the truth. He's offered proof but I can do without hearing every spit and cough.'

I shake my head.

'What about you, anyway? Want a drink?' Caroline stirs herself, looks disconsolately at the wine dregs. 'There's more in the fridge.'

'I'll get it,' I say, tugging my coat down my arms. 'You stay there.'

'I'm calling in sick to work tomorrow so I might as well be sick,' she calls after me.

I open their huge double-fronted fridge and choose one of four chilled bottles. Caroline is sufficiently mature to have more alcohol in the house than whatever she's drinking that evening and it's serving her well in a crisis. I get a glass out of the cupboard and take it through with the Chablis. Maybe quality will offset quantity.

'What now?' I ask, once we both have full glasses in hands. 'Is Graeme going to move out?'

'He can surf friends' sofas, then it's spare room Siberia, and a lot of grovelling, in that order.'

This startles me. 'You're definitely staying together?'

'Damn right we are. I'm not losing my home and throwing everything we are away over some pitiful early mid-life crisis being played out across three-star Best Westerns.'

'Oh – right.'

Her instant conviction that the relationship is worth salvaging surprises me. I wouldn't be sure of anything right now.

'Did he say sorry? Does he regret it?'

'He regretted being found out.' She sighs, heavily. 'He says so. He begged me to have him back.'

She looks over at the wedding picture on the mantelpiece. 'I never thought this'd be me, you know. Such a big fat cliché.'

'Hey. Whatever else you are, you're not fat.'

Caroline smiles, wanly. I try to think of some profound words to fit the occasion that aren't *I've always thought Graeme had a hint of The Shit*.

I admit it was mostly based on his habit of taking the piss out of Caroline's friends in the guise of 'big character' bonhomie.

'What did I do wrong, Rachel? I've had my own life and a career and I've worked at my marriage, or I thought I had. It hasn't made any difference.'

'Bollocks!' I spill some wine on my lap in the force of feeling. 'You've done nothing wrong! Like you said, there's no such thing as the perfect affair-proof marriage and none of this is your fault. Graeme has to take full responsibility.'

'Hmm. Isn't the other person a symptom of something wrong, not a cause?'

'That doesn't mean that the cause is you. If Graeme wanted more attention he shouldn't have looked for it like this.'

'Agree.'

We drink. I sense our differences more keenly than I ever have. From Caroline's perspective, if you put the effort in, the outcome should be better. I see the problem as Graeme's intrinsic Graeme-ness. When she got together with Graeme I don't think she thought he was a wonderful human being, exactly, but the right man for her. Almost like a business partner: he'd make the same investment, wanted the same return. It's not that Caroline's mercenary, she isn't. She's simply practical to her fingertips. She'd be unable to fall hopelessly in love with a penniless stoner poet. She's constitutionally incapable of being hopeless.

'Look at us all. This wasn't how it was supposed to be, was it? Weren't we meant to be all sorted out by thirty?' Caroline asks.

I smile. 'You, maybe. I don't think me and Mindy ever had a hope.'

'I turned the Hoover on, you know. So next door couldn't hear me screaming at my husband for having it off with some marketing manager. I didn't want to do the next street party knowing they'd all talked about it. I was bellowing "She's a slut and you're no better!" at him over the roar of the Dyson bagless vac. I feel so old.'

'You're not old.'

Caroline rubs her eyes, smooths her hair down. 'What you been up to this evening, anyway? Hope I didn't ruin a night out.'

'A drink with Ben,' I say, only considering the wisdom of this admission as I'm making it.

'Ben?' Caroline's face darkens. 'The two of you?'

'Olivia wanted to see a film instead.'

'What did you talk about?' Caroline leans forward, frowning.

'Nothing much. Work.'

Caroline doesn't react.

'You know, the Simon palaver,' I add.

'This is exactly what I was warning you not to do.'

'Caro, he's a friend.'

'Until he and Olivia have been at each other's throats, he gets a funny, faraway look on his oh-so-gorgeous face, you feel a bit lonely…'

'He'd never do that! Honestly. Not going to happen and I barely see him. Tonight was a total one-off.'

'Can I give you some advice? I appreciate taking relationship guidance from me right now is the ironiest of ironies.'

I nod, knowing it won't be anything I want to hear.

Caroline leans over and pours more wine into her glass. 'Make things up with Rhys. You've made your point over the wedding, it probably needed doing. Don't throw the bloke out with the bathwater. You two belong together.'

I shake my head.

'I know why you're saying this and thank you, but I wasn't happy.'

'Were you unhappy, or were you bored, and irritated with him? It comes to all relationships in the end, trust me.'

What Caroline probably thinks and doesn't want to say is: it could be Rhys, or nothing.

'It's not that. It's the way we affect each other. I wind him up and he brings me down. I don't think it's bad habits. It's like in chemistry when you put two substances together and always get the same reaction. Like that.'

'And you didn't mind for thirteen years?'

'It's not that I didn't mind ... I drifted. I avoided asking myself if it was enough and then the wedding meant there was no way of not asking myself.'

'The "happy ever after" lie has a lot to answer for,' Caroline says, staring into the middle distance. 'You're not happy ever after with anyone. You choose the person most worth persevering with, that's all. I mean, "disappearing off into the sunset together". Where everything is always bathed in a rosy glow. Am I the only one to notice the sodding problem – the whole point of a sunset is you never reach it? It's never *where you are*?'

'Am I allowed to say yes?'

Caroline smiles. 'If I ever have a daughter, this will be a fairytale-free household, let me tell you.'

'I don't expect to be happy ever after. Just happier.'

'But it all comes down to what we call happy. I think we're the generation that's spent too much time thinking about what we haven't got instead of what we do have.'

This is not the time to tangle with Caroline, I realise. She looks over.

'I was jealous of you at uni, Rach. I still am in some ways.'

This almost makes me spit my drink.

'*Me?* Why on earth ...'

'You're fun. Men think you're fun. I'm not fun. I can't help it, it's the way I am. This is why you ended up entertaining Ben in a corner at your party while I talked stamp duty with his wife. Part of me thinks that's what Graeme was looking for. Not sex. A laugh.'

'You are,' my voice thickens, 'an absolutely great laugh. Not right now, right now you're a half-pissed weepy mess. But usually.'

'Thanks,' she says, through our weak giggling. Then: 'Will you think about what I said, about Rhys?'

I nod. 'I don't think things are ever as simple on the inside as they look on the outside.'

'I know. But Rhys loves you. Really loves you, and wants a future together. I know he thinks you're the only one for him and he'd do anything for you. From where I'm sitting, that doesn't come along all that often.'

Once in a lifetime at most, I know. I've had my quota. It's my turn to reach for the bottle.

59

Rhys came round to call at my parents' house, unannounced, three weeks after I'd arrived back home from university. I was still clambering over boxes full of rolled-up posters, lever arch files and pots and pans, managing my mild depression at the anti-climax that was the end of a degree and the start of the rest of my life.

My dad let him in and their voices floated up the stairwell, Rhys having a beyond-the-strictest-call-of-duty length of conversation about the vagaries of re-tiling the downstairs bathroom. He always made an effort with them, I thought, in delayed gratitude.

'Hello,' Rhys said, when he finally appeared in the chaos of my unpacking. 'How're you doing?'

'All right, thanks,' I said. I was surprised and pleased to see him. I thought we'd made things clear – not acrimonious, just clear – the night of the ball.

I'd sat him down, by the side of the light-speckled dance floor, and explained that while I hugely appreciated his coming, it didn't fundamentally change anything. I left out the part where I'd fallen in love with someone else and shagged him, judging it gratuitous cruelty. Not to mention indecent haste. He took this fairly well, though he meekly pointed out he'd had a pint on his way to the Palace, fancied another and would be over the limit, so would I mind him crashing on my floor? I had a feeling that time was of the essence in finding Ben, but I ignored my overwhelming instinct to cut and run after him in favour of doing things properly. There would be a tomorrow. I said yes.

'How are you?' I asked, as Rhys loitered with intent.

'Yeah, good.'

'Do you want a cup of tea? Once I've done this shelf?' I was halfway through re-loading my books. 'Mind you, my mum will probably make one any second.'

Rhys came all the way in, pushing the door shut with a click.

'I've been thinking about some of the things you said, about me taking you for granted. I suppose I have been.'

I nodded, unsure how to reply.

'What are your plans now?' Rhys asked, finding a box that was sufficiently solidly filled to perch on.

'I'm going to do this journalism course, then I'm going to move back to Manchester. Get a job on the paper there.'

'Yeah?'

'Looks like a few of my friends are staying on.'

'If you want to give things with us a second chance, I'll come with you.'

'What? What about the band?'

Rhys shuffled his feet. 'Ed's saying he's going to move to London. Even if he doesn't, I reckon the writing's on the wall. And not as if I can't come back for rehearsals.'

'You'd do that for me? I didn't even think you liked Manchester much.'

'Ah, it's grown on me. So, what do you say? Fresh start. Equal partners. Flat share strictly if you say you're keen on the idea. My macaroni cheese some nights for dinner, if you're very good.'

Rhys grinned. He undeniably looked appealing, with his tarry mop of hair and black Levi denim jacket and newfound eagerness for my approval. He was a welcome trophy of my grown-up years, amid the detritus of my floral-sprigged, pine four-poster childhood bedroom.

I thought about it. I thought about another person who, I had discovered the day before, had left the country without a goodbye. The night before the graduation ball had taken on a dreamlike, did-that-really-happen quality. Maybe it was what Ben said after all: a moment of madness, as politicians have it, high emotion and high hopes but not real life. Perhaps he realised his passion for me was just fear of change, grabbing the nearest familiar thing to hand to steady himself. Grabbing it quite literally.

And Ben definitely wasn't sitting here, offering to shape his life round mine. His life was continuing on the other side of the world, very definitely without me. I had to face it. Whatever was felt and whatever had been said, the fact was, he was gone for good.

My mum shouted up from the bottom of the stairs that she'd put the kettle on, with the aim of discouraging any untoward activity. It was going to be difficult at home until I found my own place, and lonely when I did.

There was an easy path before me, and an infinitely tougher alternative. I ignored the instinct that told me which was the right one. I said yes.

60

Rhys arranges to meet me at the Ruby Lounge, the venue in the Northern Quarter where his band is playing in the mid-week local showcase slot. We can have a drink, he explains, while he's waiting for the rest of the group to arrive for the sound check. It could seem as if he's fitting me in as afterthought but I appreciate what he's thinking. We both want to meet when the meeting will have a conclusion that isn't last orders, which could be fraught with risk: either loving or fighting.

Rhys is waiting for me outside, head leaning back, one leg bent and the sole of a shoe against the wall. For a moment I don't recognise him because of his hair – he's grown the dark dye out and it's back to his natural brown. I've only ever seen that colour on his childhood photos. He hates it because it has coppery lights in it that he deems ginger. It was a month into dating before I discovered his Byronic locks came from a bottle. ('There are no cool ginger rock stars,' he used to say when I'd encourage him to go au naturel. 'Mick Hucknall?' I used to ask. 'I said *rock*, and *cool*,' he'd reply.)

356

The Ruby Lounge is a wood-floored, low ceilinged basement that looks great when lit violet by night, your ears filled with noise and senses clouded by alcohol. It's starkly odd and flat by day, like seeing a Folies Bergère showgirl with her hairnet and moisturiser on. The stage area is cluttered by a drum kit, guitars, snaking leads and a microphone stand.

I imagine staying to watch them. Seeing Rhys with his head bowed and guitar strap across his shoulder would body swap me with my teenage self, watching adoringly from the crowd, suffused with pride, almost worshipful. Maybe it all started to go wrong when he banned me from his gigs.

'Drink?' Rhys says, ducking behind the bar. 'Sit anywhere you like.'

'Coke, thanks,' I say, as he produces a couple of glasses and squirts from a gurgling soda siphon.

I slip my bag from my shoulder, find a table and get that peculiar sense of formality with someone so familiar. Rhys pulls out a stool and sits down. I see he's got some stubble, has lost weight. He looks well. Very well. I'm not proud to discover that while I'm glad he's coping, it dents my ego the tiniest bit. It's one thing to tell someone they're better off without you, it's another to be presented with the hale and hearty proof.

'You look great,' I say.

'Ta,' he says, stiffly.

'Your hair really suits you like that.'

'Yeah, well,' he says. 'Can't pretend the Clairol is yours any more, can I?'

This begs a question about who's looking in his bathroom cabinets. I only repeat: 'I like it.'

Rhys launches into house valuations and we both find refuge in talking about tedious practicalities. I get the distinct feeling we're here so he can say something he hasn't worked up to yet.

'What was happening the other day then? When I called?' he asks.

'Oh...' I still don't want to relive it. 'I feel as if I'm starring in the pilot of a show called *Everybody Hates Rachel*, hoping it doesn't get picked up for a series. You haven't acquired the powers of an omnipotent deity since we broke up, have you?'

'If I had, the Blades would have won the FA Cup and those two lipstick lesbians on our street would be asking me round for fondue.'

I laugh. 'Could happen.'

'Nah. The flat back four has been useless this season.'

We both laugh. In the wreckage of our relationship I can see the things we once liked about each other, the foundations we built the structure on. It was so long ago we're not history, we're archaeology.

Rhys glances sideways, hands clasping his elbows as he rests them on the table. He retreats from friendliness, a little.

'I've been thinking about us and I want to get something out in the open,' he says.

'Oh?'

'When things went wrong with us ... I'm not talking about the wedding, although I don't think the hassle of planning it helped.' He makes an I-haven't-finished-face as I open my mouth to object. 'It was before that. *Long* before that. Around the time you finished university. And with me, for a bit.'

My muscles tense. I wonder where this is going. I also resist the urge to point out this means he's admitting things haven't been right, which is a definite change in his position.

'I think I know why,' Rhys continues.

I try not to look very apprehensive.

'I don't know if you knew or what, but – I was seeing someone else for a while.'

Whoosh. Right out of leftfield. '*What?!* Who?'

'Marie. At The Ship.'

'The big blowsy punk fan-girl who always flirted with everyone? The barmaid?'

'She was voluptuous.'

I ignore the ill-judged gag. 'When?'

'Last few months, before you came back from university. And a little while after. It was completely over by the time we moved to Manchester.'

'Why?' Might as well get the full set of the Ws – Who, When, Where, Whatthefuck?

'She came on to me. I thought we were going to settle down after you graduated. I wasn't seeing much of you and I suppose it felt like my last chance to muck about. Which sounds shit, but there it is.'

I let this sink in. 'Did you love her?'

Rhys snorts. '*No.* I'm not just saying that. Absolutely not.'

'Did you ever consider leaving me for her?'

'Never.'

'Why?'

'It wasn't anything. We had a future. Or so I always thought.'

'Is this why you didn't like me coming to your gigs? I cramped your style with groupies?'

'No, you really did put me off. One of the reasons I never told you about Marie before is I knew you'd start suspecting me of everything. I've got no motive to lie here, have I? There's nothing else.'

And there I was, arrogantly thinking I knew the nature of the beast better than Caroline.

'Why are you telling me this?'

'It was about time, that's all. I thought you should know. Sorry I didn't tell you before, but, you know …'

'No, I don't. We've split up and you think now's the time to put this in my head?'

'I thought you might go ballistic and leave me. You've got that covered.'

'Oh Jesus, well if it's only about you and the effect on you then sure, throw it all in.'

So much for polite formality. I'd like to hurl one of the stools at him. He looks an odd combination of three-parts-mortified to one-part-gratified. As if he wanted proof I cared. It makes me even angrier.

I re-run history in my head. 'Were you going to see her the night of my grad ball? It wasn't a gig, was it?'

Rhys squirms. 'I don't remember.'

'Yes, you do.'

'OK, maybe.' He takes a sip of his Coke. 'That was bad. I came through in the end, though.'

'Sorry, am I supposed to be thankful you came back to me?'

'I never left you!'

'No, that's why it's called cheating, Rhys. You were giving me shit about coming home to you and all the time you had her on the side? It's so … scummy and low. And cheap …'

He ruffles his hair and nods, stares into his glass. I test my feelings. Upset. Very upset. How much of that upset is over the simple fact of Rhys's infidelity and how much is because it magnifies my mistake that night, I can't yet tell.

'All your friends knew? David … and Ed …?'

'Some of them had an idea, yeah.'

'They must've been laughing at me. Even more than usual.'

'No! They said I was an idiot … I half thought you might meet someone at uni. I was proving something to myself, because she was there, and I could.'

'Future-proofing against any blows I dealt to your ego?'

'Yes, that. You're better with words than me.'

'And what am I supposed to do with this information, other than churn on it and want to rip your gingery hair out?'

'I want to tell the truth. Clean slate. I always thought you'd guessed, or someone had said something,' Rhys continues. 'We had that barney over your party. Then you were different after uni. More distant. More into making the rules. And I think everything changed between us from then on. It was never quite the same again.'

'Wasn't it?'

'No. You wanted to move back to Manchester. Get away from the Sheffield circle.'

'Do you think I'm so unassertive I'd never have said anything if I'd suspected?'

'I don't know what you're thinking half the time, Rachel. "Let's have a DJ for the wedding. No, actually, let's break up" being a case in point.'

'I never knew,' I say. In retrospect, my only clue was Marie being slow to serve me at the bar, and that didn't distinguish me much from the other customers.

'I didn't tell you to hurt you, Rach, honestly. I didn't even know if it would, after all this time and with all that's happened. I want to be completely honest and hold my hands up and say, I've been crap. Cards on table. I know you don't think I can do that and so I'm saying, totally, I could've done a lot better. And you've been better than me.'

Now I wrestle with my conscience. Rhys might have been unfaithful, but there's not as much to choose between us as I'd like. Does it make it better or worse that he felt less for the other person? One thing's for sure, I don't owe him blissful ignorance any more.

'I slept with Ben at the end of uni,' I say, baldly.

Under the designer stubble, Rhys changes colour. 'Ben?'

'On my course. You know. We saw him the other day.'

'What – that bloke in town?'

'Yes.'

'When?'

'When we were split up. The night before the graduation ball.'

I see Rhys add a few things up and come to the swift conclusion that he can't push the table over and call me a faithless slag-bag.

'*Ben*,' he spits, as if it's in inverted commas, as if he might've lied about his name. 'Two-faced wanker. Nutless chimp.'

He plays with a square beer mat, knocking each of its sides against the table in turn. 'The once?'

I nod.

'That's not like you.'

'Yeah.' I feel the discomfort of Rhys's incredulous stare. 'I don't know what got into me.'

'Do you want me to draw you a diagram?'

I flinch.

'Can't have been much of a shag if you came straight back to me,' Rhys says. 'You did it to prove something?'

'Not exactly.'

'Why, then? I know you. You're not the one-night-stand sort.'

'Is a one-off worse than months?'

'I took it because it was on a plate. You would've had a reason.'

'I liked him.'

'That was why you finished with me? The first time?'

I shake my head. He tries for a laugh that comes out leaden.

'Really? Bit of a coincidence. Bye bye Rhys, hello Ben, bye bye clothes.'

'No.'

'Here I was thinking we had problems because I was playing away and it was because *you* were.'

'I didn't play away as such. We'd split up.'

'Ah, come on. I'm not for a second saying what I did was OK but we're both in our thirties so how about we act like it, eh? You sleeping with someone else within hours of ending it isn't exactly total devastation. You'd obviously worked up to it while you were with me.'

He has a point.

'You've been in touch with him again?' Rhys asks, frowning.

When I decided to come clean about this, I hadn't thought any steps ahead.

'Kind of. Bumped into him, that's all.'

'You're not seeing him again?'

'No. He's married.'

Heavy pause.

'Yet you're trying to get back into his Dior Homme trunks, are you?'

I bristle with shame. 'Of course not. I thought you didn't remember Ben.'

'Something about finding out he fumbled with my girl has brought it all flooding back. Sneaky southern *twat*.'

I notice the lack of 'ex' prefixing 'girl'. Possibly Rhys does too.

'Alright,' he says, getting himself under control. 'Alright. I might mind the thought of you two together like I'd mind a brain haemorrhage but I didn't ask you here to kick off.'

'Why did you ask me here?'

'To ask you for the last time. Let's stop this and stay together. If I was slick I'd have cued up Al Green. But I'm not, and I don't know how to work the set up in the DJ booth.'

And if I'd really thought about it, I would've known this was what it was about. Rhys wouldn't suggest an occasion like this to make either of us feel better. Not because he's nasty but because he's not one for gestures. What you see is what you get. Except when you don't see him for a while and a woman with peroxide hair, cobweb crochet and oxblood Doc Martens gets him instead. Do I want to go back? I have to ask myself all over again.

'I do love you,' Rhys adds, with evident effort, not being one for declarations either.

I think about what Caroline said, about me playing at this separation, merely being bored. It gives me a pain like the world's worst Boxing Day heartburn.

I think about how lost that date with Simon made me feel. Caroline's bleak situation. Ivor and Mindy mucking about with people they don't respect. Perhaps what Rhys and I had is as good as it gets, for most people. *We're not all lucky enough to be with our soul mates*, Ben said. How we've swapped places.

'I love you too,' I say, and I do. I always will. If I didn't, leaving Rhys would be much easier. We might've been low on fun sometimes, but he's a constant. Reliable. As Caroline said, he wants me and that's not going to change.

Rhys nods. 'Let's go on holiday. I'll even sit on a beach and get sand in my arse crack if you want to. Then we'll look at the wedding again. Maybe we should do something smaller. I always thought that reception was too big.'

'You'd want the wedding back on?'

'Yeah, of course. Why not?'

'That's more than I can promise, right now.'

Rhys hisses through clamped teeth, like he's torn a puncture. 'Either you're in or you're out. I won't be pissed about.'

I think about Rhys sat on a packing box a decade ago, making me an offer that I didn't think I had a strong enough reason to refuse. I'm about to make the same mistake again, for the same cowardly reasons. I realise it doesn't matter that I still care about Rhys, or that there's no one else out there for me, or what Caroline thinks. This isn't a sum to be added up or a least-worst option. Rhys deserves better. I deserve better.

I find my voice. 'Rhys, we're not getting back together.'

'You said you love me.'

'I do. It doesn't change the fact we're better off apart. You know that. We haven't talked like we have today for years. We might work for a while but sooner or later it'd be the same old. We love each other, we just don't bring out the best in each other.'

'You're going to throw everything away, thirteen years, for what? It's a waste.'

'Just because we didn't get married or stay together forever doesn't mean it was a waste.'

'That's exactly what it means, Rachel. Wasted effort, wasted time. This Ben. Did you love him?'

I hesitate.

'Got ya. At least this explains why he looked like someone had goosed him, the other day.'

Rhys looks down at the table, the lightly scored lines between his eyebrows deepening into a number-11-shaped groove as he frowns. I wonder what his wife's going to be like, whether his kids will be boys or girls, what he'll look like when he's old. So much to give up. No one thinks I'm doing the right thing. I feel an intergalactic loneliness, spinning off into space and untethered from the Mother Ship, watching my oxygen supplies deplete.

'I don't get it,' Rhys says, though to my surprise, not angrily. 'I don't get it. I don't get what changed.'

'I did. I don't know why. I'm sorry.'

Another silence.

Rhys leans back in his chair, produces my engagement ring from the depths of his jeans pocket and places it on the table in front of me.

'Oh no, I can't.'

'Keep it. I've got no use for it.'

Rhys stretches across the table and kisses me on the cheek. 'Good luck, Rachel.'

'Thank you,' I say, but the words catch in my throat because it has grown so tight.

Rhys sees tears on the way and stands up, making it clear our conversation is over. He ambles over to the stage area as I gather myself, head for the exit. As I turn to leave, Rhys is fiddling with the microphone stand, adjusting the height, muttering: 'One two, one two' into the bulb of the mike.

I pull the door open.

Rhys's amplified voice comes booming out: *'Pawn it and you might be able to scrape another few months at Casa Cackhole.'*

61

I'd forgotten about my childhood friend Samantha's wedding and I was able to forget it longer than I might have as my invite was sent to my parents' address. My mum was obviously uncharacteristically reluctant to remind me.

When she gets in touch to arrange a pick up for Saturday lunchtime, I face my unpreparedness, both literally and psychologically, to sit through someone else's special day. I'm going to have to bear a twelve-hour-long reminder that mine is no longer happening, alongside my parents, who will be thinking the same thing. It seems unusually cruel.

'Have you seen Rhys?' my mum says, eyeballing me in the rear view mirror while she applies another coat of mascara. We're hurtling along roads banked by lush hedgerows, heading deep into loaded footballer country.

'Yes. We met for a drink the other night,' I say. It might sound like I'm choked with emotion, in fact my trunk section is being strangled by the midnight-blue 1940s-style dress with matching bolero that Mindy forced me to buy. ('You're single at this wedding, different rules now – you must bring it and it must *stay brung*.') The bodice is currently cutting off blood supply to my legs, which has the sole benefit of meaning I can't feel how high my heels are.

A pause while my mum chooses her words, discarding those so inflammatory they will start an immediate argument. Not discarding enough for my liking.

'How was he?'

'Good, actually. Looked really well. He was playing a gig.'

'Probably putting a brave face on it.'

I grind my teeth, say nothing other than: 'Dad, can you turn up the radio, I think one of my court cases might be on …'

'On Capital?'

'Try Five Live, then!'

Sam and Tom's nuptials are taking place in a village church in Cheshire, near where they live in high-achieving splendour, the reception in a marquee in the field next door. It seems quite ambitious to do a quasi-outdoor wedding at any time of year in Britain, yet they've fallen lucky with the early summertime weather: mild and balmy. I'm glad for the small mercy that it's a contrast to my city-based wedding-that-was-never-to-be.

When we park up, I discover getting out of the back seat of a Toyota Yaris in this dress is a challenge that ought to form part of some light entertainment clips show.

'Thirty-one years of age,' my dad says, shaking his head, as I struggle like a beached beetle, legs cycling an invisible bicycle. He offers me his hand and hauls me up. We exchange a smile. Suddenly, unexpectedly, I feel a lot better. My mum is still awash with dismay but my dad's already getting over it, and some day, she'll get over it too. Who knows, I might even meet someone else they like, marry him instead. I admit it seems unlikely.

I pick my way along the gravel path through the churchyard, holding on to my dad for balance. The church is picture-postcard pretty, with weathered honey-coloured bricks and a slate spire, the athletic ushers standing outside in a tight gang of miserable solidarity at having to wear full morning dress with grey top hats, champagne-coloured cravats and striped trousers.

'Dear oh dear,' my dad mutters. 'Right Said Fred Astaire.'

'They look lovely,' my mum says.

'They look like wazzocks.'

My mum starts exclaiming with delight at seeing people she knows, buzzing over to them. I stand apart from it all, yet still close enough to overhear my name occasionally, followed by frantic shushing and hurried explanations that no, I'm not 'next'.

'This will stop happening at some point, won't it, Dad?' I say.

'Yes, of course.' Pause. 'Eventually you'll become a confirmed spinster. The same way your cousin Alan is a "confirmed bachelor".'

❤ ❤ ❤

'Stand please to welcome the bride.'

I take a sharp breath and ignore the hubbub of my parents' pitying thoughts, behind me. I feel a tug of loss and longing, yet as I see Samantha glide past in Chantilly lace, I know that if it was me, I'd be at least part-pretending. Partly is too much.

As I'm hem-hawing my way through the hymns, I wonder if I'm drifting towards a situation where I might need to Talk To Someone. A nicely-put-together man a few rows ahead glances to the side, and catching his features I think – *Ben?* Oh dear, woman. Chalk that one up to wedding fever.

We sit down for the vows. Through glimpses between bouffy teased hairdos and a forest of candy-coloured fascinators, I eyeball the handsome man a bit more, thinking, all right, I am a sad monomaniac, but it's still a freaky resemblance from the rear. Especially as replicant Ben is with a blonde woman with a haircut exactly like Olivia's …

Wait. Shit me, my life *is* a black comedy… is that *Simon*? This time there's no mistaking the Roman profile and air of arse. It's so surreal I half expect the vicar to throw off his cassock to reveal sequin pasties and a G-string, before I wake up in Rupa's bed, alarm beeping.

I fiddle with the order of service in my trembling hands and try to figure out how on earth this can be. While the well-spoken, bespectacled best man reads the Bible passage about love not vaunting itself and being puffed up, I desperately mine my memory banks for a clue. Samantha isn't a lawyer … maybe they know Tom? No, that can't be it, they've been seated on the bride's side of the church, same as us. The ushers are running this show like a military campaign, no doubt in an attempt to claw back some masculine dignity.

We watch the new Mr and Mrs walk back down the aisle and I turn nearly 180 degrees in the hope of not meeting the eyes of any of their group. Their pews empty before ours and I pretend to be looking for something lost in the depths of my tiny clutch bag as they pass. A murmur of curious voices tells me I've been spotted.

After an agonising single file shuffle outside, my parents wander off to congratulate their opposite numbers and I wonder how best to arrange myself so I look like an enfranchised, confident solo individual living an efficacious life on my own terms.

Hmm, balls to that. I do a quick feasibility study. Is leaving after the service and before the reception a huge insult...? I could claim to have been overcome by sorrow. I could take the spikes from my feet and peg it through the village, trying to flag down a cab. Only the thought of what it would do to my parents stops me.

A tap on the shoulder, and a smiling, if faintly jittery-looking Ben is in front of me. He's in a slim cut, charcoal-coloured wool suit with white shirt and black tie. He looks like he should be on one of those *Vanity Fair* gatefold covers where next-big-thing young actors are draped over each other on stepladders.

'I don't see you for ten years and suddenly you're everywhere?'

'Oh my God,' I laugh, faking amazement for the second time in recent memory. 'What on earth...?'

'You know Sam? Or Tom?'

'Samantha. Neighbours when we were kids. You?'

'Liv went to Exeter with her.'

'I didn't know Samantha did law?'

'Only for the first year. Swapped to pure maths or some other Shun The Fun subject.' He pauses. 'Simon went there too. He's here.'

'Great!' I say, with enough sarcasm for him to give me a sympathetic smile.

A crocodile of guests are picking their way towards the marquee and I suspect Ben will be persona non grata if he waits for me.

'Looks like we're all heading over for the next bit then?' he says. 'See you there.'

'Definitely,' I say, wishing the opposite was true.

As he departs I resist the urge to do a Basil Fawlty fist-shake at the place of worship we've exited: *thank you God, thank you so bloody much*. It's not enough I have to do this wedding, but I have to do it with Ben, Ben Wife and Sworn Enemy?

'My goodness, that is absolutely is the limit,' my mum hisses, as she and my dad rejoin me, my dad wearing his *batten down the hatches* face.

'What?'

'Barbara's only in the same pheasant-tail headpiece I'd bought for your wedding. And for all her snoot, it's *from Debenhams*.'

The copycat millinery momentarily crystallises the difficulty of this day for all of us.

'You know, who cares who's got what,' I say, hooking my arm through my mum's. 'Let's go find the grog.'

62

The marquee for the reception is colossal, swallowing up most of the field. The white canvas has transparent panels in the shape of arched, leaded windows, perhaps in the hope that if you screw your eyes up you might think you're looking at a vast colonial Gatsby-esque Long Island mansion instead of a tent.

We enter the usual interlude while the happy couple has endless photos taken and there's some etiquette that we're not meant to go into the Big Top without them – I see Barbara near-fainting when a guest twitches at a door flap – so we mill on the grass with the bubbly. A med student once told me that champagne nobbles you due to the speed of its absorption into the small bowel. It's not working its magic fast enough for me: I'd like it intravenously, yellow mingling with red and turning my blood a nice Tabasco orange. There's an interestingly anach-ronistic waft of fags when the smokers notice we're in a field and they can do what they like.

Trays of canapés circulate, served by embarrassed-looking teenage catering students in black aprons, as is tradition. As they're fashionable canapés, they require formal introduction.

'Here we have a quenelle of mackerel pate on gem lettuce…
this is a blini with cods' roe…'

'What are the little ones that look like jobbies?'

My dad always goes full Yorkshireman at formal events.

'That's a Medjool date stuffed with Stilton, sir.'

'To think I had a cheddar-pineapple hedgehog at my
wedding!' my dad says to the seventeen-year-old waitress, who
goes bright red, as if it might be a euphemism.

When she moves on my parents quietly grumble about the
lack of opportunities to sit down. The kind of support I'm sorely
lacking isn't for my behind, it's having friends here. They instinctively know how to form a Secret Service formation around
you, in the presence of threats. *Blue Tit Is Moving, I Repeat…*

Ben, Simon and Olivia are part of a glossy knot of haven't-
we-done-well mates, a social ring of Saturn considerably nearer
the planet of the bride and groom. Olivia's in what a man
would call 'a green dress' and Mindy would identify as a char-
treuse bias-cut spaghetti strap satin slip that's almost certainly
from Flannels and, despite flashing little flesh, totally unwearable
unless you have Olivia's sylph-like figure. Tendrils of gold wire
threaded with mother-of-pearl beads curve round her head, in
an ultra-modern, deconstructed tiara.

I wave and Ben raises a palm in return and Olivia gives me
a '*Oh Yeah, You*' cursory nod, with a flicker of lip movement
that could be taken for a smile if you were desperate, goes
back to her discussion with Simon. Simon's in stockbroker
pinstripes and throws a '*Fuck You, Forget About You*' look in my
direction. I see Ben seeing me see Simon see me. I give Ben
one of those oh-well-what-you-gonna-do smiles and he returns
it, apologetically.

I slip my jacket off in the sunshine and my mum gives a gasp. 'When did wedding guest outfits get so vampy?'

'You can't see anything,' I say, testily.

'Ooh, you get the idea though. Have you got a strapless bra or some sort of corset on?' Mum fusses with me in the way mums think they have a right to.

'Mum!'

My dad suddenly finds the view of some cows in the neighbouring field quite compelling.

If that weren't bad enough, to my abject horror, I see Ben approaching. He's already too near for me to sound the alarm without him hearing so I have to hiss '*Muuuuuum, stoppit!*' and try to wrestle away from her investigations without attracting more attention. When Ben's upon us, my mum's actually patting the underneath of my bust in some version of the panto dame boob-hoik manoeuvre that used to get a laugh for Les Dawson.

Our lines of sight lock and in a terrible moment of perfect telepathy, I mind-speak to Ben: *You Have Seen My Breasts.* In a feat of empathy I'd cherish if it were about anything else, startled Ben effortlessly, wordlessly conveys back: *Yes, I Have.* We stare at each other like roadkill caught in the headlights of a shared flashback.

'Mum, Dad, err…' I stutter, turning away from Ben in a vain effort to break the psychic link. 'This is Ben, he's…' *stroked, cupped and squeezed them…* 'married to Olivia, who went to Exeter with Sam. They both took law…' *and took my nipples in his mouth…* 'Well, Sam took it for the first year. I know Ben too because he studied…' *them and said they were beautiful…* 'with me at Manchester.' *Oh God, I said man, and chest, why didn't I just go to Norkfield and be done with it?* 'He was on English with me.'

376

And on me. And in me. It was astounding.

I roll to a close and hope I got the Things Haltingly Spoken and Things Feverishly Thought distinction right. The fact my dad doesn't appear to be suffering a terminal cardiac event suggests I just about managed it.

Ben recovers admirably for nice-to-meet-yous and shakes my dad's hand, doing the same with my mum and adding a gentlemanly peck on the cheek that makes my mum light up.

'Beautiful wedding, isn't it? Haven't they been lucky with the weather? I wanted to let you know that the champagne's on the wane so get it while the going's good.'

Vintage Ben. The Ben who hopped over the desks and started helping out on the day I met him. Given the amount of pride and dollar the parents-of-the-bride invested in this day, I doubt the Laurent Perrier's running dry. He's giving us an excuse to circulate.

'Or actually, we could bring some over?' he says to me. 'Want to give me a hand, Rachel?'

'That's very kind,' my mum says, and I hope to high hell we won't be having any *why-can't-you-see-if-he-has-any-friends* talks.

I follow Ben across the lawn. He turns to speak over his shoulder, conspiratorial.

'I wanted to promise you that Simon won't be giving you hassle,' he says, as we home in on a tray together. 'We've agreed a wide berth policy. If he does give you any shit, give me a shout, OK?'

There's a swell in my heart and alcohol in my small bowel. 'I think you might be the nicest person I've ever met.'

'Honestly?' Ben says, grinning and lifting two glasses. 'Christ. I suppose you do spend all day with murderers and rapists.'

63

The tables have been given names on the theme of New York landmarks, which is where Tom proposed. The top table is Grand Central, followed by Empire State, Queens and Rockefeller. I notice that Ben, Olivia and Simon are on Chrysler. Shiny, slender and glamorous. *Spiky*. With some sense of satire, the collection I've been grouped with is titled Staten Island.

'Might as well call it Rikers Island,' I say, pointing at the italicised place-card to Albrikt from Stockholm, who works with Tom and speaks very little English.

He nods politely and says: 'Absolute.' He has said that in response to my last three remarks. I felt for his bemusement during the best man's lengthy, PowerPoint-aided speech. Not sure how much 'children wearing colanders as hats in the 1980s' photos mean without the Metal Mickey anecdote.

To my left is a dour cousin called Ellen with allergies who I come to think of as Allergen. She scowls at the bread rolls like they're grenades giving off deadly wheat-gas and complains about every aspect of the arrangements until I decide practising the level of Swedish I learned from the chefs on *The Muppets* is preferable.

After the speeches and during the dancing, I go to talk to my parents on Central Park ('Because we're all out to pasture' – my dad) and stay there when the table is deserted for the dessert trolley queue. I'm alone with the post-prandial carnage of pink tablecloth stains, ice buckets full of water and rumpled napkins. This is far enough from the dance floor that no one will think I'm hoping to be asked, and near enough I don't look churlish. I concentrate on my phone and think: the mobile is a godsend to the self-conscious single. A text arrives from Mindy.

Caroline here, making me watch shitty film with Kevin Spacy [sic] Not any of the good ones where he's a syco [sic] something boaring [sic] with boats. The Boat Spotter. How is wedding? Does everyone love your dress?

I'm interrupted as I'm sending my reply ('*Not everyone… guess what…*') by Ben, both hands on the back of a gold banqueting hire chair. His jacket's off, tie loosened.

'May I have this dance?'

'Oh, no, I'm alright…'

'Ah, on your feet. I'm not being blown out by someone sitting there texting like a sulky teenager.'

I bristle. 'Sorry I'm not being sociable enough for you. It doesn't mean I need your pity.'

Ben screws his face up, affronted. Too late I see that he wasn't trying to ridicule me and has no idea how crappy I feel.

'What does that mean? Why would it be pity?'

I can't answer this without looking even more foolish.

'C'mon,' he says, wheedling.

I smile, grudgingly, and he grins broadly as I get to my feet. The forty-something singer in the wedding band is like a gone-to-seed Robert Palmer with a grey-blonde, pomaded pompadour.

He's belting his way confidently and tunefully through The Beatles' back catalogue as a multi-coloured lighting rig casts twisting shafts of purple, green and blue on the chequered flooring, a pin-prick starlight canopy twinkling above our heads. Nope, Rhys would not have signed this off.

'Do we have to do that?' I say, gesturing to the floor full of waltzing couples, in the one-hand-on-waist, one-arm-round-shoulder hold to 'Something'.

'Either that or clear a spot in the middle and announce the intention to breakdance, your choice. You be Run DMC and I'll be Jason Nevins.'

'Isn't this something your wife's contractually obliged to do?'

'Simon's claimed her.' Ben rolls his eyes and nods his head towards the two of them, mercifully at the far side of the floor.

'Wait, sweaty hands,' I say, rubbing them on my dress, when Ben puts his hand out to take mine.

'The angel of the north.'

What I'm really doing is clowning to take the tension out of the impending physical proximity. On the dance floor, I put my right hand on his left shoulder and hold his right hand and he puts his other hand lightly on the small of my back. I keep the rest of my body just clear of his with the muscle control of a prima ballerina.

'Why did you go off on one, just then?' Ben says, distinctly, into my ear.

In the half-light, we can have a conversation without anyone even being sure we're speaking, like spies talking behind news-papers on park benches.

'Today isn't the easiest day for me. For the parents it was going to be a two-part thing, this was the prelude to my wedding.'

'Ah, I see. Sorry. I was worried it might be Simon.'

'It's not helping, but no.'

We do a few turns before Ben adds: 'When you look sad it makes me sad, and when I get affected by something is when it officially starts mattering. The girl I knew at uni was laughing all the time.'

'That's because she was ten to thirteen years younger.'

'Oh, don't start with the age shit. When you're not texting you're as much the life and soul as you always were.'

I mumble more thanks.

'Sorry for being sweaty too,' he adds, briefly breaking hands to pull the front of his damp, and enticingly semi-transparent, shirt away from his chest.

It's actually quite hard to tolerate, but not in the way he thinks. It's all far too much of an assault on the senses, the not-unpleasant masculine body odour and the contact and the whispering in ears and the kindness and the gratitude and use of the word *lover* on stage. Given I need to take my mind off it, and given Ben's being frank, I decide to act relaxed too.

'Hey. Sorry for the tit fiddle shame. Before.'

'Oh, yeah, hah. Not your fault if they get attention. You can hardly leave them at home.'

I laugh.

Ben draws back, so I can see his poker expression: 'I mean your parents.'

'Of course.'

I laugh some more. And then, because I'm a bit 'drunkst' and needy, I say: 'We *nondescript* ladies have to try to get attention somehow.'

Again Ben draws back, this time to check my expression,

that I'm definitely quoting him. I look down at our feet.

He rearranges his hand in mine, flexing his fingers as he clasps it more firmly.

'Do you know the updated OED definition of "nondescript"?'

'No.'

'It means a complete avoidance of giving any details about an attractive woman when it's your wife requesting them. Literally. No. Description.'

'Ah.' I smile, bite my lip.

'So you know.'

'That's useful, having the lingo.'

The song ends. The singer announces: *'Thang you very mush guys thizziz a liddle numbah you may know called Toadall Eclipse of the Hard.'*

'Aw I *love* Toadall Eclipse of the Hard,' Ben says, and I can feel him shaking as we lean against each other, laughing. Across the floor, Olivia and Simon are talking, serious. How can you not find this song funny?

'You know, we're never going to win this dancing competition with my wife and Simon if we don't put some flair into it,' Ben says, holding his hand in mine out above me and pointing to the left, to indicate a twirl to the refrain *'turn around …'*

I oblige with a twirl left, and then right, and then when the song breaks into its full rawk, Ben tips me a short distance and pulls me up.

'I nearly fell out of my dress,' I gasp, as we resume the waltz-hold, in something more like an embrace because I had to put my arm round him to get my balance.

'Then we'd definitely win,' Ben says, in a half-whisper.

I glance at him in surprise and he gives me a guilty, yet slightly lascivious smile. Pissed as I am, I blush. I rest my head on his shoulder so we don't have to look at each other. This is too much. I have to cut the mood dead, the same way I did when we were feeding the ducks. In minutes, he'll be back with his wife, and I'll return to my chair on Central Park, and I have to be OK with that. *I can't be this close with you, thinking it's a one-off.*

I glance over at Simon and Olivia and he's looking directly at us, over her bronzed shoulder blade. He has a look of malevolent and completely disconcerting satisfaction.

Ben's eagerly claimed by a posh bridesmaid with a dishevelled chignon, sprigs of wilted freesia poking out at random angles, as if she's been pulled through a florist's backwards. I excuse myself to the ladies and head across the grass in the dark to the toilets. My exposed flesh goose bumps in the cold, ears ringing with disco tinnitus, heels sinking into the mud like golf tees. The Portaloos are the Porsche of Portaloos: twin stalls, piped-in music, pink dimpled Andrex and wedding flowers between the sinks. As I make my way back down the small step ladder, I see Olivia stood at the bottom, arms folded, tiara making her look like a tiny platinum Statue of Liberty.

'Hello!' I say. 'Don't worry, there's still loo roll left.'

'Can I talk to you?' Olivia says, which seems redundant given that's precisely what we're doing.

'Sure,' I say, drawing level, getting the Jangly Fear.

'Have you slept with my husband?'

'*Sorry?*' I feel as giddy and sick as if I've done that dance floor drop ten times over, after shot-gunning a whole bottle of Laurent Perrier.

'At university. Did you sleep with Ben?'

'We were friends.'

'Right. Ben tells me you have slept together. Is he lying?'

Oh God, oh God. Why did he make her this mad and set her free to hunt me? Why would they be having this conversation on a wedding dance floor, with Hall and Oates on harmonies? My mind races. Simon's face … did he know she'd been told what had happened? Why did Ben seem so casual? Why did he not warn me?

'Are you telling me my husband's lying?' Olivia repeats. 'Either way something's going on, isn't it – why would he lie?'

'No! Ben's not lying. It was only the once, it was nothing.'

A deadly silence. The throb of chatter and music from the marquee seems a long, long way in the distance. Somewhere in the surrounding blanket darkness, right on cue, an owl hoots.

'If it was nothing, I wonder why it was kept from me.' Olivia's voice sounds as jagged and dangerous as a shard of glass.

'Ben probably didn't want to upset you with something so trivial, from so long ago.'

Olivia's eyes flash like a Disney witch casting a bad spell.

'It's trivial? You think this is trivial?'

I shake my head. 'No, not to you, of course not.'

'Or are you saying it wasn't any good?'

'What?'

'Was. It. Any. *Good*?'

I may not be a lawyer, but I'm a journalist, and I know this is an attempt to extract a quote that will sound, out of context, like either gloating or mocking.

'It . . . I . . .' Mindy's TripAdvisor idea comes back to me, hardly helpful. *Great facilities, attentive service, ten out of ten, will be back!* 'We were drunk, I can't remember much.'

'I don't want you to come anywhere near me or my husband or my home ever again. Do you understand?'

'Yes.'

A pause where I hope I can decently get away from her, belt back into the Big Top, grab my things and run.

'Simon said I shouldn't trust you. He said you spent your date talking about Ben.'

I feel my first flash of anger. *That bastard.* Sod you and the pig you rode in on.

'Simon's lying,' I say.

'That's funny, he said you were the liar.'

'Well, that's a lie.' This conversation's heading towards the farcical. 'Simon also thinks I went on a date with him to investigate a kiss-and-tell story I knew nothing about at the time.'

'You're going to run my friend down?'

'I don't know how else to defend myself when he's making things up.'

I'm clammy, hands curled into fists, nails digging into my palms. My dress is digging in to me too, the balls of my feet aching. I'm suddenly very sober, long past midnight on any Cinderella moment. I know Olivia's made up her mind about me. I should still have one last try.

'I'm sorry you didn't know about this. I didn't know if Ben had told you. I didn't think it was my business to ask. But as for Simon, he's already told me I'm a piece of shit because of the Shale story. Whatever he's told you is designed to make you angrier at me. He was the one asking about Ben on our date.'

'Guess what, Rachel. Simon said you weren't being honest about only being friends with Ben. He said to get you on your own and tell you my husband had sold you out. Instant result. *Whoops*. So stand here and tell me some more about how he doesn't know what he's talking about.'

Don't worry Simon, you will be made partner. You twat.

'If you're going to take Simon's word over mine, there's nothing I can say. There's nothing inappropriate going on.'

'Like hell. What a surprise to see you with Ben on the dance floor, the second I was with Simon.'

'He asked me.'

'Hah, sure, *he's* after *you*.'

'That's not what I was …'

'Know what else Simon said about you? He said you're exactly the type of woman who starts chasing other women's husbands when she realises no one wants to marry her. You're a strictly "bed don't wed".'

The nastiness of this winds me. Bed don't wed? *The 1950s called, they want their attitudes back.* When slinging me on the fallen females reject pile, they forget the part where I chose not to get married.

'Right, OK. What a nice guy he is to say something like that. If Slime-On won't put a ring on it then I may as well end it now. I'll start putting my paperwork in order and find my father's pearl-handled revolver.'

'Oh, that's right, you're so *funny*, aren't you,' Olivia says, with whiplash-spite that turns my stomach right over.

'You're still miles out of your league, anywhere near my husband or Simon.'

As I move to walk off, Olivia adds, bitterly: 'I don't know what Ben saw in you.'

I stop, think, turn. '… Himself?'

I brace myself for Olivia to slip her L.K. Bennett mule off and give me a good shoeing.

At that second, a traumatised middle-aged lady appears silhouetted in the doorway of the Portaloos, a vision in lavender sent from heaven to bestow peace.

'Have you ever seen such lovely soap! In a Portaloo! Soap!'

64

I don't have to knock on Mindy's front door in Whalley Range as she's heard the taxi's engine and is already waiting, arms folded, as if I've overshot my curfew. She's also obviously on high alert due to my text insisting I was on my way to hers and not under any circumstances to go to bed, however much the Shipping News encouraged it. As I reach her, I see Caroline's head bobbing over her shoulder, both of them wearing forehead-crumpling expressions of concern.

'What's up?' Mindy demands.

They stand back as I sweep into the kitchen and throw my bag down on Mindy's kitchen table. I must look a state: up-do unravelling, smoky eyes gone full polecat-smudgy, problems with normal respiration.

'Olivia tricked me into admitting me and Ben slept together at university and went supernova and said I could never come near either of them ever again.'

Mindy and Caroline stare at me with dull stupefaction, as if I've blown in from another world using an alien language, which this Saturday night, I sort of have.

'Wait, wait.' Mindy holds a hand up. 'You *slept* with him?'

'Once. Right before we left university. Remember Rhys and I called it off around graduation?'

'You wily lady!' Mindy squeals. 'Why'd you never tell us? When? Where?'

'Mindy!' Caroline barks. 'What the fuck does it matter where it was?'

'I'm just trying to get the facts established!'

'At our student house. You and Caro were home the night before the grad ball? Then.'

'Why did you never tell us?' Caroline echoes Mindy, with a different intonation.

I slump down into a chair, stifling a wince at how my heat, food and booze-swollen body strains against the seams of the dress as I do so.

'It was totally unexpected. I was in love with him and I messed it up and somehow let him think I wasn't that keen and it was over before it began. Rhys walked back into the ball, Ben legged it and never took a phone call from me again, went off travelling, that was that. I've never been able to bear talking about it. It was as if, if I pretended it hadn't happened, it couldn't hurt as much.'

'Ooh God,' says Mindy, under her breath.

'And what happened with Olivia?' Caroline asks.

She looks, if not stern, then wary. This is all too much what she predicted. I outline Olivia's specific objections to me, and Simon's more general ones.

'Get tae fuck!' Mindy shouts. 'Who's he to say that? And what a bitch!'

Caroline says nothing. I put my head in my hands.

'Come on, come to the sofa,' Mindy says, guiding me. 'Those chairs aren't really for sitting, I got them because they look great with that table.'

Once I'm deposited on softer seating I feel myself under intense scrutiny.

'It was one night? Ben liked you too?' Mindy asks.

'At the time he said he loved me. He was about to go travelling, I had my post-grad course. The timing was all wrong.'

Caroline still says nothing.

'You don't have to say it, you were right,' I tell her. 'I should never have risked being Ben's friend again.'

'I don't get what you did wrong. Are you supposed to say sorry for something that happened years before he met his wife?' Mindy asks.

I chew my lip.

'Let me get this straight, have you been trying to lure Ben away?' Mindy asks.

'No, but…'

'Then I don't blame either of you for not making a thing out of it. If you'd dated before and kept it quiet now, OK, that's deception. Anything less is sparing people's feelings. No one hands over a full disclosure list at the signing of the register. It's "Don't Ask, Don't Tell."'

I laugh weakly, despite myself. 'Like gays in the US military?'

'Yeah!'

I glance at Caroline. I look back at Mindy. Am I going to say it? I've barely admitted it to myself. I am. I'm going to have to say it.

'It's a bad idea for me to be his friend because…'

390

Two pairs of eyes widen in expectation.

'…Seeing him again has made me realise the ridiculous truth. I'm still in love with him.'

Caroline and Mindy look at each other and then at me again.

'Really?' Mindy breathes.

'It's demented and tragic, I know,' I say.

'It's crazily romantic.'

'He's married, Mindy,' Caroline says, flatly.

'Yep, he's married, so it's nothing but sad and wrong,' I say, horribly aware that Caroline must feel as if she's being asked to sympathise with the kind of woman who fooled around with Graeme. 'I was stood there with Olivia insulting me thinking, I deserve this.'

'You don't deserve it!' Mindy says, but her eyes flicker towards Caroline in uncertainty.

Pause.

'Look,' Caroline addresses us both, 'you've been great about Graeme behaving like an utter dick but I feel as if you expect me to take some hard line or want to treat me with kid gloves and I'm the same person. My views are still my views and, Rachel, yes, I said I thought you should be careful of the spark between you and Ben before this, and before I became a scorned woman myself. But as for this evening, I think the row with Olivia is Ben's fault.'

Even in my relief at being excused I feel a pang of protectiveness.

'Olivia deserved to know the full history and he was the one who had a duty to tell her, not you.'

'Yeah. What were *you* supposed to say?' Mindy says. 'Hi, nice to meet you, by the way, I've had your husband?"

'And you broke off your engagement not so long ago. You're bound to be vulnerable and he's the married one. He should've known better to let things get to this point,' Caroline concludes.

Long pause. Amid all the mess of cans and worms, I feel better for having told them.

'Is she going to give me evils if I ask more questions?' Mindy points at Caroline.

'Oh, do what you like, Mindy,' Caroline says, with a shrug, though I can see she's amused. She asked for business as usual, she's got it.

'One night, ten years on, you still love him. It must've been *quite a night*?'

'Er … yes.'

'I mean. He was amazing? An amazing boff?'

'I got what you meant, Mind. Yes. He was.'

Mindy pulls her legs underneath her on the sofa, trying not to look like she's enjoying herself. Mindy loves a drama, and that goes treble for a drama that involves someone who's amazing at boffing. 'When did it change? I mean, when you were at uni and with Rhys, when did your feelings towards Ben change?'

'I don't know, exactly. It happened by degrees without me ever noticing and by the time I did, it was sort of overwhelming. I'd ignored it, and then – WHAM – he says I love you …'

'He loved Wham?' Mindy asks.

'No, "WHAM", like a cartoon explosion sound effect. He loved me …'

'Sorry, sorry! Of course. Carry on.'

'And there it was, he said it and I knew I loved him too. I thought he was so far out of my league, I hadn't even dared think it, let alone say it.'

'If he ran off, he could've had second thoughts, though?' Caroline asks, and I know she's not being unkind, just trying to take the edge off my regret.

'I'm not sure. He brought it up, when we went for a drink the other night. It was clear he thought I'd got back with Rhys at the ball and that I didn't feel the same way.'

'What did you say?!' Mindy wails, as if I keep issuing cliff-hangers from *The Young and The Restless*.

'I had to more or less go along with it. Not as if I could say, no, it was all a huge misunderstanding, I miss you every damn moment.'

'You don't know that it was a mistake,' Caroline says. 'Maybe you and Ben would've imploded in three months flat after a huge fight in a tuk tuk.'

'Maybe.'

'OK. I'm going to make cups of tea and put whisky in them,' Mindy says.

Caroline and I sit in silence for a short while, listening to Mindy pottering around in the next room.

'Aren't you going to say I told you so?' I say to Caroline. 'I deserve it and then some.'

'You didn't say that to me about Graeme.'

'You weren't remotely to blame!'

'You and Graeme have never exactly been close, I know you don't have much time for him ...' I open my mouth and Caroline shakes her head to stop me politely demurring '... but you've never said a word against him and you didn't pull him to pieces over this latest ... *transgression* or give me grief for taking him back and I appreciated it. None of us are perfect. I warned you about Ben. I thought you were going to unintentionally hurt other people. I didn't realise you were mainly hell bent on hurting yourself.'

'I knew it was doomed, Caro, I just wanted to see him again so much,' I say, mournfully.

'I know, I know. It was me opening my big mouth about seeing him at the library anyway,' Caroline says, leaning over and giving me a shoulder pat. 'He's unfinished business. It's bound to have stirred you up, him coming back when he did. Don't be too sure it's love.'

Good old Caro. She will always 'see it, say it'.

Mindy comes back in with mugs of tea. Caroline sniffs hers and wrinkles her nose. 'Jeez, what's this, eighteen per cent proof builder's?'

'My dad gave me some Glenfiddich for Christmas, I've been looking for a use for it.'

'You tipped a Scottish single malt in tea? This is a terrorist act.'

I sip mine. Hot, sweet, laced – ideal for a shock. All I need now is the marathon runner's foil cape.

'Try to remember this,' Caroline says, getting back to the topic. 'A proper relationship with Ben would've involved arguing over his crap DIY, the stage where he thinks he can do the squeeze-and-splash into the toilet when you're in the shower, and visits to Dunelm Mill.'

'Where's Dunelm Mill?' I ask.

'It's an outlet shop. My point is, the life with him you feel like you lost out on, it's perfect because it's a fantasy and it's a fantasy because it's perfect.'

Mindy places a consoling hand on my arm. 'And look at this way. What you and Ben had, one night, it was this ideal thing, like in *Casablanca* when they say *we'll always have Paris.*'

'We'll always have the Wilbraham Road boffing?'

'Yeah. With how things have turned out, you don't have to spoil it. You don't have to slowly go off each other, see the other one get senile and die.'

I sweep my sweaty fringe out of my eyes.

'The problem is, after all these years, I can't think of anyone I'd more like to slowly go off, see get senile and die than Ben.'

65

At least the maxim about newspaper people – 'short tempers, short memories' – has some truth: no one's entirely forgotten what happened with Natalie, but with each passing day, I see that if it's not quite old news yet, it's getting older every day. I can survive it.

Zoe gets her name in the *Mail* regularly. It turns out one of the 'Seven Habits of Highly Effective People' is being a shocking piece of work. I'm sure she'll end up with her own column by age thirty. She'll use it to berate venal politicians and hypocritical celebrities for lying to us, with one of those byline photos where she looks like she's staring down someone taking a dump in her garden.

Speaking of ordure and questionable hacks, Gretton's taken to bringing me a dung-coffee in the press room every morning. It's nice of him and yet it makes me mildly uncomfortable. Have I been brought so low that even Gretton feels sorry for me?

'You're more stream of piss than Jesus's sunbeam!' is a typical gee-me-up greeting.

He's also started sharing story tips, with predictably horrifying results.

'The begging and indecent exposure in 4 should be a laugh. A bag lady's been flashing people with her scary mary,' he says, this particular day. 'Arresting officer said it looked like she was giving birth to Ken Dodd.'

'You know what, Pete, I might let you apply your singular talents to that one.'

I have to get back to the flat on time as Caroline and I have concocted a plan that relies on everyone sticking to their schedules. I get home for six, Caroline's with me by quarter past, and Mindy's with us by quarter to seven, for a DVD-and-takeaway night with a twist she doesn't know about. At seven, the doorbell goes again.

'Evening!' Ivor says, as he steps inside. 'Have you really bought an Xbox?' And then: 'Oh, *what*?' as he spies Mindy.

'What's he doing here?' Mindy barks, standing up.

I insert myself between door and Ivor, herding him further into the room while I do so.

'OK. I've recently made a massive balls-up of my life, and Caroline, through no fault of her own, is experiencing some disruption also,' I say. 'We could both do with you two making friends and restoring harmony. That's not going to happen if you never speak. So, speak. Say anything you like, but you have to start speaking.'

'I'm leaving. How's that for some speaking?' Ivor says, turning.

'And if he wasn't leaving, I would be.' Mindy says with hands on hips.

'Oh for heaven's sake, the two of you,' Caroline says.

'I have nothing to say to him,' Mindy says.

'Likewise. Can I go now?' Ivor says to me.

'What, you're going to throw away years of friendship because you had a bust-up over Katya?' I say, looking from one to the other. 'Is she worth it?'

'Ask Ivor what she's worth,' Mindy says. 'Four hundred and twenty pounds a month? TV licence and bunga bunga included?'

'See?' Ivor says. 'This is pointless.'

'Stop this!' I say, suddenly a little hysterical. 'I know right now you think you can spat all you want and it'll be OK and you don't really mean it. Ivor could be hit by a bus on his way home. You never know when it could be a last chance. Talk!'

'She practically called me a sex attacker!' Ivor bellows back. 'It's nice you want to do some helping out here, but unless you can get a full, grovelling retraction from her, not gonna happen. Whether I go under a Stagecoach or not.'

'Grovelling? Kiss my arse,' Mindy says.

'Alright, alright.' Caroline gets to her feet, yanking her top over her concave stomach. 'Enough of this! Mindy, sit down.' She puts a firm hand on Mindy's shoulder and pushes her, then points a finger at Ivor, and an armchair. 'Ivor, you sit there. *Now*.'

Ivor sulkily obeys, coat still on.

She positions herself equidistant between them, standing. Caroline in full Paxman mode is an intimidating experience. I hover nearby, as if I'm studio security.

'Mindy,' Caroline says, 'Ivor did not give Katya any concession on the rent in return for kinky favours. You know that. Stop saying he did. It simply happened and he has the right to sleep with anyone he wants. He's a grown, single man. If we all passed judgement on each other's choice of bonks down the years, I think we know there'd have been a lot of ructions.'

Caroline moves her gaze.

'Ivor, Mindy gets a very hard time for her choice of boyfriends from you. You're never exactly welcoming to them. Maybe next time you see Jake, you could correct that.'

'Jake and I aren't seeing each other any more,' Mindy says.

'Whoever the next one is, then,' Caroline says.

'It's not a revolving door!' Mindy says, and Ivor looks slightly brighter.

'Sorry to hear that,' I say, to Mindy. 'About Jake, not the door.'

'OK. Jake or no Jake, if Mindy has overreacted to one indiscretion, there have been years of provocation,' Caroline says.

'I hardly think a few wind-ups are the same as branding me an abuser, do you?'

'I think you both need to say sorry and you both need to hear it. You can say it at the same time, if no one wants to go first. I'll count you in.'

'This isn't a crèche,' Ivor says to Caroline. 'What if we don't agree, no Stickle Bricks and milk?'

'I'm not going to change my opinion because of what you force him to say,' Mindy says. 'This *is* pointless.'

'At least you agree on something!' I say, optimistically.

I look in desperation towards Caroline.

'OK, you force me to do this. I'm breaking the glass and grabbing the hammer,' Caroline says, sitting down and crossing her legs.

Mindy and I frown in confusion at each other.

'I've got a theory, if anyone cares to hear it. Here's what I think is actually going on. Ivor has been in love with Mindy for years but won't do anything about it because of her ludicrous insistence on only considering men who look a certain way.

Hence the ridicule about her dates.'

I look at Ivor, who's wearing the face of a man who's raced to the airport in time for the final boarding call and found he doesn't have his passport.

'And I think Mindy's starting to realise she has similar feelings for Ivor. That's why she hates what he did with Katya so much.' Caroline turns to Mindy. 'You're not disapproving, you're jealous.'

'*What?*' Mindy says, who's the palest I've ever seen anyone with dark skin. 'I am not!'

'I'm making sense, aren't I? If we all think about this, we know it's true.' Caroline surveys the room, taking in three faces with open mouths. 'You're mad, because you're mad about each other. Isn't that right, Rachel?'

'Uh. I couldn't say. You make a convincing case …?'

'You're a bunch of …' Ivor is on his feet, wild-eyed, spluttering for words. 'Just fuck off! All of you!'

He charges out of the door.

'That stopped short of a denial,' Caroline says, looking to Mindy.

She rounds on Caroline. 'What the HELL was that?!'

'If neither of you were going to broach it, I thought I'd give it a helping hand. None of us are getting any younger here.'

'You're totally, completely out of order.'

'Am I?'

'Yes!' Mindy screams, snatching up her coat.

'You've never thought of Ivor that way?'

'No!'

'And you don't think Ivor likes you?'

'No!'

'Oh.'

400

'Well done for making a very bad situation a thousand times worse! When the fuck do you think we'll ever want to be in the same room now?'

'Don't go,' I say, weakly, as Mindy slams out the door. I hear her footsteps pounding on the steps beyond.

'That went well, I think,' I say, joining a beleaguered Caroline on the couch. 'Are you sure about what you said?'

Caroline bites her lip. 'I was. Maybe I was wrong. I overstepped the mark, didn't I?'

'If it wasn't true, it will be obscenely embarrassing to sort out.'

'And if it was true, it will be even worse?' Caroline says.

'Oh no, a diabolical third option. What if this is true of one of them and not the other? What then?'

Caroline puts a hand over her mouth. I groan and bury my head in the sofa, slap the cushions rhythmically. I re-emerge. 'I'm going after Mindy. This is my fault, I had the herd and trap idea.'

'I'd let her cool off, if I were you, but if you think it'll help . . .'

I gallop down the stairs and burst into the street. Thanks to Mindy's love of vivid colour, I spot her easily, an aubergine flag against red bricks some yards away. She's stopped still and I worry she's crying. *Shit.* I'm the one who owes a grovelling apology.

As I advance, I'm surprised to see Ivor's on the other side of her. This is good, surely? Unless they're saying dreadful, eviscerating, final sort of things to each other. Something in the position of their bodies tells me this isn't the case – it looks more like an intense tête-à-tête than the distance between two people squaring up. I watch them for a minute, unable to catch any drift or tone of their conversation. Mindy puts her arms up round Ivor's neck for a conciliatory hug and I nearly cheer.

They don't break apart.

I stare and stare in delighted disbelief until I realise I'm being a shameless voyeur and might ruin it if I'm spotted. Flying back through the flat door, I run into Caroline, who's pulling her jacket on.

'Where are you going?' I ask, breathlessly.

'You're right, best say sorry to them. That was unnecessarily sadistic. I'll say I'm unbalanced and mention Graeme and they'll feel bad enough to forgive me.'

'All right,' I say, enjoying the moment very much. 'If you can prise them apart downstairs, tell them you called it wrong.'

'They're *fighting*?' Caroline asks, aghast.

66

I thought it wouldn't be like Ben not to say goodbye the second time around, but I also knew it might not be up to him. Then a call comes during work on a Friday. It's pay day for much of the city, and we're experiencing a snap of sunshine. By half past five, the pens outside the pubs that pass as al fresco seating areas will be heaving.

'I was hoping we could meet for a quick chat,' Ben says, brusque in his awkwardness. 'I don't want to take up too much of your Friday night. Meet at the town hall steps, after work?'

I get it, neutral territory – nothing that could look like socialising. When I arrive, I see there's a French market on in Albert Square and it's a cluster of yellow-and-white striped awnings, shadowing wheels of brie, floury-looking saucisson and wooden tubs of garlic and onions. And there's a not-very-Gallic, opportunistic ice-cream van, thronged with customers.

Ben's waiting, one hand in his pocket, the other holding his briefcase. He's in a dark suit and tan shoes, looking suitably apprehensive and, inconveniently for me, as someone who'll never get to see him again, magnificent. How does he manage to get incrementally *more* handsome as time passes? I want to swipe a Calippo from a passing child to rub on my pulse points and cool my blood down.

'Hi,' I say. '*Sacre bleu!*'

'Hello. *Merde.* Great planning on my part.'

We stand looking at each other in a friendly but useless manner. Conversation needed.

'Nice brogues,' I say, pointing. *Slick like oil, Rachel.* 'My dad says only bounders wear brown shoes for business.' *And a devastatingly brilliant recovery.*

Luckily, Ben laughs.

'Funny you say that. Keep an open mind: have you ever heard the term "Ponzi scheme"?' He pretends to flip the catches on his briefcase.

We laugh. Silence again.

'Uhm. Obviously, you know what I want to talk about,' Ben says.

I nod, nervously. 'In general.'

Across the square, an accordion starts up, accompanied by some throaty singing from a Bejams Edith Piaf. *Non, je ne regrette rien* … Je regrette plus da loads, actually.

'Do you know St John's Gardens? Part two of Ben's Parks and Recreations tour.'

'I think I do … lead the way.'

As we walk down Deansgate, Ben learns more than he could've ever wanted to about the subtleties of 'intent to supply' and I pick up some opinions about cuts to legal aid.

'This is beautiful,' I say, when we get to St John's, a verdant oasis tucked behind Castlefield Museum.

'Isn't it. It used to be the site of a church, I think.'

It occurs to me Ben might've been walking in his lunch hours because he has a lot on his mind. St John's is mercifully near-deserted, it being happy hour. We take a seat on one of the circle of benches that ring the memorial cross. Ben puts his briefcase down.

'I didn't see you leave the wedding…?'

'No. I, uh, thought it best if I went quickly.'

'I'm really sorry. I want to apologise, for both of us. Liv had no right to put you on the spot like that, and I should've told her first. You've ended up in the middle of something that's nothing to do with you and it's not fair. I can see that even if Liv can't right now.'

'I'm sorry I dropped you in it when she asked me. She said you had told her.'

Ben looks stricken. 'She never asked me directly so I never said anything. That was all. If I'd thought for a moment she would ask you, I'd have put her in the picture first and spared you both the slanging match.'

'I understand why you didn't tell her about uni. It wasn't as if we went out with each other.'

Ben squirms some more. 'That's what I said to myself, but it was lying by omission. If Liv was inviting some old friend round for dinner, I wouldn't want her to leave the carnal knowledge detail out. I wouldn't want her to pull a lawyer's "you didn't ask the right questions" on me, as her husband.'

I don't know how to answer this without making it sound like I'm knocking Olivia.

'It was Simon who told her to ask me,' I offer, instead.

'Yeah. We had another situation, a while back. Oh,' he rubs

405

his face, wearily, 'I was going to talk in non-specifics, but fuck it. Back in the day, when Liv and I were first engaged, Simon declared his undying love. To her, obviously.'

This news is in the category of surprise-but-not-a-shock. In all Simon's searching for proof of my Significant Other, deep down I recognised the symptoms. All signs pointed to Olivia, if I'd been looking.

'He did?'

'She told me straight away. Everything was sorted out and we stayed friends.'

'That was who he meant by the married woman who went back to her husband?'

'They weren't involved. What he said to you makes me worry what went on in his head. I suppose he had to change some details so you didn't twig, but still… When you told me that had been discussed on your date, I should've realised he was going to make trouble. I naïvely hoped he was clearing the decks.'

'Right.'

'Afterwards, Liv and I agreed total honesty had to be the policy between us. I broke a promise in not doing the same about you. Not that I'm suggesting it's a similar situation,' he adds, hurriedly. 'But Simon took it upon himself to start insinuating he stopped dating you because he thought there was something going on between us. He blamed you for the story and I think he blamed me for putting you in touch, then taking your side. Stirring with Liv called to him on all kinds of levels.'

'That's *so*…'

'I know,' Ben says. 'I don't want to upset you too much if I say I have my doubts about that date you had. I'm sure he was attracted to you anyway.'

I put a hand up. 'Please, no bother. I honestly don't care that Simon wasn't interested in my sparkling personality. I wondered why he fished lots about you.'

'Yeah. I suspect he was working out if you could be used to drive a wedge from the start.'

'And he accused me of having ulterior motives!'

'Quite. Bastard. It's not lost on me he wouldn't have had as much success if I'd not been so lazy. As for Liv, it's safe to say he doesn't have a chance whether I'm around or not.'

Ben looks like he didn't mean to say 'or not', and ploughs on: 'I've told Liv everything about us now, anyway, so…'

'I thought I managed that?'

'No, everything,' Ben says, quietly and firmly, turning to face me more fully. 'My side. I know it wasn't the same for you and I stressed that to Liv. I don't think it made it much easier to hear.'

It wasn't the same for you. There it is. The mistake I can never correct, the words I can't take back. Or the words I can't add.

I summon all the decency I possess, which takes five or six seconds. 'I hope you two are OK. You don't have to say what you're going to say. I know that you have to cut me off, completely, and I understand.'

'I appreciate you saying, that…' Ben pauses. 'Liv's left.'

'*What?* When?'

What I really want to ask is – left you?

'Few days ago. We've been rowing over other things and she'd been threatening to go back to London.'

I struggle to catch up. *Olivia's gone. Does this change everything?*

'Liv's not settled in Manchester, says she doesn't want to bring kids up here. You know about our disagreement over the house thing. She put a transfer at work in motion, only told me it was for definite when she'd packed her bags.'

'I'm sorry.' I'm not anything. I'm in freefall, wondering where I'll land.

'I don't know how long it's going to take for me to find something down there. I can't simply transfer. I'm not as senior as she is.'

Not left Ben? Left the north.

'You're going too?'

'Yes.'

'You're OK with going? You've talked about it?'

Ben gives me a thin smile. 'Sometimes you have to put what's right to one side and do what's necessary. She isn't coming back, no matter what I say, which means I can't stay.'

I notice there's no mention of the Didsbury house. I guess in obscenely loaded world, selling one isn't a prerequisite for buying another.

'Well,' I say, with lead in my belly, 'Manchester's going to miss you.'

Ben sighs. 'I'm going to miss Manchester. It's been great to be back.'

I hesitate. 'Are you going to take the house from her parents?'

He hangs his head.

'I don't know. It's not a price I want to pay for keeping my relationship together but it looks like that is the price, whether I like it or not. Please don't ask me any more questions. I feel depressed about the answers.'

'Sure,' I say. 'Sorry.'

His head snaps up again. 'Tell me this, Rachel, did you ever think being a proper adult would be this hard?'

408

'I think I thought once I got finals out of the way, it would be plain sailing to the family plot. All downhill sledging.'

'Exactly,' Ben laughs. 'Going downhill sounds about right. If I'd known what was in store, I wouldn't have moaned about Old English so much.'

We grin at each other. My ribs ache.

'It's been lovely to see you again,' he says. 'Shame you can't say the same about me and mine. First Simon goes off at you, then Liv. I bet you wish you'd never started learning Italian and visiting that library.'

The lie that restarted everything. It's my turn to speak, to insist no, it's been wonderful to see him too and then let him go as if it's easy for me. Yet Olivia's gone. They might not stay together even if he does move down there. He might decide not to move, if all the facts are made available to him. This could be it. This could be a second chance, and it's going to melt away forever if I don't seize it and show the mettle I failed to the first time round. *Put what's right to one side and do what's necessary*, wasn't that what Ben was saying?

'There's something I have to tell you.'

I hope to see some glimmer of recognition in his eyes to make this easier. He's totally impassive. 'OK.'

'I didn't bump into you by chance that night at the library. Caroline told me she'd seen you there and I was waiting for you, hoping to see you.'

Ben frowns.

'I've thought about you so much during the last ten years. I've never had what we had with anyone else. I don't know how I failed to convince you how I felt, back then. If you're leaving now and you're not sure you want to, you should know that I still love you. I'm in love with you, Ben.'

My words hang in the space between us and I can't quite believe they're my own.

Ben's eyes narrow. 'This is a joke, isn't it? You're winding me up? 'Cos it's in really poor taste.'

'I mean every word. Surely you know I wouldn't joke about this?'

He stares at me. Before he speaks, he takes a deep breath, as if about to swing something heavy.

'Liv said this was what you were doing. My wife said I'd let someone into our life who was trying to break us up. I called her paranoid and ridiculous. I defended you and your good intentions to the hilt and I've been sat here apologising to you and criticising her behaviour. You're telling me she was right all along?'

'I wasn't trying to break you up—'

'Then why are you telling me you're in love with me? What am I supposed to do?' Ben exclaims. 'Why did you even come looking for me?!'

'I . . . I couldn't stop myself.'

He pauses, a log-jammed pause, as if he has so many things to hurl at me he has to stop to sort them into order of priority.

'I can't believe this. No wonder my wife's walked out on me. Do you honestly think I'm the type of man to put the small matter of being married to one side for a while? That I'd go, well she's down there, I'm up here for a bit, I'll take this opportunity and cheat on her?'

'No! I wasn't talking about an affair.'

'What then?' Ben stares me down. 'I'm married. I intend on staying that way.'

I gulp and slump as if I've been shot. 'OK.'

'I'm sorry about you and Rhys. You're not yourself at the moment. I get that. But if I'd thought you thought this was in any way ...' he scrambles for the word '... *romantic*, I'd have run a mile. God, what kind of impression have I given you?'

I could honestly lean over and retch into the shrubbery from sheer humiliation.

'It's not your fault. It's just. You said Liv had left ...' I trail off.

I comprehend what he's thinking, from his appalled expression, as clearly as if he had more of Rupa's gold letters to spell it out on a wall. *What makes you think I'd be interested if I wasn't married?*

I should've known. It became such a cherished memory I couldn't allow the possibility that Ben's passing interest in me was a glitch in space and time, an anomaly, a freak occurrence, the sort of youthful folly you look back on like using Lambrini as a mixer, or MC Hammer pants. I allowed myself the fantasy that being married to Olivia was the reason he wasn't with me. Now that's gone too.

Ben clears his throat. 'You don't want me, anyway. You're upset after breaking up with Rhys. In fact, I think we've been here before, haven't we? Deja bloody vu.'

'No!' I cry. 'He arrived at the ball and you disappeared.'

'I didn't want to cause a scene by standing there with him. I assumed you'd make your choice. There wasn't going to be a duel.'

I'm almost struggling to get my breath now, to get the words out. 'I didn't get a chance to choose you. You went. I couldn't bear to leave Rhys standing there. He deserved better than that.'

'Even staying the night?'

'What?'

'The next day I walked to your house, early, to check. His car was outside.'

'Yes, he stayed over, strictly on the floor. I couldn't throw him out on the street. We talked, he slept, he left, and I went to yours first thing and found you'd gone back to London. You wouldn't take phone calls from me, you didn't reply to my letter. That was it. Over.'

Ben says nothing.

'Then one day when I rang, I got Abi.'

He winces at this. 'She wouldn't have meant it.'

'She wasn't nasty. In fact it was the kindest thing, probably. She told me you'd brought the date of your travelling forward and she didn't understand why I kept calling when you obviously weren't going to talk to me. What was I supposed to do? Come down and camp on your doorstep? I was desperate enough but by then I was sure *you'd* had second thoughts...'

Ben shakes his head. He doesn't want to rake this over, I know. I've not left him much option. He fiddles with the handle on his briefcase, as if reassuring himself he'll be able to make a swift getaway.

'I didn't know what you were thinking. For the entire time at university, really. Rhys dominated you, and you let him. Sometimes I thought what I felt might be mutual, but other time...and I knew you didn't mean for us to end up in bed. I couldn't tell where your head was afterwards, even though you said nice things. I had to give you some breathing space so you could make a decision. And you did.'

'I didn't.' I shake my head. 'Or not the one you think I did.'

'Hang on, you were with the bloke all this time. You got engaged. Are you honestly saying that wasn't your choice?'

'I'm not proud of this, but I fell back into being with Rhys. I thought I was a good person to spare him finding out what had happened, the night of the ball. In the end it was much, much crueller. For everyone.'

Ben stares at me. He opens his mouth, closes it. Then says: 'OK, even so, for three years I gave you all the signs I could, without actually jumping on you. You think with rose-tinted hindsight that you were unlucky, but when I was available you were undecided. Anything you can't have any more starts to look more appealing.'

'I never decided I didn't want you. I never would.'

'It was a decision by default. Which is how you seem to make your decisions, by not making them. They happen to you.'

The justice of this hits me like a tin of Spam in a swinging sock. I want to contradict it, with every bone in my body and fibre of my being, but sometimes, there's not enough fresh evidence to appeal.

'I'm sorry I ran off,' Ben says. 'That was poor. Bloody hell. Maybe I've got more of my dad about me than I'd like to think.'

We sit in silence again. With the whole truth you're supposed to feel some completion – *closure*, as they say in California. I feel more hopeless than ever. And what's the point of arguing about who's at fault, anyway? We are where we are. Not as if we're going to come to a different conclusion about the past and suddenly present day outcomes will be altered.

'How did seeing Simon fit in?' Ben asks, eventually.

'He was interested, it was flattering. You'd said I was nonde-script.' This is perhaps too much honesty about my thought processes. 'For about five minutes, I thought it was possible. It was a way of staying around you, I guess.'

'You were using him?'

'Not intentionally.'

413

'That's going to be on your headstone. Here Lies Rachel Woodford. Not Intentionally.' He smiles. 'Mind you, it's about time Simon was on the receiving end.'

His voice is steadier but his eyes keep darting towards me, as if I'm a mesmerising, gruesome museum exhibit: a mummified body with burnt-paper skin and eye-sockets like the wizened scoops left by peach stones.

'If you hadn't told me Olivia had left, I'd have never said any of this. I'd have let you go.'

He ruffles his hair, tiredly. 'Yeah, I know. It's never a good idea to be mates with someone you want more from. Take it from a man with bitter experience.'

We sit in silence.

'I wish I had a time machine,' I say, in a tone of voice that's meant to sound wry and comes out plain defeated.

'So do I,' Ben says, then waits for the right beat to add. 'I'd go to Leeds University.'

My laughter mechanism is broken. Also: too true.

'I'd better be going,' he says, getting up. I nod miserably, getting up as well, fighting an urge to grab him by the lapels and beg.

'Goodbye.' I try to sound brave, and fail.

'Come on.' Ben turns back. 'You'll be OK.'

'I'll miss you.' I hear the crack in my voice, the desperation, *why don't you care the way I care*, even though he's told me he doesn't, I can't accept it.

'Oh, Ron…' Ben finally looks sad.

The unexpected resurrection of my nickname sends silent tears rolling down my face. It'll all end in tears, Caroline said, or if she didn't use those exact words, that's what she meant.

'What were you going to say to me?' I wipe my cheeks with

the heel of my hand, 'Graduation ball, on the dance floor?'

'I don't remember.'

'Oh.' Hard gulp.

'Look, I do. But. It doesn't matter.'

'It does to me. Please, Ben.'

He looks doubtful about obliging me, and with good reason, as I'm apparently on the verge of nervous collapse. He looks around to ascertain we're still alone, apart from the barefoot guy with his tie wrapped round his forehead, doing tai chi underneath the statue.

'I was going to tell you,' he says, softly, 'I'd given my tickets away for the travelling so we could rebook the whole thing when you could come too. I didn't change the date I left. I bought new tickets and went on my own.'

I stare at him through swimming eyes. This is pretty much unbearable. He looks upset and steps forward as if he's going to touch my arm, but his hand drops to his side.

'Something I want in return,' Ben says, voice still low.

'Yes. Anything.'

'Please don't come looking for me again.'

And in a few purposeful strides, he's gone. I bet he had to discipline himself not to run. What a finale.

I walk round and round the park, trying to get my face under control before I go back out in public. The broken heart I can't do anything about. I test my eyesight by reading the inscription on the cross. In this tranquil space, it calmly notes: 'Around lie the remains of more than twenty-two thousand people'.

How apt. The blossoming idyll is in fact a well-fertilised graveyard.

67

'He's going to go back down south and live in this giant gilded cage bought by his in-laws and be miserable,' I say, entering the forty-eighth minute of pointless rehashing with Caroline as abused, patient audience of one. She's already listened to it all the way to Tatton Park, her reward for driving me here.

I'm shouldering a wicker picnic basket, she's carrying the gingham oilskin blanket and cool bag full of clinking bottles. It was Caroline's birthday last week and she nominated a classical concert and fireworks here as her celebration, making us book tickets what feels like a lifetime ago. It confirms the greatness of Caroline's mind: the day's dawned, she has Mindy and Ivor AWOL, status unknown, and Rachel, status, wreck. Visa card debits and a sense of duty are all that's knitting us together.

She and Mindy have already heard the tale, of course. I called them individually. I had to concede it didn't have much of a twist. They both listened with the kind of mounting apprehension you get in the horror genre when the teenagers announce 'It's nothing but superstition' and go down to the old boat house holding tiki torches.

'Mmm,' Caroline says, throwing the blanket out, testing the ground underneath for lumps with the toe of her shoe. 'You don't know that he's going to be miserable.'

I put the basket down, plop in an ungainly heap onto the rug.

'No,' I say. 'No. A house, though. No one should force their partner to do something that makes them feel that compromised, surely?'

'Rachel. It doesn't matter if she's mixing him Paraquat Martinis. He's told you he loves her and he doesn't love you. You have to let this go. I say that as someone who definitely loves you.'

Caroline pulls a bottle of Prosecco out of the bag and hands me a couple of plastic goblets, the sort with screw-in bases. I wish alcohol helped. It tastes like paraffin and sizzles in my gut like it's cauterising an open wound. In general, I feel as if my very essence has been through a document shredder.

'This was never going to have a happy ending,' Caroline says, gently, uncorking the bottle with a snap of the wrist and tipping it to one of the glasses. 'You need to start a new story. Accept Mindy's help with the online dating thing.'

'Do you think they're coming, by the way?'

We agreed we owed Mindy and Ivor some distance and respect. We didn't tell them what I'd seen or ask them any more about Caroline's allegations. Caroline texted them both to check they were still coming today and they both confirmed. A sign, we agreed, that positive things might've happened, but it's very hard to say.

At that moment, Mindy, clad in floral-patterned tights and fuschia waterproof, appears. Caroline waves with her free hand. When Mindy reaches us we say our hellos but she's inscrutable which is very unnerving when it's the most scrutable woman in the world.

'Shall I say my sorrys when Ivor's here too?' Caroline asks, as I hand her glass over.

'I suppose,' Mindy says, casually, sipping the froth before it spills. 'Did he say he'd be here?'

'Well, yes,' Caroline says, faintly perturbed.

She and I exchange a look. Who knows what I saw outside the flat. There's five minutes of stilted small talk about Mindy's latest business proposal before Ivor lollops through the crowd, identifiable from the air by the so-very-Ivor thin sports jacket with tangerine chevrons he's in.

'Wotcher,' I say, shading puffy eyes against the sun.

'Afternoon.'

We assemble a drink for him.

'Let's get this done,' Caroline says, once Ivor is cross-legged with beverage. 'I am completely, utterly, abjectly sorry for what I said. I was wrong and it was wrong. Please, please accept my apology.' Caroline looks from Mindy to Ivor. 'And not that I want to emotionally blackmail you but it's my birthday week, and tomorrow I start sessions at Relate with my faithless husband so, you know, cut me some slack.'

Ivor looks blank. Mindy pulls up clumps of grass and sprinkles the blades back down in heaps, gazing off towards the stage.

'We've talked and we think what you did was pretty awful but we think you should be embarrassed about it, not us,' Ivor says. 'What you two didn't know and Mindy and I did know, is... I've been fighting this for a while. It's time I said something. I'm gay.'

'Seriously?' I blurt. 'You're gay?'

'Yeah. That's why Mindy was angry with me about Katya. She said it was time I owned who I am. Caroline accusing me of fancying another woman – not helpful in the whole *coming out* process.'

'Oh good God, Ivor, I'm so sorry. Not sorry that you're gay, I mean. Sorry again for what I did. How long have you known?' Caroline says, one hand to her chest.

Ivor shakes his head. 'Long enough that it's time I stopped hiding from it.'

'And I'm sorry, it was my idea to ambush you two,' I say. 'Ivor, I only wish you'd told us before. It doesn't make any difference.'

He nods.

'Have you ... got a boyfriend?' I sound like a sixty-something at the Women's Institute trying to make sense of this new craze called dogging that doesn't involve dogs, or that BDSM *isn't* a driving school. The homosexuality announcement is so utterly unexpected that I can't sync sense and mouth.

'Nah. Not that far along with it. Just ... you know, lots of meaningless cock I trawl for at Manto's.'

I definitely don't have a Post-It note in the relevant section of Debrett's to hand on this so I turn to Mindy and reiterate my apology. She's throwing back her Prosecco, merely wiping her mouth and nodding curt acknowledgement.

'Well, I say cock, cock *and* arse, I haven't decided which side of the bargain I prefer being on yet,' Ivor continues.

Caroline and I nod, sip our drinks for something to do. There's a disconnect between the genteel surroundings and the frank nature of our conversation. You shouldn't be thinking about whether your friend prefers being a bottom or a top with rough trade while watching three generations of a family sharing Earl Grey from a Thermos.

'Sorry,' Ivor says. 'I've been going to a support group and once the walls of communication come down, they really come crashing down, if you know what I mean.'

'Did you not want to tell us before?' Caroline asks. 'Not that I'm complaining. I wish we could've been there for you.'

'I nearly told you both, once. We were watching a film with Matt Damon and he was scaling a building—'

'*The Bourne Identity*,' Mindy says.

'Thanks Mindy, yes, *The Bourne Identity*, and I nearly said *what a fierce BUM. I'd scuttle that rotten!* It nearly popped out. Then I remembered myself.'

'And it's a film about someone forgetting who they are,' Mindy says.

'I had never considered that irony,' Ivor says. 'Perhaps that was the subconscious influence. What's in the picnic basket then? Any Scotch eggs?'

Caroline appears grateful for the distraction and starts rustling through it, pulling out Lakeland Tupperware.

'Oh, too many salads. I'm not that gay,' Ivor says.

Mindy squeezes his arm.

There's something niggling me and with the arm squeeze, I identify what it is.

'Hang on,' I say. '*Hang on*. Mindy knew. *Mindy?* How on earth did you get her to keep a secret?'

A pregnant pause. Ivor is freeze-framed with a breadstick halfway to gob.

'Aha! Got you! Surprise! We're totally dating!' Mindy squeals.

Caroline and I look at each other and then back at Ivor, who's broken into the broad grin of the evil swine.

'Ivor!' I shriek. 'A fake coming out, then going back in? Bit tasteless!'

Ivor collapses in on himself with laughter. 'Your faces, woo hoo …' he chokes. 'Fierce bum, haha.'

Caroline puts fingers to temples. 'Ivor, you're *not* gay? And you and Mindy *are* seeing each other?'

'No I'm not … and yes we are,' Ivor says, glancing at Mindy.

Our eyes move to Mindy. She's wearing a shy smile. She never looks shy. This is amazing.

'I knew I was right!' Caroline cries.

'And contrition for humiliating us lasted, what, four minutes?' Ivor says. 'You absolutely deserved this retaliation.'

Caroline hands me her glass, then stretches across and kisses him on the cheek, doing the same with Mindy. 'I am so, so pleased for you two.'

'I can't believe you're going back in the closet,' I say to Ivor.

'There's no closet, Woodford, OK? I am a hundred per cent lady lover. Got a qualification in hetero from Peterborough Academy of Smooth and everything.'

'We haven't done it yet though,' Mindy says. 'That's gonna be weird.'

Ivor knocks a palm against his forehead.

'Mindy! We were winning this embarrassment contest until you said that!'

'Sorry. It's what I'd be thinking about though, if I was them.'

They laugh, with a touch of self-consciousness. They sound different.

'This is fantastic news, apart from the fact you're not allowed to say you'll never see each other again if you break up. Are we agreed?' I ask.

'We have talked about that. We think it might've been one of the reasons we took so long to get around to this,' Mindy says, with another shy look. It occurs to me she's experiencing the novel sensation of going out with someone she actually loves. That's what was missing.

'We'd have to work out a timeshare where you both retained your stake and we scheduled around it,' Caroline says. 'But it might never happen. Me and Rach might be aunties to gorgeous cocoa-skinned gaudily dressed children.' She sticks her tongue in her cheek.

'May I pour you a nice warm cup of shut the fuck up?' Ivor says.

I propose a toast. 'To Ivor and Mindy. With names and taste in clothes like yours, you were always destined to be a couple.'

We clink plastic glasses.

'And to Caroline's fifty-third,' Ivor says, looking around us at a sea of silver hair.

68

I pack away my textbook and mumble my goodbyes to my class mates before heading out into the mucky weather. I started taking an Italian night class at the university. There's about a half a dozen international students and me, mumbling our way through pidgin Italian with a very bright, fair and entirely English tutor, nothing like the undulating Gina Lollobrigida character of my imagination.

Clouds that were soft, smoky pencil smudges this afternoon have dissolved into spattering rain. Despite the persistent drizzle and my next engagement requiring me not to look bedraggled, I decide to walk. I pass Central Library, the dome illuminated in a *Close Encounters* way, as if it might start whirring, chiming and spin off into the night sky. I stand and gaze at it for a few moments, shivering, clutching the collars of my coat together. I hurry down the streets as the rain gathers pace, speckling my face and making me blink. In the twinkly sanctuary of the café-bar I find a table in the far corner, by the window and below *The Wizard Of Oz* poster.

'We've got mulled wine on the go, if you fancy it?' says the art college waitress, pulling the pencil from her floppy ponytail as she takes my order. 'It's so nasty out there we thought we needed it.'

'Ooh, go on then,' I say, as if it's contraband, like the naughty old granny dipso I'm surely fated to become.

It arrives in a glass on a saucer, a paper napkin folded underneath to catch the drips. I got here just in time: the rain's being picked up by the wind and hurled sideways, cascading down in waves as if we're inside a car wash.

These last weeks have been fairly awful. Tonight I don't feel so bad. I'm empty but energised. The sort of light-headedness I imagine you get on a fast at an ashram, when you tell yourself it's the toxins leaving your body as opposed to it starting to digest itself.

I'm back to factory settings. Clean slate, start again, only way is up, as the great philosopher Yazz said.

Rhys called me last night to tell me he'd met someone else, Claire. She's started working at his company. She might be moving in, and did I mind it being so soon? I surprised myself by not only saying I didn't mind, but meaning it. He sounded like he wanted to gush, and that's not the Rhys I know – she's already having an effect I didn't. Rhys doesn't need my blessing or permission, he explained, but I still have a key and some things in the loft. I knew it was more than that. He was excited and wanted to share it with me. And although he said we had nothing to show for thirteen years, I think that's something.

Caroline's gone down to a four-day week at work, spending the other one volunteering at worthy inner-city projects. She *loves* it. God knows what all those public-sector poverty tsars are going to do for an income when she solves poverty and moves on to the next task though. Our old Friday foursome nights have become Saturdays. Friday is her and Graeme's night together, as their counsellor says they must 'set aside time to value their bond and reconnect'. Mindy and I agreed we've got to redouble our efforts with Graeme for her sake. It helps that he's suitably chastened enough not to take the mickey out of us as much as before.

Meanwhile, Katya's in Colombia, Ivor doesn't have lost week-ends in Vice City and Mindy doesn't spend any time worrying about Detroit techno. They've never revealed precisely what went on that day Caroline dropped the truth bomb on them, which is mind-bending restraint in Mindy's case. I did get one thing out of her. She tells me she caught up with him, they looked at each other, and: 'We just knew. We knew it was true without either of us saying a word.' Those two, not saying a word to each other. Incredible in itself.

Mindy still refuses to completely revise her theory of attraction. She's altered the terms: now it's based on whether you've seen someone *in their pants*, claiming if she'd known Ivor had good muscle definition she'd have said she was up for it sooner. No one believes her. They are ridiculously, sickeningly happy, though they are considerate enough not to show it, if they can help it. I'd miss their bickering too much.

I let Mindy sign me up to My Single Friend. She insisted after she said my forays online 'were like Gerald Ratner with a sherry decanter'. ('Have you spellchecked it?' Ivor asked me. 'One of Mindy's own ads said she was a fan of jizz instead of jazz. Mind you, *big* response.')

'Rachel?'

A tall, dark-haired man with a lot of water on his face stands in front of me.

'Yes! Hi! Gregor?'

He sits, slapping down a wrinkled newspaper that I gather has been on his head in lieu of an umbrella.

'What would you like to drink?' I say.

'Have they got a menu?'

He plucks a printed slip of paper from a wooden block on the table and studies it. I try very very hard not to study his hair, and fail. What. The. Blazes …? It's a pronounced, obsidian-black widow's peak. What's most distracting, however, is it isn't apparently made of hair. It's like … Velcro, or some scalp-based equivalent of astro-turf. It looks *sewn on*.

While we make introductory chat and Gregor asks for a lager, I feel irritation bubbling up, and then feel guilty for feeling irritated in case his hair fell out due to a trauma and he was misled by his follicular regeneration specialist and his wife left him over it. Seriously, though: why not put the plugs deal upfront? All his photos were artily-lit to conceal it. Surely it'd be wiser to filter the Hammer Horror enthusiasts, avoiding disappointment for everyone? I mean. There was well-meant Mindy bullshit about beauty in my resume, but my properly-lit pictures were there as a visual corrective aid.

Stop being so superficial, I tell myself, personality is what counts. Personality is what you're here to enjoy.

'What's the concert you're going on to?' I ask.

'Michael Ball. A collection of show tunes. "Aspects of Love", and so on. Do you get down to the West End much?'

'Erm. No. I always mean to—'

'Oh, you should, you should. It's a fantastic night out, you know? Great entertainment.'

The waitress brings Gregor his pint and I notice he doesn't say thank you, or even acknowledge her. How early are you allowed to say: *this is never gonna work?*

'Why's a nice girl like you single, then?'

'Can nice girls not be single?'

'It was a compliment, if you're going to throw it back in my face ...'

'Uhm, OK, thanks. That's a big question ...'

His line of sight flickers to my chest while I'm talking and suddenly I'm sixteen years old, out with a boy who thinks he can look at chests and not be noticed doing it. Maybe it's a nervous tic and he's not doing that at all. I'm only wearing a dark sweater dress, after all, it's not as if it's revealing.

'... Why are you single?' I ask.

Gregor blows his cheeks out. 'Working long hours. International travel.'

'Right. For the bank.'

'I can pull down twenty, thirty K in bonuses in a good year. They want their pound of flesh, har har.'

At the word 'flesh' his eyes slither south again. He is! He's copping a goggle! Unbelievable.

Half an hour later, I am giving sincere thanks to the work ethic of Andrew Lloyd Webber that Gregor's gig starts early.

'This has been fun. Feel free to call me,' he says, tucking his chair back under the table. 'If I'm Stateside it might go to vee-mail but I'll pick it up.'

'Mmm, hmm,' I say, making the emphatic closed-mouth smile with vigorous nod that means *yuh-huh, on a nippy day in hell.*

427

I could concede defeat and go home. That seems too much like setting a precedent that being out alone isn't fun, and being alone isn't good. I order another drink and make a note to self to bring a book next time.

Here's what I've decided. I will always miss Ben. I will always wonder what might have been if I'd said: 'Thanks for coming, Rhys, good effort, nice touch with the Brilliantine, but please excuse me while I pursue the man I'm really in love with.' But despite how dreadful that day in St John's was, I can't regret what I said to Ben. At least I tried. Rachel's maxim: fail again, fail differently.

Some people end up with their soul mates, like Mindy and Ivor. Some people end up with partners they can work at being happy with, like Caroline and Graeme. Some get second chances at getting it right, like Rhys and Claire. Some people get who they deserve, like Lucy and Matt. Some people will forever be a mystery, like Lucas and Natalie. He got cleared, they're back together, no further statements will be made. Other people, of which I might be one, end up on their own. And that's fine. I'll be all right.

I make a decision: I will book a trip to Rome for my wedding-day-that-wasn't. And I will speak Italian. Some.

69

I'm prodding at the slice of orange and cinnamon stick floating on top of my wine with my teaspoon when the chair opposite me scrapes across the floor.

'Is this seat taken?'

I look up. The spoon clatters into the saucer.

'The weather is end-of-the-world *Blade Runner* out there, isn't it? I'd forgotten the north-west's capacity to chuck it on you.'

I continue to stare blankly at Ben as he drapes his coat over the back of the chair. He doesn't look very soggy. He looks as per, as if he saved the world in time to make the appointment with his tailor.

'Saw you outside the library and followed you,' he says. 'You took the most roundabout route here, you know that? Then I sat over there in the corner and watched you in a creepy manner.' Ben peers into my glass. 'Any booze in that?'

'Yes.'

'Good-oh.'

'Are you here to serve me some kind of cease-and-desist special lawyer papers?'

'No, I'm going to get another drink. Ah, fantastic — same as her? Yeah, cheers.'

He confirms his order through standard café-bar semaphore with the waitress.

'Who was that with you, then?' he asks.

As I understand precisely nothing about what's happening, I'll answer the questions I'm given.

'Gregor.'

'New fella?'

'Uh. No. He likes musical theatre and looked at my tits every twelve minutes.'

Ben wrinkles his nose. 'Amateur hour. Everyone knows you pick up what you can on the periphery of your vision and assemble the 3D with imagination.'

I shake my head as the urge to laugh battles with my extreme bafflement.

'But you're dating again?'

'Badly, but yes.'

'Glad to hear it.'

Ben says thank you for his wine, picks up his glass, takes a sip. It's then I spot the small but telling detail about his left hand. He sees that I see. He sets the cup back down.

'Liv and I are getting a divorce. I went down to London and we talked for a long time about what had gone wrong and decided it couldn't be fixed. It had nothing to do with any aggro at the wedding, I should say. That was more the death throes. It had been staring us in the face since before Manchester. We were playing for time, moving north, really.'

'I'm so sorry, Ben.'

I discover I am sorry. Very, very sorry, and sad for him. I

wish I could say for sure I'd have felt that way before all self-interest was gone, I don't know that's true. What I do know, confirmed to me with Rhys's latest news, is that when you love someone, you want their happiness even when it's not going to involve you. Even when it *depends* on your lack of involvement.

'So am I.'

'You must be devastated.'

'In a way, it was worse when I knew it might happen, or it should happen, and we hadn't said it. I'm very sad, but resigned. This is better than tearing lumps out of one another until there's nothing left. You must know what I mean?'

I think about Rhys. 'Yes, I do.'

'Mulled wine,' Ben takes another sip. 'Quite nice, if wildly unseasonal.'

'Are you staying in Manchester?'

'Yes, I am.'

'Ben,' I say, cautiously. 'If you're here to say it's OK to be friends now you're separated… I'm not sure I can be. We've had two goes at it and neither of them has ended well. I mean, friends can do things like write My Single Friend pitches for each other, like Mindy did for me. If I had to write yours, I'd be saying you're the most sexist man I've ever met. And reeks. Wear a hazmat suit for copulation.'

Ben pretends to sniff his armpit and deadpans: 'Now you tell me?'

'You know what I mean. I can't be your dating buddy, or meet your new girlfriends. It's not going to work.'

'Mmm.' Ben fishes the cinnamon stick out of his drink between finger and thumb and puts it on the edge of the saucer. 'That belongs in pot pourri only.'

I can't tell how my words have been taken. It was hard to say, and hard-won wisdom.

'About being friends. I happen to agree it wouldn't work. I was angry when I last saw you. Only at myself, when I thought about it. You ought to know that I left that night of the ball because I was so sure – so *scared* – you'd pick Rhys over me, I didn't risk sticking around to see it happen. I dodged your calls for the same reason. I thought it was just confirming the bad news. I told myself that if it had been me you'd have torn after me at the Palace. But you'd told me how you felt and I had no business playing games, getting you to prove it. I never saw it from your point of view. You weren't indecisive, I was insecure. Then later when I heard for sure you were back with Rhys, I told myself there, that's the proof, I was right to doubt you. Until we were sat in that park, I'd never faced the fact I might've brought the situation about. I realised what a total idiot I'd been.'

He takes a sip of his drink. I'm not sure I can withstand going over this again. It's like rewinding a traffic camera clip of an accident.

'Then when I was honest with myself about the past, I could be honest with myself about the present. I started out with the wrong intentions, wanting to prove things to you in my stupid wounded pride.'

'What can you have needed to prove to me?'

'That I didn't mind what had happened. That I didn't ever think about you or wish things had turned out differently. Pretty soon the plan started to go wrong and we were sat in here with me trying not to wail *do you know you broke my heart, bitch.*'

Ben smiles to make it clear this is an ironic bitch, not an actual bitch.

432

'And I wanted to save you from Simon's oily grasp … a bit too much. The thing is, seeing you again, it's all been based on a misunderstanding. I was sure it was safe to be friends. I thought I couldn't possibly fall in love with you again, and I was right.'

He takes a breath.

'Please,' I interrupt, desperately. 'If you want to tell me you've come to realise you care for me as a second sister, that's nice but I don't want to hear it. Put it in a card with some bull-rushes on it and post it. With Deepest Sympathy For Your Loss Of Sex Appeal.'

'I was right I couldn't fall in love with you. Because I never fell out of love with you.'

'*What?*'

'It's true,' Ben says, cheerfully. 'Seems once was enough to infect me. From then on you've been lying dormant, like a virus. Or an incurable chronic condition that flares up from time to time.'

A long pause, where life transforms from black-and-white to colour.

'I'm eczema?'

Ben beams. 'Eczema of the heart. That's it. Psoriasis of the soul.'

The whole world is one table by a window in a café-bar in Manchester and the person sitting opposite me. If joy could be seen by the Hubble, tonight scientists would record a peculiar iridescence on an island north of the equator.

'In view of this, I wanted to ask you on a date. Are you free tonight?'

'Uh,' my mind's so overloaded I can only make simpleton sounds, 'yes.'

'Great! God, you're on your second man of the night while I'm out of practice at this. Do I have to pretend to love cats, old movies and getting caught in the rain? Wait, no – Rachel Fact, she doesn't like it when people say they like "old films". There's good ones and bad ones. If someone said they liked 'new films' you'd think they were stupid.'

'Did I say that?'

'First year of university.'

'I can't believe you remember that.'

'When it comes to you, I'm blessed with total recall. So no need for this.' Ben pretends to rub his neck and steal a glance below my neckline. I start gurgling with laughter. He taps the side of his head: 'All up here. Don't you worry.'

He puts his hand over mine. This is real.

'I should have so much to say, and I can't think of anything to say,' I burble.

I see the waitress with the pencil in her hair giving us that *nice couple* smile again. *If only you knew.*

'You can answer the unspoken question hanging over us about what we do next,' Ben says.

'Is there one?'

'Yeah. Do you want to get some dinner?'

As we leave the café, I ask: 'Is it OK for us to be out together?'

'How d'ya mean? Have you got an electronic tag?'

'As a …' I'm going to say couple and then I think it sounds a bit presumptuous after 175mls of lukewarm rioja '…as a – you know. The two of us.'

434

He stops. 'As a couple? We've waited a very long time for a first date. I don't see how anything we do can be considered rushing. I hope from what we said in there that you're ... my girlfriend. Aren't you?'

'Yes!' *Girlfriend. Boyfriend. A couple!* 'If you honestly want a woman who is currently described on an internet dating site as "a proper lol".'

'It's pathetic, I knew I did from that first moment we met. It was ... not love at first sight exactly, but − familiarity. Like: oh, hello, *it's you*. It's going to be you. Game over.'

I feel as if I'm going to burst. 'I can't believe I get to be with you at last.'

He leans down and kisses me, one hand on the back of my head, fingers woven into my hair, our mouths warm and red wine blackcurrant-flavoured while the air around us is rinsed-clean cold. Like old times, it has a whole body effect on me but the reunion isn't like a recovered memory. It feels brand new. I put my arms around him, underneath his unbuttoned coat, and hold him, reassuring myself he's solid.

We walk on, hand-in-hand. Passers-by don't know this is an everyday miracle. I want to stop them and say something.

'If anyone asks how we got together, it'll be the most difficult tale to tell ever,' I babble. 'Most people can say "We met at the office Christmas party. We both liked spelunking and hip-hop. We have two kids."'

'Well, tell them we met at university.'

'It doesn't do it justice. You have to chart the whole thing. I might write it down in a diary, in case there's ever any grandkids.'

'The story would start in Freshers' Week and come up to

435

date and finish, when, tonight?'

'Of course,' I say. 'This has been the most important evening of all, really.'

'What would the last line say?'

'Oh dear. I don't know. Something corny about the wait being worth it and "Then I went for Chinatown dim sum with him and to top it all off, he's fairly competent with chopsticks"?'

'Nah, unless that's code it's a total anti-climax. We're English graduates, for God's sake, we can do better. Think about the legacy, the weight of history. It's got to inspire. How about: "And then he did it to her and she loved it"?'

I glance sideways to catch the look on his face. I keep mine straight.

'Yeah, that could work...'

So that's it.
Rachel and Ben's story has been told.

But if you love what you've read, turn the page for some more brilliant writing from Mhairi. She's a journalist too y'know, and if you've got any smarts at all you'll follow her on Twitter @MhairiMcF or visit www.mhairimcfarlane.com.

Mhairi's next book will hit the shelves in December 2013.

THE ULTIMATE CELEBRITY INTERVIEW!

I am so sick of reading this interview. You read it all the time, constantly, year in, year out, in every glossy magazine and Sunday supplement. It's founded on the twin principles that a) people who act are the most fascinating beings on the planet, and b) that we, the readers, are totally credulous, awed plebians. The dumbstruck interviewer acts only as a conduit to divinity, drinking in their shuddering magnificence and recording their sub-adolescent witterings as if it's brainy gold. We're now at the stage where an actor or actress would have to take a shit on the reporter's notebook to get a less-than-howlingly-sycophantic write-up. (Or maybe not. HE'S WHERE IT'S SCAT!) I'm convinced by now there's a template. It goes like this.

Beauty, brains and Braun

An actress bounds into the East London photographic studio, slightly out of breath, fizzing with the energy of Silvio Berlusconi on Horny Goat Weed at an 18-year-old's swim party. 'I just gave a homeless man outside a twenty pound note, and now I'm worrying he'd have rather had it in two tens,' she says, huge eyes widening in a luminously fresh face, as she puts down her vintage handbag and leather-bound copy of *Anna Karenina* ('I'm obsessed with Tolstoy; it's a weakness, I need to widen my contemporary reading') in a flurry of activity that lights up the room and makes all heads turn. 'Oh, no. I hope he's OK,' she says, fretting extravagantly over this act of incredibly charming philanthropic spontaneity I'm choosing to include here for colour but that she obviously had no idea could end up in the article.

The issue of the Handily Timed Tramp is resolved when a menial is despatched to offer him change and to pick up her favourite snack, Minstrels. An actress who eats?! I ask, incredulous, as she unselfconsciously shovels in great handfuls while having her hair and make-up done. 'Oh, I eat like a pig, I love cooking for my boyfriend,' she says, adjusting her navy wool crepe Jil Sander dress over her tiny size six frame, which she maintains by consuming shitloads of food and walking to appointments. 'I'm really boring; I don't like all those red carpet events. I love staying in and putting on pyjamas and making a massive casserole for my friends. I'm such a down-to-earth, homely, generous goof! This is so embarrassing to admit.'

So, I say, once she's finished showing pictures of her dogs on her phone to everyone because she's completely unstarry and prepared to talk about herself to unimportant people, was it a difficult decision to choose to play Eva Braun, as she's a controversial figure? She suddenly looks serious. 'Obviously people have their views on what she did but really I just approached her as a character, as a story. You know, before anything else she was just a woman, in love with a man, trying to make a life for herself in Nazi Germany.' Did she do much research? 'I avoided reading anything about her because I didn't want my performance to be affected by other peoples' opinions. You know, I wanted to get to the emotional truth. That's your job, as an actor.'

While I'm being admitted to her intellectual salon and everything I thought I knew is being turned on its head, I have to ask, because the answer will help all of us, would she consider herself a feminist? 'Uhm,' she says, with the pause of someone who chooses their words very carefully, her perfect brow creasing. 'I'm not…part of a cause or a movement or anything. I'm just a person. So I'd say I'm definitely female. But I'm not a "feminist" as such because I'm too independent-minded to be part of something. You know?'

She finishes all her ideas with 'you know?' The phrase contains a note of yearning, to find and make connections, and it strikes me that she's desperate to be understood, but she has learned to wear the struggle lightly. Yet she effortlessly metamorphoses from Thinker to Model once she's dressed in a retro ironic bikini and ironic heels for the '50s-themed photoshoot that sends up the notion of a 'pin-up', pulling faces where she pretends to double take at the sight of her own tits while talking on a Bakelite telephone. Yet even in vintage costume she's absolutely modern, in control of her image, of how she wants to be seen – when she vetoes some iced bun props on the basis that 'It's a bit slutty *Calendar Girls*' everyone on set who doesn't want to be fired instantly agrees that she is right.

As she stands patiently while wardrobe people fuss with the ironic see-through baby doll negligee for the next slyly subversive picture, she explains how she hopes her role as Braun will see her considered for more serious parts. 'Casting agents, they do tend to think, she looks a certain way, that's all she can do. But things are changing. Look at Judi Dench. I'd like a career like hers. Old women are so inspiring.'

Now Hollywood is calling, it says here in the publicity material I was given. Can she see herself in blockbusters? 'God, that'd be so weird!' she laughs, revealing perfect teeth. 'I'm not sure I'd want to be, you know, Meryl Streep famous because then your life's not your own. I'm going back next week for the endless slog of auditions but I don't want it that much. They judge you on how you look and how well you can act, it's very pressuring. When you get rejected a lot you start to realise it's a very fake existence. And I'd miss my dogs!'

And with that, she's gone, in a gust of her signature scent. ('You like it?' her eyes light up. 'It's bespoke! They mix it for you at this amazing atelier in the Loire Valley. I'll send you their details.' True to form her PA mails me a day later, and I discover it costs more than the moon. Only someone unmaterialistic could assume a journalist's salary could cover it. I get a glimpse of what it's like to live like her, whimsically, in the moment, seeing so few limitations).

But what IS her life? It's simple, crazy and complicated, veering from casseroles to film premieres and Tolstoy and a pair of Basset Hounds called Pearl and Dean, and yet she takes all the madness in her faux-python Stella McCartney slingback-shod stride. It's only after she's left, in a moment of aching symbolism that poignantly encapsulates this entire encounter, that I notice she's left me most of her bag of Minstrels. A gesture of such heartbreaking kindness that I might die wanking.

THE GRACIOUS HACIENDA DRINKING GAME

A recent letter from Tom Cruise's lawyer, advising a publication that he had a 'gracious and loving family home' recalled the text of many a wonderfully sycophantic magazine article, or scenes in an MTV Cribs tour round a chintzy celebrity cack pile.

'Gracious' is a Beano comic imaginary word: always written, never spoken. 'How's your house?' 'OK, pretty gracious. Come round sometime. It's also loving.'

It occurs to me that there are so many key features that crop up time and again, you could play a kind of Obscenely Blingy Horror Shack Interiors drinking game and get nicely pissed.

You'd think that having the kind of wealth that allows you to jizz funds around Harrods like Formula One champagne would mean an incredible diversity of result. However, it seems there's an aesthetic ubiquity in the upper price bracket to rival that of IKEA's Miserly Landlord range.

Yes, YES I know MTV Cribs has been around awhile. But if, like me, you enjoy drinking booze, watching reruns, and leafing through nouveau riche Casa 'Shoulda Gone To Specsavers' mansion photo-shoots, this tick list is always gold. Like a rapper's keeping-it-ghetto bath tub.

KOI

There must be a pond and it must feature Koi Carp, the landed gentry's 'roided goldfish. A beginner's spotter badge, award self one shot of Dooley's.

'This Is Where the Magic Happens'

Mandatory phrase when being shown the recording studio in Cribs. If one's tour guide is a member of Maroon 5, or in Fred Durst-ian oversized shorts, it's not so much magic, as necromancy.

Servant Sighting

'Our lives wouldn't run without her, she's part of the family' or similar, if being narrated to interviewer by willowy patrician blonde at her 'Barbados hideaway'. Except presumably, most family members aren't tasked with refilling the loo roll pyramid and required to give four weeks' notice if they wish to leave. In Cribs, this is a bashful-looking middle-aged Hispanic woman who our ebullient host grabs, hugs and shouts: 'I call her Mama!' Well, unlike 'The Person Who Cif Lemon Mousses the Thunder Box for Money' it has the benefit of brevity.

Showcase For Workless Wife's Startlingly Appalling Taste

Ushered into a lounge that features beige box pelmets, Regency stripe swags, tasselled tie-backs, a Warholian triptych of the Queen, a suspended flat screen TV and a kidney-shaped glass coffee table with lions' feet, we're told 'My wife did all of this' in an admiring tone that implies this isn't a highly defama-tory statement.

'We've gone for a kinda country house, rustic, Ye Olde English feel...' she says, clad in Juicy Couture trackie, in the blistering sunshine of the Hollywood Hills in a terracotta-washed Mexican style bungalow surrounded by palm trees. And the aim is to transport us, in this one room, to the Cotswolds?

Breaking news: you've dropped two mill to pull off the same standard of illusion as Duty Free lagged Brits rofling through airport terminals in sombreros.

There was a particularly splendid example of the 'misguided pride in own DIY' genre when Joan Collins welcomed *Hello!* into her Manhattan penthouse master suite, an aggressive whole-room pattern-matched vexatious twanging of the optic nerve; Jackson Pollock meets Heathrow Sheraton Classic Double circa 1988.

She announced, imperiously: 'I have an eye.' That you keep in a drawer, like a marble? USE TWO.

Turkey Bacon: So Many Questions

Casually introduced in fridge contents inventory, as if it's not a paradoxical mindbender and affront to gustatory dignity.

What in the name of all that is holy is 'turkey bacon'? Why can't Americans see a thing, without trying to transpose it into turkey? Why have so much cash you could hire the White House lawn for a barbecue, and then eat not-actual bacon? Why consume a meat-hybrid that, if made flesh ('Behold God's abomination: Wattle Pig!') you would run from screaming, not chasing with a mandolin slicer?

Is this the dream? You become an NBA superstar, platinum seller or American Idol judge in a sprawling estate the size of Wigan. Beautiful partner, brace of kids, at the very pinnacle – the thin air summit of success – where you then get so light headed that you ask your private chef to toss a skin graft flap of reformed smoked poultry to shrink in a skillet?

Turkey is not for winners. Turkey is for people who find chicken too exciting. To try to make bacon out of it is fucking demented.

Artefact That Reminds Them Of Where It All Began

Must be in a glass case. Extra shot awarded if it's in a Temple To Thine Ego room full of trophies, awards, skateboards nailed to walls, framed photos of owner doing finger guns with wheel-chair-bound confused Bob Hope, etc.

My Friends, Who I Have For Money

A loose affiliation of Entourage-style hangers on must be cluttering up the overstuffed sofa playing video games, or hanging around the island unit in the kitchen, waiting to do on-camera high fives. They have, of course, been 'there from the beginning.' The beginning of your being loaded.

This 'hired homies' technique was later adopted by makers of Jamie Oliver programmes. Little known fact: he calls everyone onscreen 'tiger' because he doesn't know their names. Even his nan. That's a Central Casting stunt nan if ever I saw one. Let's just see if she turns up as Aaron Craze's, too.

Specially Commissioned 'Art'

Because no one would embark on painting something that shit without being paid up front.

Once on Cribs, a tour guide showed us his haunting oil painting of Tupac Shakur being baptised by Martin Luther King. 'It came from an idea I had,' he mused, 'That Tupac Shakur could've been baptised by Martin Luther King.' Rendering Ali G instantly satirically obsolete, he then put on a wolf fur coat and started howling.

It was the finest ten minutes of telly ever.

Untouched Kitchen That Cost 40 Grand

'I love to cook!' says our WWF wrestler host, holding a spatula upside down and waving it vaguely in the direction of a range that still has a fine coating of brick dust from the kitchen fitter's work.

'Yeah, I do egg white omelettes, and other stuff. Wolfgang Puck gave me a private lesson, it was wild. I can do sauces. All the sauces.'

Ah yes, Puck's saucing masterclass: the red one, the brown one, and the white one. The classic French jus trio for feasts of TURKEY BACON.

There must also be a double-door fridge large enough to store a dead body, holding only neatly stacked cans of Gatorade.

'Original Stone Tiles From Milan Are The Weapon Of Choice In The Luxe Bathroom'

Not strictly relevant: I once proof read an interiors piece containing this phrase from the designer. I now realise I devised this whole feature idea just so I could share this.

THINGS WE DON'T NEED TO SEE IN ROM COMS ANYMORE

I love rom coms.

After being inspired by *Drive*, I even worked up my own treatment for a film called *Human Man,* where Ryan Gosling is a human man. It's a bit sketchy on plot but there are roles for Emma Stone, a longhaired kitten and fleeting willy.

However, too often, myself and fellow genre enthusiasts find ourselves in Cineworld foyer bellowing, what in all that is holy was THAT?

The same misconceptions about 'what women find fun' crop up continually, and I think it's time to resolve some confusion.

And yes, Sumner Redstone, holding on Line One, I will take your call to talk about *Human Man* further. Right after my nap.

You're Good At Your Job? Good Luck With That Sex You Were Planning On Having, Ever!

When was the meeting held that agreed 'professionally effica-cious = frigid'? If you're remotely competent, it's a given you'll be seeing no action whatsoever.

Or if you are, it's with a pin-striped Mr Wrong who we see in an early montage where they're both standing up during breakfast and talking on their cell phones, juggling cups of filter coffee and eating croissants, because we all know that's how Hitler got started.

In *The Proposal*, Sandra Bullock is Don DeLillo's literary agent, but has become so power-addled penis-repelling she has to blackmail men to marry her. Obviously, she must stay by a lake with people who wear plaid and be told her values are warped.

(NB: Fragrant lady-jobs, such as florist, pediatrician or curator at MOMA, may not turn your uterus into a stingray, according to latest findings in *The Lancet*.)

When a woman becomes more successful during the film, she must also be told her values have warped. In *The Devil Wears Prada,* Anne Hathaway's magazine internship costs her the relationship with New York chef boyfriend, Adrian Grenier.

Woah, wait – rewind? Yes, those notoriously time-rich, short-order cooks in The City That Never Sleeps. How unfortunate for ambitious Anne that her boyo got a job in The Restaurant That Closes At 8p.m. So You Can Go And Be Pious With Your Partner.

It's Zagat rated. Try the horseballs.

'Tis Pity She's A Porker

Memo Fox Searchlight, et al: seeing sensationally attractive women heckled about their appearance is not reassuring or enjoyable as schadenfreude. It's depressing and bewildering.

Martine McCutcheon being sent up for phantom lardarsery in *Love Actually* was a noteworthy low.

In *She's All That*, bonsai supermodel Rachael Leigh Cook is rendered the nuclear option in schoolyard games of 'would you rather' simply because she's arty and wears dungarees.

All of which makes us feel that if we could climb into this universe, we'd have the effect of The Scarecrow in *Batman Begins*, when the psychotropic gas pumps out and all you see is a screaming sack with wormy eyes.

The Eighth Habit Of Highly Effective Females: Telling Their Paymaster To Piss Up A Rope

As plot devices go, this is pretty sci-fi. Heroine flies kamikaze mission with her salary and comes out on top, as she is so pure that she sees and speaks truth with a child's innocence.

Trans: it's only OK to get the great job if you win it by default by acting like a bit of a div.

Extra points in busting the bogus-o-meter if the unlikely promotion is awarded by a crumbly Emperor Palpatine of a CEO in a spotty bow-tie, who suddenly magically transforms from a ruthless capitalist into a benign grandpa with his favourite granddaughter.

'My God, Matilda Perspicacity, you're RIGHT, I AM a massive wanker. I see now how you stole my nephew's heart, by telling him he's a bit of a wanker too. I'm firing all these sycophantic fools and making you Head of Everything.'

Cue Katy Perry's Firework and shareholders doing a conga round the boardroom with Tampax Pearls sticking out of ears.

He's been nobbing someone else? This is a wakeup call. TO LOOK TO YOUR OWN CONDUCT.

Mentions here for *He's Just Not That Into You* and *Sex and the City 2*.

Obviously, SATC 2 was a human rights atrocity of considerable proportions and I can't say much while all our legal proceedings remain active.

However.

Miranda's husband was scuttling a waitress, and the whole tenor of the storyline was that it was her fault for being too much of a shrew while juggling parenthood and a job that ran the family's lifestyle.

Alfred, fetch me my gun. No, the larger one.

Bitch Gotta Make Rent There Is No Way Bitch Is Making

In *Sliding Doors*, Gwyneth Paltrow was footing what looked like a Knightsbridge pied-à-terre and supporting a wastrel novelist boyfriend — by flogging lunchtime sandwiches. What were her price points on those baguettes, and was she selling them to concussed Saudi princes?

In *Confessions of a Shopaholic*, Becky Bloomwood's freakonomics saw a staff journalist amass a designer wardrobe a Kardashian would deem 'a bit vulgar', then sell it second-hand in an auction and clear her debt with ease.

Who knew that garish Clown Porn rags were a canny investment?

That's why we've seen so little of Su Pollard lately! She's in Cap Ferrat, drinking champagne out of a jewelled conch shell.

Of Course I'm An Unholy Twat: My Dead Gay Aunt Only Has One Leg!

Wherein our hero gets enriched, or excused, due to a Secret Pain. Just write us a sympathetic character; there's no need for this Second Act, Get Out Of Jail Free revelation. Or if there is, maybe ask selves why.

For example, in the otherwise-great *Friends with Benefits,* Justin Timberlake's preppy shagger acquires sudden depth because his dad has Hollywood Alzheimer's.

A gentler variant of dementia, Hollywood Alzheimer's does not cause you to take a shit in a shopping centre or shout 'Are you an Arab?' at the district nurse.

Hollywood Alzheimer's sufferers bark the odd non-sequitur but drift into lucidity long enough to deliver homilies about finding your one true love, and to help their sons nail Mila Kunis.

In *The Ugly Truth*, we discover Gerard Butler had to be a raving chauvinist jebend because a woman once broke up with him first, or something.

Bear in mind, by this point in the running time we really need Gerard to prove he's being used as a skin puppet for the demonic bidding of a dead murderer.

You were *dumped*, broheem? That's all you got?

In case you're not catching enough of a whiff of what I think of *The Ugly Truth*, it's a film that needs to fuck the fuck off while it's fucking off and then come back, purely so it can fuck off again. ('Roger Ebert Is Away').

However, in terms of muddled redemption, nothing beats batshit reactionary fable *Pretty Woman*, in which Richard Gere's prostitute-boffing asset stripper reaches the denouement of a spiritual journey where he ... builds big warships.

HOW IS THERE ROOM IN YOUR BODY FOR THAT HUGE HEART?

It's possible *Pretty Woman* was conceived originally not as a romance, but a portrait of what a Bond villain does in his downtime. Think about it: Edward lives in a hotel penthouse, has his own plane, likes the opera, polo and hot tubbing with call girls.

The man's a nine iron, a can of Halfords metallic paint and a pair of plus fours away from Goldfinger.

 GOODBYE